THE JOPPENBERGH JUMP

A NOVEL

Mark Morganstern

The Joppenbergh Jump

ISBN: 978-1-7337464-2-7
Library of Congress Control Number: 2020932250

Antique postcard image of Joppenbergh courtesy Rosendale Library

Cover design by Bryan Maloney
Author photo by Brent Robison

RECITAL PUBLISHING
Woodstock, NY 12498
www.recitalpublishing.com

Recital Publishing is an imprint of the online podcast The Strange Recital.
Fiction that questions the nature of reality
www.thestrangerecital.com

Contents

Acknowledgments and Dedications

Thank you to my family: Susan, forever—you know what for, for which I cannot ever repay; Lily, aka Pippi Long-stocking with apps, my second keeper; Harry, the builder, machinist, fierce and loyal; and Chef Luke in SoCal, creating small plate magic paired with stunning wines. I was AWOL while writing the story, even selfish, but please believe me…you have always been the real subject matter of my life.

To Edward Rus Springer for your editorial heavy lifting, setting the clock right, taming the chaos, and your exasperated encouragement. You stacked the building blocks of the book in the right order while I was spinning yarns that required further orchestration on your part.

To Brent Robison, author, editor, publisher, and friend, for the fine-focused, finished edit, an essential and beautifully executed task, for your indefatigable support and your open-hearted belief that the book *was* a book.

To the well-tempered Knights of the Abundant Mug Round Table (on Fridays at *the cafe*): Tom G., Tom S., Richard K., Richard L., Dennis D., E. Rus Springer, as mentioned above, and Benny T., the pasta king and original card designer, who summed up our most esoteric exchanges on lit and art, aka Life, wisely, with a Spinoza-esque quip: "It is what it is."

And to the ancient mountain, a glacier's offspring, called Joppenbergh, which called to me and stoked my fictional mind into action.

I have been lucky.

"There are mountains in this world, Everest the slayer, the volcanic Kilimanjaro, and then there is this mountain, my mountain, alive, magical, and divine."

—*Coot Ronald Friedman*
Sergeant E5, US Army, Retired

Prologue

Coot Friedman here, Coot Ronald Friedman, *CRF*, in case you want to buy me a monogrammed hoodie or some silk boxers. Sergeant E5, CR Friedman, US Army, retired, weapons specialist / supply clerk. Afghanistan and Iraq Wars Veteran on permanent disability. Sharp shooter, ex-deer hunter, mushroom forager, wildlife guide, survivor of a previous wild life; handyman, poet, friend to all who befriend me, and ghost talker.

I am also a "borderline alcoholic with a marked case of PTSD," according to Dr. Montaigne Fung at the Albany Stratton VA Medical Center. Zip Code 12208, in case you're planning a field trip with the kids. Dr. Fung, who graduated from a not quite prestigious medical college in Karnataka, also diagnosed me with "transient epileptic amnesia," but a gaggle of kindly VA nurses, and a few supportive maintenance staff, anecdotally decided I was just *unusual*. Despite Fung's impromptu diagnoses, despite everything, and there's been a shit load of everything, I feel pretty damn good.

Dr. Montaigne Fung, *Monte*…he hated it when I called him that, insisted that I couldn't differentiate between fact and fiction. That I couldn't even fill out a medical intake form honestly. No shit, like who does? How many cigarettes do you smoke a day? Oh, just one, a short one, the size of a gherkin pickle. How many drinks do you have a day? Oh, just one, a glass of beer, *out of a glass the size of a fish tank.*

Fung can think whatever he wants. It's the truth I believe in. Truth in whatever forms it takes. When it sprouts up out of the ground, sweet, green, and tender, or when it

1

lands on your head like a safe full of Confederate bills and Mardi Gras beads. The truth oozes out of the details like a squished cockroach, no matter how skewed or wobbly the details are. I also believe that it's not a waste of time to mine for fool's gold. Or to watch Yetis in tuxedos break-dancing on curbs and sewer covers. Why? Because I've seen them do it.

I don't care what Dr. Fung says about me. I'm no liar. I'm going to tell you the truth. I'm going to tell you the truth about war, friendship, and love. I'm going to tell you everything that happened in this way unique place I live in, and the people. People of every weird cut and wild curl you could imagine. I'm going to tell you about how I came back home, fucked up from war, and how my best friends, a pharmacist, a ghost, and a sacred mountain saved my ass so many times I lost track. And how I got handed a 14-karat life the chances of me ever having were minus nil.

As previously stated I am a veteran on permanent disability. 100% disability as a matter of fact. My symptoms include, but are not limited to, lapses of memory, nervous glitches, episodes, some of mythic proportions, and an inability to keep my mouth shut when it would save my ass from a beat-down. My symptoms are the result of a head injury I sustained in Afghanistan. I mentioned that I was a supply clerk and a damn good one at that. I knew where everything was, the entire inventory, every last Beretta 9mm, Colt M4 Carbine, and Basic Issue M16, locked up tight in a nine-digit combination safe. I knew where they were and I knew how to use them. I recorded all of their serial numbers on a computer and memorized the most requested items before I got hit in the head.

It didn't matter if you were a supply clerk, or a mess tent cook. If a firefight broke out in the front yard of our compound, you'd get your ass out there and do what you had to do. One night during a mortar attack an entire shelf of steel-toed boots came unhinged and rocked over on top of me. I was buried under them and must have taken at least six hits directly to my head, like I was kicked in the head six times with steel-toed boots, sizes eight to fourteen. I was out cold for two days straight. The medics didn't know if I would wake up again. At the very least I had a severe concussion, possibly minor brain damage.

While I was out of the office I dreamt or imagined some very strange shit. Apparitions faded in and out, sad, crazed, and hostile visitors tormented me. My poor mother appeared, regarding me with a sense of loss and uselessness. She stood there disconsolately and pointed at the burn hole I'd made in her new French provincial sofa. I'd been home on leave and fell asleep with a doobie in my hand. That sin was compounded by the fact it had taken her and my dad three years to save up enough money for their living room set—it was their dream furniture. To this day, I can't sit on a sofa. A chair, a stool, on a rug maybe, but no sofas.

Next was Mr. Warwick, my high school biology teacher, in his stained lab coat and amoeba tie. He reiterated that I was a genetic mistake, something nature would eventually correct. Enemy fire almost took care of that.

I saw a large pulsating letter F, which was my overall high school average. Except for English. Even though Mrs. Ramstein hated me, I escaped her sterile little planet and weed-dry pedagogy. I managed to score in the upper percentile of the Regents ELA. There was something about books that caught me right away. I was and am a reader. I read everything I got my hands on. I was the only student who showed up with the *New York Times* in my gym bag everyday. The *Times* did a better job educating me than public school ever could have. I was addicted to the smell of the print and loved the smart look of Arial they used for their sans-serif font. It made everything. Even bad news was more interesting to read.

The last visitor I encountered in my unconscious state appeared in a swirl of cotton candy pink light, a beatific figure in a gold lamé robe, doused in the saccharine cologne of sagaciousness. He waved a white-gloved hand over my face. He said, "Not just yet. Not just yet, my son." Then he grabbed my throat and choked the hell out of me until I came to screaming, and threw up on the nurse. This all-knowing guy, Mr. Gold Robe, is a frequent flyer through my psyche. He shows up during my episodes to "assist" me back into reality. He helps me snap out of whatever I'm caught up in.

Doctor Montaigne Fung theorized that Gold Robe symbolized my father. Why would my father want to strangle me? Fung's theory was that my father and I had an unresolved competition for the sexual possession of my mother. The old Oedipus two-step thing; screw that. Fung insisted that was the root cause of my illness besides the other misplaced diagnoses he'd pinned on me. He must have cracked that one out of a fortune cookie. When I asked Fung if I could see his medical license he got sullen, then annoyed. "You will never adjust to civilian life without medication and intense therapy," he seethed. The bastard; I'd already struggled enough to get thoughts like that out of my head. Hell is other people telling you what you fear most.

Whoever Gold Robe is, like I said, he shows up at my desperate times and acts as a threatening catalyst to shock me through the immediate crisis. And there have been many of them. And when I think about it, Fung resembles Gold Robe more than my father. And if there was an untoward element of sexual possession it was probably Fung trying to screw with my head. All things being oxymoron, the guy who patches your flat tire puts a curse on the other three or something like that.

Part 1: Returning Home, Damaged

Since Fung lacked any authority to keep me for further observation, I slipped out of the ward and left him in Albany to analyze me in absentia. I hopped a bus going south back to my town. Well, my hamlet. We're not big enough to qualify as a town. We're a small town inside of a town like an egg yolk inside of an egg. There are about seven thousand souls here, some living, some not so alive. We're snug in a mysterious region, tucked away in a bend in the Hudson River Valley. The hamlet... it's also called a village, though some insist on calling it a town because size matters. Whatever. We're situated along a circuitous creek called the Rondout, rich in farmland and apple orchards, located just west of Hank Hudson's Great River of discovery. We're practically the doormat to the Catskill Mountains, which I like to call the Magic-hills.

We're in a quaint setting similar to that of Mr. R. V. Winkle, in the days when officious, natty Dutchmen like that prick, Jew-hater, Peter Stuyvesant ruled Manhattan Island. I love those Washington Irving stories about the early Dutch settlers. I must have read all of them at least five times. I did mention that I was a poet, right? And here, for your enjoyment, I give you my Rip Van Winkle poem, first published in the local Penny Saver, Sunday supplement:

> *RIPPED*
> *And like Rip,*
> *I withdrew deeper*
> *Into the dim tavern*
> *Against the shrill cries*
> *Of her voice*

Not a great poem maybe, but poems are not so easy to make. But any man who's done a long-term sentence with a certain type of female will relate to this ditty. This one is actually about my first wife, her name withheld due to some unresolved litigation from a few years ago. Anyway, she's the tarantula who ran off with a snake and gave birth to a puff adder. And that's being kind. She took everything I had at the time, which was good because I had nothing. But there's no need to go into that here. Suffice to say it prompted me to write a poem about Rip.

But what am I talking about? What I need to do is tell you about the mountain. There are mountains in this world, Everest the slayer, the volcanic Kilimanjaro, and then there is this mountain, my mountain, alive, magical, and divine. Joppenbergh, named after our town's founding father, Jacobus Rutsen. He named the mountain, as these modest types do, after himself. Joppenbergh, Jacob's Mountain. It's the king of Ulster County, a mountain of carbonate bedrock (Paleozoic days) overlain with deposited material, pockets of till, and talus. It's situated on the west end of town and towers about four hundred and ninety-five-plus feet above the Rondout Creek and Route 213 West. It's the backdrop of the town and, though not known to any but the *sensitive*, it's the living soul of this place.

There are disappearing streams up there, sinkholes, cliffs, ravines, crevices, and gaping cave mouths one should not enter—no designer of theme parks could have come up with this one. To say that it's a second home to me is to say nothing. It's my place of salvation, my temple. And there's something else up there, certain stone personages I'll tell you about shortly. I'm at peace when I roam through its world of mist, rocky woods, overhung shelves of ancient stone, man-made and forbidding mines, red fox, deer, deer ticks, bears, sometimes in close proximity, wild turkeys, and circling eagles and red tails above.

And it was up there on Joppenbergh that I met Kurt Geary late one fall afternoon—maybe it was spring. I should say I met Kurt in his incorporeal state. Kurt, my ghost bro and spirit guide, the poor bastard. I was deer hunting with no luck as usual when I felt something cool touch my arm. When I re-entered my skin I'd jumped out of he introduced himself to me in a most cordial manner.

He needed to tell his story and I looked like the right person to listen. Kurt Geary was a homeboy and had lived here in the days when the ski jump was first built. He took to it immediately and soon became a record-holding ski jumper; he sailed along at two hundred and fifteen feet above the run, traveling forty-five feet through the air. Though not an Olympic record in 1924, when the committee recognized Ski Flying as a legitimate sport, Kurt was definitely a contender. He used to tell his teammates that he felt more comfortable V styling high over the hill, preparing for a perfect-score Telemark landing, than he did drinking Miner's Punch in the Tea Room. He was a custom binding maker and a daredevil.

The guys who attempted the Joppenbergh Jump—early on before technology improved and made the sport safer with wider and longer skis—were steel-nerved, thrill-seeking crazy men looking to gain some altitude above bad marriages and chaotic financial times. Not that it paid anything to fly through the air, just the currency of exhilaration. And they had to cover at least sixty feet airborne to qualify for the Olympics—a long shot.

Kurt should have stayed with his team that day, his last day. He had the next jump, and was up to break his previous record. It was the State Championship Ski Jump, February 25, 1928. But Kurt heard something call him that day and it made him leave the jump. It was the daredevil within who'd recently inhabited a reckless corridor of his mind. Kurt quit the slope and circled around to the other side of the mountain that overlooked the Iron Wonder.

Kurt loved climbing as much as skiing. He'd scaled most of the walls of the Shawangunk Ridge, and had summited Sam's Point and Gertrude's Nose a dozen times. But this was a different challenge. Man versus architecture. The Iron Wonder, a massive train trestle, built in 1872, was considered to be an architectural feat at the time. It existed for the sole purpose of carrying out the natural cement dug out of the mines on Joppenbergh. They mined it almost to the point of collapse. And there were some horrific cave-ins and miraculous saves.

That day, instead of taking the jump, Kurt lowered himself down the treacherous rock walls, negotiating sharp outcroppings and loose stones. He threw a long line out, hooked on to a girder, and then guided himself down until he got a decent foothold. First he had to work his way over to the middle of the trestle before he could begin his ascent in earnest. Kurt made steady progress going up. From the ground below he looked like a small action figure climbing a giant erector set that reflected the sun's glorious face in the creek. He was feeling exhilarated about the hoopla it caused with the spectators who'd gathered to watch his stunt. Then one of his carabiners suspiciously snapped. The other one held fast to his harness as he swung out in a wobbly arc. He was momentarily suspended at the apex, but then gracefully swung back in. His rope snagged on a girder, tightened fast, and propelled him into a beam where he smashed his head open.

He was left suspended there, as brain matter and globs of blood drifted down into the Rondout Creek far below. The alarm was sounded, and the winch was laboriously rolled out onto the tracks. When it was in place, a volunteer fireman was suspended from a cable and lowered slowly to retrieve Kurt's body. Meanwhile, he swung back and forth, a sad ornament for all to see, including his garrulous, drunken father, emerging from the Tea Room. Euphemistically branded, the Tea Room was attached to the old Central Hotel where the miners were housed. They drank hard in the Tea Room and proposed romantic "excavations and elevations" to the "ladies" who congregated there. Ladies who were aware of the men's carnal appetites, and their own need to fill their embroidered purses.

It was a strange place, The Tea Room, where after hours, in the gloom, a lone maid or a barkeep would come upon the two white-haired ladies, perhaps sisters, dancing together in white tattered dresses, observed by a gallery of floating heads. Or below in the storage room where staff reported seeing miner's legs walking around without a torso. It was this room that Kurt's father tripped out of to see his son hanging lifeless over the creek. And later that night he exited the world of the living with a shotgun blast to his calcified heart.

After the accident, Kurt Geary, or rather Kurt's spectral self, was left to float around the ledge overlooking the trestle where he'd been dispatched. On my frequent explorations of the mountain I commiserate with Kurt over his misfortune. I am quite fond of him. We catch up on town gossip, which he is well-equipped to do, having since kept a watch on Main Street for the last eighty-eight years. "It helps to float," he says. He tries to look out for me, gives advice when he thinks I'm "sprinting into the void," which is often the case. Of all the nonpersons I've met he's the closest one to me; he's all spirit and I love him.

Wait, I'm getting ahead of myself, or maybe behind; for most of us time can't be reckoned with, we just know that we're ripping uncontrollably through it. Anyway, that day after I'd escaped Fung's toxic gravitational pull and made it home, the first thing I did was hike up the mountain to give thanks. I felt shaky, but exuberant, liberated, like I was walking above the path, observing the flora and fauna beneath my feet. Home.

When I reached the summit I looked around to see if Kurt might be in the vicinity. I wanted some company, some support. I started down the cliff side making my way cautiously, glad that my body, every muscle, my fingers and toes remembered which rock to grasp, which branch was safe to take hold of. Belaying, rope systems, and bouldering techniques are for less qualified climbers, not to brag. I only resort to those devices if I become inadvertently impaired. And this is not a good place to be goofy stoned. You could disappear up here.

When I got to the squeeze I shoved myself through then sat down and did the ass scramble slide about fifteen yards. I got up, positioned myself against an ash tree and scanned with my bird glasses. And there they were as ever, centuries old, distinctive stone visages, all seven of them. I nodded and thanked each one silently. I sensed their acknowledgement and approval of my return. I had tried to describe these carved faces, their temperament and power, to Dr. Fung in the brief window of time I thought I could trust him. He interpreted it as just another manifestation of my unbridled psychosis. But they're real, the master work of a receding glacier, ancient stone inhabited by entities humans can't decipher: Raging Tom, Jasper, Hooded Parrot, Grinder, Banana Nose, Stoner Van Etten, and the lovely Vanita, the lone feminine presence of the group. Each one possesses its own power and authority, like the Greek gods, except these are made of stone. I'd taken the liberty to christen each one, though they are in no way denominational. It was only after the advent of belief systems, aka religions, that murder was introduced into the innocent world, twenty-four seven.

I'm not sure how long I stood there observing them, struggling to intuit what I sensed were messages and presentiments about the hamlet that lay sleeping below. A warning of some kind. Something about the fate of the residents, the assurance of our future, or not. I had hoped to be relieved but a sharp edge of concern knifed my head as I realized I was the only one who would know about this. Therefore, I would bear some responsibility. I bowed my head to them in thanks, and then began a treacherous descent down the wildest part of the mountain in the dark.

Somewhat scratched and bruised I found myself alone on Main Street, or so I thought. I felt completely spent and dehydrated, slightly disoriented, and in much need of a pint of high-octane beer. Then I heard a honk and a rattle. How could they have possibly known I'd returned? Maybe one of them had spotted me earlier in the afternoon when I'd slipped into town. But there they were marching toward me. The Shad Town Improvement Brass Band and Social Club.

Among other things our hamlet is referred to as the Festival Town. And the town band does not miss a single opportunity to perform. They fulfill a sociological aspect that supports and serves our needs very well. They are, in a sense, a satellite zeitgeist orbiting the place, accompanying our journey through time, which runs from prehistory to right about now, and maybe what comes after.

I froze in place as they marched toward me. This was an unwelcome assault that I was ill-equipped to bear. I needed quiet...sanctuary. I needed a beer, not this. When they reached me they split off and formed a circle around me. The band's leader, Beaming Dove, a diminutive powerhouse, stood erect before me in her marching whites. She made a snappy salute to me, then struck her snare drum once and counted off. They played their version of "America the Beautiful." This was uncharacteristic as Beaming Dove is a staunch pacifist and avoids all things that hint of rabid patriotism or unbridled militarism. She was making an exception. It was a bit off-key and ragtag, but the melody, the overwhelming sentiment was there. And there I stood. I recognized their faces, I knew these people, just as I'd recognized the faces on the mountain. But the faces I saw now were the ones of my brothers, the ones I'd served with and left behind. The real heroes. The ones who wouldn't be coming back. The ones who wouldn't be honored as I was mistakenly being honored now. The faces blurred in the street lights as I wept uncontrollably. My tears spilled into a drain, an open wound in the middle of my chest that isn't actually there. And I asked myself if I even had a right to be alive.

I don't remember much more about that night. I wandered into the park and slept for a couple of hours in the pavilion. I awoke in terrible pain and had a crushing feeling of dread that I'd miscalculated my situation. That I wasn't of this place anymore, an outcast with no alternative place to go to. I ran through the streets, desperate. I had to find him. He was the only one who could possibly tether me here, keep me from floating away into a terrifying and stagnant bardo. But it was the middle of the night; his pharmacy would be closed, but I couldn't remember where he lived. All the little shit details I remembered, and I forgot where his house was.

I looked through the pharmacy windows. The Rx light glowed dully on the back wall. Nobody home. I pulled the floor mat up from the entrance of his shop and covered myself with it. Then I scuttled under the bench he kept there for people waiting for prescriptions. I slept a few hours.

Zeitzer found me there in the morning and practically dragged me into the shop and began forcing cups of hot coffee into me. He laid me on a hospital bed, a rental, and covered me with blankets. "Coot, you're home. Why didn't you tell me you were coming? I would have picked you up."

"I guess I didn't think. Sorry."

"You OK? Do you want some aspirin?"

"No, I'm good." I felt like a child in the bed with this middle-aged man taking care of me. I must have fallen back to sleep. When I woke up again he slid a tray in front of me. Pancakes and bacon and more coffee. I almost cried. I ate as if I'd been starving, and I think I was. He wouldn't let me get out of bed until he took my blood pressure, which is usually pretty low. There's so much to say about Zeitzer. If you're lucky, in your lifetime you have a friend like him. I was starting to feel back in the world.

"What are you going to do?"

"What do you mean?

"You're going to need some work, right?"

"Yeah, I'll start looking." But he hired me on the spot. Before I enlisted, I'd done a lot of odd jobs in town, for Zeitzer and almost everyone else in town. He wanted me to organize his shelves, clean out the basement, and inventory everything but the medications. I wasn't allowed in the dispensing area unless I'm vacuuming the rug. He offered me minimum wage plus.

"Why don't you go to the community college and get your Associate degree in English literature? You still write poetry, don't you?"

"Yeah, I should do that."

It was not even noon yet, but he closed the shop and

invited me to go with him. I think he wanted to keep an eye on me, and make sure my re-entrance into the hamlet went smoothly. We walked a block and then went into Fay's Cut, Curl, Lash, & Trim–Unisex on Main Street. Fay flailed a towel over a reclining salon chair and sent hair flying. Zeitzer slid into the chair and sighed like a weight was coming off his body. I sat in a chair with my head under a nail-polish-red hair dryer. I was still kind of shaky and just stared through a bristling shaft of sunlight, kind of lost in it. I watched a hair float around the room like a fuzzy comet. Then it fluttered to the floor. In the end gravity always gets it, every strand, every one of them. Salt and pepper, gray, black, blond, red, straight and curly, all kinds—kid's hair, old people's hair.

Fay started right in with her usual on Zeitzer, really giving it to him. "Don't you think we've taken Christ out of Christmas?" she says to him. "Don't you think we've become a Godless nation?" I've heard this before from so many devout types that it's futile to point out the cliché. I hate clichés, but I do like repetition—that's how you learn something thoroughly. I watched Zeitzer squirm, a hostage in her barber's chair. Fay punctuates her words by jabbing her trimming shears next to his ear. "Christ *jab* out *jab* of *jab* Christmas *jab jab*."

Everyone in town gets the same treatment. Fay's service includes a diatribe—it's part of the haircut, the unwritten agreement. God speaks through her comb. Fay Bunny Nichols will accuse you, and enlighten you about the Lord and the joy of faith as she snips and shapes your hair for this and the next life to come. And she'll shout out a husky hallelujah every so often.

Zeitzer made his customary polite reply. "Well Fay, you know I don't really follow any religion—no religion at all, actually. Jonah, my boy, is married to an unaffiliated Episcopalian travel agent." Zeitzer didn't mention that Jonah's spouse was a guy named Kenny and that the wedding theme, besides love and commitment, was exotic cuisine from around the world. The catering bill was astronomical. Estranged from his wife, Zeitzer had invited me to attend his son's wedding with him. It was amazing, but the exotic Croatian beer knocked me on my ass.

Between the Christ talk and snipping, Fay asked how Zeitzer's wife was doing. He didn't tell her that Hannah, had gone radical-boogie-on-Jewish-woman and relocated to a kibbutz on the outskirts of Bat Yam in Israel. Once there she cared for olive trees and dates and had virtual action dates with kibbutzniks of all shapes and sizes. Anything for the cause.

Hannah told Zeitzer before she left him that he just wasn't an "exciting guy." He told me, with much hesitation, that one night after an unsuccessful performance in bed she stormed into the bathroom to get her vibrator, and said, "You're a pharmacist for Christ sake. Get some drugs." That's not fair. He's one of the best humans I've ever known. Everyone malfunctions once in a while. I should know.

Fay liked to swivel the chair around dramatically and look Z dead in the eye with her steel gray marbles, an aura of tiny red flames flickering damningly around the pupils. "I will pray for you, Mr. Zeitzer. I will pray for your soul and your progeny. And I will pray that we be spared the darkness that's descended upon this town." She'd sweep a weathered hand across the stained storefront window, with its display of fishing hooks, hunting knives, and dated Norman Rockwell calendars, as if to scoot the evil back down into the sewer or wherever it had come from.

Poor Zeitzer, he's about as confrontational as a Woolly Bear. He has a reputation for being straight up and generous. More than once I've seen him pick up a co-pay for some elder who couldn't afford his meds. He also pitched in to help replace the roof on the senior housing building on Route 32. I will only buy my rolling papers and Shag tobacco from him, as I do a bit of mixing and compounding myself.

Fay finally released him from the salon chair. He thanked her and tipped generously. Once we got outside he ran his hands through his hair. Fay had done so much preaching she'd cut his hair down to nothing. "There's something about a haircut that makes me hungry. Let's go over to Bebe's."

"I feel like I just ate all those pancakes and bacon."

He stepped back and looked me up and down. "You should eat some more."

I was actually glad to be going to Bebe's. She and her little cafe are considered to be a town anchor, at least for those who value it. It's the best food around unless you're craving a burger. Then you go to Bull's Boxcar. There are two spray-painted, luminous gold fryolators, wrapped in blinking midget Christmas lights, rotating in the front display windows of the Sprouting Affair. Each one with a hand-painted sign: 1) FRY ME A RIVER and 2) WHAT, ME FRY? This harkens back to when Bebe first arrived, a feisty Hoboken refugee fleeing gentrification, the scourge of our profit-driven republic. Bebe had decided to recreate the cafe she'd made famous in Hoboken, but some cranky bastards on the town board went after her with a meat cleaver, and she came close to not being approved.

True, it didn't help the way she responded to them, but they had it coming. Bebe is the hard-working, strong-willed daughter of a New Jersey bricklayer and a mother who'd waited tables in Atlantic City when Bebe's dad had been laid off for a year. Her mom, as strong a woman as her daughter, did it to help cover the mortgage, until the dad went back to work. Bebe isn't one to mince her words. She can spice them up with cayenne pepper real quick.

The exchange with the building commission was confrontational. The crotchety old timers were frightened; they resisted the new wave rolling in. They told her that they wouldn't approve a fryolator in a wood framed building. And to be approved she'd have to install a costly sprinkler system as well, and have it inspected by the town code enforcement officer who was basically a for-cash Dracula with a tape measure and a flashlight.

A fryolator is standard restaurant equipment, a burn and fire hazard as well. Bebe said, and I remember it word for word, "I don't need a fryolator to make Moroccan Chickpea Stew, Tofu or Seitan Buffalo Wings, or Mexican Fajitas, never mind Black Beans in Sweet and Sour Caribbean Sauce." Of course, none of these dishes would have appealed to anyone sitting on the commission. She may as well have said Shepherd's Pie Laced with Spicy Goat Turds.

Vic Nichols, Fay's even more devout husband, didn't like the sound of Seitan; it reminded him of the devil. Bebe explained, "Seitan is basically wheat meat, a kind of textured protein. It's chewy. With the right ingredients, people find it satisfying."

Vic persisted and got testy, his usual manner of welcoming new folks to our town. He said something about "you people," and Bebe got heated up: "You're all still on the Animal Farm diet. This town oozes with fat and gravy. The obesity epidemic is off the charts. It's time to clean it up. At least have a choice for Christ's sake." There was an uncomfortable silence in the room except for the ruffling of agendas and scraping of chairs shuffling back as a group

The Joppenbergh Jump 19

of affronted plus-size folks got up and left the meeting in haste.

Bonnie Flair, who had stage four intestinal cancer at the time, stood and addressed the board: "Jesus Christ, Vic, she's not opening a nuclear facility. It's just specialized cuisine for...you know...those people."

Three months to the day after her battle with the board, Bebe's Sprouting Affair celebrated its grand opening with an overripe zucchini, pumpkin, and tomato mosh pit in the backyard. It took Bebe all day to put the ingredients through a blender. A small crowd took turns sliding into and wallowing in the goo to let the essential vegetable matter and juices soak in and boost their immune systems.

Unfortunately, Bonnie Flair died that night. As an impromptu memorial, the next night we sat around Bebe's fire pit and shared a joint and a few beers. Bebe said that Bonnie was a standup woman; she admired her. That she'd single-handedly gotten her café approved. "I wish she'd been eating here, she would have lived a lot longer."

Where was I? Oh yeah, I was telling you about when Zeitzer and I were at Bebe's recovering from his severe haircut and Fay's fundamentalist outpouring. Z always gets the Zen Platter, says it keeps his blood pressure normal. I have the Spicy Black Bean Chili, Stuffed Cornbread. Both are delicious and even come with a salad and Bebe's homemade Yang Sea Dressing. I could drink that stuff out of the bottle.

Z had obviously been thinking about Fay's sermon. He said that he'd given her words some thought. "I'm not opposed to the idea of having a soul, though I'm not aware of possessing one either. I don't doubt that each of us has one, like a car has a battery—it makes sense." He dumped hot sauce on his platter. Everything's better with hot sauce.

"It's like your shadow," I said. "You can see it on the

side, but you can't pick it up and hold it. It's just...there. One time I dreamed that I held my soul like a crying baby in my arms." Z gave me an uncertain look.

"Hmm...what do you think Fay meant, Coot?"

"By what?" I said.

"You know, the darkness that's descended upon our town."

"Oh that, you know Fay. She senses darkness descending upon us quarterly. Last August, you remember, maybe July? I was home on leave and a big, battered truck with Delaware plates, and tinted gangster windows showed up, a Mr. Softee? That set her off good. She said the music put the kids in a trance and they ran after that truck like little hypnotized heathens." She maintained that there was no mention of ice cream in the Bible. I did a little research at the library and learned that King Solomon was fond of iced drinks during harvesting time, if that matters.

Speaking of sweets, we must have been starving that day. Z got the chocolate espresso cake, and I got key lime pie, my favorite. Chocolate makes me blow up like an inner tube; it makes me terribly sick. Swelling, hives, diarrhea; that's the worst. Chocolate is my enemy. You wouldn't want to be around me after I ate chocolate. But both desserts are very filling.

"I don't remember the Mr. Softee truck."

"She didn't like the tune that came out of the truck. The music spooked Fay because the speaker was cracked or something and made it sound distorted, like underwater circus music. I looked it up in the library—there's a whole history on Mr. Softee. It's supposed to be a light-hearted ditty in a 6/8 time signature." I sang it for him: "The creamiest dreamiest ice cream treat you get from Mr. Softee." Z considered that for a moment, a glint of recognition from childhood brightening his face. He took a credit card from his wallet and placed it over the check.

Delcie, the waiflike waitress, snatched the card from the table. "You should do open mic," she said. "Coot Friedman sings Mr. Softee's one and only hit." Delcie is a pert and snappy girl and always has an answer for everyone—nothing gets by her. I'd asked her out once. She'd told me that her life was devoted to animal rescue, though I'd seen her on the back of Cal Darnell's Harley more than once. I told her that we all needed rescuing some time. She said that I'd be too tough to domesticate. "Go on, try it, rescue me," I said.

"The kennel's full. Maybe next spring," she said, prancing off with our dishes.

"Can I ask you something?" Zeitzer nodded in his embarrassed, affable way. "All that crap Fay was saying. She knows damn well you're Jewish. She probably thinks your people killed Christ, or something stupid like that. Well, are you uncomfortable about it, being Jewish? I don't mean anything by that. Is that why you don't cop to it?"

"You know, Coot, Fay's a good woman; she's just zealous about her beliefs. I'm not going to change barbers because of that. Did you know that she does the neighborhood girls' hair for half price on prom nights?"

"But those God-awful pamphlets she gives to the kids," I said. They depict the Savior with a gladiator's physique, a man with a beautiful head of hair, thick black curls sprawling over his white robe across his broad shoulders. Not a hint of Sephardic shading in his complexion or an odd angle to his nose. It looks like the work of a Hollywood makeup artist. The kind of thing you see painted on velvet canvases at gas stations.

"I know," Zeitzer exhaled heavily, "but we make allowances for kindness like that. She means well."

He studied his chocolate-smeared napkin, as if divining something, then slid his plate to the side. "I have a tenuous relationship with religion and ethnic culture in general. I try to avoid all signs and traits that identify me with a specific tribe. Hmm, tribe, just the word itself. The very connotation of tribes... their purpose seems to be that they are at war, one tribe versus another. Look at the bloodbath in the Middle East, you saw it, Coot. Thank God you got out alive. God? I said God." He chuckled softly. "We're still trying to Christianize the heathens as if there was only one true belief. If pressed, I'd say that I am a Universalist, but I don't go to meetings. Besides, it's the Muslims and the gays who are getting it in the neck these days. Open season on those poor folks. The Jews are kind of getting a pass for a change. But I don't get comfortable. Anti-semitism is a favorite old card they like to play from time to time."

"Yeah," I agreed, "Imagine if you were a gay Muslim?"

He didn't hear me; he was studying something in the front of his mind.

"I remember when I was about ten. My aunt had a cleaning woman, a Black woman, Dorothy. She came to her house once a week. My aunt would prepare her lunch for her, a tuna sandwich and a glass of milk. The same every time. After Dorothy left, I watched my aunt pour boiling water into her milk glass. That image of her sterilizing the Black woman's glass stayed with me. I knew at age ten that I would never judge people by their skin color. My criteria for judging people are to what extent they are or are not stupid and vicious, and usually the two go together hand in hand."

This was a strong statement coming from Zeitzer. He got quiet, kind of fell into himself. I listened to Bebe chopping vegetables in the kitchen. She was like a machine; she could reduce a pile of carrots, celery, and onions into a sizzling frying pan-full in half a minute. Delcie swept away the dessert plates with a mischievous smile, rather content. "Thank you very much, gents." Zeitzer always leaves more than a twenty percent tip.

We got up and shook hands. I felt grateful that this man was my friend. He was like the guys I'd served with. We had each other's backs. He always gives an extra little sincere squeeze at the end of a handshake—much appreciated. And I knew I might have to count on him, enlist his help for whatever was going to come down, whatever it was those stone faces warned me about on the mountain. I felt uneasy, frightened about what might happen.

Or maybe I was just stuffed. Bebe serves trucker-size portions of food.

Part 2: Pinballing into a Life

One of her biggest culinary fans, and personal admirers, is Rudolph of Melrose Hall. He was sitting in front of a huge platter of nachos with a large scoop of sour cream as Z and I were leaving after lunch that day. Bebe prepares her nachos with texturized vegetable protein to give it a bit of meat extender—satisfying and chewy.

Rudolph is a fairly new resident at Melrose Hall, which is a client residence, basically a group home. The building is perched at the foot of the mountain behind the municipal parking lot and looks as if it might have emerged from the rock behind it, like a slide-out RV. Periodically, a boulder or broken-off lump will come loose and land on the roof, sending the clients scurrying. And none of them will attempt ascending the mountain as it is believed to be haunted or evil.

Rudolph gets his SSI check the last week of the month, so Bebe extends him credit that rarely gets repaid. He's an exotic specimen. His family emigrated from Russia when he was a child and he was raised by his uncle in Brighton Beach. It's not clear how he zeroed in on our hamlet. Probably another social services transfer. Once here, he pursued his interests: game boxes, prophesying, putting spells on people (or so he claimed), and romance. The organic apple of his eye turned out to be Bebe. He begged her to marry him.

One time I was doing some woodwork repair on the back porch off of her kitchen. I saw him sneak in behind her and wrap his arms around her while she was bending over the oven. If it had been anyone else they would have gotten her heavy duty spatula imprinted on their forehead. I couldn't

24

help watching him put the moves on her. She's a tall girl and he's a short stocky guy, with enameled shiny black hair like a ventriloquist's doll. He has a wide, shark-like mouth under a thin, wispy moustache. He speaks fluent Russian and plays keyboards. What else would a girl want? Bebe turned and gently slid out of his grasp.

A few minutes later he was in the dining room in front of a platter of pasta and butter, a small haystack; he could eat bowls of the stuff. And of course coffee punctuated by multiple smoke breaks. Coffee is the certified fuel that drives the residents of Melrose Hall. It exacerbates a host of facial tics, irritability, and general edginess.

Bebe is without a doubt, the most generous woman I've ever met, definitely to a fault. She won't let anyone go hungry. Maybe it's the cruel memory from when her dad was out of work and the gaunt personage of hunger that was an uninvited guest railing at their kitchen table. That probably explains her massive portions. Her lasagna alone has achieved distinction throughout the valley. It's about the size of a man's ten and a half loafer. It feeds two large adults, three small adults, or four children. It inspired me to write a poem about it, first published on a napkin at the coffee bar of Barnes and Noble in Kingston. It's short, but people find it amusing.

> LASAGNE
> Eat lasagna;
> Don't get it
> On ya.

Z and Bebe are my support, my closest friends except for Kurt, which is a whole different thing. But it got me thinking about other kinds of relationship. Other than my first wife, the tarantula, I hadn't really ever known the true love of a woman, what that might feel like. And then, not long after that day at Bebe's with Zeitzer I found out.

I was still into hunting then, hadn't lost my taste for it yet, another fucking debacle, which resulted in some bloodletting on my part, a stupid mistake. I was getting my gear together to go up the mountain. I was loading my quiver and missed. I shoved and arrow tip into my thigh. Not just any arrow tip, but a Victory Arch Gold Tip Pro Hunter 3555 that ran me a hundred and fifty dollars for a dozen. These arrows are like acupuncturists needles; they almost go in by themselves. I would have screamed in pain, but no one was around to hear me. I ripped more flesh open pulling it out of my thigh, poured some Iodine on it, then stupidly bandaged it up and waited. I figured it would heal on its own. It didn't.

Two days later I was in the ER at Benedictine. My thigh was red up to my crotch and down to my knee. A young intern, Dr. Gorseki , shoved a needle full of antibiotics next to the wound just to get me started. It was a new record in pain, almost medieval. He bandaged it properly as he lectured me about the risk I'd taken, then he gave me a script for Ciprofloxacin, a serious antibiotic. Basically, if I didn't take all of them, he said I could die. Then he asked me if I was happy at home.

"I'm glad to finally be home."

He leaned in closer to me. "Do you feel safe in your home?"

The dude was going for something. I sensed a Fung style assault coming at me. "I feel safe in my home." I said this steadily to make it clear that I felt safe.

He lowered his voice for the next practiced question. Dr. Gorseki cleared his throat. "Do you ever think of…harming yourself?"

I looked down at the bandage on my thigh, which was becoming crimson with blood at the edges. "If I were going to do something to myself it wouldn't by be sticking an arrow in my thigh." Then a quick video flashed through my head, back over there. I could have bought it any day back there. If they couldn't do it to me, and Christ knows they tried, why would I do it to myself? Though some guys had. It's that hard.

I limped home and lay in bed for five days and couldn't keep anything down. Z infused me with gallons of water and made sure I took all of the meds on top of homeopathic remedies he made for me. Finally, the antibiotic capsules caught up to the little infectious bastards in my bloodstream. I was feeling better and suddenly ravenous.

I went back to Benedictine for the follow up with the Dr. Gorseki, but went immediately to the cafeteria. She was behind me in the line and I didn't even notice her at first. She watched me ordering macaroni and cheese, a baked potato with sour cream and bacon bits, a slab of baked ham, oozing brown sugar and raisins, two inflated dinner rolls, and maple walnut bread pudding topped with a globe of whipped cream. When I paid and headed for a table she asked me if I were carbo-loading for a triathlon. We sat down together as there was only one table left with seats. I devoured my platter with a serving fork that I'd popped out of the sliced pork roast pan. I used a soup spoon for the rest of it.

I have to mention here that I find standard-sized flatware annoying in that food escapes off of them so easily. I also prefer to eat from a bowl to help contain the food. I feel so strongly about eating this way that I submitted a poem to a journal called *Your Little Ditties, Hooray!* It's really political. Who laid down the law as to what utensils we should eat with? The friggin' English, of course. I give the poem partially here now, which was summarily rejected by *Your Little Ditties, Hooray!* This was perhaps because I submitted it delicately scratched with an extra fine point Sharpie

on three sheets of Seventh Generation Toilet Paper. I refuse
to be a slave to literary convention.

KNOW THIS
I like a wide bowl,
Noodles and meat corralled,
Nestled in a pool of glistening sauce.
Chuck the flat dish,
Morsels scooting over the edge,
Like brainless lemmings...etc. (Copyrights).

You get the idea. It's like I always fear that my food is
going to be abruptly taken away from me. Another post-
Afghani holdover.

I was eating so ravenously that I almost forgot she was
there. When I looked up into her face I dropped my spoon
and splattered gravy on both of us. I felt something like
a handspring in my thoracic cage. "What is it?" she said.
"Are you all right?"

"It's...you," I said. "What's your name?"

"Margaret." It seemed like a plain name for such an
exotic, heavenly creature.

She asked me my name. I told her.

She said, "That can't be your name."

She asked me why I was there; I told her about my arrow
wound accident. She didn't seem convinced.

"What do you do for a living?"

I said, with a big mouthful, "I'm a hunter...and a poet."
She gazed at me. I sensed that she knew me without knowing me as I did her. Or at least I certainly wanted to.
I returned her gaze with intense interest, one appetite
instantly displaced by another.

She was there to assist in a delivery. She explained that
she was a doula, a midwife's assistant, that she was in
school to become a midwife, and would soon be certified
in New York State and Massachusetts. She said this with

such passion that I was suddenly rooting for her, proud of her. Then for some reason I made an inappropriate comparison to the Sorcerer's Apprentice, my brain like scrambled sweetmeats. "What if you delivered the baby and more and more of them just kept popping out like the buckets of water that the broom fetched after Mickey Mouse put a spell on it? What would you do?"

She stared at me. "You're an unusual man."

I went for it. "I'm going to tell you something. I am half in love with you now and I think I'm going to be all the way in love with you…forever."

Her eyes, hazel, with yellow-orange highlights like chips of candy corn, widened, and then softened.

I put my hand on top of hers. She slid hers away, but not quickly. Her beeper went off. "Baby's coming."

"Coffee here tomorrow, same time," I called as she rushed off.

She called back, her stunning hair flailing behind her "I don't know."

Early next morning, I bathed scrupulously with a bar of Yardley English Lavender Soap. I love that smell; good Brit stuff. I got there early and claimed a table far away from the clutter of the service line. I lay a bouquet of Prunus Mei on the table. Prunus Mei is Latin for Plum Blossom, and not easily found in the neighborhood. I had to bus all over the county until I found a florist who had them. They cost fifty-four bucks. But they were beautiful, shades of pink and white, a blissful fragrance, and resilient to winter weather. I suspected that Margaret was exactly that kind of flower.

I ran back to the dessert bar and grabbed the best uninspired pastry they offered. I bought coffee to go with it, which she later traded in for herbal tea. I should have guessed she was a tea lady. Herbal tea gives me hives.

She looked nervous when she arrived, scanned the room quickly. Obviously relieved, she turned away. I stood and waved, hopeful. Reluctantly, she made her way to the table. "Thank you for coming," I said stupidly, as if I were selling her Shaklee Products.

She stood there staring at the flowers. "Those are the kind that grow in my mother's country. How could you know that?"

"I didn't know. But they remind me of you."

"You're full of shit. You don't know me." A sickening wave of fear flashed in her face. "Have you been stalking me?" She got up.

Something snapped in my heart. "No...no, I would never do something like that...hurt you? God no!" I was almost crying.

She sat back down and was quiet, deep in herself for a few minutes.

"I'd never do that. I..." I almost said, "I love you."

"You don't know where I'm from. It's hard...where I come from."

"Your people come from far away?" I asked. She gave me the "you just failed your SAT" look.

"You are completely weird and inappropriate. Nothing you do or say passes for normal behavior."

"Normal?"

"My normal." But then, for the next lucky forty-five minutes she told me about herself, her early limited years in the deep South, and her escape from it. I listened as if I were privy to the secrets of the universe, peeking at her thighs and breasts.

Her life, she told me, is dedicated to bringing babies into the world, healthy, happy babies. She is immersed in the birth process, prenatal care, birthing, after birth, the whole front end of life's journey. She'd studied it at some farm in rural Tennessee led by a birthing guru woman who smoked cigarillos and drank black tea nonstop. This woman, Glea, wrote the book on home birth. She's been arrested for her "unorthodox" birth practices a few times, like allowing women to labor until they're ready to deliver their babies.

There's something about the South. They think birth is only possible with the assistance of a corpulent obstetrician in tasseled loafers, wielding a pair of stainless steel forceps. A small-hearted man who resents postponing a date on the golf links. And if the woman doesn't have insurance to cover her birth, tough shit.

It annoyed the hell out of her that I took notes as she spoke. "I want to remember every single thing about you." She parried all my romantic talk without flinching, but she didn't run away, which was a warm hand over my heart.

She came from Southern Georgia; her accent is delicious peach cobbler with a shot of Kalua. She is the only child of a Taiwanese mother who after thirty years in the States only learned a small shopping list of words; therefore, Margaret was fluent in Taiwanese. Her father, Aldo, is a Sicilian who first came to the States as part of a circus act, The Flying Cannones. He was the smallest of three men, so he got to climb up their limbs to the top and shoot his arms out heroically. Then he'd flip off the guy's shoulders and land flat on his feet. He cooks in an Asian Fusion restaurant, and does janitorial work at the college.

As a result of the cross pollination of In-Su and Aldo, Margaret looks African-American—gorgeous, kinky hair, sculpted lips, light coffee skin—which translates to "Black girl in cracker land."

At fourteen, she enrolled herself in the Valdosta College library, where her father cleaned after hours as a second job. Margaret read about three quarters of the tomes until she got to midwifery. She devoured that shelf, made a list on her legal pad, and birded out of Atlanta on her eighteenth birthday with the babysitting money she'd earned from kindly white folk who occasionally, by mistake, referred to her as "girl."

She told her parents the night before. Her mother burned incense, prayed, and lit candles to the Buddha. Aldo sat on the front steps chain smoking, and conversing with his dead mother in Sicilian, whose opinion it was to let the girl go have her own life. He could be cursed if he held her back. Margaret's exit ceremony consisted of placing an orange before the Buddha and kissing the Virgin's hands multiple times just to be sure.

The sad consensus was that she should follow her heart, leave their not-so-beloved, prejudiced, and crime-ridden town for a life in Fort Lee, New Jersey, where her Aunt Pei-chun ran a successful hair and nail salon.

Unlike In-Su, Pei-chun Americanized herself immediately upon arrival in the states. Her entire staff was required to wear red, white, and blue workout uniforms. Prominently displayed in her window was a modified Statue of Liberty lounging in a chair as her hair and toenails were done by little Taiwanese dolls. The sign said: "You Have a Right to Remain Beautiful."

So Margaret, who might have been cast aside, relegated to sit by the stove in some gentlewoman's kitchen between "service," was saved, reborn to eventually bring hundreds of babies into the world—the woman I love. The American, Asian, Sicilian Dream born once again. She promised to visit them often, but the average salary of a doula, unless she assists delivering quintuplets twice a week, is about the same as a side man in a mid-level boogie band, maybe less.

After Margaret's initial suspicion of me at the hospital I decided I'd do everything I could to win her trust. In fact I couldn't imagine a future for myself without her in it.

Gradually, over time, I sort of won her over, or she just got used to me hanging around. I'd do things for her; surprise her with my cosmic thoughtfulness, love being as political as redistricting. For example, I was summoned by the VA, not the one in Albany, not Fung's jurisdiction, but New York City, the mothership VA. There was a glitch in my records, their fault, but I had to produce myself; you know, the *habeas corpus* thing.

When I arrived, I was muscled into a basement office and given a battery of tests, the mental kind. I knew they were trying to cut costs like most government agencies and I figured I was fucked. If I lost my benefits I wouldn't make it on my part time jobs, definitely not sweeping up hair for Fay. The shrink told me that there was no way to fake out the test; they'd know if I was bullshitting. So, seven hundred cards with a question or a statement on each one. If you answered yes, it goes down on the right. If it's a no, it goes to the left. Seven hundred, what were the odds? I played it completely straight, figured I didn't have choice. The questions were not indistinct or cryptic like I thought they'd be. They were simple, like: I'd like to hurt a police officer if I could. No. My mother deserves to be punished. No. I'd like to position myself to be alone with the President. No. For Christ sake, this was psychotic Monopoly. I have a couple issues, but I'm not out to hurt anyone.

Anyway, a month later I got a letter from the VA. They bumped up my entitlement by five percent and included a prescription for Trifluoperazine, aka Stelazine, and suggested I take one tablet a day with lots of water. I'd tried one once at a party, just to be sociable. It felt like my brain had been hijacked by a gorilla in a Zip car. None of that shit for me.

The slight increase in my VA benefits helped, but I still kept my odd jobs, which seem to get odder as time passed.

One of them, the worst one I had, was as a Walmart free food sample guy for their Taste and Tips program. I wore a white shirt, green apron and cap, so I looked like one of their aliens. I stood behind an elevated tray and offered slices of flavored salami, buffalo, mango, etc., and neon-colored cheese cubes cut perfectly like dice on whole grain crackers.

The folks who rushed up to me for samples were like: Hi, I'm a storage container for cholesterol—feed me! But I was soon terminated for an obvious lack of zeal for the job and for sneaking bits and pieces. I figured for what they were paying me they should at least provide lunch, toxic as it was. I was caught on the surveillance video, which they played for me in slow motion in the manager's office. Slow motion, I guess to emphasis my crime. It was just missing a cinema noir soundtrack. But they paid me for the day...magnanimous.

Shit, I did it again. Fuck Walmart and the rest of that trivial crap. I was talking about something thoughtful I did for Margaret to win her over. I left the VA that day, it was snowing or raining. I guess it was a wintry mix. I had my big camouflage umbrella with me so there was much bumping, jostling, and swearing from my fellow pedestrians. I figured I had enough time before the next Pine Hill Trailways bus north to accomplish my mission. I made my way into the New York Public Library, a cathedral of knowledge that rivals any of the great institutions of Europe. I climbed the sacred marble stairs and made a smart salute to the pair of lions, Patience and Fortitude, who didn't bother to roar but yawned with disinterest at my sudden appearance.

I spoke to a baby faced young man at the desk. He asked me if I was a veteran as I had on a pair of worn, but clean fatigues. Based on my service, which he thanked me for,

I was allowed a pass into the Rare Books Division. I told him I was researching war. "Which one?" he asked.

"All of them," I said.

But I was really looking for something else, a reference to something I'd spotted in Margaret's papers, a very old book. A woman who vaguely resembled my high school English teacher, Mrs. Ramstein, approached me with obvious distaste, like who the hell let him in here? She wanted to know how she could help me, though she really didn't. I described the book and she nodded incredulously, turned a blunt heel, and I followed her. She put on a pair of thin cotton gloves, deactivated an alarm, then unlocked a drawer and slid it open. There it was, a sixteenth-century midwifery text, resting on some purple material, perhaps velvet. The gold title was all but faded. I could barely make out the word Ipswich, purported to be the oldest town in Britain. A dry aroma of old paper wafted up. "Why do you want it?" Her voice was like Brasso on an open sore.

"I'm studying to be a midwife." Her harsh snort of laughter drew attention from the other scholars in the room. I tried to make nice, share a bit of knowledge: "You know, there is speculation that the Virgin Mary was attended by a midwife. But her name is lost in time." Her harrumph was crushing. I'd never heard someone actually harrumph before. She could have harrumphed for a living. I asked her to turn some of the pages, which she did reluctantly, as if I'd asked her to spread sun tan lotion over my back.

I saw the words I wanted and quickly shot them on my iPhone camera, which was the equivalent of rare book molestation. She shoved the drawer in quickly and tapped her belt alerting the security guards.

I hardly got out my apology and explanation when they grabbed me on either side and escorted me out of the room and the building. They stood guard waiting for my disappearance into the churning throng below. I descended the steps, looked back, and shrugged helplessly at Patience and Fortitude. Their disgusted expressions revealed that they held me in rank contempt, lacking the qualities of either of their virtuous names. So, I descended the marble stairs wondering how I could accomplish what it was I planned for Margaret.

I was running late now and did something completely uncharacteristic and expensive; I took a cab to Port Authority so I wouldn't miss my bus. I was anxious to get back upstate to the rocks and trees, mammals, snakes and snapping turtles, and of course, the spooks. The driver had the heat cranked up like a Persian Sauna, but it felt good. Momentarily, insulated, shielded from the onslaught, the crushing action of the city, the greatest show on earth, I molded into the seat for a bit of peaceful luxury and closed my eyes and tried to visualize it. I hoped I'd got it; I was afraid I'd screwed it up in my haste.

I slid my fingers over the screen until the text was large and legible, and read: "A midwife should have a hawk's eye, a lady's hand, and a lion's heart." The noble, the courageous feline who protects the mother and child. I exhaled heavily and texted the words to Zeitzer so there'd be no chance of losing them. He texted back. "Are you off your meds?"

I shot back, "I don't take meds."

"Hmm, something to consider."

Safely ensconced back in the hamlet, I awoke the next day and remembered that for some damn reason we don't have a jewelry store. This is curious considering all the folks who collect rocks, fossils, and coins. They make really nice necklaces and stuff. I didn't have a choice; I'd have to go to Woodstock where no request is ever too esoteric to grant, if you have the cash.

I showed up at Rhinestones to Gold on an overcast Monday or Tuesday, as I figured there'd be less foot traffic in town. I got there ten minutes early and the sales girl told me that Judy Dazzle, the owner's professional name, was upstairs finishing her chai.

Meanwhile, the girl treated me to the usual lack of interest you get from the clerks in those shops. The dismissive attitude is a result of the residual fairy dust stirred up from the great festival of '69. The cannabis-infused dust settled upon their psyches and elevated them and their sacred village to a state of royalty on hallowed ground. The inhabitants, even those still alive after the fact of the "concert," take on the persona of post-festival elites. I tried a little conversation. "Think it'll snow?"

She considered that for a few moments and said, "It snows sometimes." Oh well, a complete sentence anyway.

Judy Dazzle emerged from the staircase donned in a thick sheepskin robe, sparkling and studded with synthetic gems, best I could tell. She was a large gal and went in for black eye makeup and a very red mouth, like she was there to sing Drolla in Wagner's *Die Feen*. Her earrings, a mass of brass rectangles and triangles touched her shoulders and might have doubled as mobiles. She summed me up as probably good for no more than four hundred dollars, which happened to be what I had to spend. I outlined the project to her, showed her the words I'd scribbled on the paper: "A midwife should have a hawk's eye, a lady's hand, and a lion's heart." I said I wanted it on an ankle bracelet.

She slapped it on the counter. "You want me to get all that on an ankle bracelet? You're crazy." Nice sales pitch.

"Yes, and I'd like it in old English lettering as well."

"That ain't fucking happening."

"Maybe I should try another jeweler."

"Look, Chris, Coot, whatever your name is, you don't know bupkis about engraving. Even if I could get it on an anklet you'd need the Hubble Telescope to read it." She exhaled, exasperated. We sat there a galaxy apart. The salesgirl looked up from her text message and observed us with supreme disinterest, listlessly chewing gum, a creature more oriented for the pasture, not a dynamic career in sales. It occurred to me she might be Judy's daughter.

"How about this?" She grabbed a pencil and drew what looked like the outline of a newborn or an amoeba, about an inch and three quarters around. "It would have to be a necklace. I could get it on that. It'd still be small, but legible. English lettering, no way."

We stared at each other for a while. The shop bell rang; the girl resisted her inertia and moved toward the door.

"White gold?" I asked.

"Fifteen hundred, at least."

"Sterling silver?"

"Five hundred."

That could work, but Margaret was gold and I wanted gold.

She read me like a midway carnie guy. "Maybe I could do it for eight hundred."

"For white gold?" I felt her reeling me in. I had a couple of collector's items, not described herein, that I could sell for the other four hundred.

"White gold," she hissed, conspiratorially, as if we were highwaymen about to rob Lord Sedgwick of his purse and his life.

"How sturdy would it be? It couldn't break, could it?"

She answered with a degree of solemnity, "Everything breaks if you don't take care of it."

I didn't want to give up the idea of an ankle bracelet.

I still had hopes of fastening the clasp around Margaret's graceful ankle. "I'll think about it."

I felt kind of trapped. Either I dealt with Dame Judy Dazzle or I'd have to make the dreaded pilgrimage to Revere Jewelers in Kingston. There was a guy there I'd heard about who made stunning creations out of galvanized garbage cans—very talented. I figured he could handle an anklet or necklace if there was no other choice.

When I left Ms. Dazzle I stopped to pay homage in the village green. There was a drum circle in progress, jubilant people of varying rhythmic ability, but all confirmed in their bliss. I listened and the drums said: 'Don't go to Kingston.' Good advice. Kingston triggers my most severe episodes.

I determined that I would have to trade with Dame Judy Dazzle. She made it clear that she would not lift a finger until she had a cash deposit of seven hundred dollars. I would pay the last hundred when I picked it up the merchandise. Failure to produce the final payment would result in her summarily melting the item in front of me and retaining my deposit. She seems to get off on authority.

I was very excited and spent the next few days selling off a couple of items that I won't mention. I got my finances in order. Then, on a warm spring morning, or mid-summer, who knows, with the promise of rebirthing of the green, with a bag of green cash and some green buds rustling around a green pill bottle, I set out for what I'd begun to refer to as Soupstock, as soup stock is at least nourishing and it mitigated my emotional turmoil about the town.

Zeitzer, in a generous, but forgetful moment, had mistakenly loaned me his Passat. So I traveled in luxury that day, turning right onto Route 375, Levon Helm Memorial Boulevard, the Yellow Brick Road so many had travelled before me in search of peace, piece of ass, acid, pot, and misunderstanding that passes for temporary arrangements. "Hey, man, I got some friends down the road. Like they'd be here but they don't have legs. Could you buy them some legs?"

Besides the green buds I'd partaken of before exiting the hamlet, my ear buds throbbed with "*and put the load right back on me.*" I was feeling light and airy, the car gliding about a half foot above the pavement. The trooper must have been parked at the Hurley Ridge Market. I didn't even notice the bank of flashing LED lights until the siren cut through the music. The obvious outcome of this adventure requires no further explanation, except to say that the trooper, for some reason, in his movements, waddling back and forth to his cruiser, and his facial expressions, reminded me of a blond duck, which I found hilarious. When he asked me for my license and registration, both of them AWOL, an additional infraction, I quacked at him and laughed uncontrollably.

The court appearance resulted in seven hundred and seventy-five dollars in fines and a suspension of my previously temporary suspended license now *in perpetuity*, the only motorist in New York State to earn this distinction. I am not even allowed to operate a riding lawn mower in Ulster County. My VA ID card spared me a month or so in lock up. Thankfully, there is the Pine Hill Trailways bus as mentioned earlier.

Zeitzer was initially peeved at me for this stunt, but he is a kind and forgiving man. For retribution I cleaned out his archival garage over a two-week period for free. If you need your garage cleaned out, I'm the guy. I detailed the floor, polished the tires on his car, sorted, and put his tools and everything else in order, stacked and tied up piles of *Mother Jones* magazines and recycled them. He was amazed at the job I'd done. The garage actually shined, if you can believe that a garage can shine. And he paid me two hundred dollars anyway. He is the most munificent person I've ever known.

At least I was free, but broke, my money gone to pay for my dumbass behavior. There would be no gold, silver, or galvanized garbage can, ankle bracelet or necklace. It was now out of the picture. I devised a last-ditch plan to deliver the saying about midwives to Margaret. I thought it was a novel idea. It would have to be on a cake. I would have to put all my eggs into one of the town baker's creations. But there would be a rude price to pay for it.

Coltaire, a notorious and spiteful baker, terrorized the town on a regular basis. He seemed to go off every time the fire siren sounded. He was at war with the town govern-ment, its inhabitants, and even his customers if they didn't present in a manner acceptable to him.

The bell tinkled ominously behind me. Through the glass case with its display of ornamental pastries, I saw Coltaire leaning over the oven. He withdrew a tray of perfectly browned Kouign-amann, aka butter cake. Why the hell couldn't he make a croissant? He carried the tray toward me then lifted it up to a shelf that displayed a plaster bust of Saint Honoré, the French patron saint of bakers, and whispered a few husky words to it. So, the guy for all his madness had a bit of religion in him. Bless this muffin oh Lord, our God. He set the tray gently on the counter, obvi-ously pleased with his work. And it did smell heavenly. "What the fuck do you want?" Ah, the welcoming shop-keeper.

"Got any coffee...please?"

"You know where it is." I went to the row of carafes and poured a cup of French Roast. It actually smelled good this time.

"Did you change your coffee?" I asked.

"You writing a fucking review?" Gently he removed each of the Kouign-amann with a spatula and set them on a thin white plate.

"It's good," I said, after tasting it.

"It's Café Bustelo, espresso style, if you really care to know."

"That's not French," I said.

Coltaire puffed out his chest and assumed his full portly height and glared at me. "You're not French. Two dollars."

I stood before the cash register and paid. Then I placed the crumpled piece of paper on the counter. "What the fuck is that?"

"I'd like you to put this on a cake."

"Get the fuck out of here."

"I'm serious, the way you decorate your cakes, your handwriting is...perfect for this."

"Are you fucking with me?"

"I'm not. You do beautiful lettering." The compliment caught him off guard and he softened a bit.

He considered my request for a few moments. "This won't be free, you know."

"I'll clean out your basement."

"You've been in my basement? Have you been there when I'm not home?" You had to admire the man's paranoia. It was fully realized.

We settled finally. I would keep the Route 213 traffic grime off of his wide shop picture window for two months. I thought that was fair. Then he started talking about different kinds of lettering and seemed to warm up to the project.

"How about old English lettering?"

"I hate the English."

"Yeah, I hear ya."

It was a long two months. I kept his store windows spotless and he kept adding on additional chores. I washed the cement steps leading up to his shop like a Bavarian scrub woman. I unloaded and stacked bags of flour in the store room. I cleaned the toilet and sinks and filled the potholes in his parking lot. I even did his laundry a few times. The amount of work I did paid for the cake three times over. But it was worth it.

Finally, he made it. On the appointed day at the precise time, Zeitzer and I presented ourselves before Coltaire. He looked upon us as something unfit for his aristocratic eyes, though we were all peasants and we knew it. He'd put a silk cloth over the multi-colored glass cake dome and wouldn't remove it until he had our complete attention. He described how he'd shaped the flowers by hand, and how delicately he'd formed the letters. He stepped back and withdrew from his apron pocket his master airbrush. He placed it between his legs so it pointed at us, and said defiantly. "With this, I make art."

Zeitzer and I acknowledged his superiority so he'd get on with the unveiling. He whisked the silk cloth away and Zeitzer gasped. I just stared at it, my heart pounding like a love drum. The letters were perfectly formed: A midwife should have a hawk's eye, a lady's hand, and a lion's heart.

"You are an artist," Zeitzer told him. Coltaire didn't hear him. He'd lowered his other hand and began to slowly stroke the shaft of his air gun. He stared at the cake, his eyes glazed over. Zeitzer and I exchanged "what the fuck" glances. We were momentarily trapped in an appalling tableau. I kind of felt sorry for the poor bastard. He made Pygmalion look like a camp counselor. Cautiously, I reached under the glass platform and slid it toward the end of the counter. This snapped Coltaire out of his reverie, to employ a euphemistic term, and he slammed the air gun down.

"Stop, that's my cake dome."

"I promise I'll bring it back." To put that creation into a cardboard box seemed like a travesty. We went back and forth about the dome. Finally, Zeitzer offered and Coltaire agreed to a fifty dollar deposit.

Outside, we drank in the fall air like a healing elixir after our brush with Coltaire's psyche. I think it was fall. It's always some goddamn season. I opened the trunk and we set the cake into a crate I'd prepared. It was lined inside and outside with bubble wrap. I attached three elastic bands to handles on the crate and looped them around the spare tire braces. Then I placed two-by-fours at angles so the crate could not possibly slide around. The cake was secure, gently cradled and safe, barring a tractor trailer mishap. Never has a cake been transported with such care, much less psychosis. We started out for Margaret's house.

Zeitzer, per my request, had set up the meeting. I sat in the car sweating as I watched him carry the cake up to her door. It weighed about nine pounds with the pedestal. He stalled on the second step and I thought he was going to drop the friggin' thing. She let him in and I sat there for the next fifteen minutes watching my shattered life pass before my eyes. What the hell could he be doing? I knew that she was fond of him and considered him a good influence on me. But I was dying there and already needed another shower though I had bathed meticulously with Old Spice Body Wash that morning in anticipation of our meeting. Finally, he came out and got back in the car.

"What?" I snapped. "She doesn't want to see me? What'd she say about the cake?"

Zeitzer exhaled, not quite completely exasperated. "All you have to do is go in there. She's accepted you. Coot, just do it, and don't do anything else for Christ's sake."

I was sweating. It came to me that this was perhaps the

most important moment in my life. What if I fucked up? I froze; I couldn't grasp the door handle.

Z gave me a little shove, "Go."

"Will you wait for me?"

"Jesus, Coot. I don't know…OK, I'll get coffee."

"I need you nearby. This is…Margaret."

He softened up. "I know about this, Coot. I know about…"

"What, Z? What are you saying?"

"I know about wanting someone."

"What's going on? You seeing someone?"

This time he shoved me a little harder. "Get out of my car."

The door was open. Margaret was in the kitchen leaning against the sink. She seemed to be deep in thought. I stopped in the doorway. The cake was on the table with a knife and two plates. I know we both read the inscription more than once: *A midwife should have a hawk's eye, a lady's hand, and a lion's heart.* And in her case, a solid left hook that could take me out if I got stupid.

There was something off about her, not her usual, which was to give a command, like "Coot, chop the onions."

I moved toward her. I will not describe the rest of the evening, but just say that I will never have another one like it. There could not be two of them in a light year. After…we put away about a third of the cake. Ironically, Coltaire's insane and perverted mastery worked wonders on both of us. I'd say that we ate my words, but they weren't mine. They'd been scribed centuries ago and now dedicated to Margaret. There were other words, unspoken but understood…that time and the mountain had moved and our lives had changed.

I completely lost track of time. It might have been three hours later. Z was sleeping in the car. I was crushed by a wave of guilt that I'd made him wait for me. He was a little grumpy. "Christ sake, Coot. You've got to get your license back."

It struck me violently in the car on the way home. I began to sweat profusely, and my stomach churned like a washing machine. "Pull over, now!"

Zeitzer slammed on the breaks. I jumped out and hurled on the sidewalk, couldn't make it to the lawn. Zeitzer parked and ran over to me with a wad of Kleenex. "Coot, what the hell is wrong?"

"Coltaire, the bastard must have used chocolate in the cake. I said no chocolate. I think I said that." I found out later that he'd used white chocolate for the lettering because he could control its flow better. I was so excited about the gift and presenting it to Margaret that I might not have mentioned it. My stomach felt like it was about to explode. And it went on from there, Zeitzer stopping every other block to let me relieve myself on bushes and lawns, in trash cans, and alleyways all the way back to the hamlet. I left an unfortunate, toxic trail behind me—no further description required.

Suffice to say I threw all my clothes in the trash when I got home and poured a rain collection container over myself before I went into the house. It went on like this for the next twenty-four hours. Margaret was anxious but I couldn't see her in this condition. I was too ashamed after her tender welcoming of me. I still couldn't believe that it had happened. Zeitzer told her he'd ordered me a medical bracelet: ALLERGIC TO CHOCOLATE.

Reverse alchemy instructs us that gold can be turned into silver and then into cake. I realized after the fact that it could have been written on a rusted license plate. It was the words that mattered. I should have stayed in the hamlet. I could have saved myself the stress and precarious travel to locations that unleash my demons.

Both towns, Kingston and Woodstock, present unique challenges for me, mainly to do with their inhabitants. Back in the hamlet we can't afford pretense, airs, or attitude. Tourists are not in awe of us; they walk around like they're at a game farm. And it's live and let live, no matter how crazy you are. The last time I was in Kingston I got caught in the Wellness Bar, formerly The Peg Leg, and had to wait out one of my worst episodes. I'd only had a couple Old Speckled Hens, a fine English Ale from the Morland Brewery in Oxfordshire.

Then, unannounced, it started. From the far end of the bar I saw a hen strutting defiantly toward me, and another one coming down the other way. They bumped breasts, upsetting my pint glass, then proceeded to pose threateningly at each other. Suddenly there were four of them involved in a hostile skirmish right there on the bar. I glanced at Noreen and she pantomimed, "Do you want another beer?" The hens were obviously invisible to her. But clearly they were there to rumble.

I recalled the Morland Breweries line of products: Old Speckled Hen, Old Crafty Hen, Old Golden Hen, and Old Happy Hen, but not so happy at the moment. More like Old Good and Pissed Off Hen. They went at it, feathers flying. Old Crafty Hen bitch-slapped me with her wing and I spit out a feather. This went on for a while until I noticed flickering lights at the windows. Flames shooting up high the entire length of the six foot casement windows of the tavern.

I was in the old Colonial section of town like I said—in days of yore, The Peg Leg, in honor of Peter Stuyvesant, who'd employed his prosthesis to assault the testicles of a Jewish merchant. Old Pete was not a fan of ethnic minorities. He's also the guy who believed he derived his authority from God, "not from a few ignorant subjects." Friggin' Dutch, I'd piss in their wooden shoes if I got a chance. Well, one of them anyway.

The flames caught the attention of the warring hens and they looked at each other like, "What the fuck, a barbecue?" And they were outta there, leaving a few hen droppings next to my glass.

I felt pressure against my knee and cocked my head to the left. Seated, snug up against me was a British Redcoat, complete with the tri-corner hat, white breeches, leggings, and boots. His face was red and bloated like he'd had a hissy fit.

"Pretty little fire, isn't it?" he said.

"Are you talking to me?" I asked.

"I'm telling you and all you bastard Colonists it's over."

"What's over?"

"Your pathetic little party—your revolution." I looked around for Noreen to see if she noticed the guy. Now she was dressed in a Colonial barmaid's outfit with a peek-a-boo blouse, stacking pewter mugs on a shelf instead of glassware. She gave me a coquettish wench wink, much appreciated.

Holy shit, I thought, it's 1777 and the Brits are burning Kingston. They'd done that to punish the Colonists for supplying our Revolutionary troops with food. The whole area was rich in farmland and there was plenty left over for our soldiers. Almost the entire Stockade area would be torched. That's why the capital wound up in Albany. But what the hell could I do about it?

The musket he'd rested against the bar was a toy, a squirrel gun, compared to the shit I'd given out from the supply room in Kandahar. And the guy was starting to piss me off.

"Check it out, Lord Nelson, or whoever you are, you

bastards made us ship everything we made here back to you, and you taxed us anyway." Then I thought, just like our government does now. I hate taxes. I think people should be able to keep what they earn. I was starting to get back some of my patriotic mojo. "You assholes lost the war anyway."

"Lost?" He was incredulous. "We are the greatest Army on earth."

"Yeah? Just one of our Abrams Tanks would have taken all of you bastards out at once."

"What? Abrams Tanks? Are you mad, sir?"

"And your strategy sucked as well," I added for good measure.

He was sputtering now, "See here, Major General John Vaughn is a brilliant strategist. Look," he pointed to the flames in the window, "he burns your little encampment now!"

"Great strategy? You bastards lined up like friggin' penguins in red jackets and we took you out."

"This is sedition! You will hang for this, sir."

Oh yeah, how would he know all this? He was still in 1777. Shit, so was I, at least for the moment, and I was talking to him.

He banged his fist on the bar. "A brandy, girl. A brandy, now!"

I felt something pressing against my right thigh. It was the knee of my good friend, Mr. Gold Robe, dressed for a night on the town. Between his white gloves he caressed a Cosmo topped with a flowered drink umbrella. "Nice place, huh?" He took a sip, then reached for my throat. "You little shit." He'd gotten less spiritual than he used to be. I went down fast, smacking my forehead against the bar.

When I righted myself I was dizzy, but the room seemed

to be back to normal. *Au revoir* to my companions, or rather *cheerio, dickhead*. Good old Noreen approached me with a pint glass, not a pewter mug, and said, "Try the Stone Delicious IPA; it kills."

And it did, with a hint of grapefruit no less. I switched to it immediately lest the hens come home to roost again.

What really oppresses me about Kingston, maybe I should say New Kingston, is the creature known as the hipster. And on they have come, as arrogant, disaffected, demanding, and with as much a sense of entitlement as the worst of the old Brits.

In fact, not long after my episode in the Wellness Bar I had a kind of hallucination. It happened around Passover; maybe it was Thanksgiving. I don't know. Instead of lamb's blood painted on the doorposts, all the hipster apartments and lofts would have an "H" spray painted on the façade and just those places would get torched.

I'd hire actors to dress up like Revolutionary War British soldiers to light 'em up. Kind of a replay on how the Colonists, dressed as Native Americans, had tossed the Earl Gray Tea into Boston Harbor. It's how it works. You make them think someone else did it.

Gentrification—the word sticks in my throat like a toothpick. By definition it's yet another throwback to Merry Old England. A gentleman expects a commoner to step out of his way even if it's into a stream of raw sewage running through the street. The gentrification of Brooklyn and other borough neighborhoods is a socio-economic disaster for our brothers and sisters of lesser means. And it's a slap in the face to the immigrants who built that great city, tunneled the holes out for the subway system, welded steel girders in the sky for the downtown towers, now aggressively encroaching on uptown, coaxed by the Yen and the Won. Phantom money structures menacing the pedestrians on 59th Street, and the mariners launching their fragile boats across the Conservatory waters in the park.

The hipsters come north with great expectations and a sacred belief in their divine entitlement. They buy or rent what seems like cheap real estate compared to the city, don their plaid shirts and party hats, and go in search of the perfect latte. This is not a sustainable system. Lifestyle is not work product. Posing is not creativity and does not contribute to the good of the commonwealth.

What really kills me is when they refer to themselves as expats. Ex-fucking-pats. That drives me *Equus africanus asinus* nuts, aka donkey shit. Yeah, like they're Gertrude's lost boys and girls tripping around Paris in the twenties. Yeah, those expats drank themselves into early graves, messed up bars, ruined marriages, crashed parties, used up a lot of people, fucked up pianos, but they produced something. They added prodigiously to the world's larder of significant art. Restoring a brownstone for a couple of brats from New Rochelle has to be weighed against the human cost of exclusion. It's "Removal," the new March of Tears. And fuck 'em if they don't hear the solitary strain of sorrow, of hu-fucking-manity.

But screw all that. There are people walking this earth so authentic and true that all the pop synthetic crap doesn't matter. I mean people like Z and Margaret. And I actually had her. Margaret was mine between bouts of distrust. She doesn't completely trust men. And I don't blame her.

Her last relationship, not long after she came North, was with an Iranian convenience store and gas station magnate in Northern Jersey, an unlikely match, for a woman who cherished her freedom above all else.

I won't mention the name of the town, stick my neck out as it were. He used to threaten her with moving them back to Iran where she'd become a proper, obedient Muslim wife, wear a hijab, the whole nine yards. He thought, with her cream and coffee complexion, he could pass her off as at least Turkish, who knows maybe even from Miami, to explain her exotic features. She wouldn't be allowed to talk very much anyway.

He, Hamzah, didn't know something about her that I know all too well. The woman is constructed of durable, rustproof steel, carbon-coated and reinforced. That's just her body. Her mind, her reasoning capacity, her instantaneous ability to take your inventory, her sense of complete and utter self-determination, is like a tightly wound barbed-wire ball in a bear trap inside a shark cage, and that's when she's just feeling mellow. Hamzah's threat of an Iranian honeymoon in his tribal village engaged her mettle. The gears shot into quick propulsion and she was gone by evening prayer time, didn't even vacuum his rug.

To cover her tracks and assure permanent disengagement and supreme autonomy she had her girlfriend's husband, a mid-level accountant at the IRS, visit Hamzah one morning, after a series of letterhead mail abuses, to take a look at his books. He even sneaked a call in from the office to provide an official caller ID that he hoped would never be detected. He used a colleague's phone number to do this. The crappy government issue Ford Focus he showed up in helped.

Like most books there were accounting errors that smelled of missing cash, but this one suggested there were transcontinental banking deposits such as, The Central Bank of the Islamic Republic of Iran. This unnerved the guy to the point of diarrhea because if this impropriety popped up on someone's laptop at headquarters, an eyebrow the size of the St. Louis Arch would be raised. He and Hamzah could wind up sharing a fifty-year suite at Leavenworth, or so he imagined.

Still, he followed through. His wife lobbied hard for him to help Margaret. A persuasive woman, she agreed to play pony girl for a series of weekends, not described herein. Despite a couple of Hamzah's thugs in the office, patting handguns under their Burberry Modern Fit Wool Silk suits, not exactly the attire a modest Muslim worships in, he managed to cinch it based on a particular expenditure, a donation. There was no way the new playground at the mosque could go for five and a half million dollars. "The monkey bars must be solid platinum," he said. This resulted in short guttural laughter and increased suit jacket patting.

After the meeting Hamzah promptly dropped his all-points bulletin on Margaret and was forced to keep a closer eye on his shops and clean up his bookkeeping practices. He never understood why the IRS didn't follow through with an audit and make him pay a hefty fine. They didn't even deport some of his shadow employees. It definitely put a fly in his babaganoush.

Speaking of culinary delights, Margaret's second passion is cooking. She will occasionally make me a wicked good meal of Gua-bao Pork and Shitake Goreng over rice or eel noodles. I bring the Tsingtao Beer, which is perfect with these molten hot dishes. It also gives me the opportunity to make my usual toast before dinner: "Tsingtao and get funky." Margaret always says that was funny the first thirty times. Permanence is not a discussion topic, birth sure is. She can go on about it until I get morning sickness. I understand about the permanence thing, the Eastern philosophies cover that in spades. And I can't talk permanence when I can't exactly explain what it is I do for a living. "Odd jobs, hunter, certainly not poet," is not part of her lexicon. She likes things cut and dried, everything on the table.

She once let me take her on the table...divine. It's none of your business. Let's just say that when she takes action, she takes it thoroughly, and with a tender violence that shakes my core—nothing is to be taken for granted. It's as if she possess the power of hundreds of women whose babies have awoken in her hands.

I've never loved or will love any woman but her. She knows it; I know it. She is capable of using this information against me like a geek in a batting cage. I hold her in esteem, like Harriet Tubman or Serena Williams. She is, at five-nine, an Amazon of sculpted beauty and physical grace.

One time, just one time, after a hot-pot that got me lapping water from the sink faucet, she made some offhand remark about bestowing a child upon me, which she of course would deliver, while giving me terse and succinct directions. It was a mad July night, I think, maybe November, and I went dairy-swirl frozen in the bed next to her. "What?" she said, "What's wrong?"

"My dream," I gagged. I'd do it if I got the whole package. Her, her earthly body, and the baby, Wonder Girl-bot, no doubt. But I don't think I convinced her. She never mentioned it again, and broke up with me multiple times in between. But she's the one. The misguided past excursions I've taken with other ladies, before I knew her—they're all just blank canvases. She's the one I'd like to paint my masterpiece on, if she'd let me.

After the baby thing, during one of my summary dismissals, and being denied bed privileges anyway, I took a few nights off, kind of a self-banishment as it were. I left her to ruminate about my true character. She must have wondered what kind of father I would be. Could I even do it?

In the wild it's the lioness that does the hunting while the male sits on his duff waiting for cheeseburgers. A random thought, but it fits Margaret. She wants to be the aggressor; I'm down with that. There is something deep in her character, something that sticks her like a sewing needle. She will never settle for just an ordinary guy, despite her background, her desire for "normal." As much as she can't tolerate my waywardness she won't completely reject it.

I had retreated up the mountain, my place of refuge and meditation. There was rumbling and lighting that night, pebbles and stones tumbling down around stumps and vines, intimations that soon there will be a finale to what seems to percolate in this town. I sensed a climax, a termination; *ne plus ultra* is not far off.

My go-to place on the mountain is the Ruined Cottage. Not Wordsworth's, with "…four naked walls / That stared upon each other," but similar. As I thought about the poem, I remembered that it was about a woman named Margaret. The woman who stayed in the cottage and waited. A great fucking poem. Loss, devotion, and misery, the only subjects worth writing about.

My ruined cottage is an abandoned brick outbuilding, a pump house, the roof ripped open to the elements, the rest soon to give up its shredded blue tarp. The structure emerges early on the trail, situated at an angle that beckons, and startles the traveler, just before the rise that takes you by twists and turns, tripping roots, and stubborn boulders to the summit of Joppenbergh Mountain.

A local artist had spray painted Dr. Eckleburg eagle eyes on the presenting walls that watch for intruders. And there had been some recent activity, witnessed by discarded cans of Busch, a non-beer, and a nest of cigarette butts. The entrance lacks a door so any approach on foot, hoof, or underbelly sounds the alarm.

A treasure of remnants from the mining days: a dead

electrical board with a thick cable running up and over the roof. Looks like enough juice to run a small Dead festival. There is a pump, maybe five hundred pounds with a series of pipes, levers, and handles that provided water to cool the kilns. The bricks that comprise the walls are mostly in place, the product of the sprawling Hutton Yard braced up against the shore of the Hudson.

Modern decorations have been added to adorn this recent antiquity. Inside, fading illegible chalk markings proclaim the undying love of someone for someone, but the heart is obvious. "Pussy Riot" broadcasts loud and clear, pulsates, thanks to iridescent spray paint. And long may they live and live free—more bastards, the Russians. Here's history and government in ten words: Kill them or lock them up in a hole forever. Think about it. When was the last time the bastards got in touch with you to ask you how you're doing?

When I'm up there, I sleep on a thick piece of foam I've dragged up the trail, covered with two Army issue sleeping bags and a quilt with wild horses embroidered that my grandmother, thinking it might be cold, mailed to Afghanistan.

And for all this, the not-so-mild PTSD and recurring dream of the girl I almost didn't "save" from those savage assholes, and for the sorrow of Wordsworth's Margaret, who wasted away in her Ruined Cottage for the love of he who went off to soldier, and for her dead babe.

Talk about being attached to a sense of place, home; that's where you want to die. This is where I go to remember, to meditate, to suffer dreams that beg sanity. It's where I go when the noise and the rattle of the hamlet becomes a cudgel to my compromised skull. And where I go when Chief Cruickshank needs to have a little chat with me.

I camped out here for two weeks last February, or was

it December. At night the snow sifted through the roof like a manger scene, but with just one jackass in there, me. A veteran, a vet is what I'm called, a person who went where no one else wanted to go, did things no one else would do, bonded with other men in a complex, deep friendship, incomparable to any other human relationship you can imagine—ultimate altruism. That's why some of us go back; we can't find the same kind of intensity or truth out here.

But you pay for it...the girl...always the girl, the recurring dream. It's one of the things that haunt me, and it almost got me court martialed. An impropriety involving a deal gone bad for some forbidden Kandahar schnapps. I left base without permission and headed about two miles west. I was out of my league with these border rats. First we sat in front of their tent and drank tea. Their women served us. I noticed that they were all bruised, obviously beaten and abused, couldn't lift their eyes up from the ground.

So, instead of buying the hooch, I lectured them on human kindness: that you don't beat up on women; it didn't make you a man, it made you a scummy bastard. I should have been on suicide watch. After the translator shared that with them, they took my tea cup and beat the shit out of me, stole my cash, my boots, my M16, and shoved a young girl on top of me, who they apparently had no more use for.

I hated myself; remorse was not even a default position. I limped back to camp with this...child, carried her most of the way when she'd passed out from exhaustion. I presented myself before my boss, Colonel Cortez, and pleaded with him to let me find a way to make it right for the girl, Abessa, as I understood her name to be.

Miraculously, incredibly, in an unmilitary fashion, he allowed me to escort her to Kabul where there was a branch of Catholic Charities running an orphanage for girls. They even managed to place some of them in good homes in the states with Afghani families or any family that met the criteria, mainly in the metropolitan area. Cortez even let me borrow a jeep, which broke down five miles from the town. I knew when I left it with the smiling crew at the Good Guy Repair Center I'd never see it again anyway.

I had to find food and water for both of us after our rations ran out. All the time she stared at me, a terrified, misused child. When would I beat her, rape her, cut her throat?

We got there. The nun, Sister Lisa, spoke Farsi and English. I explained most everything; editing out the parts that pertain to my mortal soul, the one I can't feel. They took her in, whisked her inside before anything could go wrong, but she resisted just before they got her past the threshold. She stared at me, frail, fucked over by the tribal fathers who should have delivered her from evil, whom I'd have killed on the spot, her dried lips moving.

Something, a small piece of ordinance unhinged, searing the inside of my chest and I began to sob. Sobbing in front of Sister Lisa and this girl. I sobbed and I bowed to the girl repeatedly because I didn't know what else to do, how else to say goodbye. I bowed, I think, because it was the only way I could honor her life, acknowledge the possibility that she might have a life, maybe even a good one. Maybe she'd get out of this hellhole one day. The connection was such, the fact of our escape, and her ultimate safety was like a thin blue fiber optic line connected between her solar plexus and mine.

Sister Lisa stepped up and made the sign of the cross on my chest. She blessed me, a first, as I know from my mother on her deathbed, that they'd forgotten to baptize me, being one of nine children. I bowed to her once more, a pathetic example of the American soldier. There was no, "You're welcome, miss, just doing my job."

Late that night, whatever time it was, I dragged myself into the village center where I'd left the Jeep; the garage, as I expected, was vacant. There was a cracked fountain with a cement statue of some patriarch; I'd begun to hate all of them. I dropped down and shoved my head in the water, forcing myself to keep it submerged, experimenting to see if drowning could be an intentional act. Finally, I jerked my head up gasping for air, because there's no choice. I said to that uncompromising stone face, "I would have died for that girl. What do you motherfuckers do for anyone?"

There is nothing in my life, nor will there ever be, of more importance than saving that child. And what confluence of luck helped me do it? Maybe that's what that aura reader / barroom queen in Virginia was hinting at. Whoever I am, and I admit that I may not be that much, I would have died for that little girl.

I must have passed out slumped against the cool stone. I was awakened, not gently, by a group of village elders who dragged me away from there to avoid detection and a swift knife to the gut. I was fed, clothed in local duds, armed with a map with neat Arabic lettering that I couldn't read, and sent back to my base with Allah's blessing. So, I thought at sunup, Jeepless, soulless, heading into the blinding glare of a naked, charbroiling day, sinking into the life-sucking sand, *You got some mercy you lousy bastard...just get me get back alive. And this time I promise, I'll stop fucking up.*

I realized, as I faced the inferno and a possible finale, that there was, unaccountably, a song in my head. A goddamn song. Why? My friend Mary, when she came through the hamlet once a year to play The Miner's Theater and Performance Art Space, she always sang this song she wrote called "Mercy Now." When I first heard it and every time after, I'd slip out the side door to be alone, overpowered with the feeling that sang gave me. And not just me, everyone who heard it. It was one of those quiet songs that did slow open heart surgery on you. It made you want to give mercy and ask for it as well.

And it made me sorry. Sorry for the brothers I lost in Helmand Province. Sorry for everyone who hurt, everyone who died in terrible pain, who died alone, the ones who'd lost their minds to whatever and couldn't experience, couldn't take in this vast, shocking, penetrating beauty that presents itself in rich colors every moment we walk on the earth.

That is the core of it, what I'm trying to embrace before I revert back to my selfish, addictive ways. I get to walk around and see this vibrant show when I'm not too stupid and self-involved to let it all come in. And, more important, I get a chance to do something for someone.

People cried when Mary sang that curiously complex, but simple, shattering song. And I heard it in my head now all the way back to base, even though I did not know how to get there. She sang it to me. It was like an aural compass. I know that Mary saved my life. So, I guess I know two good things.

And I'll carry those things with me for the rest of my life. Abessa...Mary...and my Margaret, my three muses that give and take life from me. I feel them operating me with silk strings, pulling, twisting my soul into a figure eight. The soul I can't see or taste.

This one is for Margaret. I think it's my most Wordsworthian attempt. And I'm giving you the whole thing. Screw the copyrights.

MARGARET
Obsidian Goddess, long

I served your temple, held
Gold chalice to your lips,
Lift silk over tortile curls,
Taste with supplicant's lips
Your nectar, divine tonic,
For which Helen's war was waged
I kiss the entrance of life,
Oh, sacred canal
Whence no soul returns
Bliss to enter, when Rose
Or Flower moon prevail,
And the Goddess yield...
Creation, high or low
Its form may be,
Afore final night,
May know
A spark—Paradise to hold,
And then to let go

It was first published on a writing sample that was rejected, along with my application to Bard College. I didn't think they'd reject a veteran. I'd decided to kick it up a notch and apply to their writing program, prestigious bastards. The woman who administered my entrance exam was a Bard matron who'd stayed on after she'd graduated and got to torment applicants who applied to the program.

She tried to throw me a small bone. She thought I might be good at writing jingles, like for commercials. There was a certain "sing-song quality" she found in my work that was "kind of charming." Of course I'd already had a hundred ideas for jingles. I told her about one, a very cool idea for a commercial to promote asparagus, perhaps not the most popular vegetable compared to french fries. I'd sent it out to both the San Joaquin and National Asparagus Festivals in California and Michigan, respectively.

It goes like this: everything is clouded in mist with mysterious music in the background. Slowly a thick, green asparagus missile, a spliff, lifts up off a launch pad, sparks flying. Suddenly it rips into the sky and the music from *Hair* (remember *Hair*?) comes up loud. They sing: "This is the dawning of the Age of Asparagus, The Age of Asparagus, A-s-p-a-r-a-g-u-s."

Get it? You see the green asparagus careening into the stars. It suggests that you'll be powerful if you eat asparagus. You'll blast off on fuel infused with n-butanol, antioxidants, and fiber. And, get this, it's good for a hangover—I'm sold. The stuff shields liver cells. What's not to like? I always order a side of asparagus when fine dining. Problem is most bars don't offer asparagus, just Slim Jims, beer nuts, and blue hard boiled eggs. I thought it would at least fly in California. "Hair" for Christ sake!

Anyway, I sweated bullets over Margaret's poem. Zeitzer said it was beautiful and it was their loss to turn down a talent like mine. But the bastards didn't let me in. It's as Romantic as anything Wordsworth ever penned and Margaret's a colossal beauty compared to some of those faded English *ladies* he got down with. They were all so wimpy and asthmatic.

Don't get me wrong, he's a great poet. He couldn't help that he was English, those wormy little White bastards with their tea and cakes, fox killers, high manners, and disdain for the lower class. They were fond of hanging derelicts and the mentally ill. Their treatment of the Irish was unforgivable—you don't fucking starve people—one potato, two potato at a time.

Yeah, English History, not so pretty. At this point I'm more focused on local history. This place drips with it. That's what motivated me to pay a visit to the town historian, Doe Gottlieb. That and a need for an infusion of cash.

I could always count on her for a cleaning project or two. Doe's office is conveniently located just off Main Street.

Not a lot of folks stop by to see Doe. She has a bit of a strange reputation. She's solitary, always alone. You'll see her walking along the berm at night, or maybe at the farmer's market. She'll grab a few items then disappear, an Eleanor Rigby type.

After I helped sort some files and vacuum a few years of dust off some crates waiting to be sorted, I followed her upstairs to her office. She rummaged through a filing cabinet bursting with records and took out a picture. "That's Colonel Jacobus Rutsen, our town's founder," she said with distant reverence. "He named the mountain after himself, Joppenbergh. It means Jacob's Mount."

She backed toward me, "I think I got a deer tick hiking up there yesterday, will ya look?" I took the magnifying glass off her desk as she flipped her hair up. "See anything?"

"Nothing yet." She kind of leaned back into me until she was up against me.

"Move up a bit," I said, getting uncertain about just what kind of tick this might be.

"Coot, do you think my hair looks OK? I mean, should I do something with it?"

"I guess you should wash it once in a while, I guess," was all I could think to say.

"See anything?"

"Just a tattoo—who's Andy?" I was seeing more of her neck than I needed to.

"Andy was…a man. A man who loved me very much—don't laugh."

"I'm not." I've learned not to laugh at people. That's one of the meanest things you can do. I think some pretty bad things about some people. I guess that's not any better.

Doe's office window faced the mountain and I looked up at it. The rounded dome, cracked with fissures, protruded and was spiked through with evergreens tilting precariously over the side. It seemed always to be quaking slightly, ready to let rip with a killing rock slide. There was definitely something going on up there.

"Well?"

"What?"

"Ticks, tick! Do you see a tick?"

I let her bob flop down and took a step back. "No, unless it's so tiny—deer ticks are tiny."

She spun around and faced me full on. She has a square face; her mouth and nose and eyes are at an uneven distance from one another as if her features had been twirled on a potter's wheel, flung out, and then settled where they landed, the effect not wholly displeasing.

"Do you want to kiss me, Coot?"

I sensed that this was coming and hadn't yet come up with a plan of action; well, inaction. "I'd be glad to do more sorting for you," I said weakly.

She stiffened, and then stepped away, giving me one last Picasso glance with her cubist features. She sat at her desk and took up her pince nez, all official now, picked up a glass unicorn, peered through it, and rattled off the facts as if she were channeling: "Rutsen was a merchant. He came down here from Albany in 1680, Colonel Jacobus Rutsen. Our first settler." Her tone was sarcastic. "He bought the place from a Lenape Indian for a nickel. He is regarded as our founder because it didn't count that the natives were here first, which is how history operates.

"Rutsen explored the lands, mapped them out, and claimed them as his own. He especially noted the mountain that rises above the Creek and appropriated it as well. In the colonial, explorer spirit he named it after himself: Jacob's

Mount. Others call it Jacob's Nose or Jobsenbright. Three hundred and sixty years later it's Joppenbergh. And it's as magical, strange, and haunted as any pre-revolutionary site in the country."

"You've got some memory, Doe."

She set the unicorn down and said, "You got a girl, Coot? You got someone?"

"Well, I'm kind of ...between, you know." I shuffled a little; I hate it when I do that.

"You've got a jones for that little ho at the café, don't you? Everyone knows it."

"You mean Delcie, she's just...I don't know, a waitress."

Doe picked up a random file from a box and opened it. "You need anymore history?" she asked.

"No thanks," I said, backing up a few steps.

"Then you are."

"What?" I asked.

"History."

A thought came to me; I'd leave her some venison steaks when I got my first buck in the fall. I didn't want to part like that, her mad at me because I didn't respond. I still had hope, like a kid searching a gumball machine for the magic eye, that Margaret would roll her hard-coated sweet surface into my mouth for keeps.

"You know," I said, "I don't pay any attention to that crap Gil Fashion says about you. You know your stuff." Her cool dismissal turned into a threatening scowl.

"Gil Fashion isn't fit to be something stuck on the bottom of my shoe."

I nodded sympathetically. Doe had beat out Gil for the job of town historian because she had an Associate degree and didn't display the level of obsession Gil did. She has issues but manages to keep them at bay in the backpages of her personal history.

Gil, on the other hand, had taken up a crusade against her, contradicting her credibility, knowledge, and the old documents she collected and displayed under glass at the library. He went around town lecturing about the town's true history to anyone who'd listen. Not many did. He did everything he could to soil Doe's reputation, her authenticity as a historian. Despite his ugly presence she remained true to her office and only dealt with facts. Their feud didn't cause much of a stir, but attests to the point that we are the town of, among other things, doppelgangers: the historian and the shadow historian.

Doe dismissed me. "Get out." I wasn't complying, so she was done with me. I glanced at her on the way out. Her features seemed to have reshuffled during our exchange, her nose more to the left, her mouth tipped up, both eyes at odd angles. More like Modigliani I decided.

Key lime pie. It just popped into my head. I needed something a little sweet after my acerbic treatment from Doe. I ordered it with a cup of black coffee. Delcie, usually the perky, saucy elf, carried the tray like she was in a funeral procession. "What's going on?"

"Nothing."

"Something is. You're not you."

Tears streamed down her face, perfect and translucent they dropped into my coffee and on top of my pie. "I'm...pregnant. And Cal won't marry me. I can't tell my parents. They'll disown me."

"Jesus, Delc, Cal's an asshole. You want me to try and talk to him?"

"If you want to go to Vancouver."

"The asshole ran away?"

"He's taking a bike trip to think it over. His mother lives there. He ran home to his mother just like a little boy," she shrieked, and wiped her nose on her sleeve.

"Fucking asshole." I wanted to go find him, and then what?

"Coot, what should I do?"

"You've got to talk to Margaret. She'll think of something." Knowing Margaret I figured she'd offer to deliver Delcie's baby for free, nurse it, and then let her move in with us. It sounded like it was way too late for a Morning After pill. I didn't want to ask her how far along she was. She retreated to the wait station.

Poor Delcie, her folks were straight up fundamentalists of some sort. Abstinence was the only one-way road you could take. They'd probably throw her out of the house for sure.

I left Bebe's and headed home. I figured I'd get Margaret on this right away. But I got sidetracked by a sickening image. A mangled bicycle like a black and white photograph of a crime scene. And it was a crime. The bastard Gerhardt intentionally drove his Dodge Ram 2500 Diesel Truck (blood red) with a Snow Chief Package over Brock's bike. Brock, Gerhardt's own kid, for Christ sake! Brock had just a split second to eject himself over a guardrail into a patch of Witch Hazel before the impact.

Brock is a nervous, delicate kind of guy; he constantly squints and looks at you askance, never straight on, even while riding his bike, always on his bike until it got mangled. He volunteers at the Food Pantry and Angel Food. He does a great job. He's at his best when he's doing something for someone else.

I've made use of the food pantry when I've run low on supplies. I'm particularly fond of the Campbell's Chunky Healthy Request line, convenient when I'm on bivouac. They even make a low-fat and cholesterol-free Chicken WonTon Soup, surprisingly good.

Brock's dad, Gerhardt, is the kind of asshole who'd take

out his own kid because he seems effeminate. Gerhardt is the assistant fire chief and experiences life as if he's shooting hot vinegar through his hose. Mucho macho with a grasshopper's brain, he's everything Brock isn't. If the two of them were weather patterns, the dad would be a hail storm of ball-bearing stones. Brock is a kind, soft spring shower. Suffice to say he lives on the geographical farthest point on the map from his father's house.

Brock's mom visits him with home cooked meals and want ads. She secretly wants him to go to seminary school. He'd be "protected" that way—she told me. Every time I see her she's got a new bruise on her face. Beating up on women is the lowest scumbag form a man can take. And he beat the hell out of Brock as well. I don't know why she didn't take her son and get out. Some day Gerhardt is going to get his.

Not long after that, Brock completely lost it, attempted suicide and was shuttled off to Burnt Hills for an extended engagement—the poor bastard. If you're not too bad off it can be handled in-house over at Benedictine. But if you really scratch the devil's ass, it's Burnt Hills. "Where's Brenda?" someone might say. "Haven't seen her in about a month." The answer might be, "Oh, she's burnt out in Burnt Hills." Not exactly a professional diagnosis.

Anyway, I already knew Brock's story. He was one of my "spillers," one of a group of people who singled me out to spill their guts. They figured it was safe, a crazy veteran who wouldn't remember anything anyway. But I do remember everything, sort of. He had to get it off his chest before it killed him, and he tried to anyway.

When did he tell me? I think it was last fall. I remember leaves blowing around, maybe it was newspapers. He spotted me in Willow Kiln Park, my default office, where I receive people and examine acorns for orange grubs. He still had his bike. He took a Schlitz Tall Boy out of his backpack and offered it to me. Someone had left it as a donation at the food pantry, not my first choice, but one needs to be thankful for waving grains. We sat at a picnic table under an Incense Cedar near the trailhead, a bucolic moment, except for his story.

He was terribly agitated. I offered him a sip, but he wouldn't take it. When he was in his mid-twenties, he'd run away from home, away from his abusive father, and joined a cult in the South American rainforest. It was an extreme "Goddess" cult that worshipped Mother Earth. He agreed, after chewing a few too many coca leaves, to participate in a ritual where the men in the cult mutilated their testicles, with a little help from a painted priestess. The purpose of this ritual was to prevent the men from imposing male dominance on the earth, nature, or on all things "Goddess," a terrible irony as Brock is as gentle as a baby blanket suffused with fabric softener.

Afterwards, the goddesses dressed them up in ceremonial robes and prepared a special feast for the mutilated men, rich with dark leafy greens to help replace red blood cells, not a fair trade in my opinion. There are probably better ways to save the rainforest, like making a donation to Greenpeace or eating at the Rain Forest Café. He cried; I almost retched, but controlled myself.

"My father doesn't know. He just thinks I'm gay." The look on his face reminded me of villagers I'd seen who'd survived attacks by the Taliban, complete devastation.

"You know, Brock," I said, "nuts are overrated anyway. Most guys I know rarely put them to good use. When we'd take fire in Afghanistan we just shit our pants." He was responding to this, so I added, "Manning up isn't just getting it up. It's the way you carry yourself in the world. It's what's in here." I tapped my chest and hoped that I wasn't too full of shit. But I had to say something useful to him. He was drowning. I couldn't just leave him like that, a very broken civilian. I wanted to go find Gerhardt and wrap his hose around his neck in an Alpine Butterfly.

About a month later Brock attempted suicide and ended up at Burnt Hills. I wished he'd talked to me first. I might have been able to talk him out of it. But he was desperate. You tend to lose self-esteem when your own father tries to kill you. All I could think of was how I could nail Gerhardt.

I keep thinking I should get a bus to Burnt Hills and visit him. But what could I bring him? He can't have it back. None of us can get back what we've lost: time, people, limbs, nuts and bolts, love, hell yes, love. That's the hard one; when love's gone you struggle to hang on to it, to carry it with you the best you can, but it's like trying to cup hundred-year-old cognac with your hands. You run with the precious stuff, but it trickles through your fingers until you lose all of it.

Speaking of confessions, I would never reveal the horrific details of the treatment I underwent in Helmand Province. But here they are: I made the mistake of squatting on the ground—there was no place else to go. Even the desert sand there is out to get you. It's a bad fungus that can only be treated with diluted bleach. It's called Dalkin and it's worse than an ass transplant.

Around this time, October (might have been May), Gil Fashion went off again on Doe Gottlieb. He got up on his soap box, a red milk crate, and began an incoherent rant against her. Gil was just a bookworm; he memorized facts then delivered them in skewed torrents because his recall wasn't all that good. History for Gil was more about passion, who did what to whom, which pretty much is history. But he maintained that Doe makes up her facts or relies on

the internet for our town history without even fact-check-
ing it.

This time he was dressed in traditional Lenape clothing.
Let's get this right: Len-AH-pay. The Lenape, aka the
Delaware Indians, were living here in peace before Jacob
Rutsen and the rest of the murderous white Europeans
arrived, the beginning of the long kiss of death for the
Native Americans. Let's face it, we live on stolen, blood-
fertilized land. The blood of the tribes. So there's Gil in
a breechclout, moccasins, bone and shell wrist and ankle
bracelets. He'd coated his skin with some make up, a reddish tone.

"Rutsen stole the land from them, stole it. Who was
Jacob Rutsen, you ask? Besides a thief. He's a megaloma-
niac, that's what he is! He settled the town all right, settled my ass. Cheated the Lenapes. A militarist, that's what
he is: a captain, major, lieutenant, and colonel of the Ulster
and Dutchess County troops. 1700 for those who care, ah
shit. Ya see that mountain there?" He pointed up above
the façade of the theater. "Only an egomaniac would name
it after himself, a man who spawned seven children in
his own image. He entertained Washington at Hardenbergh
Hall with dainties and wine in that fancy neighborhood.
Where is he now? You want to know?" No one asked.
"He's dead, and you know what marks his grave?" No one
asked. "Two small iron posts, that's what. Go find em." Gil
seemed overwhelmed, at a loss. He slumped on top of his
milk crate, the native coating sweating down his torso from
his effort.

As usual, Gil had his head up his ass about the facts.
If you go past the library on Central Avenue just pass
Josephine Avenue there's a little broken down cemetery.
The biggest grave marker in there, about five feet high, has
a plaque on it: JACOB RUTSEN, 1650 – 1730. How Gil

could have missed that is a shocker. Faux town historian, not so much oxymoron as moron.

Gil's second mistake that day was that he chose to make his presentation on the sidewalk in front of the bakery, Le Raide Éclair, whose hair-trigger proprietor, Clotaire, guards his property and business like three-headed Cerberus guards the entrance to Hades. Clotaire is a hell of a baker, he's just out of his fucking mind—obvious to me the first day he opened and I went to buy a baguette and welcome the dude. The bastard didn't have any baguettes; he didn't like them, too common or something.

What he had were all these little fruit pastries on doilies, and cheese rolls, petit sandwiches, and soft puffy cookies. I hate puffy cookies. The coffee tasted like friggin' Maxwell House, and it turned out it was. I spied the empty can in the trash. The motherfucker didn't even recycle. And, get this, no espresso. No espresso?! My favorite breakfast besides oatmeal with raisins, a teaspoon of brown sugar, and a heavy stout, is a croissant and an espresso, the stronger the better. Just Maxwell House? Bebe serves good strong organic coffee, the only decent cup in town.

So Coltaire charged out the door; he's a big boy, a linebacker in his baker whites and coifed blondish-white hair. The word is he was a consummate soccer thug and an unmitigated womanizer in his hometown of Mittelbergheim, home to the Mittelbergheim Maulers. They prided themselves in inflicting as many injuries on their opponents as they did goals. Especially when they were tanked up on the local Grand Cru Zotzenberg—a fine *vin de pays,* but it ain't no IPA. The welcome bell tinkled as he went after Gil and kicked the milk crate out from under him. So much for freedom of speech. No *"Bonjour, comment allez-vous?"* Just kicked it, and Gil falls on his faux Native American ass.

By then there was a crowd of about twenty of us gathered and we helped Gil off the sidewalk. He was understandably pissed and yelled: "You asshole, fucking asshole. Never shopping here again. Go back to Frogville or wherever the fuck you came from." Coltaire, who doesn't require incitement, went off on Gil flailing a frosting knife, smeared with what looked like his delicious raspberry frosting. Say what you will, the guy was a frosting genius. He could make frosting out of industrial lubricants.

Suddenly, there was a low rumbling noise coiling down the street and everyone stopped and looked toward the mountain. "See," Gil shrieked, "you'll pay for this, Frenchie! You'll pay." Slowly we dispersed, except Coltaire who continued to slash away at the mountain. He cursed it out: "*Nana, vagin, de pus.*"

Gil threw a half-hearted punch at Coltaire. I took his arm and guided him across the street. "Coot, what the hell is he saying?"

"I think he's calling the mountain a pussy—not a good idea."

I resented Coltaire calling this noble mountain names. It is my sacred duty to steward this great peak, this unique summit, this majestic pinnacle that is so much more than a pile of stone. It is the very buttress that supports the span of centuries that resulted in this diverse enclave, this odd tribe of misfits who inhabit this place and its purlieu.

And the most dire threat to the mountain came recently from the very people sworn to protect it—the town board. Like most towns our politics are low and dirty. Our supervisor is a big man; we call him "The Shirt." That's because his shirts never completely cover his belly, so there's always an elliptical red and hairy presentation at the top of his pants. We're not friends. He tolerates me because I'm here, just another veteran off the tax roll. I think he equates me with other municipal burdens, such as snow and trash removal.

The Shirt is the quintessential politician. He struggles to appear like he's accomplishing great things for the town. Recently he lucked out. He managed to secure a state grant to replace our hundred-year-old leaking water main. A coup, of sorts.

But the constant digging and filling-in has made the town a dust bowl, an unpaved rough road, wind-whipped and lacking only sagebrush. A fleet of Caterpillar equipment rips and tears up Main Street. Backhoes, loaders, excavators, pipe layers, skidders, and trucks greet the men who fire them up in plumes of diesel hell. Man-made machinery, prehistoric iron beasts, insatiable for the street and earth beneath it. They dig up, replace, and reconnect pipes to each building. Then cover it with an uneven blotch of tar that will be replaced with permanent asphalt in the promised spring.

But the real culprit is his brute brother, "The Digger." The Digger hates me because I oppose most of his slim-brained projects that come before the Planning Board, the other august town institution that's likely to approve any heinous development that arises. Like The Digger's proposal to lay tracks along the berm above the Rondout Creek. Horses or a tractor would give people rides in old cement carts, attended to by folks in miner garb of the day. Boots, picks and axes, the whole deal.

The problem was that the berm was built by the Army Corps of Engineers to keep Main Street from flooding, as it had as recently as 1958. They concluded that the weight of the tracks, tractor or horses, and cars and riders would cause an undue stress on the protective structure. It was nixed out of the chute. It didn't even make it into the chute. At the public input portion of the hearing I suggested we could have hookers and a whisky cart at the end of the line if we really wanted to capture the flavor of the period. The Digger stepped on my foot hard as he left the meeting and said, "I'm going to take you apart, asshole."

The Digger, whose real name is Berry, is called The Digger because he owns an excavation business and will dig anywhere, anytime, with or without permits, through septic systems or buried electrical lines. One time he was five feet down a protected species habitat before the DEC arrived and made him fill up the hole. Somehow the fine never got paid. The Shirt saw to that.

The Shirt thought he was pretty crafty, keeping little brother Digger out of trouble. But he was no match for a gaggle of carpetbaggers who descended upon the town and decided that our lakes, our life giving water, was fair game for a gated luxury housing community and an exclusive spa.

These guys thought that they were ultra slick. Nobody even noticed them slither into town. Never mind that they'd never built or completed a project before. They seemed to think that being incorporated was enough. And they had a bag of investors' bucks to throw around. They promised the town a new fire truck and various perks to camouflage the screw job they intended. But the first thing they did was to challenge their tax assessment. They got a break. No one else did.

The lake in question was a pristine body known as Lake Lydia, part of a connected three lake chain, Lake Lydia, Lake Louise, and Lake Lillian, (someone's kids' names from the rusty turn of the century), hence The Three Sisters. It's loaded with geological bonuses, including Karst geology, a network of fragile underground caverns with water flowing like a world-class water park. You could pollute it with just a few septic mishaps. Not something most developers lose sleep over. And we all live on top of this goddamn thing. It's our friggin' water.

One time I ran into this officer from the State Fish and Wildlife Department on the mountain. We discussed the ill conceived project. In particular its threat to drinking water. He summed it up. "You can't drink oil." You make a few million now and die of thirst later. Of course the corporations are buying up all the reservoirs and selling it to us as plastic bottled drinking water, the bastards.

At the first town board meeting to take up the developer's proposal, I spoke during the timed public input. I was a wee bit sloshed and angry at the codgers who couldn't wait to rubber-stamp the project. Their guiding principle was that something had to happen. And it didn't matter what, or how much environmental chaos it caused. And everything stemmed from nativism. Nativism is a local cancer designed to protect the long term inhabitants' interests, the assholes who've been here the longest. Time served, in other words.

So, I had my two minutes. I decided to one up the nativists. "My name's Coot R. Friedman and I've lived here since the last Ice Age tore us out a new asshole. I vehemently oppose this project."

"Anything else, Mr. Friedman?"

"Yes, one more thing. I do not subscribe to the idea that the rich shall inherit the earth." Officer Boice already had his hand on my arm escorting me out of the meeting. He stifled a belly laugh as I said, "This project is shit soufflé with piss biscuits. Bon appétit."

"Good night, Mr. Friedman."

The Digger was in the front row sitting with the developers, glaring at me because he knew that I knew about his little plan. Jason from the highway department had clued me in because the Digger had done an excavation project at his neighbor's house and managed to flood Jason's patio, terminating his collection of guinea pigs and rabbits and his new Napoleon Legend LA300 Gas Grill, just over eight hundred dollars. Jason had saved fifteen dollars on it by turning down the insurance policy.

The Digger supported the Lake Lydia development because he has his own project in mind. He figured that once all those rich people moved into Lake Lydia they'd want entertainment, besides the spa, the hiking trails, the paddle boats, the four-star restaurants, and the interpretive center. He wanted to build a DuPlex Drive-In on top of Joppenbergh, complete with a concession stand. And he wanted to build a road going up there, some four hundred ninety feet up the mountain. All this without even a parking plan. Never mind that there's only room for one lane, or two narrow lanes if everyone had a Mini Cooper.

And if the Lake Lydia debacle got approved, The Digger, with a little help from brother The Shirt, might actually realize his dream. Our nightmare. Nepotism taken to the bleakest extreme. And as a last touch, a *pièce de résistance*, he would position the screens so that motorists and hikers could see images along Route 213 and Binnewater Road as they approached their gated community. This would entice them, stir up a bit of nostalgia. Imagine seeing Daffy Duck cavorting over the screen or hearing Woody Woodpecker's inane trademark laugh echoing off the mountain. Even the DEC, which has played fast and loose in recent times, because of a pro-development governor, wouldn't roll over for something like this one. The Digger blamed me and swore revenge.

And he did get revenge, but I retaliated in a way that turned my stomach. At heart I'm a pacifist, but there are a few bastards I'd take out without a nose hair of remorse.

Like those assholes who abused Abessa. And Gerhardt; the asshole tried to kill his own son.

We were both in the Box Car one night. The Digger didn't notice me because he was drunk and busy displaying his racist under-armor. He was telling a story about a Niggy Poo and a Tight Ass Jew. It was a kind of sing-song performance outlining the dumbass, asswipe stereotypic poisonous lies the legions of the ignorant like to believe about these folks. I was glad Zeitzer wasn't there to hear this shit. And there are only four Black people in town. One of them, my friend Clarence the cook, was watching this unfold from the kitchen service window, his kind, sweaty face shining, framed in the window with a helpless expression, abandonment, and heated anger. I knew that I was going to have to answer The Digger for him.

The Digger kept it up, "Niggy-Poo and Tight-Ass Jew, they went out ta dinna. Ha, ha, ha." Big Digger laugh. I counted three more "Niggy-Poos," then I said to Ray, the owner. "It's your place, shut the asshole up." The asshole's stool scraped back. He was quick for a big guy.

"You talking to me, queer?" Slowly his drunken features focused as he realized it was me.

"I'm talking to Ray, not you."

"Get up, faggot!" I looked back in the window. Tears were streaming down Clarence's face, moving his head back and forth, pleading with me, "No." He glowed in the window light, a symbol of three hundred years of abuse and still more of the same shit. That's the thing with me, maybe a bad habit, but when I see a face like that, Clarence, Abessa, I react, maybe because I can't stand the idea of helplessness. There's got to be some friggin' help somewhere.

I got up and said, "This isn't cracker land. Shut the fuck up."

I was a bit drunk myself and was trying to recall a defensive move I'd learned in hand-to-hand combat. Then I heard the cracking sound against my nose, the force of which scuttled me under the pool table, messing up the green indoor-outdoor carpet. Thick drops of blood dripped from my nostrils, some back into my throat. For a while I just heard noises, voices, like I was dreaming. Then it got crowded under there. Gold Robe crouched over me dabbing a handkerchief at my nose. "You going to let him do that to you? Are you going to forgive him? Will you always be the town trash can? Poor Coot." He slid his hands up to my throat. I knocked them away.

"Fuck you, Gold Robe." It took me awhile to crawl out from under the table, get on my feet and access the immediate surroundings. When I was ready I got in range and whispered, "Hey, Digger." He looked up like he was hearing voices and started to turn around. I brought the thick end of the cue stick down against the left side of his head forcing his right ear into the pint glass; smashing it to bits. He was drinking Bud Lite anyway, poor choice. Both sides of his face bled out onto the bar as folks got out of the way and Greg threw bar towels down and scooped ice over his head.

I think that's when I started to black out, but not before I saw Clarence coming toward me with the first aid kit. Our eyes locked, his head nodded in a sympathetic greeting. I raised my hand to welcome him, then I was gone. That's when my psycho hunter kicked in.

I remember now I was warned that I could be a candidate for anterograde amnesia after my run-in with the steel toed-boots. Anterograde is better than global amnesia where you lose everything. But having endured that traumatic brain injury and after The Digger smashed my nose into my head, and of course the four pints of beer, I was ripe for a bit of memory loss.

But apparently my procedural memory kicked in and took care of business. I found myself the next day back in the Ruined Cottage in my gear, camouflage pants and jacket, my Ten Point in my gloved hand. I felt frozen at first and slowly began to move my limbs. Everything ached and my head beat like a bongo drum. I searched my pocket for some Advil. Finally, I got myself into a standing position. I took a pill and washed it down with some rain water. I squinted into the afternoon light and judged it to be about two o'clock.

I remembered the altercation with The Digger. I figured if I'd killed him they would have come to get me by now. I was sure he was hurting. He had it coming. I remembered everything up to the point I blacked out. I also remembered that I'd promised Doe Gottlieb some venison steaks in the fall. Well, I'd promised her in my head. I didn't say it. Being as I was suited up and armed I said, to no one in particular, "I guess I'll go hunting."

I followed a familiar deer path for about two hours. There were more pellets, coyote, and raccoon droppings than I've ever noticed before. But not one buck. Just a disdainful skunk that took its time crossing my path. There could have been a few deer bedding in the weeds and bushes, which makes them almost invisible. I passed through the funnel area, the narrow strip of land they like to walk through and decided to try my luck on the summit just above the outcropping faces, the ancient stone fathers and mother of the town.

I heard something rustle, caught a flash of white, spun around, my bow drawn for a quick, decisive shot at what I thought would be a whitetail. Instead, it was Fay Nichols flat out cold, her white dress flapping like a flag, her mouth wide open like she'd seen a ghost or was dead, or both. "Fay," I yelled, "shit." I scooped her up; she was breathing. I started down carefully, lots of boulders, roots, and loose sand, still there from the Ice Age. Fay is a slight woman but she's tall and lanky; it felt like her body was put together with pipe cleaners. I had a time of it keeping my bow and backpack on, feet firm on the ground and eyes on the sky.

Some turkey vultures, and an albino black vulture that hangs out by the ball field circled over us thoughtfully. Maybe they didn't think we'd make it down alive. Well, we did, but not before Fay's eyes shot open, those steel gray marbles, an aura of tiny red flames flickering damningly around the pupils—all systems go. She looked at my face and screamed.

I must have applied some Camo Face Paint in preparation to hunt. Scary enough, but it was mixed with dried blood and my nose felt pushed to one side. When she got done screaming in my face, terrified, she recognized me. Then she launched straight away into a rant: "Coot, I saw her! I saw the Virgin! Just like they did after the rock slide." She squeezed my arms with surprising strength. "I saw her, Coot." She passed out again.

I kept going; the harsh steam-engine noise in my ears was my own struggle to breath. I knew what she was referring to, but she had it all wrong. After the December 1899 cave-in, thanks to tunneling the shit out of the mountain, there was a series of landslides, including the Black Smoke Mine Shaft network, and that was a pisser. About a week later the tourists arrived with cameras to gawk at the debris that blocked Route 213. One guy, Fleming or something, snapped a picture that purported to depict the Madonna, inciting the Christians into a feeding frenzy. This kind of crap offends me because you know sure as hell that when one team, be they Catholics, Muslims, or Jews, think they've witnessed a miracle, well all the other teams are odd man out. They use it against them. I did the research: everywhere in America, at least once a day, some whack job sees the Virgin's image in a pancake.

Fay comes back on line, "Think of it, Coot. The Holy Mother!" I tried to think about it. Should I tell her she wasn't even near the "sighting?" She could only have seen it, if it was even there, from the road. Maybe she saw it in a pile of bear squat, pareidolia accounting for the phenomenon. But I've learned that fanatic believers are not troubled by facts; that's the beauty of faith, or so it seems, as long as they don't kill you if you don't agree with them.

I scanned her face, but couldn't see it because her dress was hitched up over it displaying not a bad pair of legs for a mature lady. I leaned over and pulled the hem down with my teeth, none of this effort comfortable, as the next terrible thought slid into to my focus, illuminated by the flashing red lights and yipping sirens down below. Word must have gotten out that she'd come up here. What would they do when they saw me transporting her apparently lifeless body into Willow Kiln Park? A few feet to my left, posed by a black walnut tree, I saw what sure as hell looked like my tenth grade English teacher, Mrs. Ramstein. She was holding up a thin book, regarding me with disdain. "Coot," she said in her acerbic teacher's voice, "Do you think it was morally wrong for George to kill Lenny at the end of the story?"

I gave her the same wise-ass answer I'd given all those years ago: "I think he should have shot Curly instead. The little bastard deserved it." Much to her dismay, I scored a ninety-five that year because I aced the Regents. I wasn't in school half of the time, but that didn't stop me from reading. I'd get amazingly vivid pictures in my head when I read. Stories are the nuts.

"The Virgin, Coot, I saw her." There was some repose in Fay's face now; some peace had come over her as if a long desired goal had been attained even if it wasn't real.

I stopped to catch my breath. Her face was flushed. "Yeah," I said, "the Madonna, why not." What the hell do I know?

They were at the trailhead waiting for us. The town cops, the state troopers, and the EMT's. Ray must have called 911 after my tussle with The Digger. I figured the EMT's were there for me after the beat-down I got. I was about to drop Fay and glad they were there. They hustled up with the stretcher and lifted her out of my arms, laid her down, secured the straps, and whisked her into the ambulance. We stood there staring at each other. The relief I felt was huge. I just wanted to collapse. Finally, Officer Boice called out, "You all right, Coot?"

"Sure, anybody got a beer?" I stumbled by them. Chief Cruickshank took my arm. Now what?

"Your friend, The Digger, he's in bad shape. He's got a bandage all the way around his head, real thick." He grinned. None of us were fans of The Digger. And we just barely tolerated The Shirt.

From that day on, the experience with Fay, the "run-in" with the Virgin, I don't know what, but I lost my taste for hunting. I would never kill another thing, not even an ant. Maybe I'd become a Jain. But I didn't forget my promise to Doe. I went foraging one afternoon and filled half a grocery bag with bolete mushrooms. The only white caps I saw had already released their spores and would taste like rotted shoe leather. Definitely not Knaust brand, picked by elves.

She accepted the offering and made us something called Zypraska, a Polish dish of gravy from rendered pork fat, onions and peppers, garlic, flour and spices, served over egg noodles. She even baked a loaf of pumpernickel bread spread with fresh churned butter from the Farmer's Market. Dessert was unnecessary. I scored a case of Firestone Walker Union Jack IPA, not cheap, but so worth it—anything brewed west of Chicago is killer, and we killed quite a few of them. She has an upstairs apartment on Cooper Avenue; her porch overlooks the trestle and creek way below.

When I got there, she'd lit a bunch of candles and everything smelled of anticipated romance, which wasn't my primary objective, I told myself. You get lonely; you do things you shouldn't do. We didn't talk much history that night, but things did mushroom, so to speak. It was not my intention to cheat on Margaret even if she didn't want anything to do with me.

And I don't think I did. The Zypraska was aromatic and intoxicating. I may have picked a few party mushrooms with the boletes by mistake. That and the regiment of IPA's involuntarily shuttered my eyes at one point. I must have passed out. When I awoke the next day I hid in the bathroom and conducted a discreet inspection of my body parts. I determined that I not participated in an amorous act, nor could I have, given the legion of bottles next to the sink. In this case alcohol had acted as a sexual deterrent. Still, the machete of remorse hacked away at my conscience.

When I got to the bridge by to St. Peter's I sat down on the retaining wall and stared at the angel in the stained glass window. Something about her drew me in. She was beautiful and free of all the earthly crap I wallow in. As I studied her face, her lips moved. The face transitioned; it was Margaret, my lovely Margaret's face. I heard her say, "Loser," she said, "You're a loser. Why do you keep doing things like this?"

I staggered onto the bridge and tried to catch my reflection in the water slipping swiftly underneath, but the water churned in circles hissing up at me, "Loser." My own creek judged me harshly. I followed the line of the blunt steeple, with its dull cross pointing heavenward, and determined that I'd go see Margaret, even if it was for the last time. She'd stopped answering her phone. I guess she was done with me. She either had to take me, damaged goods and all, or tell me to go to hell, like she had a hundred times before.

But something was happening that was different than the usual telepathic hurdy gurdy in my head. It, whatever it was, surged through my body, as the roiling water did under the bridge. I felt as if I'd be knocked off of my misguided feet. Was I having a stroke?

Epiphany is not a word that applies to someone like me. When someone tells me that they had an epiphany at a Yoga retreat, I think it's bullshit. If you're really going to have one why can't it be when shopping for cereal? But I believe that's what happened; the rushing water, Margaret's angel face, the steeple urging me to look up at heavenly bodies, the throbbing endless blue sky, and my rock-bottom loser life. What was I doing here anyway? There comes a day when it's all got to have some meaning. And the meaning mule-kicked me in the head—a burst of shocking clarity. Margaret was and would be the only thing that mattered in my life. I would erect the Temple of Margaret and worship in it for the rest of my days. My devotion was absolute. Now I had to go find her.

Zeitzer agreed to take me. He never denied me. We just had to go after he closed the pharmacy. I could have taken the bus there, but I felt too freaked out. At that point I didn't know a season from a day or a week. It's just time, and the picture changes to fit the earth's rotation. I go on instinct; I stumble along.

Like I said, Margaret doesn't live in the hamlet, but she's

not too far away, over in the college town near the Wallkill River, sister to the Rondout. We got there around seven-thirty and it was already dark, late fall, probably. I knew I should have called first, but she wasn't picking up anyway. Zeitzer left me off and went to Stop & Shop, said he'd back in about an hour. I knocked for a while and waited, looked in the windows; it was dark.

This girl with crazy red hair came down the sidewalk. "I'm Evie, you looking for Margaret?"

"Yes, very much."

She started crying. "The bastards took her."

"Who, the police?"

"They looked foreign, maybe Indian, I don't know," she sobbed.

I lost strength in my legs; my stomach flipped. "What else, anything?"

"They were...rough with her. I came out with my boyfriend and they pushed him around, told us to go back inside."

"Did you call the police?"

"As soon as they left."

"And?"

"The cops had no idea what was going on."

"What were they driving?" I was completely mechanical now, speaking in a lifeless tone, extracting what facts there might be.

"A Mercedes, a big one, black, H something 7. I don't remember the plate number, we were scared."

"State?"

"Jersey, my boyfriend's from Jersey. Who are you? Are you Margaret's friend?"

I was done talking, my throat tight like a tourniquet was wrapped around it. Now I knew why she hadn't called, she couldn't. The bastards got her. I waited at the curb, my eyes darting wildly from car to car; where the fuck was Zeitzer?

When I spotted his car I dove into the front seat. "I'm a pharmacist, Coot, I don't do this sort of thing…espionage, or whatever." His hands were trembling on the wheel. We didn't speak again until we passed Mahwah on the Garden State Parkway. "I'm not military. I haven't had training. I'm a pharmacist," he repeated. "Coot, are you listening? These guys could hurt us, they really could."

"I think I know how to handle this."

His glance was incredulous. "We're not dealing with fools, Coot. These guys are zealots, fanatics. They'd think nothing of …of taking us out." For some stupid reason that made me laugh, which unsettled poor Zeitzer even more. I've got this thing like when someone says something I add words to it or change it in my head. When he said "take us out," I thought, yeah, and show us a good time. Stupid.

I tapped another unfiltered Pall Mall out of the pack, lit two and handed him one. We'd been chain smoking them since the rest stop at Woodbury Commons. Neither of us smoked, well just weed; he'd quit fifteen years ago, but I just got them and started smoking, kind of like preparation for the firing squad.

"I think I know how to do this."

"Jesus Christ, Coot,…my people don't do this kind of work." He had a coughing fit. "You couldn't get filters?"

"I know one of your people who does." Something maniacal had overtaken me. I wasn't right in the head since the epiphany. Shit, I wasn't right in the head way before that too. Who the hell did I think I was? Was I starting to see a pattern here? Hadn't I done my share of rescuing people? I put that thought away. I'd get Margaret back, or…what? I had no business bringing Zeitzer into this. We were at the Montclair exit. By then we were both pale and sick from the smokes and wished someone would shoot us—plenty of time for that later.

But I had done my homework. I'd gone through Margaret's phone once while she was showering and copied everything to save for a rainy day, maybe a bloody day. I checked the address and cell against what I had on my phone and called from the car. It was one of those large-porch, three-story, old and opulent New Jersey palaces. After a minute a light blinked on and off inside a huge window.

Zeitzer waited in the car, fidgeting nervously with the radio as he craned his neck around every which way, not looking too nonchalant. The woman who let me in was plump, excessively white, and dressed in an equestrian outfit with beaded white cowgirl boots and gold buckles. She was nervous as hell—we all were. As my eyes adjusted to the dimness of the room I noticed various pieces of equipment used in horse training, well pony training. Her husband was out, working late. The IRS never sleeps.

We stared at each other, strange creatures from the same planet. She handed me a piece of paper. I read it. "You could have texted it to me."

"We have too much to lose. Paul, my husband, said the house has a security system and at least one of his men patrolling all the time."

"OK." I couldn't help wondering what Margaret had lost already. What if she were out of the country? My reach was limited, and the game would be over. It would all be over.

"This might help." She showed me a number on her phone. "It's Paul's private number at work. Call him when you get to Englewood. They're busting his house in the morning, early, six AM."

"Whose busting it?"

"I shouldn't be telling you this, but she's my friend. I

haven't slept since you called me. After Margaret got away from him and nothing happened, he went back to his usual. He's sent a ton of money to Iran or Iraq. He might be involved with…"

In an instant I understood what it meant to feel ice water in your blood.

"I'm not saying any more. We could lose everything."

I moved toward the door. "Do what you can," she said. "Paul will help. Who are you anyway?"

"That's the problem. I'm nobody." I turned back to her. "Are you sure, six AM?" How could this shit be happening?

"Paul said."

Zeitzer wasn't in the car. Holy shit. "Zeitzer, Zeitzer," I whispered. He came out of the bushes holding his crotch.

"I peed my pants. I couldn't help it, Coot. I'm sorry." I put my arm around him and don't think I've loved any other human more than him at that moment.

"We're not done," I said as soothingly as I could, "and I think we might have some help." I finished the thought in my head, "if I don't fuck this up as usual." I checked the phone; it was four thirty-five AM, not long until six, if these fuckers were punctual. And what good was that going to do us anyway? I directed Zeitzer to a diner I'd frequented when I'd taken basic training at Fort Dix. He went straight to the cigarette machine and bought another pack of Pall Malls.

"Now you've got me addicted, Coot." He gave me a look of distrust, disbelief, and utter devotion.

We slid into a coffin-sized booth under arctic air conditioning.

"Why do they keep these places so cold?"

"It helps keep everything erect." I pointed to the seven-foot revolving chrome display case with its glass door and brass handle. Inside were confections, pies and cakes six to seven inches in height, the size of a good man's dick. "I think they have a special air pump that gets the meringue and whipped cream up that high and solid enough to support those big-ass strawberries."

"I don't think I've ever been in a Jersey diner."

"Nothing like it."

He reached across the table and grabbed my hand. "Coot, what the hell are we going to do? What are we doing here? This is not..."

"I know, you're a pharmacist," I said gently. "But you're more than that Z, way more." I pulled out one of the oversized paper napkins and slid it in front of him. "If I can talk to them, we might not have to do anything." Good luck with that, I thought. Meanwhile, Paul never answered his phone; he didn't want anything to do with this. He was probably out shopping for more equestrian fetish items, sequined harnesses, etc. Whatever, I don't judge that kind of stuff.

We got to Englewood early and circled the block several times confirming the address on each orbit. It was a stupidly imposing, columned McMansion. On the last circle I scanned the driveway with my bird-watching glass. There was just enough light creeping in to make out the Mercedes emblem and the plate, "Hamzah-7," I chuckled.

"What?"

"They can't help themselves. They get here and as much as they hate us they customize their license plates. Hamzah-7. He has seven convenience stores and gas stations."

Suddenly, my stomach rebelled. I opened the door and heaved violently on someone's well maintained Zinnias. Zeitzer, the chocolate freak he is, had talked me into the chocolate pudding pie, with a thick graham cracker crust, topped with three inches of whipped cream, finished with rivulets of hot fudge and maraschino cherries. I think I mentioned that chocolate makes me blow up. It does more than that. I was going to need a toilet real soon.

I sat up and wiped my mouth and turned to Zeitzer. He was cloud white and a thin line of saliva inched down his chin. At the window was a guy with a Remington Model 870 police 12-gauge shotgun, its fourteen inch barrel resting against Zeitzer's left temple. I turned slowly; there was a companion one on my side as well, and my nose pushed the barrel aside so it was aiming into my mouth.

I said, "Good morning, CID. Glad you're here."

"Out, asshole." Another one opened the door. I slid out carefully. There was one at the back window aiming at the front seat. I didn't have the luxury of time to explain to Z that the CID was the armed unit of the IRS.

The guy in back of the car said, "Did he say CID?"

Someone grabbed my shirt collar and shoved me over the hood. They were already prying open the trunk with a steel bar. Zeitzer would surely have released the trunk lock if they'd asked nicely. I felt two barrels at either side of my head.

"Easy there, those babies are speedfeed ribbed black forend."

"Who the fuck is this guy?" There was some quick movement of boots on the ground as they cuffed me, dragged me three cars back and threw me into the side door of a communications van.

"Leave the guy in the car alone," I said as evenly as I could, about to shit my pants. Damn chocolate pie, and I could have had key lime…

"Good Morning, Sergeant Friedman."

"That was fast."

He patted the laptop. "Not as fast as you becoming a

casualty of this action, or disappearing 'til the end of time."
He shot a look at his watch, a chunk of black steel that
was probably way more than just a timepiece. The machine
beeped and he studied the screen, considered what he'd
read for a moment, took a handgun out of a drawer and
placed it on his lap. "Say's here you were a fuck-up, Friedman…but you took some risks to help other people. That's
touching."

"Is that really CID protocol, all pricks all the time?" He
lifted the weapon and twirled it with his index finger. A real
fucking cowboy. I knew that the CID was the shoot 'em up
contingent of the IRS. Hamzah was about to have quite a
wake up call.

He stopped twirling; the barrel came to rest in the proximity of my heart about two feet away. "You seem to be
acquainted with the 870's we use. How's that?"

"Wilson Combat Ghost Ring Rear Sight." How the fuck
did I remember that? Good inventory keeping practices. He
worked hard to suppress his surprise; his cheek twitched: a
good sign, or trigger time.

"What the hell were they doing there?"

"US Army Special Forces. You happen to have a bathroom in here?"

He smiled, "Can't help you with that. You saw them
there? Answer me."

"Sure, I saw them. They were handy for things that go
bump in the night."

He nodded. "You shoot one?"

"Just at a can."

He looked skeptical, pressed a control on his watch; two
of them almost ripped the door off the hinges.

"Listen to me, I think there's a women in there. She's got
nothing to do with this…she's innocent." Fuck, did I sound
too desperate? He considered this for a moment.

"All right, soldier, who is she?"

"She's…my wife…my fiancé, Margaret." He nodded and they dragged me to another car, threw me in the trunk and slammed it shut. I thought I heard them laughing. And this is the way the world ends, in darkness, hopelessness, and fear. I listened to see if shots were being fired or perhaps an early morning delivery truck had backfired. Then it came over me. What if they killed her in their zeal to perform their duty, get all the bad guys, especially if there was a connection to… I got as far as the letter "I." It was getting warm, the air less gracious. A "soldier" without options, I slowly put myself into a state of hibernation like the New York State Snapping Turtle in winter.

Maybe it was an hour and a half later. They opened the trunk, I squinted into what I judged to be still an early morning sun. This time two of them lifted me out, careful not to smash my head. They set me down like I was a porcelain doll—finally a little respect. I struggled to orient myself. The guy who'd played gun tag with me in the van walked by. "Your story checked out, otherwise…" he held his forefinger and thumb up and gave me a playful "bang" behind my ear.

The impact was like it had been a real bullet when I saw that Margaret was standing in front of me and dressed head to toe in a full black hijab, not her color. I don't know who embraced who first, but we were there. "Did they hurt you? They didn't hurt you, did they?" My eyes were scanning the ground for a spare 870. Maybe I could make it to the car or the van and say *goodnight* to Hamzah. She was hanging on to me like a lifeline. Every ache and pain in my body smoothed out; I'd been kicked around a lot lately. "Did that bastard do anything to you?"

She shook her head no. We stood there, I don't know for how long. Finally, the cars and vans pulled away, long and black, like a funeral procession. We glanced at them. "You'll never see him again." They secured the house, five of them with service-issued revolvers, nice lawn ornaments, better than gnomes. We were almost alone.

Half a block up I saw Zeitzer leaning on the back of his silver VW Passat, lighting up another Pall Mall with a bit of swagger. He'd actually taken off his suit jacket and thrown it over his shoulder in a cocky pose. And he was smiling like he'd just got the Mega Millions Winning Numbers, all the right ones.

"How did you convince them?"

I was feeling the sweet milk of success—soon she'd be mine for keeps, I hoped. But like I've mentioned, Margaret could turn on you in a blink like a rabid muskrat; draw blood first, then ask questions. "Strategy, military know how," I said. At that moment the residue of the high-rise chocolate pudding pie decided to evacuate at the other end, making for less than a hero's welcome. I've got to stay away from chocolate.

A month later, maybe a few months, I was back in the hamlet without any repercussions from the CID. What would they want with me anyway? I was just some jerk-off GI Joe who happened to be on location when they arrived to do what they didn't want anyone else to see them do. But I was thankful they got Margaret out; they let us go. They could easily have done us some long-term harm.

As usual we were on and off again. But the on again episodes had intensified. When we made love, we dug further in and made serious love. There was more purpose to it as if we were trying to go deeper and find the place, the thing in the other person that would complete the connection, cement us together, as it were. Of course, after an exchange of hyper-passion that revealed our best animal selves, Margaret went at me, all chinchilla teeth and claws, for a lapse in decorum, which need not be described here.

But here it is. We were having a lovely Italian feast at Bambino's. We were half way through a kale and white bean soup and breaded pork chops, a salad featuring a brilliant swath of anchovy paste sprinkled with truffles, and a regiment of Peroni Beers.

Peroni offers a premium lager. At 5.1% alcohol per volume it was voted thirteenth best selling beer in the UK in 2010. Think of it. The UK is to fine beer what Willie Wonka was to milk chocolate, ugh, did I say chocolate?

Anyway, I was buzzed, loving my girl and the Peroni's. Later on, I penned a lyric to that fine brew. As with other of my works, I caste it in the rap idiom. It is an urban style that I have much respect for, a new language of poetry. I wrote it at the library, but forgot to save it on the computer. All I could remember was the title. It was called Nastro Azzurro. My plan was to publish it—pin it, actually, to the bulletin board.

Whenever we celebrate, Margaret likes to go to Bambino's. Maybe it's because their grandchildren roam around the place with impunity. Ma and Pa Bambino are like lovable cherubs who stepped out of a Caravaggio. Why I started talking about dictators in that candlelit setting of romance, fragrances, dreams of lust and love, I don't know. But I went off on Mussolini for some reason, referred to him as a murderous little Italian bastard, nothing but an inconsequential breadcrumb, a butchering Sicilian. I got this thing about dictators.

Somehow this reminded her of Aldo, her dad, down in Southern Georgia. He'd been laid off from his college cleaning job and there was a sudden loss of income. Things were not going well and they might lose the house, lacking a final mortgage payment of just forty-five hundred dollars.

If they made the payment they'd own it free and clear. And Margaret couldn't help them. She'd managed to save eight hundred dollars toward her next used car. The whole thing just blew up; she accused me of hating her father and his culture, disrespecting her mother, disparaging her childhood, and cruelty to animals, especially chinchillas. She said that she couldn't tolerate my insensitivity. It got all out of proportion and it was all my fault.

After that debacle I slunk back up to the Ruined Cottage, completely withdrawn. I ate morels, and containers of rice and beans Bebe dropped off without asking. Not many cafes deliver up a mountain. And I caught spring water that slid, pure and freezing, down a rock face. I think I was in a self-imposed retreat lacking insight. This went on for maybe ten days.

I was like Wordsworth's London Beggar, a blind man (I did say lack of insight) with a paper pinned to my chest telling the story of the man I am, a loser, a snapped vet who can't maintain a relationship. I'm just an emblem, just another one of them who saw action and returned damaged. But unlike the poet, I didn't feel admonished; I felt nothing. Then I remembered the five thousand dollars, and a ring of rosy glee like Bittersweet vine circled my head.

Just before I'd been discharged, they offered me (and strongly suggested I take) a five thousand dollar insurance policy, as I would need it for psychiatric expenses if my benefits ran out. The payment would come out of my disability pension and I wouldn't even notice it. I was in a giddy and agreeing mood at the time and signed the papers, though I didn't know who the hell to leave the money to. Now if I could find the papers and get myself to a VA office and cash it in, I could send the dough to Georgia and maybe get straight with Margaret again, maybe. I still had scratch marks on my psychic chest and arms from her attack.

A week later I walked out of the office and got into Zeitzer's Passat and showed him an official blue check for five thousand five hundred dollars. They'd given me interest. We went to Zietzer's bank and he cashed it, then on to the post office to buy a money order. On the way there I reviewed the numbers and addresses I'd lifted from Margaret's phone and called Georgia. A woman answered: "In-Su! In-Su!"

"Hi, are you Margaret's mother?"

"In-Su!"

I said, "In-Su," thinking that meant hello.

"I In-Su. Who you?"

I remembered. "This is...New York State Prize Services."

"Who this?"

"New York State Prize Services. You've won some money."

"Money, need money...who this?"

"Congratulations...your daughter bought you a winning ticket. You've won four thousand eight hundred dollars." I couldn't give it all up. I still had to live: groceries, staples, beer.

"Money, need money."

"I...we're mailing you a money order for the amount I mentioned. You can...pay your mortgage."

"Mortgage, need money, who this?"

"Do you have a checking account to put the money in to?"

"Husband do."

"Aldo will pay the mortgage, right?" Shit, I shouldn't have said his name.

"Aldo pay, need money, who this?"

"This is Mr. Friedman, I'm sending you the money order."

"Send money, who this?"

I signed off. Would the money actually get into their account and the mortgage get paid? I decided that it would. One thing I know about our species, self-interest operates almost one hundred percent of the time. Zeitzer eyed me, his forefinger tapping the steering wheel. "That was not exactly polished."

I had a dream that night, whatever night it was. Margaret and I were faced off on Main Street. She was dressed in a cowgirl outfit with a stethoscope slung over her shoulder. She wore a six-pointed sheriff's badge, and she was packing a holstered gun. When she drew it on me I was surprised. A Ruger SASS Tricked-out Vaqueros, an Old West replica, but enough to blow your nuts off. I felt for my piece, not that I would have ever drawn on her. I realized that I was naked, nothing on, not even a pair of sandals. She smiled wickedly at my predicament. "Thought you'd take care of it. Didn't you, Coot?"

"Take care of what?"

"The mortgage, you slimy bastard." It was definitely a dream. Margaret would never talk that way to me.

I was naked, but I started to sweat. "I was trying to help."

"Help who?"

"You...you're folks."

"You were trying to help yourself. You think I'd come back to you? You pathetic bastard."

I was getting tired of crying, even in my dreams. "I love you...Margaret!"

"All you love is your dick and your beer. That's what you love."

I sank to my knees. She stood over me and aimed point blank at my head. "I love you." She pulled the trigger and a little stick slid out of the barrel with a little flag attached to it, which I suspected would say Bang! But it wasn't. It was a money order. The one I'd mailed to In-Su and Aldo. She struck a match on the bottom of her boot heel and lit it up. I followed the black ash as it drifted to the pavement and began to disintegrate. I was disappearing. Everything I'd hoped for went up in smoke.

I awoke from that nightmare into some geological trouble. The next few days brought sudden tree falls, much rumbling, rock slides, moaning noises, and banshee shrieks—probably coyotes, usually fearless creatures, disturbed by the events. Some of the townsfolk were convinced that the mountain was going to finally blow. The mountain could implode on itself if the pillars the miners had carved out gave way. Some had deep cracks in them.

Brad Breslaw, giver of lame theories, speculated that the entire town, the houses, the people living in them, the stores and bars, the movie theater would be plowed into the Rondout. Kind of like The Last Days of Pompeii, but without the lava and overacting. The highway department was kept busy clearing dirt and gravel off Main Street. People were consulting their insurance agents. Fay was running all over town waving her Bible like an overdue invoice. The darkness she'd been counting on would finally descend; the wicked would be punished, paving the way for the Rapture.

Why is it always the followers of the saints and the gods, the zealots; they're the ones who do the most damage? They make you pay. You look at those medieval angelic paintings of Mary; she looks like a kind and reasonable woman, a bit of an introvert, not a screamer, someone you'd like to have a nice cup of tea with. Just think, if she'd been wearing earbuds at that crucial moment she wouldn't have been impregnated. And the world, as we've come to know it, would have been a safer place for atheists.

I have previously described the various faces carved into the west side of the mountain…haven't I? I meant to describe them in more detail. Well, they run the gamut: erudite, monstrous, fierce, sublime, goofy, raging, and nondescript. Kind of like the Seven Dwarves carved in stone. If you stand three quarters out on the trestle with your bird glasses you make out their distinct individual faces. Depending on the crisis or how delicate the situation is you address one or all of them, named here again, alphabetically for ease of memorization: Banana Nose, Grinder, Hooded Parrot, Jasper, Raging Tom, Stoner Van Etten, and Vanita. Vanita is the only discernible female face as there is softness to her countenance as she drishti-gazes out toward the Shawangunks, and displays two artistically formed boulder breasts below her neck. A fine artist that glacier was.

I have climbed them many times, rested upon them, rolled a spliff and fantasized about nursing. These great visages, though not complete bodies, rival the forms of Easter Island. They act as our firewall, our benevolent protectors, the in and out box of our daily monkey business. They are the receivers of cosmic communications, threats from the realm below, and bits of divine gossip.

Like that day they really came through. It was December 19, 1899 when the Black Smoke Mine shaft network caved in. First, they thought one hundred and fifty miners had been inside. But all one hundred and fifty were outside eating lunch, an ideal metaphor for a town that's been out to lunch for at least one hundred and fifty years. I'm sure that the collective consciousness of those slabs of cracked stone saved those miners' lives.

They've overseen centuries of progress, war, and human endeavor, profound and stupid. They anchor this place and stoically guide us beings who live beneath their shadow, despite our stupidity, dishonesty, greed, and the occasional act of nobility. When they finally beckoned me to climb up for a powwow, I didn't hesitate, though I didn't quite make it to a face-to-face as I tend to miss a lot of appointments.

I suited up in my hunting gear, but this time I was hunting for meaning and truth, and an answer to what would or wouldn't be with me and Margaret—they could tell me. I checked the batteries in my head lamp and slid my eight-inch gutting knife into its sheath. As soon as I started up I wished I'd put on long johns. The leaves, almost all down by now, and the twigs snapped and crunched under my boots. But the stones were smooth and slippery, especially with the leaves hugging them in the damp night air. I stopped to listen every few moments in case someone was following me, an old habit, one that saved my life a few times.

When I reached the summit I dropped my backpack and uncoiled the rope. I secured it around two of the most solid looking Trees of Heaven, three times, fastened the rope around my waist, then threaded it through the pulley and tested it hard. I figured if things didn't work out at least it was a Tree of Heaven, just for good luck—not that I believe that stuff for a moment. I do believe in luck, and I've had some.

I'd have to lower myself down carefully along the rock face, and over multiple rough out-thrusts that crouched like knife-wielding gargoyles vying for a piece of me. I felt for a safe foothold then inched along a narrow ledge until I reached a point where I could make out the visages. Each of them seemed to bear their usual expression except Raging Tom who looked more pissed off than usual. I double-checked the rope around my waist and eased down, marking each bit of progress with a piece of orange chalk—I'd have to return the same way I came. I'd be able to pull myself up with the gear I brought and muscle the rest if need be. I paused on the ledge and took a couple of tokes to calm my nerves and help concentrate. The air was colder now and throwing a serious chill on my back, which was already sweated up from exertion.

I made it over about fifteen feet and noticed an opening about ten feet in height and wide enough for two men to enter shoulder to shoulder. It was like a huge niche; it even had an arched top, the kind you see in old cathedrals. I'd never noticed it before when I scanned the mountain with my bird glasses. It might have just appeared as a shadow. There are countless nooks and crannies there. It was one long step away from where I was, and I had to think about it. There could be a bear in there or a Timber Rattler, neither in a welcoming mode with chips and onion dip.

I grabbed my flashlight from the tool belt and held it out as far as I could, shaking it to alert any creature therein. A couple bats flapped out wildly, one brushing my ear, which almost made me drop the light. From what I saw, they looked healthy, no white nose syndrome—a good thing. I waited until my heart stopped pounding, reached down and grabbed a paper weight size rock and tossed it in—nothing. I realized that I was off mission but something was drawing me into the niche. Finally, I put tension on the rope, made it secure, grabbed hold of a rough ledge, my fingers slipping off loose pebbles, then took a giant step and swung myself into the opening.

"Evening, Coot." I jumped and had to catch myself from falling off the edge. It was Kurt Geary, Kurt's shade hovering in front of me. "What brings you up here tonight?" There was no body or mouth, just a cloudy shape like a transparent freezer bag, but I could hear his voice well enough.

I was gasping for breath. "Jesus, I didn't know you'd be here."

"Where else would I be?" His voice was wistful, sad.

"Right."

"Going spelunking, Coot?"

"No, I'm..." Shit...I didn't know. I was having one of my episodes, forgetting where I was at the worst possible time. This went on for about six minutes. I was out of it but conscious enough not to take a step out of the opening into a final elevator ride, about twenty floors down, express, and with sharp and blunt objects on the way.

Then along came my friend in the gold chiffon robe and white gloves. "You've made it to the summit, Coot. But can you achieve your mission?" I hated how he was always talking that kind of shit to me. As if it helped. He placed his hands firm on my shoulders and said, "You've proven yourself a worthy man. But now you must reveal your true spirit." He slid his hands up to my neck and started choking me to death. I wrenched out of his grip and placed a hard knee into his robe near the vicinity of his perceptive testicles. He made a pained look and said, "That's not cricket." Then he was gone.

I snapped back alert and ready for what was next. He did that much for me. But I cursed him, "You asshole."

"You calling me an asshole?" Kurt asked. He'd materialized somewhat more and I could see his ski outfit and the smashed-in part of his head and the bird-like features of his face, like a bird of prey, but vulnerable.

"Kurt, I wouldn't call you that. It's my problem."

"I have a problem, Coot."

I felt so bad for the guy, but what the hell could I do?

I noticed a little cloud in front of my mouth—condensed breath; it was freezing in there and my hands were numb, not useful for climbing back up the rock face to safety. The sky was going crazy. There was a dubious waxing crescent moon that cast a morose glare over the trees, boulders, and rugged terrain. The stars whirled about like pinwheels of white, pink, and blue light in a blur. They flaunted their celestial stuff like a virtual Van Gogh, while beneath them a shower of shooting stars like searing white spokes filled in the blanks. I thought maybe I'd read something about the Leonid Meteor Shower; was that tonight? I tilted my head lamp at my wrist, November seventeenth. "Shit, it's 11:30 already. Was I out that long?"

"Got an appointment, Coot?"

"Leo's taking a shit."

"Who's Leo?"

"The constellation Leo. They seem to emerge from that radiant point in the sky."

"I don't have to shit anymore."

How fucking sad it must be to be dead, especially if you're still around, and know that you're dead.

"Can I do anything for you, Kurt?"

"Promise to invite me."

"To what, my funeral?"

"Just promise, Coot, I need something."

"Sure, whatever, everybody's invited—what the fuck?" My funeral probably would be sooner than later anyway.

That seemed to satisfy him; I observed a quieting in his static energy. "Look around. You might find something you need."

That riveted the Stones tune into my head and I couldn't stop hearing it: "But if you try sometimes you just might find you get what you need. Oh yeah."

I'd been so preoccupied with Kurt, the light show, and figuring out how I was going to save my ass, that I hadn't even examined the niche or cave, whatever it was I found myself in. I turned up my headlamp up to bright and focused my flashlight at the walls. Each section of the wall was a different color, decidedly earth tones, a combination of granite, marble, and of course limestone. I would not have suspected it. But it all blended in perfectly as if some prehistoric decorator had done his cave over. I pressed my palms solid on the wall and felt it, a slight trembling at first, almost a rhythmic quaking, a constant pulse that sounded like someone was striking a low-tuned tympani. "It's beating. I can hear it. It's…the heart of the mountain…the fucking thing is alive." But didn't I always know that?

"Everything has a heart."

I looked at Kurt, tears distorting my vision. "Is that what I'm supposed to find out, Kurt? That everything has a heart?"

"Look down there."

There were little phosphorescent puddles winking on the floor and small luminous icicles protruding from the lower walls. "This is crazy shit."

"Down there."

I knelt down, gasped and scuttled back. There was a gaping four-foot slot in the wall that went to…who the hell knows? I could have been mailed into oblivion if I hadn't seen it. The caves were famous for slippery entrances that conveyed the unaware caver into an ice bath without a handy ladder to extract oneself. "What the fuck is that?"

Suddenly, there was a sizzling sound that reminded me of when a power pole was struck in a thunderstorm and a live wire falls into water. It was Kurt; he was lighting up like a pinball machine and his specter was bouncing off the walls. "Are you all right?" What the hell do you do for ghost first aid?

"Gotta go." And he was gone; he didn't fly away; he didn't melt like the Wicked Witch. He was just gone.

Wherever it was that he went or was summoned to I hoped there would be some help for him. I sat there, exhausted, clinically frightened, and soaking my ass in a phosphorescent puddle trying to figure out my next move.

There aren't many moves to make in a situation like this, somewhere deep in Wackoville. It was as if all the strands of weirdness that connected the hamlet, and the folks in it, wound themselves around my body, and trapped me. I waited, helpless, for the spider's fang to puncture my carotid artery.

Suddenly a flash of light filled the wide slot and flickered, momentarily blinding me. It was like a movie screen juicing up for a double feature. I knelt down and peered into the opening while I flattened my body out and dug my toes in as best I could, considering it was rock. I stayed near the side with one palm pushing against the wall so I could push back hard if I had to. I felt something weird on my butt and reached back and touched a small chunk of ice. The puddle I'd sat in had frozen. "Now I have a frozen ass, not a lame ass, a frozen ass—mother fuck!"

There was movement and more lights below, and small plump white objects were floating down there like a choreographed snow storm. And there was movement between and under the white balls or whatever they were. I stared until I saw them, red caps and slippers, green jumpsuits with buckled belts, white beards, red cheeks, and twisted noses—elves, hundreds of them. They were chasing what I suddenly recognized as Puffball Mushrooms and chopping and sawing them and putting them into colorful cans.

"Holy shit." I'd read about in a book I'd borrowed from Doe. I was looking at the Herman and Warren Knausts' Cavern Mushroom operation, but with the elves freed from the can labels and chasing the floating mushrooms around with cleavers and saws. This was, I knew, circa 1936. Somewhere in the back of my sputtering brain the word flashback popped up, but I was too far into the show to care.

The mushrooms and the elves and cans slowly slid to

the right, making way for the town band marching in dis-
orderly ranks from the left. A cymbal crash, honking trombones, the contingent of drums, the shrill arpeggios of a
flute, the muffled guitar, "honk, toot, bang, crash, strum!"
How the hell could the band have gotten in there? It struck
me. They would have had to come down from Iron Mountain, the name the Knaust Brothers gave to the cave after
they were finished with the mushroom business. It's the
biggest below-ground storage facility in the country,
maybe the world. There had to be a subterranean route
from Iron Mountain leading to Joppenbergh. Mind fuck!

The band was playing "This Land is Your Land." I
scoped out the guitar player. Tall, thin; was it Woody
Guthrie himself? I thought: You're having a flashback and
you may freeze to death. Get out now.

I couldn't stop myself. The band marched by followed
by two elves pushing a baby carriage. I squinted to see as
the scene darkened. A little face encircled in a pink bonnet,
cherub lips, and a small hand waved up at me. She waved
at me. Was it Abessa's way of telling me she'd had a child?
Then pain, intense torturous pain as if I were being beaten
with shovels. I'd waited too long and didn't think I was
going to get out of this one. They'd find me up here like
Frozen Man with pouch of weed instead of tools. The voice
was firm, "Get up, fuckhead, and move! Now!"

I came down from the mountain pretty beat up. I stumbled and fell, skinning my hands, adding to my physical
trauma. My hair was spiked up and white with frost, and
the only tablets, not of commandments, I carried in my
backpack, were Advil for a future hangover.

Zeitzer was there at the base of the mountain, waiting for
me in the park. His eyes widened as I approached. I was

shivering and disheveled. He seemed uncertain about me. "What is it Z?"

"You look...transformed."

"Just the usual bullshit."

He stared at me and waited. "What?"

"You have to take better care of yourself, Coot."

"I know."

"You've got good reason to."

"What? Zeitzer, what is it?"

"Margaret's pregnant."

This time it was more like a sledgehammer to the chest. I mouthed the question, "Mine?"

He nodded back, "Who else would it be?"

"For sure?"

"She's sure. It's yours, Coot."

I stammered, "What does she want?"

"You should ask her that."

"Does she want to see me? What'd she say?"

"I think you better see her right away."

"Would you mind giving me a ride?"

Neither of us spoke in the car. He parked and we just sat there for a while. He put his hand on my forearm and squeezed it. "She wants to see you." I started to slide out. He held on. "Coot...be smart. This is your moment." I felt my throat constricting. "Go get her."

"Thank you. I..."

He rested his head on the steering wheel. He had his own concerns; his own losses to contend with. I was just draining the guy...being a selfish bastard.

"Go on, Coot. She's waiting," he said.

I took in a breath and I went in. Her face glowed and was slightly more full, probably from the refined pregnancy juices sluicing through her veins. Her expression reported no trace of anger or disappointment. She just gazed at me as if I were an object of meditation.

I didn't speak; I wasn't even sure that I could. I stared at her knowing that I would never see anything as beautiful as this again. And the vague thought that I was somehow expected, hopefully welcome, made my heart pound. I remember now that she didn't speak either.

I followed her to the dining room table. The back forty of my brain was clicking away as usual. I had about two hundred thousand years of biology working for me. The seed, the family, mommy and daddy. And the absence of anyone else around who might step in. I was one lucky bastard.

Then I noticed that she had prepared a lovely meal. She'd made portions of ba-wan, oyster omelets, glutinous rice and sausage, and kidney. The aromas floating about the room were more than holy. There was even a selection of the best Taiwanese Beer on ice. Being with child, she would only drink Formosa Oolong Bay Jong Tea.

We must have spoken during dinner, but I don't know about what. Of course, there was plenty of baby talk. She'd already filed her birth plan and I was to be a foot soldier to help execute it to the letter of her law—no longer at war for my country or against myself.

I must have asked...begged Margaret to marry me that night. Two days later I got a certified letter from her, in which she specifically outlined all the terms and vows of the marriage contract. She could have been a great divorce lawyer. I had to sign it and initial certain condemning passages. Basically, if anything went wrong my nuts would be in a vice grip with her turning the handle.

I signed up, happily. I got her, and the baby to come, which she insisted would be a powerful, independent thinker, a girl of course. She even took my last name for the baby as a legal point, and an extra layer of protection, so

I'd be responsible for child support should it come to pass, in perpetuity—fine with me. Though I didn't think that the chump change I made from part-time jobs would go too far. But I was so happy I felt enveloped in a universal air hug.

Margaret's sense of propriety demanded that we get married immediately. It was a small, intimate affair. Margaret looked beyond stunning in her traditional Taiwanese wedding dress, wound blue silk with a little extra room for what was coming. I wore a blue bandsman's uniform I'd gotten from a friend, complete with yellow tassels and medals including my Sharp Shooter medal. I was going for the Sergeant Pepper look even though it had gone down decades earlier.

Just before the town justice arrived, Margaret cried because her parents couldn't be there. She missed them terribly and wished there was some way to move them up north closer to her. I thought that might be a mixed blessing, but told her I wanted them here as well—anything for her.

Bebe was the bridesmaid and Z stood by my side. He said it was one of the proudest days of his life.

Ironically, Margaret wasn't the only pregnant woman there. Delcie looked like she was ready to pop any moment. Despite that, she served food and bussed the tables, followed closely by an overly solicitous Cal Darnell, who'd come to his senses in Vancouver and returned to make her an honest woman. It was actually Cal's mom who brought him to his senses with a sharp clap against his head. She'd be goddamned if he'd cheat her out of a grandchild.

When he'd called her from the road, Delcie told him that there was at least one man who'd offered to take her as she was, baby and all, if he wasn't interested. She didn't tell Cal that the suitor was Rudolph of Melrose Hall. Rudolph's plan was to petition the group home leader to allow Delcie to move in. He'd share his room with her. He'd take care of the baby and Delcie would work at Bebe's. Rudolph also had some extravagant ideas about a honeymoon that didn't get articulated, much less budgeted for.

It wasn't until after the ceremony that I noticed Kurt hovering over Bebe's appetizers longingly. Her staff at the Sprouting Affair had gone all out. When I went to take a leak he appeared in the stall. "You know why I'm here, Coot?"

"To watch me take a leak?"

"You don't remember, that night on the mountain…you invited me. I asked you and you did." I didn't remember anything except I almost died, and had reached a point beyond physical exhaustion hoisting my stupid ass up the stone wall to the top, which was made more dangerous with dew. That, and that the town band had marched through a secret corridor in the mountain, and that insanity was what passed for homeostasis in my playbook.

"You really don't remember. I was recalled. I lit up, and then vanished. But your invitation somehow made it possible. I had to establish a connection before I'm allowed to leave here properly."

I listened attentively, but it was my wedding day and I didn't feel like being away from Margaret. I didn't want to do anything that might upset her. I just wanted to be…happy. I realized that I was happy, a recent and purely unique feeling I'd been accorded for no particular reason.

"Coot, I need to tell you something."

"What?" I backed away from the latrine. It flushed. I noticed that it was not a self-flushing unit. "Did you do that?"

"Oh, yes. Sorry…you're welcome."

"Rutsen had a treasure chest. Did you know that?"

"Rutsen, Jacob Rutsen?"

"Yes, it's full of gold coins, pewter spoons, dandy and ball buttons, deeds—probably no good, but who knows—and some valuable ladies' jewelry he obtained excelling at poker. Worth a fortune, Coot. It's...shit. It's happening again." His form got hot; he was leaving me with intense feeling.

It was as if he'd just been unplugged; he was gone. Something kept misfiring in his circuitry. They, whoever the hell they were, should have more expertise with this shit. We just can't seem to get it right—living or dead.

Part 3: Seeking Firmer Ground

Margaret's nesting instinct in preparation for the baby could have been compared to a NASA rocket launch. No detail was unattended to. I was immediately put to work using all of my skills. I built a self-rocking cradle out of cherry wood, with a little motor that swayed it gently. I did this simultaneously as I repainted our bedroom and sanded the floor and stained it. I collected and rid the house of all chemicals, though Margaret was almost totally organic. Some dinner guest had left a small bottle of palm oil in the cabinet. She commanded me to remove it as if were a radioactive isotope. I didn't know that palm oil could kill you. And how would the baby get exposed to it anyway? But I obeyed.

Margaret's pregnancy was textbook perfect. The birth was something else: thirty hours of labor, spells of nausea, constant warnings and threats from the doctor that they couldn't risk leaving the baby in for too long. There could be stress on the child. Every time they brought the ultrasound she threw them out of the room. I stood between her and the staff, repeating her instructions. One moment I had to prepare myself for was when the baby finally came. I was not to, under any circumstances, allow the nurses to whisk the baby away and perform tests, etc. She rode the waves of her contractions with power and such dignity that, as terrified as I was, I couldn't have been more in awe of her.

When the baby finally came to us I caught her in my hands, held her up and instinctively smelled her. I don't know why. I experienced a feeling I will never forget. I can only describe it as "being welded into the great chain of humanity." I was finally there. And being in this rarefied place I felt the full impact of life as it opened before me, sacred and unfathomable. And death as well, in other holy moments like this when I had witnessed my comrades pass. I was forced deep inward to hushed space…sacrosanct.

"Here, Coot. Give her to me. Our girl." I wiped my eyes on the sheet.

The next morning, we went home, a family. I told as many people as I could, strangers, anybody, "I have a wife and a child." Margaret already knew her name: Valkyrie Margaret Friedman, VMF in case you want to get her some monogrammed rompers. Val is her nickname. Margaret wanted to endow her with a name that would put men on notice when she grew up. Valkyrie. Right from the get-go she'd command respect. She'd be like…well, like Margaret. Then a discordant thought took hold of me. What if one day she met a man like me? I committed myself to be the best father I could. I owed them both nothing less than that.

From day one I was Val's playmate, wagon-puller, story-teller, companion, fellow explorer, confidant, and clown. I could get her to smile at two months. Margaret would have to snatch her away to nurse her. I'd fidget, and not know what to do until I got her back. Margaret didn't say, but I could tell she approved of my parenting, the advanced degree I'd always craved.

I was shocked when her first birthday came. I started building a castle out of balsa wood. I planned turrets, a drawbridge, an extravagant plan, even a moat. Margaret said that a one-year old didn't need a castle. Instead we invited Z to a special dinner. Margaret said we should invite Bebe as well. Again, she was sad that her folks couldn't be there, especially now that Val was with us. In-Su sent a traditional gift of money wrapped in red paper, and a delicately fashioned pair of gold earrings. I couldn't image piercing Val's ears. It seemed brutal. Margaret put them away for when the time came that Val could make her own decisions.

And so it went. It was, I think, the happiest time of my life. I was freed up from all my rumination and self-involvement. Caring for my little girl was not a chore. It was an honor I never would have expected. I wheeled her all over town, stopping at the stores and the library to show her off.

I think it was mid July, probably a Sunday. It was the annual Mermaid Parade, and the hamlet was buzzing. The lady mermaids seemed to be in competition as to who could show the most midriff with the most midriff. Everything else was covered in sequinned and shiny materials, a rainbow selection of hair colors. There were mermen as well and gaggles of kids dressed in nautical fashion. Of course the Shad Town Brass Band was marching under the direction of Beaming Dove. The composition of the band had changed again. There was a sousaphone now and two more girl trombone players plus the usual saxophones.

The obligatory tambourine was played by a kindly woman who at one time had traveled with and kept her finger on the pulse of what became known as the beat poets. She writes and recites her poetry in that style of Ginsberg and Corso. There is a legion of folks, and she is one of them, that remind us of past culture, the greatness of the road and the word. And after years of travel, stints at Esalen, and West Coast escapades, she felt herself, as many have before her, summoned to the hamlet beneath the magical mountain where dreams can thrive, both kinds, sweet and nightmare.

Also in attendance was the Senatorial Puppet Bazaar with a towering seahorse, mermaid heads, ships, and drowning men. All doused with pounds of glitter, shimmering and sparkling in the intense sunlight. Their leader was a slight professorial woman who played trumpet and had the same wide-eyed look of constant shock that her puppets had. Per protocol for a circus, which this was, everything to the minutest detail was exaggerated.

I pulled Val along in a little wagon resting on a heap of shredded green sheets. She was decked out in a violet outfit complete with a mermaid tail so she couldn't walk. Her hair was pulled to one side and tied in shiny ribbons. I'd rigged up a battery-driven bubble machine with dyed water so beautiful blue-green sea bubbles floated around her as we marched. A good number of folks snapped their cell phones at this cute little girl, unaware that she knew, or at least had been told, that there are six thousand and eighty yards in a nautical league. I started us off on a study of oceanography right after I read her an abridged version of *Moby Dick*. Call me bubbles.

And so it went, parades, celebrations, birthday parties, mud pies, cookies, all the bright and tender-hearted celebrations of childhood. Older folks would stop us on the street and peer into Val's carriage and admire her. They'd lament, "You better enjoy every moment while she's young. It goes fast."

And it was going fast. At two years my baby speaks: "Dada, Dada, look." Dada, she calls me Dada. I've been called Coothead, asshole, numb nuts, whack job, soldier, and other names, but never Dada, which is fine with me.

"What, baby?" We were sitting in Willow Kiln Park. I'd wheeled her over from our house on Fairview. It's a steep hill but it's part of my exercise regimen. I was getting in shape. It's better to jog than crawl out of a bar, notwithstanding Boxer's Day. When she was at story hour I'd run up the hill to the IGA in Tillson, pick up a few items for dinner and jog back leisurely. Margaret was usually at a training or a birth; she was a licensed midwife now. She'd planted a small patch of hops in our garden, a concession, so I could attempt some home brewing. She'd leave me a list of chores, but usually I'd wind up just playing with Val. We had more high teas with her dolls and stuffed animals than the Queen of England. Her snow bear can absorb twelve cups of tea without leaking. I'd hang him on the line to dry afterwards.

"Dada, see mutton."

"Mountain, baby. That's a mountain."

"Big mutton."

"Yes, sweet, big mountain."

"You mutton dada." She pointed a precious pink index finger at me. "You mutton, Dada." She pointed to my left. "Friend, Dada...you friend." Kurt relaxed, taking in the warm rays of this spring morning with us, as usual. Somehow he was more at peace those days. And who wouldn't be on this quintessential spring day, so fresh, clear, a promise that comes true. "I like mutton, Dada."

"Mutton loves you, baby."

"Dada friend! Dada..." Margaret doesn't like it when the baby refers to Kurt. It's our secret.

Something was going on with Kurt. His form shifted from the bench to a few feet away next to a willow tree. I sensed he wanted a private moment with me. His voice sounded like it was being transmitted through a two-inch speaker in a whisper.

"Listen, Coot, I'm going. I thought I'd have more time. They're letting me go." So much for the promise in the air.

"Where? Why are you going?" Next to Margaret, Val, and Zeitzer, I love Kurt—we're a family. "Don't do this to me, man." He was Val's godfather; I'd asked him after she was born. Actually, Zeitzer was also her godfather, but

I didn't tell him about Kurt. But what was I saying; he'd been gone a long time ago.

How do you hug a ghost? I stood there with my arms around his gummy protoplasm, nervous that I might be drafted into the ranks of the afterlife.

He whispered in my ear. "Listen, Coot. It's already happening." I felt a shift in his energy force. "Coot, listen to me. Rutsen...the treasure chest."

"Rutsen, Jacob Rutsen?"

"Yes, I told you at your wedding. Worth a fortune..."

"I don't care about that. Tell me you're okay, that you're going some place that's...good." His voice sputtered out like it was interrupted in a lightning storm, and then cracked back in.

"It's near the...Coot!" His form got hot; he was leaving me with intense feeling. "Near the horse farm, after the honey bee warning. It's near a...look for a...black..." I clasped the air where he'd been...empty.

"Kurt, don't go." But he was gone; he was free. He was finally free. I could feel a cool breeze cleanse my face, perfumed with a relaxing bouquet of juniper. And I was glad for him. I jumped and threw my arms up to the sky. I jumped.

"Dada jump!" She squealed, "Jump Dada, jump!"

In the aftermath of Kurt's sudden departure I spaced out what he'd said. It wasn't until Zeitzer and I dropped Margaret and Val at Stewart Airport that I remembered about the treasure. Margaret and Val were going to Valdosta so Val could meet her grandparents for the first time.

I wasn't invited. I was to continue my odd jobs, keep up the garden, though I think there was a frost. I was to stay out of the Box Car. But I was allowed to go bowling with Zeitzer. He'd taken up the sport for no apparent reason. He seemed to have more energy than before, an inexplicable vitality, a bounce in his step, for such a cautious and thoughtful man. By the way, the beer they serve in the alleys is fizzy trout urine.

It was at the bowling alley that he revealed to me that he'd been seeing Bebe for about half a year. He confessed this with much embarrassment and agitation. He'd asked her to move in with him. Talk about inviting a panther into the house, and a hot one at that. He wanted my approval. "Z, I'm happy for you. She's a great lady."

"You think it's all right?"

"It's very all right; it's beautiful."

"We're...close."

"I'll bet you are." I punched him playfully on the shoulder.

"I heard from Hannah," he stammered.

Who the hell is Hannah? Then I remembered his ex who'd moved to Israel to tend olive trees and pursue romantic interests. "What'd she want?"

"She wants a Gett."

"What the hell is that?"

"A Gett, a Jewish divorce."

"Seriously? You don't owe her anything."

"I know...but I was rude."

"You don't know how to be rude. You're the best man I know. You and Kurt."

He winced; he didn't like it when I talked ghosts. "So, what'd you tell her?"

He got all sheepish and whispered, as if I could hear over the crashing of pins and the PA system announcing half-price pizzas and pitchers of characterless beer. "I told her to Gett fucked." He actually turned red.

"Well, sounds like she does that anyway."

"And I don't care." After he said that I suddenly saw a different man. He was confident, an older man who'd grown up, grown into his skin and surpassed all the bullshit he'd been through in his earlier years. A satisfied man, he'd scored the prize, Bebe. And I was ashamed, and looked down at my green-marbled, lady's twelve-pound bowling ball, for all the times I stared at her ass when she passed through the dining room. The lucky bastard.

"Mr. Zeitzer," I said, and bowed, "You are a lousy bowler."

Truth be known, I was glad to be excluded from Margaret's Valdosta homecoming. But I didn't mind being her parents' mortgage bailout angel. That gesture, that small manipulative act of generosity bound Margaret to me for life. Rescuing her from Hamzah was just a field exercise; it earned half of her heart, though it was more fun, when she wasn't trying to kill me. The mortgage payment got me the other half; though I made sure we stayed out of Italian restaurants. And I didn't want to do ten days of "Who this?" Margaret explained that her parents wouldn't understand me anyway. No problem. What I remembered that next morning, and said to the lush studio portrait I'd won at a drawing from Hannaford, of my lovely Margaret and Val, "It's time for Daddy to go treasure hunting."

It took much convincing to get Zeitzer to don his hiking boots, dig out his metal detector, and accept the premise that there was a treasure trove stowed somewhere in the woods based on the word of a spook. He didn't know it, but I intended to split the whole thing with him. He always had my back no matter what crazy shit I'd gotten him into. If it contained everything Kurt said, there would be more than enough to pay for Val's college and for Margaret to visit her folks whenever she wanted to. Hell, we could even buy them a new house. We could even hire an ESL teacher for In-Su.

Zeitzer insisted on spraying us both down with a flea and

tick concoction he'd made, what with Lyme Disease rampant up and down the valley. He wore a red wool sweater and carried a hiking stick. His backpack was full of egg salad sandwiches, some Trefoils—Girl Scout shortbread cookies (no chocolate)—and bottles of spring water. He'd even packed a small first aid kit, always the professional. He reminded me of the guy from The Sound of Music.

In all the years he'd lived here he never been up the mountain. He was a bit nervous having seen me come down from there so many times looking like I'd been mauled by a bear. And there are bears, but mostly of the shy kind.

"Coot, remember, I'm a pharmacist, not a mountaineer."

"Don't worry, Z. It won't be anything like Jersey. I promise."

"What if we get lost?"

"I practically live up here. I know every inch of it."

"We'll break for lunch, right?"

"Of course. This will be as civilized as a Viennese coffee house."

He looked uncertain, but started following me up the access trail. We headed up the backside, past the ravine on the right where the wide cross-path opened up, a four corners. I always felt like I could hear colonists marching through this area.

"What's that?" he asked.

"That's a pile of old antennas and wood platforms they've been bringing down. Everyone used to get their TV reception from up there, but not anymore."

Just then a small brown rabbit darted across the path a few feet in front of us followed fiercely by a careening red-tailed hawk with a wingspan of about sixty inches, a serious contender. We could feel the wind shear coming off the bird's body. It dug its talons into the creature and flew vertically up with it. Dinner on the wing.

"It's wild up here." He didn't know how wild it could get up here. What was it Doe had said about the mountain? It's as magical, strange, and haunted as any pre-revolutionary site in the country. Z was visibly shaken. We watched the red-tail transport its prey to the upper branches of a distant sycamore tree where there were probably three or four chicks waiting for dinner to be ripped apart and served. "Really wild," he added, nervously.

We continued climbing up, avoiding ruts, stepping over polished stones that had sat on the bottom of a stream at one time. Through the trees off to the left was a great flat wall of stone which looked like the side of a surreal apartment building without windows and a roof top garden of trees. The power lines followed the massive poles high above us. The path was steep now and the wind picked up as we ascended. I could hear him breathing hard behind me. I stopped to let him catch his breath. "How much further?"

"Not far. We turn in at the horse farm and honey bee sign."

"Honey bees? I didn't know they were here."

"It's just a sign to scare trespassers."

"We're going to trespass?"

"It's the only way in, don't worry."

"Really, Coot, this is not my cup of tea."

I didn't mean to laugh but his anachronistic saying cracked me up. After about fifteen minutes of a steep climb we reached the entrance. He hesitated at first, looked back down the trail and then followed me in. I knew he didn't want to go back alone. We walked for a while until we reached the pile of tires and jump rails. I led us west along the far ledge of the mountain well above Binnewater Road. He stopped.

"Lunchtime."

"OK, Z." I was anxious to press on and see if we could find it, but he was ready for lunch. We ate our sandwiches and cookies and talked about some of the dumb-ass, lame adventures we'd shared. All we needed was a jug, a harmonica, and a pipe. I wouldn't have minded a couple of hits off some Bo-Bo I'd stashed in my pocket. But I couldn't do it in front of Z. Somehow I'd earned his good opinion and I wouldn't do anything to screw that up.

A chill moved in across the terrain and we both felt it. "Let's proceed," I said calmly. It got more rocky from there and thorny. We were sort of bushwhacking sideways and up. We had a clear view way out to the majestic Shawangunks. The sun's driver had whipped up the horses and the chariot was moving quickly west and would soon set. And, of course, I was starting to feel engaged, my word for weird-as-shit. Not good. "Is that thing on?" I asked him.

He fiddled with the controls and it beeped. "It's working, I think." Then it started going off like crazy. Of course, I thought, there's probably metal debris all over the mountain. How would we know pieces of piping, boiler parts, bolts and nails, from a metal box containing a fortune in treasure? He was scanning over the rocks and thorn bushes when the disk caught between two stones, wedged in tight, and catapulted him over it on to his face.

"Shit. Z, are you OK?"

"Oh, Christ. It's my ankle. My ankle and my knee." A wave of panic cut through as I clamped my hands around his ankle and felt it. There was a bump there. His knee seemed alright, but he said he could feel it up to his knee. That was, I thought, because his friggin' ankle was broken. And it was my fault. Holy shit!

It would be dark pretty soon and I had to do something. "Let me use your cell." I'd forgotten mine. I reached into his pocket under him and pulled it out; the case was completely smashed in as it had landed on a rock. It was either broken or there was no service. We were already too far on the west side of the mountain to go back the easy way. There was no easy way now. "I fucked up, Z. I'm sorry."

"It's all right, Coot." Even in pain and a whole world of trouble coming down on us he was more of a man than I'll ever be. "Can you find my glasses?"

"Sure." I crawled around looking for them. I saw something glinting in a thorn bush. I reached in and got them. My hand came out scratched and bleeding. The left lens was gone. Shit. "Z, a lens is missing. I'm sorry." Shadows were spreading over the landscape, painting us into a disquieting scene. I did a quick scan with my flashlight. Nothing. I got him to sit up and he bent the twisted frame to fit over his nose and ears. I noticed a gash on his forehead and reached for the First Aid Kit. He blinked, adjusting to the distorted image it must have made.

"I'll keep one eye on you, Coot."

"I've got to get you out of here." I took off my shirt and cut strips out of it with my knife. When I had enough I wrapped them snug around his ankle. "Let's see if you can stand on it." I eased him up into a standing position. "Can you take a step?" He did and groaned.

"How far do we have to go?"

"A ways...some ways, Z." I had to at least try to get him to the Ruined Cottage. We'd have four walls there and I could make a fire. There was no way we were getting back down tonight. I put his arm over my shoulder and we took four steps. He collapsed under me groaning in pain. Fear, bad fear can feel like a blade ripping up the inside of your guts right into your mouth and split your tongue like a snake. Fear and acknowledgement. I felt like I was being closed in by a warehouse elevator door without a sensor, relentless. I knew what I had to do.

"Coot, head back down and get some help. I'll be fine."

"That's not happening." I knew how cold it gets up here at night, not a good spot for waiting. I looked around, pulled out my pocket ax and started chopping. I made a sturdy hiking pole. Just one; I had Zeitzer's hiking stick as a second. I rolled out a piece of rope and cut it. Then I sat him up and strapped my backpack onto his back. I got on all fours. "Get on my back and put your arms over my shoulders."

"I'm not doing that. You can't carry me." I was starting to feel more engaged; an episode was definitely looming. I reasoned that this plan was as good as any, as we were already screwed.

I had never raised my voice to him before. But I did. "Do it!" I shouted. I waited, bracing myself until I felt him struggle and then get on. "Pull yourself up higher." He did and I tied his arms and wrists, snug but not too tight around me. Holding both sticks in my left hand I held on to a tree and shimmed myself up with an effort that left me sweating with my forehead against the bark. I took several slow, deep breaths and started heading up. We had to get to the top and then start down to reach the shelter. The next half hour or whatever it was could be compared to Mel Gibson's *The Passion of the Christ*, except a demented, flashbacking, atheist veteran carries a Jew on his back to the top of an iconic Catskill landmark. No lack of irony there. And Mel, the crazy bastard.

Somehow I made it to the top, vomiting on the moss and ferns. I untied the ropes I'd used to secure Z, then collapsed on the flat surface overlooking the trestle. I knew that I couldn't carry him down to the shelter. Desperate I ran some Plan B scenarios through my head, which were preceded by an oncoming episode. My head felt like a dryer with hot confetti flying around inside it. I leaned on my side, my back drenched from Z's weight on me. I unsheathed my knife because it was pressing into my leg. "Coot, what are you doing?"

"What do you mean?"

"The knife, I thought…nothing."

What did he think I was going to do? I'd never hurt him. I'd sacrifice my life for a guy like that. I rolled over. He handed me a water bottle; I poured it over my face and I lay there staring up at the stars, which had it going on. A number bloomed in my head:

thirty-five degrees north latitude, the same as Albuquerque, but not—the difference being the lack of light pollution. It was sweet home Afghanistan. Holy fuck! It came back fast. There was Orion and his retinue of bright winter stars. The brightest one, Sirius, sporting a bluish tinge. And Canopus, the yellowish-white one. And a million in the back up chorus.

Somehow I felt at home, but at the time I would have done anything to get out of there. I blinked to see if the stars would still be there. They were, but so was a beautiful young woman in a lavender perahan and Punjabi trousers. She kneeled and placed my head in her lap and held a cup to my lips. Sheer Chai. I remembered it from the villages and cafés, when it was possible to visit one without an insurgent hiding under the table. She smiled. I gazed at her, something awakening in me. Slowly her face came into focus. It was the little girl, now a woman, who I'd almost died with in the desert on the way back from the bastards who'd abused her. "Abessa?"

"Shhh. Is all right."

"Abessa, you're safe? You got out?"

"Yes, sisters managed get me out on National Guard flight that helps Catholic Charities. I'm eighteen now. Is my English good? They taught me."

"Your English is beautiful."

"I go to college now." Her laugh had a delicate ring to it like finger cymbals.

"Thank God," I heard myself say. "You're free…are you happy?"

"I am very happy."

"You knew that I never would have hurt you?" I needed to make sure she knew that.

She nodded that she knew, her beautiful black hair falling over her shoulders. I noticed that she was wearing an onyx cross, no doubt a gift from the sisters.

"Did they let you go to school?"

"Yes, I'm studying to be a teacher." She was actually here telling me the good things about her life. "And when I have my first child, I will name him Coot."

"That might not go over so well with your people." I whispered. I didn't ask what she'd name the child if it was a girl. But Abessa is a beautiful name.

She bowed her head. "Bless you, Coot Friedman."

"Abessa, it is really you…? Do you still have the wound?" She slipped the perahan off of her shoulder. There was the burn mark, dark and hateful. They'd branded her. "I should have taken the bastards out when I had the chance."

She placed her index finger over my lips. "You are not a murderer. You are not like them."

Maybe it was the cold air, lying on stone, the night full on, but I was shaking violently, freezing and shaking. When I opened my eyes again I saw Zeitzer. He was pushing me so hard I was sliding around. "Coot, are you OK? What's going on?" Instantly, I looked around for Abessa.

"Abessa, where are you? Did you see her, Z, Abessa...a young girl...?"

He stared at me with profound sadness. "No, Coot. There's nobody here. Just us." Then something rustled in the bushes; an owl sent out its mellow question, always the same one. "And we need to do something pretty soon." There was fear in his voice.

I was deeply mourning the lost presence of Abessa. Had I really saved her? Was she safe somewhere in the States? How could I find her? But the working corkscrew of necessity ripped at my guts.

"Z, help me up."

"I can't get up myself." Then I remembered my Plan B. I was going to make a fire up here, big enough to attract attention and get it called in. We'd have the fire company up here soon enough. They'd have to hike in, hopefully with at least one stretcher and medical supplies. Maybe a beer if I got really lucky.

The bushes rustled and I heard whinnying and snorting, and gravel shuffling around. Z grabbed his hiking stick and held it protectively toward the noise. She stepped out of the shadows, huge, muscular, and stunning. Z scuttled back, jabbing the stick at her. "Get back. Get away."

I was still pretty disoriented from the episode, which seemed too real to discount. I wanted to believe that Abessa was safe and happy. I didn't trust myself at the moment. I'd have to research it later. "Z, do you see a horse?"

"Yes, don't you? It's huge and I don't think it's very friendly." He scuttled back and leaned against a pine tree. He looked terrified. I turned over, got on my knees and pushed myself up, agony shooting through my limbs. I was still shaking and unsteady on my feet. I grabbed the backpack and unzipped it. There was a row of shortbread cookies left. I took two and held out my palm.

"Come here, girl. Come and get 'em." She waited, observing us. "Come on, girl. You remember me. I know you do." She stepped closer, her hooves the size of anvils. She was a Noriker draft horse, chestnut colored and huge, a powerful beast, a thousand pounds of animal. She lowered her muzzle and gently accepted the offering from my palm. "That's a good girl." I gave her a few more and slide my hand alongside her head and stroked her. "You're a good girl, aren't you? Z, I'd like you to meet a friend. This is the Countess Von Heidelberg."

"She's a giant. How do you know she won't hurt you?"

"You wouldn't do that, would you baby?" I fed her another cookie then wrapped my arms around her head, as much of it as I could reach. I pressed my cheek to her.

"Jesus, Coot, you're something else."

"Cheer up, Z. Our taxi is here."

He considered that for a moment. "No, no way. I'm not getting on that thing. If I fell off I'd wind up in a body cast."

"She won't let you. I know this horse. I brought her back to the farm once when she'd gotten as far as Main Street. She was eating apples out of a bin at the farmers' market. She must have polished off thirty of them. It'll be a smooth ride. She's sure-footed and she'll go slow." He sat there shaking his head, dismal about his options.

Finally, he said, "Help me up." I lifted him and helped him hobble over to her. "Just for the record, I'm scared shitless. And this *is* worse than Jersey. You said it wouldn't be." He let out a hysterical shriek of nervousness, perhaps to dispel his mood. The Countess stomped her hoof. "You have to be quiet with her. Quiet and gentle." He put his arms up over her back, which barely reached, as she stood a good seven feet tall. I lifted with all my strength until he slid on to her. "Get your leg over the other side."

"I can't."

"You have to. Do it." He did. Then I had to get on. I reached up and touched her soft muzzle.

"Come here, girl." I held a cookie and she followed me to a boulder that was about four feet high. I climbed on top and then mounted her. She stood completely still, compliant and good. I reached around and hugged her neck and fed her the cookie. I took one of the remaining pieces of rope and put it around her neck. I didn't pull it. It was just something to hold on to. Gently, I brushed her ribs with my boots. "Come on, girl. Let's go down. Let's go down. Nice and slow." She carried us down in the pitch dark, except for the stars, which had reverted to their old Joppenbergh Mountain patterns. Much appreciated.

We descended the mountain which has come to own me and determine the fortune of our town, past and present, the sacred place that seems to define us. We rode upon a noble horse with a royal name, who stepped artfully over roots and stones like a prima ballerina, my friend behind me grasping my waist frantically until I almost couldn't breathe. There was something more than heroic happening at that moment. Something beyond what I knew. The words appeared like pulsing neon: life-affirming... vitality...a miracle in the pitch dark of some season I didn't even recognize anymore. But it all felt like home.

"This is pretty fucking cool, Z. What do you think?"

He was shaking and squeezed me tighter. "I never told you. I have equinophobia."

"You're afraid of horses?"

"Yes, horses. Not pigs." Finally, about twenty minutes later, we reached the trailhead and reentered the park. Had we been eggs there wouldn't have been a single crack. I rewarded the Countess with the remaining cookies and stroked her muscular neck gently. I would call the farm so they could come down with a trailer and bring her home, though I wouldn't have minded riding her back up there.

As we crossed into the parking lot under the lights I saw two large passenger vans, the kind that carries about nine to twelve clients at a time. Their high beams were on. One was parked in front of Zeitzer's car, the other in the back, both almost touching the bumpers. Obviously, the intention was that he wouldn't be able to leave.

"Z, do you see that? The vans around your car?" I wanted to make sure I wasn't being flung into another episode.

"Of course I see that. Get me off of here." I guided the Countess next to a picnic table and helped him slide on to it. He hopped on one foot, sat down and moaned, then clamped his hands around his ankle.

We watched them get out of the vans. I'm used to the surreal, it's my mailing address, but this was reeling with the surreal. Black was the dominant color. The men wore long black coats and hats, some wore round fur hats, white shirts buttoned all the way up—no hairy chest display. They sported curled side locks and long beards. The women wore modest, loose fitting long dresses and flat shoes. Their clothes seemed to be layered on them, so it gave the impression that they were a half size larger than the men. There were about eighteen or twenty of them, including the children, smaller versions in black. I was still sitting on the Countess.

Zeitzer sat groaning at the picnic table. Watching them approach, I sensed that there would be a cultural divide here, perhaps with some bitter disagreement. I wracked my brain to remember if I'd ever seen these folks before and how could I have offended them? What could they possibly want with us anyway?

A large, well-layered woman stepped forward. She wore

a fur hat or headdress. Three of the children followed behind, tugging on her skirt. The Countess backed up a few steps, snorted, and stamped her hoof, slightly indignant. Somehow this personage challenged her royal authority. I glanced at Zeitzer. He appeared to be folding into himself, imploding. "Z, what's up? You know these people?"

The woman, the spokesperson I assumed, came close, her fists clenched. "Norman!" Her voice boomed and reverberated off of the kiln walls. It had the dreaded authority of ancient wisdom tinged with a harsh contemporary tone, a warning that the listener, the supplicant was about to get pussy whipped. "Norman, answer me."

"Who the fuck is Norman?" I asked Z.

Zeitzer hung his head and made a long study of the ground in front of him, looking for a convenient rabbit hole to escape through. I ran the name through my fragmented mind. Norman? It stopped at an image of a framed license I'd seen in Z's pharmacy. I even retrieved some of the language..."Having attained a competent level in the art of compounding...We therefore confirm and...to Norman Herschel Zeitzer." I never called him anything but Z or Zeitzer. The other names didn't fit him. And I hadn't even remembered them until now.

She moved forward within striking range and The Countess Von Heidelberg clearly sensed that her territory was being invaded. She reared up as the stout, heavily dressed woman in front of us shouted, "Norman, I want a Gett!"

Holy shit, I realized that this was Z's ex, Hannah, and she'd come loaded for bear; well, loaded for Gett anyway. And she'd brought her community with her. I scanned the side of the van and couldn't read the Hebrew words, but it definitely displayed the words Crown Heights. I pieced it together. She must have moved back from Israel and settled in a Hasidic community in Brooklyn and reproduced. She wanted the Gett because Mr. Lucky, whoever he was, was waiting to marry her. And these folks have lots of old rules. Like Catholics, but without torture and body piercings. You got to admire them for that.

The three munchkins attached to her skirt were chanting, "Gett, Gett, Gett." I knew from Z that she was no stranger to... let's say freelance coitus for lack of a better term. So what was the deal? I didn't think these folks were allowed to procreate or hook up until they'd gone through proper channels, unloading the previous partner.

As this ribbon of logic ticked through my head, I observed an ultra big boy emerging from the van in full regalia. Slowly, laboriously, he made his way up to the front of the crowd. We could hear him panting as he sallied forth. Finally he arrived and stood solid as a joshua tree next to Hannah. His demeanor suggested that he was to be an integral part of the proceedings, whatever they were. By this point Z had curled up into a fetal position on the picnic table.

I sensed that Z was about to get his ass kicked and he was going to need representation against the charges which I was sure were about to be levied against him. I slid off the Countess, stumbled forward, and landed before his highly polished shoes, about size eleven. I stood quickly and assumed an air of borrowed jurisprudence.

One of the young men placed a folding chair behind the big man and he sat down with a throaty discharge of relief, "Ahhh." The walk from the van had taxed him. We stood there listening to him breathe for a full minute, his barrel chest lifting with exertion. About ten of the young men formed a tight semi circle around him. Between his hoarse breaths an owl queried: *Who are you? Who are you?* His breathing accelerated and his huge chest heaved under his garments. He was either allergic to our pine trees or he was asthmatic. One of the men handed him an inhaler and he took three deep hits from it.

Gradually, his breathing eased and he swabbed his mouth and nose with his handkerchief. He held me in a steady, slightly bemused gaze. "I see that you've gotten off your high horse, mister." Oh, a regular comedian. A brief titter skipped through the crowd. I didn't have an answer for that, so I said nothing. In fact, I didn't know what to say to this guy. Nothing presented itself at the moment, and that worried me.

The young man, who'd taken back the inhaler, said, or rather proclaimed to me, in order to dispel my ignorance. "This is Rabbi Shmuel Yetzel Moshkovitz."

I bowed to him, not having a clue of the correct protocol. "Sir." I almost saluted him. It never goes away.

"Rabbi, address him as Rabbi," the young man instructed.

"Rabbi, I am honored to meet you." Duh! Oh yeah. "I am Coot Ronald Friedman."

"You may sit, Coop."

"My name is Coot, not Coop." The young man snapped open another folding chair with the authority of a lion tamer's whip.

"I prefer to stand, sir…Rabbi, sir." I realized that the sir thing was a throwback from old court appearances where sir was the prescribed response to authority.

"Tell me, Mr. Coop Ronald Friedman, are you Jewish?"

Was he mispronouncing my name on purpose? Some kind of strategy to trip me up? "I don't think so." Shit, why'd I say that? Wouldn't I know if I were Jewish? And I stopped myself from saying, "No, but my best friend is." Poor Z, he was in much pain.

"Are you familiar with the Talmud? Do you know anything about our laws?"

"I know that I've often been on the wrong side of the law." Shit, I was way off my game. I'd need to do much better than this or Zeitzer was going to get screwed.

"Hmm, an honest man," he exhaled.

"Coot, I need a doctor." Z was writhing on the table.

A young woman stepped forward from behind the men and turned to Shmuel, her head bent down in servitude. He nodded approval and she trotted back to the van. "Belvah is a nurse-practitioner. She will see what she can do for you, Mr. Zeitzer." His tone implied that this was not the only address he'd make to him on this queer night.

Hannah leaned over him. "Norman, you disrespected me. You know I have to have a Gett to move on." She knew what she wanted, but I suspected that she'd already moved way on, judging from the kids in tow.

Moshkovitz looked at me with a face full of "Well, what do you have to say?"

Meanwhile, Belvah returned with her medical bag, two blankets and a pillow. She got Z to lie on his back with the pillow under his head and then covered him. She slipped on her exam gloves, took her scissors and cut his pants off at the knee. Then she cut off my shirt strips and tossed them. She conducted her exam as Hannah continued to berate him. "You couldn't even get it up, you schmo." A few of the woman giggled.

Moshkovitz intervened, "Shh, that is not our way."

Belvah reported, "It's not broken. A bad sprain. His knee is bruised from hitting something." She slathered some ointment over Z's ankle and wrapped an ACE bandage around it, then clamped an ice pack on to reduce the swelling. She helped him lift his head and popped a painkiller in his mouth, then handed him a water bottle. I suspected she had already broken a covenant by touching the flesh of a man's ankle, even with latex gloves on. She wasn't going to pour water in his mouth like the woman at the well, but she at least provided it.

I realized that I didn't have a shirt on. I'd sacrificed it for the cause. My chest was sweat stained, matted with horse hair, dirty, and scratched by thorn bushes. I noticed the younger girls seemed to be staring at my chest. Something way off of their menu. I felt embarrassed. Once again, I looked the crazed freak who'd been voted off the island. I thought it might be a good time to confer with my client. I whispered to him, "Z, what the fuck am I supposed to do here?"

"Just give me a few minutes. Let the medicine work. My ankle's killing me. She gave me Oxycontin. I'm going to be zoned out, but I'll do it." I wanted to ask Belvah if she had any more. But I couldn't jeopardize my credibility as an amateur legal counsel. A voice in my head said, "What credibility?"

"I think we can work this out," I said, just glimpsing a possible idea.

The Rabbi snorted. "He has to tell her. The man has to do it. He must initiate the procedure." Suddenly they produced a folding table and two more chairs. They placed it in front of him, and draped a silky tablecloth with blue Hebrew lettering and yellow fringes hanging down. He motioned for me to sit down. One of them placed some Challah bread and wine on the table, and a jar of Vita Pickled Herring in Cream Sauce. He blessed the offering silently, then sliced the bread on a cutting board and distributed four pieces of herring.

I observed it suspiciously and wondered if I was supposed to bark like a seal. We broke bread, I guess. Then the wine. I knew there was such a thing as kosher beer, but that would not be part of this deal. He poured wine into crystal glasses, some nice hardware. He said the prayer for the wine. I toasted him, but he took my hand and lifted it up toward the sky. I got it; we were drinking to the Man himself, the big daddy up there who should have been laughing his ass off by now. The wine warmed my chest and released the built-up hours of exhaustion I'd denied until this point. I was starving and thirsty. I shoved the bread into my mouth. Some of his crew nodded approval. Maybe, I was thinking, it might be cool to be a Hasid for a semester or two.

"You are, I think, an unusual man, Coop. You seem both knowledgeable, but perhaps a bit reckless." Now I was getting my fortune told.

I gestured toward Z. "He is a very good man, even if he…left his religion."

The Reb considered this, then said, "He took up with another woman before he properly released his wife so she could remarry. He lives with a…"

"A shiksa," I finished it for him. I wanted him to know I'd been around.

"A non-Jewish woman," he corrected. "I don't use the term you just used. It's derogatory."

"How did you know he was with another woman? How did you know we'd be here?"

"One of our associates delivers olives to your cheese shop. He hears all the gossip. The woman there, Myra. She's a communicator. And she keeps an eye on you, Coop. You have a certain reputation in this town."

I felt a sudden wave of camaraderie with this guy and said, "Just for the record I hate people who hate your people. I hate haters. That man," I nodded toward Z, "Jewish or lapsed or whatever he is, is the best friend I've ever had. In some ways he's saved my life."

His eyes widened and he motioned for more wine—much appreciated. "You are a loyal friend, Coop."

"That's Coot, Rabbi. And yes, I'd take a hit for him." We sat there in this strange night, two men from not even different planets, but galaxies, commiserating on things we might never agree on in the light of day.

"Coot, help me up." I helped Z sit up, swing his legs over the table. I got him on his feet and he didn't complain. Then I helped him over to a folding chair. These guys must have stopped at Ikea on the way up Route 17. I could tell that the Oxy had kicked in. His eyes were glazed. He reached for the bottle.

Reb Moshkovitz pressed his hand down with a meaty paw. "You have a duty to perform to your wife first."

Suddenly, a car skidded into the parking lot and braked hard, leaving a trail of dust that floated up into the street lights. A tall woman with streaked blond hair and overalls got out and ran over to us. Bebe threw her arms around Zeitzer. "What the hell happened to you? What were you doing up there?" She glared at me, then looked around at the congregation. "What? This is my husband." At that pronouncement there was no fan big enough for this shit to hit. The Reb signaled and two more folding chairs appeared.

Hannah muscled up to her. "This is your husband?" She grabbed Z and yanked him out of his chair, which caused him to cry out in pain. "Agunah, you made me an agunah?" I inserted myself between them and she popped me in the jaw. Bebe was on her like a Jersey street fighter. The men quickly separated them, but not before Bebe swung a solid left hook that bloodied Hannah's mouth. The women hustled Hannah back into their group and comforted her. So, here we were, one big, unhappy family listening to Hannah whimper. My jaw ached.

It must have been midnight by now and the moon

refused to gaze down on this scene of human folly. Rather, she wrapped herself in a gauzy shawl and turned away to think her own somber thoughts. And when you think about what the moon has witnessed since day one: our proud march through the millennia, with our stupidity and endless brutality, you just want to send her a condolence card. If she were applying for another job, she might write: *Dependable satellite available to orbit a peaceful planet. Experienced. References upon request.*

"We have an issue to discuss here," Moshkovitz said. He started wheezing again, and the inhaler bearer was there. The Rabbi took three more hits.

"There might be several issues to discuss here," I said. "And maybe not all covered by Jewish law." He squirmed a bit. Finally, I'd made a point. The wine had helped jump start my mental motor. Zeitzer was sagging in his chair, a faint smile on his lips. After the fact he'd probably be glad this went down while he was stoned. I guessed that an agunah meant that she was a wronged woman, or maybe, if Z was remarried it might be a problem for her to get a Gett.

"I'm taking him to the hospital." Bebe started to pick him up, but he was dead weight.

"Maybe not just yet," I suggested.

"This happened because of you." She was fuming. "You're his best friend? And you always get him in this...stuff." This was adding om to ominous.

"I'm sorry. I'm a fuck up."

"Miss, please sit down. We mean no harm to your husband. My intention is that each of your needs shall be honored." Moshkovitz was all charm now and succeeded in calming her for the moment. He signaled and they guided Hannah to the table and sat her on the opposite side of Bebe, whom she glared at.

I took a moment to parse out how this might go down.

Bebe knew that Zeitzer was still married to Hannah, at least in the eyes of Hasidic Law. But she was as secular as a coffee mug, and couldn't care less. Zeitzer had escaped the fold long ago.

Obviously, Hannah hadn't known that Z had married Bebe and neither had I for that matter, which made me feel left out, kind of hurt. I would have wanted to stand with him. And when the hell had they gotten married anyway? How did I miss that? Maybe during one of my sojourns at the Ruined Cottage. But if Z married Bebe before he gave Hannah a divorce, why was it ok for Hannah to reproduce three times, or so it seemed, before she'd gotten a religious divorce. Was that part covered in their laws?

"Rabbi, I think there might be a compromise here. It seems that the horse has been put before the cart or something like that." That reminded me. I needed to borrow a cell phone so I could call the farm and get the Countess picked up. I looked over where she'd been, but she was gone, probably back up the mountain, knowing every step of the way, and every tasty bit of grass and herbs, heading home. "God bless you, Countess." I love that horse.

Moshkovitz raised his hand and another chair appeared at the table. A bespectacled young man sat down with a parchment and a pen. His beard was so long it dipped into the herring cream sauce. It was starting to get crowded at the table.

"The document has been prepared. It just remains to be signed."

"With your indulgence, Rabbi. I'd like to read it first."

"Of course," he made a coy smile, and slid it across to me."

It took me a few moments before I realized it wasn't written in English. "It's…in…Hebrew," I observed.

"What, you're expecting Old Norse?" He chuckled good naturedly.

"I object," I said, not sure exactly what I objected to.

Suddenly, he was all business. "These are serious charges, Mr. Friedman. If your friend does not grant her a Gett she is *agunah*, still married, a chained woman."

"What about having children out of wedlock?"

He seemed to be anticipating that one. "Children born out of wedlock are not *mamzerim*. There is no stigma."

"*Mamzerim*?"

"Bastards, but we don't call children bastards, Mr. Friedman."

"Neither do I, Moshkovitz." We glared at each other. Some of the feathers and the side locks of his crew looked a bit ruffled.

"Look, Coop, you may not be aware of the Gett Law, Domestic Relations Law Number 253. Under this law in New York State a man cannot refuse to give the woman a Gett."

"Seriously? I mean that's all she wants, right?"

"I think we've been over this."

I glanced at Z. He seemed to be teetering in and out of consciousness, not being accustomed to a little help from our friends.

I held up the parchment. "How do I know that's all that this says, that she's not going to take him to the cleaners afterwards?"

He gave me a kind of shark smile. "You don't trust me?" Meanwhile, more wine, bread, and some appetizers appeared on the table. Between the food, hands, and the scribe it was pretty crowded.

"Is this what you do for a Gett ceremony? Have a meal?" I asked.

"We should go hungry? *Fress*, my friends, eat."

I leaned toward Z and spoke in his ear. "Z, I think this is legitimate. All you have to do is tell her that you divorce her and sign the paper. Can you do that? Z, do you hear me? Z!"

"Yeah, ok. Who? Who do I tell?"

"Hannah. Just tell Hannah you divorce her. It's simple."

"Hammer, I vorce you...vorce..."

"Jesus, Z, say, Hannah, I divorce you. Do it."

"Hamma, I vorce you."

Moshkovitz nodded that Z's pronouncement was accepted. I held Z's hand and helped guide the pen across the parchment. "Done!" Hannah leaped up, knocking her chair back and threw her arms around Moshkovitz.

"You?" I said. "You and Hannah..?"

"What, I should be denied love and the blessing of children?" She found his mouth through the thick beard and kissed him passionately.

The crew cheered "Mazel tov." And there we were, a disparate, unlikely gathering of far flung, far out souls, communing over kosher snacks, celebrating the beginning and the ending of a marriage. We placed yet another indelible stamp in the passport of insanity, to gain re-admittance to a distant and strange country—our very own.

After the vans retreated to Crown Heights, Bebe decided that Z, reeling with Oxycontin, couldn't drive. Z slumped in the back seat slurring the lyrics to "Oh Freedom." Where in his patchwork history he'd come across that Pentecostal gem I have no idea.

I was so tired when she dropped me off I walked into the screen door. I think I was already asleep. I woke up in Val's little bed surrounded by her stuffed toys, my arms wrapped around Friend Teddy; that's what she called him.

It had been eight days since they'd gone to Georgia. I missed them terribly. I called every day just to hear their voices. For a woman with limited English, In-Su loved to answer the phone.

"Who this?"

"It's Coot, Val's daddy."

"Who this?"

"Margaret, Margaret, is she there?"

"Margaret here. Who this?"

Two days later I awoke in a panic remembering that I was supposed to be at JFK in three hours to pick them up. I had a hazy recollection that Bebe had mentioned it between choruses of Z's freedom from bondage song that night after the Gett.

Zeitzer had agreed to drive us to the airport, but there was an influenza outbreak at the senior citizen housing apartments. He kept the pharmacy open all night with a doctor on site, giving out medicine and shots. He'd arranged for Bebe to take me. She had the day off and I was still banned from operating a motorized vehicle in the state, and would be for a long time.

I dressed quickly and downed half a quart of milk, the sour taste of which reminded me I had neglected to shop before they got back. Nothing delighted Val more than a huge bowl of fresh fruit on the kitchen table. She especially loved "cidtress," anything from Florida. Personally, I'm a plum guy.

I ran to the door and there was Bebe holding up her cell phone, ready to feed it to me. "I've been calling you for an hour and a half, Coot. What the hell are you doing?"

She insisted on taking I-684 down to the Saw Mill River Parkway, and she drove like a demon, which made me nervous on top of my excitement to see my girls, and get them back home under the protective eyes of the mountain.

I made small talk. "When did you and Z get married? I really wished I'd been there."

"Jesus, Coot, you were there. You passed out after the open bar closed."

Profoundly embarrassed, I said, "Was it a nice ceremony?"

She softened, "It was beautiful. And forget what that cow said. In bed, the man is a reptile." There was a spicy dash of pride in her voice. She was referring to his ex, Hannah, who claimed he couldn't get it up. We both dropped into an uncomfortable silence after that disclosure.

"Z's quite a guy," I finally said. "Any new specials?" I asked, to make conversation, get away from the reptile thing. Though secretly I was like, "You go, Z. Slither on, brother."

"I made a mushroom-walnut paté, with goat cheese on Crostini. You really care about this sort of thing? I thought you were mainly a Slim Jim and beer guy."

"I have eclectic taste," I said, defensively.

We made it to JFK just in time to pull up to arriving flights at Delta. There was a string of uniformed women working around the cars. "Move it! Let's go! You, move the car!" Welcome to New York City.

I spotted Margaret. Her expression was one of having just returned from a Druids funeral. She was holding Baby Val up, who was waving her creamy little hand at me. My heart melted, then froze. Standing beside Margaret were two miniature folks, one dark, a fedora pulled over his eyes, smoking a cigarette, the other obviously an Asian woman with the shadow of a moustache. She was wearing a t-shirt over her coat. "I Love New York." Jesus Christ, she brought them with her.

"Move it, now." The officer leaned toward Bebe's window, taking up a lot of cubic inches. "You hear me." Bebe swerved to right about fifteen feet. I jumped out and grabbed their luggage and hurled it into the trunk. I took the car seat and threw it in. We pulled out as the officer approached with her ticket pad.

No one said a word. I couldn't even kiss Margaret or hug my baby. Holy fuck! My heart spun like a food processor stuffed with a load of fiery garlic and horseradish root. We got on to the Van Wyck Express, but it wasn't before we hit the Whitestone Bridge that my breathing normalized.

I said a weak, "Welcome home."

"This is my mother, In-Su."

"Who this?" I knew that was coming.

"I told you, mother. Coot's my husband. Daddy, this is Coot."

I slid my crushed hand out from under the car seat across my lap and offered it to the little man next to me. I was squished between her parents in the back seat with Val's car seat numbing my leg. He grabbed my hand and shook it fiercely.

"You are great man, Cooch, I hear all about you from Maggie. Good man, father, provider."

"Uh, thank you, Aldo. I try…call me Coot."

"Very generous, you take us in time of need."

"This New York?" In-Su made a face like she'd eaten bad eels.

"It gets prettier upstate, Mama."

"Time of need?" I repeated cautiously.

"The bank foreclosed on their house, Coot." Steely means cold, determined, and hard. But her voice was beyond steely; it had murder in it. "Your check bounced." Moments of time can sometimes be measured in centuries.

It wasn't until we passed Ossining that I asked, "The check bounced?"

Margaret stared straight ahead at the line of traffic making its way up the Saw Mill. I could feel the frost coming off of her body.

"It bounced?" I asked again.

"What part of that don't you understand?"

"I'll call the VA tomorrow. It has to be a mistake."

"Mistake." She said it in one word, which dealt a death blow to my body, both physical and psychic.

I was her mistake. Her voice was bitter. Life, everything I thought I had, vanished in one word. I'd fucked everything up again. How did this happen?

Bebe said, "I'm so sorry."

Margaret whispered it, "Sorry." A word that expresses sorrow—a bullet to the head.

Margaret put her parents up in our room, our love nest. She took the day bed in the den. Val of course had her little princess bed and I slept next to her on the floor with a blanket for a mattress. I knew better than to attempt an entry into the den. At present it was not a demilitarized zone. I slept poorly on the floor and would have been more comfortable in the Ruined Cottage. I wanted to go there and try to figure things out. Something about this just didn't add up. You send a check for x amount of money through the US Mail and it's supposed to get there; that's the promise.

In-Su snored like a stone crusher. It kept me up for hours. When I finally passed out I dreamed that I was wandering around an antebellum mansion. There was no furniture, knick knacks, or anything. But in each room was one of Val's stuffed animals, mutilated, paws and tails torn off, eyes gouged out. Howls of pain echoed through the hallways and cavernous rooms. In the last room I stumbled into my old friend Mr. Gold Robe assaulting a stuffed panda bear. He was tearing at it viciously, lasciviously. "You fucking pervert." He turned to me. It looked like he'd drawn blood from it. There were red streaks on his lips and chin. He held it up and smiled.

"You want some of this, Coot? Go ahead. It's yours—you own it."

I cat-lunged on him and took him by the throat. "You're done, bastard." I started squeezing.

"Go on, kill me. You're killing yourself. Who do you think I am? I'm just a piece of your shit rotten brain, troop."

"Then I'll kill myself." A weapon's specialist without a weapon is not much of a threat. But I had my fists and raw rage for this guy who'd tormented me for so long, even if he wasn't real. He was something that needed getting rid of. And it was time. I woke up pounding the floor, my fists bruised with the impact. "You bastard."

Val's Little Mermaid clock said it was already eleven AM. I checked her bed. She was gone. I ran through the house and to each room, afraid I'd find mutilated stuffed animals. I scanned the kitchen and then the back porch.

They were in the backyard watching Aldo perform tricks. I was dazed. I stood there in my boxer shorts, not monogrammed, and shaking all over. I watched the scene. He walked on his hands, did backflips, and sprung himself off the grass with only the strength of his arms.

Baby Val laughed and clapped her hands. She had her own private circus to watch. The guy was amazing, sixty-two and he was doing backflips. In-Su sipped from Val's Wonder Woman tumbler. Margaret had made them a large pitcher of mimosas—it must have been a Sunday. In-Su was sucking hers down, a human sump pump. "More, more," she urged Margaret. She laughed in staccato bursts, her grackle cackle. Margaret poured out more for her mother, her face as grim as it had been at the airport. I watched, wishing like I even felt like a mimosa, wishing that things could go back to where they were. I'd lost my life.

Then it happened. Aldo was walking on his hands over

the blue stone I'd painstaking laid over the patio in the design of a rocket ship. Something fell out of his pocket and floated in a zigzagging pattern and came to rest between the dahlias. I walked over and picked it up. It was a money order for five thousand five hundred dollars, signed by a certain C. R. Friedman. The word "Prize" was written in the memo. I looked on the back; it wasn't endorsed. I stood there perhaps a full minute, aware that the sun was warming my shoulders and offering some much needed illumination. I strolled over to Margaret, gently deposited the instrument on her lap, picked up a glass of mimosa, and went inside for a rebirthing shower. It was the best shower I've ever had.

On my way back out, I made a nice display of donuts on a tray. I was feeling a bit festive, refreshed and exonerated. I was not guilty. Guilt is crows eating roadkill, and you're not the crow. I flashed for a moment on Stanley K., triumphant in his silk pajamas, waving them over his head. I thought better of that and dropped the attitude, and assumed the role of gracious host to my peculiar in-laws, as peculiar as it was for me to consider anyone else peculiar.

Poor Aldo was on his knees in a position of prayer before Margaret and In-Su. He was crying and begging for forgiveness. Baby Val seemed to think this was the clown part of the circus and laughed hysterically. For a moment, it troubled me to see how easily entertained she was. She tried to climb up on his shoulders as he confessed and apologized. The gist of it was, he couldn't stand living so far away from his little girl, Margaret, especially now with a beautiful granddaughter, "Ciao bella, ciao bella."

He had no life in Georgia; he'd no family left. There were hardly any Italians in their town. In-Su was reclusive and they never went out. He said that the place was an intellectual vacuum. That surprised me. But I found out later that he'd read the Inferno multiple times, and in Italian. He compared life in Valdosta to one of the levels of Dante's hell. He'd even written some liner notes in his copy, which he shared with me later. The money order was his ticket out of there to upstate New York. He concluded with what sounded like the strains of a tragic opera. "I dowanna die in Georgia. God help me." I was with Aldo on that one. In-Su cradled his head in her lap and stroked his thinning, but still black hair.

When I approached them they looked like terrified orphans, and I was the all powerful landlord about to pass judgment on them. I placed the tray of donuts on the table and smiled. "It's OK. Have a donut."

Our eyes met. Margaret has an interesting dynamic when she relinquishes one frame of mind for another. She goes from running lava to the sweetest cream-filled pastry you've ever had. She melts in upon herself then opens her pastel petals and it's spring again. The look I read upon her face restored what little faith I have in my own ability to do the right thing, to be a good husband and father. There was, I hoped, a gleam, a promise of blissful intimacy to come, should we ever find ourselves alone in a darkened room again, now that we had Aldo and In-Su on board.

Baby Val had grabbed and munched a donut and vampire jelly dribbled out of her mouth on to her chin. That caused me to flash back on the nightmare I'd had, the violent end I'd handed to Gold Robe—hopefully I was done with him. In that terrifying moment, when I said, "Then I'll kill myself." That frightened me, but I was killing the part of myself that haunted me. I realized that something had changed, something toxic had leached out of the soles of my feet.

There was suddenly more room in my lungs to inhale

this brilliant morning. And my eyes told me, as I gazed upon my wife and daughter, that I had finally…hopefully managed to heal that part of my mind that had tormented and crippled me. I just stared at them and said, inwardly, and to the world that had returned to me, without postage due for a change, every hopeful scrap of paper I'd sent out to it, "You are my life."

Zeitzer hatched a brilliant plan to take care of our housing problems, all of them. First, he contacted the senior center in town. He had good cred with them for donating to fix the roof and assisting them through the influenza epidemic, which had unfortunately opened up a few vacancies. But it was good fortune for Aldo and In-Su. It was arranged, that after Fresh Start, Inc. took care of the mess and odor of a cat that had been overlooked in a closet when the tenants were wheeled out, Aldo and In-Su would take up residence. It was a big win.

I washed and waxed Z's car for him. Margaret's folks were a short walk away and we suddenly had built-in babysitters. They couldn't get enough of Val. Though it did annoy me when Baby Val started saying "Who this?" with Taiwanese inflection. I was certain that within a month or two she'd be able to order food at the Taiwanese restaurant in Newburgh, in Taiwanese. My little girl's a genius.

Next, Z contacted the bank in Valdosta and offered to pay off the mortgage in full. Just in case they didn't really want to acquire the house, which was supposed to be on the modest side anyway. Mr. Howard, the bank manager, whom Zeitzer described as a "not so coy cracker," said that they'd already foreclosed and the house was on the market. It was a done deal. Clearly, Mr. Howard thought there'd be a juicy profit on the horizon.

But Z had a Plan B. His Great Aunt Sylvia had left him a condo in St. Petersburg. Z is a true mystery man. People keep appearing from his past. He'd never seen the property for painful and personal reasons, which he shared with me later on. But he dangled it in front of the bank's real estate department, telling them he was ready to sell—couldn't they work something out?

Mr. Howard said he needed to assess the value of the condo, find out what condition it was in, make sure the deed was in order, and all the paperwork as it should be. And then he'd get back to Z. He dispatched a team to St. Pete's and everything was put on hold. The result turned out to be another case of the blades of the fan not powerful enough to distribute the shit that was about to hit it.

I stopped in the pharmacy a few days later to buy rolling papers and diapers. "You have a great Aunt Sylvia?"

"Well, yes I do, Coot. I think I only met her once. It's vague. She may have had me confused with my brother Stuart in Nanuet."

"You have a brother? Jesus Z, who else is there in your secret family?"

"My brother's a travel agent. He was the normal one, Stuart, the preferred one. He...stayed with the tribe. I couldn't handle it. Sylvia probably meant to leave the condo to him, but she was probably so out of it by the time she passed she might have left it to me by mistake. Maybe she left it to both of us...I don't know."

"Wouldn't you have some paper work on that?" He looked blank. "Do you think the bank will go for the condo deal?"

"I don't know; I've never seen it."

"You haven't stayed there, or gone on vacation?"

Z scribbled his initials on a pill bottle and tossed it into an alphabetized plastic organizer to await pick up. "I've never been to Florida...and won't be going."

"Because?"

He came around the counter and started straightening out magazines on the rack. "Because it's the Elephant's Graveyard."

"What?"

"It's where you go to die, Coot. Like elephants, but they're less demanding. I prefer to spend my time here."

"Z, that's irrational. There's the Everglades, the Keys. Citrus fruit. There's some very cool shit down there."

"Are you calling me irrational, he who communes with ghosts?"

"They're preferable to a lot of people in this town…not you," I added quickly. I followed him to the front door where he flipped a sign over that said Back in Ten Minutes. He slid the bolt and we headed to the back of the store and outside on to the loading dock that overlooked the Rondout Creek and some stubbly open fields. The road to the right of the creek curved attractively until it turned a bend and disappeared. In the distance was the squat brick water treatment plant with faded bricks rouging up the horizon. The scene was altogether a lesser Van Gogh, but striking. He slid a Pall Mall out of his shirt pocket and lit it.

"Go ahead," he said. "I know you have a joint in your pocket." He held the flame out for me. We sat next to each other on lawn chairs. "I thought you were done with cigarettes," I said.

"I have one every once in a while. It reminds me of our crusade in Jersey when we rescued Margaret. You provided an opportunity for me to be…I don't know…to be a real guy." He blew smoke out and watched it dissipate toward the creek. "We could have gotten our asses kicked."

"Yeah, I kind of did. And as a matter of fact, you're way more than a guy. There's no one like you in this town or the whole fucking state."

He kind of missed the compliment, as he was pensive; he was reflecting on something.

"Is there any place in the world you would never go?"

"That's an easy one. The Middle East—done with that."

"That's how I feel about Florida. Never."

"You mean because of the climate?

"No… shuffleboard."

"Z, I'm the one smoking weed. What are you talking about?"

"I've watched them play it on YouTube, my people. They get all dressed up for it, period costumes, old time stuff. They play on regulation deck courts, six feet wide, fifty-two feet long. They use poles with pronged ends so that the blocks or pucks fit into them perfectly. They spread a powder or something, silicone actually, so the pucks slide smoothly and quickly. And these folks look happy. At least for a while."

I had no doubt that what he'd said was an accurate description of the sport. "OK, what about it?"

"What I see when I watch them play is a coffin on a steel rail, slowly inching ahead toward a Power-Pak II Plus – Smoke-Buster 166."

"And that is…?"

"That is the number one cremator in the world. One hundred minutes or less cremation time. You ride down the rail sealed in the coffin, naked on your back until you start to feel the heat on your feet."

"Jesus Christ, Z…I didn't know you felt so strong about it." The poor bastard must have researched it. Suddenly, I wasn't high. I just wanted to jump into the creek and let the waves churn over me. "Yeah Z, I get it. No Florida—no fucking way."

We sat there quiet for awhile, me checking him out from the side of my eye. It really was the worst thing for him. I guess we all have the worst thing that could happen. Mine is I never want to hurt Margaret or Val. I never want to let them down, but I always feel like I might, even by accident. That's my death by fire. That's what burns the soles of my heels.

It was about a week, or maybe a month later, after Aldo and In-Su had settled comfortably into senior housing, the hamlet was abuzz with the news. The Chamber of Commerce announced a competition for a sculpture representing the town's history, featuring our contribution of natural cement that went into building so much of the state. It made sense, since our hydraulic cement built so many structures in New York City, including the Thruway, and beyond, that there should be a monument erected toward the west end of town by the cave entrance where the volunteer fire department pumps water into their tanker truck. They decided to review proposals for the project.

Immediately, the town artists, and there's one in every other house and apartment, started submitting designs. One, a ten foot high block of cement was ruled out without exception. It was just a block of cement. It got the point across but it was minimalist, not emotive enough. The chamber wanted something that showed the freewheeling pioneer spirit of the town. Something vital. Something that also hinted at our contribution to the Revolutionary War, which was mainly hiding from the enemy.

Eventually, it was Clark Furey who won the design contest. He'd just gotten out of rehab, was attending NA meetings nonstop, and was proud that he'd kicked opioids, but was hooked on Diet Coke and Swisher Sweets Natural Filtered Cigarillos, Natural Grape. He was bursting with creativity, almost self-immolating. He completed his creation in a manic week.

The Shirt and the rest of the town board and most of the

inhabitants assembled at the highway department garage because the ceiling is twelve feet tall and could house his work, which was ten and a quarter feet high, bigger than life. Clark scurried around the massive thing scribbling and crossing out items on his checklist. Then three trombones from the Shad Town Band gave a fanfare. They hoisted the giant painter's drop cloth from the top of a cherry picker, but it got stuck on the rafters. Vin, one of the young volunteers, climbed out on the arm and released it. And there it was.

"Ladies and gentleman," Clark, announced. "I give you our historic Joppenbergh Mountain miner. A goddamn American Hero."

The statue's head was heroic, the size of a medicine ball, carved oak, which gave him a slightly middle-Eastern cast. His cheek bones were pronounced. He was looking determinedly to the side of his right shoulder, the pick handle resting on his left shoulder. His gaze was reminiscent of the determined David about to take on the mighty Goliath. The veins and muscles in his neck pulsed with energy. He wore the traditional miner's helmet with a headlamp that actually lit up. "Two doubles A's. It's good for three months. We just have to change them," Clark said. "Or I could install a solar light sensor. I'd need a small budget for that."

"Yeah," Brad Breslaw sneered, "how about a revolving reflector lamp like a lighthouse for the kayaks out in the creek over there."

There were some guffaws and chuckling which ended abruptly as folks took in the rest of the spectacle. He had installed knee-high black boots on his creation, made from old truck tire tread. He'd treated them with an industrial, all-weather coating to protect them from the elements. The jeans were painted a noble blue like they'd just come out of the wash. The gold zipper, a foot long, gleamed and was prominent.

But what really caused a stir was what rested next to the zipper. Clark must have inserted a piece of PVC pipe in there. His sculpture was endowed with a massive member that could not be ignored. It was in fact, the focal point of the statue. All eyes were drawn to it automatically.

Doe went up first and touched it, not without a bit of appreciation. "And what the hell is this? There's no written record of the miners'…whatever, in our town history."

Clark pointed his pen at it like he was giving a lecture / demo. "That's his baby-making miner's pipe."

Fay was next. She marched furiously up to it and covered it with her Bible, barely. She stuttered, "Smut, blasphemy; it's…idolatry. It's genital worship! We won't have this in our town."

I could see that the Shirt was canvassing the crowd to see what tact he should take, which way the wind was blowing. He was a man of no original thinking. "Well, uh," he cleared his throat. Clark this is a miner if I've ever seen one—a miner's miner, I dare say. Uh, but maybe you could make a slight adjustment to the…design. Maybe a little less…"

"Dick," Clark yelled. He clamped his hand over it. "Don't you people see? This is what we are. These men went into the mines and worked like pack animals. They mined, they ate, they drank hard, and they fucked. Otherwise you all wouldn't be here ridiculing it, goddamn it. His dick," and Clark patted it, "is as integral to the process as his pick and shovel is." All the dick patting was beginning to seem like a tribal rite on some Polynesian island.

The Shirt took a furtive step forward. "Now look, Clark. No one here is saying what you did isn't…uh…monumental. It's just…"

Clark spread out his arms and took a defensive stance in front of his creation. "Don't no one come closer. I mean it. Stay back."

The Shirt was visibly nervous. "Clark, don't be unreasonable."

Clark grabbed an iron bar off of the truck and swung it around. "Someone's gonna get their fucking head broke," he warned.

I felt a nudge from behind and a voice whispered, "Do something, Coot, please." It was Bebe. Whenever the top boils off the pot in this whacked kitchen they expect me to do something about it. I walked toward him slowly without a speck of aggression. He was perspiring and the bar was slipping in his hands. When I got close enough I cupped my hands around his ear and said: "As far as I'm concerned there's never enough dick." A smile spread across his agitated face. "These people don't know shit about art. Come on, man. Let's go get a beer."

Then I said to the crowd. "How about we cover up this fine piece of art for now. Let's everyone go home and sleep on it. We can talk about it later." And I added under my breath, "About modifications."

At first they just stared at us, two of the least esteemed men in the hamlet. Then they slowly filed out of the garage, perhaps a bit disappointed that there hadn't been more fireworks. Knowing these folks as I did, I figured they'd wait until Clark went back to rehab, which was his pattern, and then one of the town artists would modify the sculpture's offensive feature. It wouldn't be like taking a hammer to the Pietá.

I led Clark outside and Zeitzer drove us to the Box Car. We had a shot and a beer. Clark assured me that it was OK for him to have a drink since he'd finished sixty days of rehab and was clean as a whistle. The man wasn't a slave to logic. Z had an iced tea. Clark was considerably calmed down by now. He admired his eighteen ounce mug of Spaten Lager, not the top of the German line, but a soft golden brew with tiny refreshing bubbles rising up, each a message of hope.

"Man," he said. "I'd like to stick my dick in that."

"Slim Jim?" I offered, to get him to stop thinking about his dick.

He took a long draught off his beer and belched. "I hear you got a Jones for that Rutsen guy. What's his name?"

"Jacobus."

"Yeah, that's him. Didn't he do something in town?"

"He settled it in 1680."

"Yeah, whatever. I saw him over at the Culinarians' Home when I fixed their fountain. Big ass fountain. I got it to shoot up five feet higher…like a total ejaculation." The guy just didn't stop.

"There's no way you saw him."

"There's some way elderly dude over there dressed in kinky old Dutch rags. They call him Jakie Boy. Crazier than a coot. Uh, oh, sorry Coot."

"The guys been dead for over three hundred years. No way."

"Yeah, and he looks it. The dude can hardly stand up. Crawls around like a turtle." Clark consumed the rest of his beer in a nanosecond and looked to see if I was buying him another.

I determined then and there that I'd have to visit the Culinarians' Home. Stranger shit has happened in this burgh. Of course it couldn't actually be Rutsen. But then again there was Kurt. I saw him and felt him when he was with me. And at the moment I missed him and his guidance very much. Z gave me his baleful look when he knows I'm about to go off chasing shadows.

I made an appointment for the following day to tour the Culinarians' Home under the pretext that my mother-in-law, In-Su, was interested in a retirement community nearby so her granddaughter could visit. I didn't mention this to Margaret or In-Su.

The place was beyond bucolic, rolling hills, farmland, well-tended walkways for strolling or wheeling, the Wallkill River sluicing peacefully south. Everything you'd want to stare at while you waited for La Santa Muerte to pull your dance card. And the food, as the name implies, was high quality grub. The aromas wafting from the kitchen were definitely creative codger cuisine of the highest order. The director, Mr. Tupper, was a genial guy and unequivocally excited to show me around. He stopped in the walnut-paneled dining room and posed, his outstretched arms presenting the windows.

"Look, Mr. Friedman: leaded, stained-glass windows. And look outside. Open fields, a flowing stream, granite cliffs." I doubted there was much cliff-climbing going on. "Evergreens and hardwoods that protect migrating birds. Terraces and gardens. Just look."

His voice went up an octave when he said that. I was looking. I gazed out the windows for the obligatory amount of time. But I was looking for an old Dutchman, whom by standards of science and reality, couldn't exist. Yet this is the locale where the hobgoblin takes tea with a miner whose spirit refuses to vacate until the last load of rock is trundled down the mountain and into the kiln.

Mr. Tupper insisted on showing me all four bathrooms, pointing out how they were retrofitted for any and all handicaps. There were handrails all the way around, rubber mats to avoid slipping on a wet surface, raised toilet seats that lifted you gently from the back to help the user up into a standing position, and then flushed automatically. You could almost take a dump even if you didn't have arms or legs. A resident could also pull a convenient cord with his/her teeth, or just yell, and a kind attendant would come and do the requisite wiping. I didn't ask Tupper if they powdered them afterwards.

We sat in his office and he pressured me to close the deal with a check. I told him I needed to think a bit more but was leaning in a pro-check direction. I asked if he minded if I wandered around the property before I left to soak in some of that abundant spiritual comfort the place offered their guests. He walked me out to the fountain and said goodbye and, "Look at this." I looked again and noticed some movement in the garden off to the left of the access road. We shook hands and said goodbye.

I jogged down the road and entered through a creaking gate and followed a path a few yards up to a metal bench where a little guy was carefully lowering himself down. A quintessential Dutch garden gnome. He clasped his hands and stared at them. I asked if he minded and took a seat on the opposite end of the bench. He didn't respond. He was reciting something. I strained to hear what he was saying. "Tschirky, Tschirky, Tschirky." Well, at least he knew where he was. The home was located at 71 Old Tschirky Road. A strange name, but after all, a strange place.

I went straight for it, "Are you Jackie Boy?" No response. I waited a few moments and dropped the J.R. bomb. "Jacobus Rutsen?" He twitched. "Rutsen?" He twitched again. Holy shit. Maybe it was just palsy. He looked ancient. He climbed up out of his reverie like an old toad out of a dark pond and took me in with pasty blue eyes.

"Oscar, is that you?" Who the hell is Oscar?

"I'm Coot, Coot Friedman. I came to ask you where you buried your treasure, if you don't mind."

"Oscar, you'll be late for the trolley." He coughed. His voice was a dry reed. "OK," I played along. "I'm Oscar. What trolley?"

"The steamer...for the steamer." The guy was agitated at my lack of knowledge as to where I was supposed to be going. And trolleys were way gone since the twenties, except for the trolley museum in Kingston. He kept his eyes on me, disgusted. "Powell, Mary Powell...the steamer." A nut cracked open in my head. The Hudson River Day Line circa 1885 had a steamer that went from Kingston to New York. That's how people got there, the steamer or the train. I'd read about the Mary Powell on a placemat in some fish house in Eddyville. The golden age of steamers. Some were like floating palaces. But what did that have to do with buried treasure?

He was looking up to his left and nodding at something. "Yes," he rasped, "always the veal, always." It was like he was ordering dinner. Then it struck me, a stamp on my forehead, Veal Oscar. The Dutchman was channeling from 1889, Oscar Tschirky, Oscar of the Waldorf-Astoria. I'd read about him in a book Doe loaned me about turn-of-the-century high life in New York City. I don't remember why I was interested in it, but it seemed cool. All those rich bastards strutting around flicking cigar ashes into silver ashtrays.

And Oscar was maitre'd at the Waldorf-Astoria as well as a culinary inventor. He came up with the Waldorf salad, Thousand Island dressing, and, though unconfirmed, he helped develop the preparation for eggs Benedict. I read that there is still a relish bottle in the lobby of the hotel with his picture on it.

He's kind of like Chef Boyardee, aka Ettore Boiardi, the Italian immigrant who had a famous restaurant in Cleveland (1928). His dishes were in such demand he sold his raviolis and meatballs in cans all over the world. There's a statue of the guy in Omaha, Nebraska. Maybe Cleveland didn't want it.

I couldn't believe I was remembering all this shit. It was just oozing up under the floorboard of my brain. There are times when I can't remember where I took off my boots. Or I'll find my toothbrush in the crockpot.

Oscar Tschirky was an urbane guy, a transplanted Swiss gentleman who'd migrated to New Paltz to build a home on a spectacular piece of property, with breathtaking views, and a sense of peace. He wound up rubbing shoulders with the most powerful families and leaders of the day. He over-saw the daily operation of the Waldorf like he was royalty himself. He even moved into the hotel after his wife died in 1929. But it wasn't until 1942 that his property became a retirement home for chefs. And I was trying to talk to a guy who thought I was Oscar and who I doubted was Jacobus Rutsen. So we were even.

Still, I tried again, "Rutsen?" He twitched. "Are you Jacobus Rutsen?" I spoke quietly because I didn't want to stress the guy out. He could pop off at any moment. "Did you bury your treasure on Joppenbergh Mountain?"

"Joppenbergh?" He said it vacantly. "Joppenbergh?" The name seemed to have some distant significance to him. Of course if he'd lived here for decades or centuries why would he remember anything?

"Treasure?"

"Yes, do you know anything about any treasure?"

He struggled to stand up. I helped him and handed him his cane. He walked further into the garden. I held his arm. We strolled, or rather crawled, toward an ornate mar-ble bird bath, an accommodation for the migrating birds who passed through on their way to greener pastures. He stopped at the bath and with effort lifted his cane and jabbed it in, and swirled the water around. There were maybe a hundred or more gold Sacagawea, James Polk, Zachary Taylor, and silver Susan B. Anthony coins swishing around the bottom along with colorful marbles, cat's eyes and bull's eyes. A light was mounted on a post above to show it off at night if anyone cared to observe the attraction. The birds wouldn't have to search too hard for a drink of water.

So, there we were, Jackie Boy, or whoever he was, stirring the coins and marbles around. He managed a smile; the activity seemed to give him contentment. He said, "Oscar...treasure. The treasure, Oscar." I calculated that I had wasted two hours there, but for some reason I didn't regret it. I like old guys like Jackie Boy.

A few days after my visit to the Culinarians' Home, I slipped into the Box Car for a quick burger. Margaret was intent that Val would be raised on an all organic vegan diet, therefore those were the only kind of meals served in our home. It was all delicious, but I was starting to feel vague for lack of protein. Hence my craving for a bleu-cheese burger with waffle fries injected with ketchup.

I was shocked to see Doe and Gil snuggled up close at a table toward the back of the room, the dark corner, hidden behind the jukebox. They looked blissful, connected like chains on a snow tire. I guess it was inevitable that they would hook up, hate being such an attracting force. Together they could rectify local history.

I'd say that she has mighty peculiar taste in men, except I'd almost drunk at her well not so long ago, and I couldn't criticize. Though I had repented my near miss, I carried my guilt around like a millstone. My only defense was that I thought I might never have Margaret for sure. She'd rejected me so many times. I'd just be another lost vet wandering the streets. Loneliness, if you've tasted it, is a cold steel hook that hangs you out to dry. It can draw the life out of a person over time. So we do anything we can not to be lonely.

Still, it brought me up short comparing myself to Gil Fashion. All we had in common was our uncommon minds. But I was happy for Doe and wanted to contribute something to her newfound relationship. I wanted to contribute to her happiness.

I wanted it to be something handmade and indigenous. I had an idea. Back when I'd cleaned out Zeitzer's garage for that traffic infraction, I found a beautiful old wooden jewelry box. It looked expensive. I asked Zeitzer if I should throw it out. "I don't care. Take it if you want it." It was unusual for him to give a short answer. He never used a cold tone like that with me.

When I opened it, it played a tune from *Fiddler on the Roof*. "Sunrise Sunset," to be exact. It choked me up as I realized it must have been his wife's. He'd probably given it to her when things were good between them. No wonder he'd bristled at my question.

The box was empty. But I pulled the felt cushion out just to see if there was any mildew on the inside that would need treating. There was a picture of the two of them. They were in bathing suits facing the shore, a turquoise ocean behind them under a tropical blue sky. Their heads tilted toward one other. Their expressions were blissful, their connection palpable, their devotion to each other unquestionable. I guessed that they were on their honeymoon. This was a picture of love, and what the hell was I going to do with it?

I didn't think Zeitzer would appreciate me giving it back to him. I tried to put in the recycling bin at the post office, but I couldn't. There was something about it that should be honored, preserved. I wound up slipping it into the donation box at St. Peter's. Catholics are always up for a new relic.

I've got this theory...well, it's an unproven formula actually. It goes like this: the amount of love you have for a person, and that person for you, is doubled to the negative lack of love when that love goes bad or is withdrawn. Let L stand for love. X stands for the amount of love. And -2X stands for the amount of love lost, which is twice that first given. At least that's how if feels. LOL stands for loss of love. Hence the formula XL > -2X / LOL = shit. Ergo shit = shit. I might have to rework the formula, but I believe there's some substance to it. And that's why you feel like shit when someone dumps you.

Anyway, I wanted to decorate the music box and give it to Doe. So, I went to the source, the place where all things converge, where magic is still possible, where the living bargain with the dead. I went up the mountain with my collection kit, scissors, knife, rubber gloves, and plastic baggies. I was up there so long it got dark by the time I was finished.

I had harvested the samples: oak acorns, just the beret caps, red and white oak leaves sans orange grubs, quaking aspen leaf, sycamore bark, some potato-chip bark, a handful of long, soft needles from a white pine, Russian olive, peanut butter and jelly, some Asian mushrooms, and Hen of the Woods, couldn't do without that. Got back to my room and arranged the various flora, fauna, and fungi on a piece of paper the same size as the top of the jewelry box. When I was satisfied, I reached for my trusty glue gun, the only kind I ever want to shoot again. I must have been up half the night assembling it. I finished it off with clear spray hobby shellac, which dries in just minutes.

When I woke up the next morning I did a double espresso with a soup spoon of brown sugar and two chipped Advils. Caffeine and Advil work nice in concert together. Then I looked at the jewelry box sitting on the kitchen table, the sunlight practically making it appear to float. The various clippings and pieces gave a warm glow from the shellac. I slipped the card inside. I'd written a short poem to both of them, not disclosed here because it's private, but it had to do with reconciling their history, burying the hatchet, stuff like that, wedding card prose—I could have done that for a living. Carefully, I placed it in the cardboard box I'd filled with Styrofoam peanuts.

I checked my phone to make sure it was a weekday, so her office would be open. Sometimes she was out collecting artifacts or at meetings with the Chamber of Commerce to brainstorm about what the next festival would be. In early August it could be Wiggle Your Toes Day dedicated to your poor piggies always trapped in your shoes. Or, my preference, Tapioca Pudding Day. Why? First because it's not chocolate pudding, yuck. And I realized why I like it so much. It's the cassava root in it that creates those small, tiny balls that gives it a unique texture. Yum.

I was excited about the gift and certainly a bit proud that I'd made it with my own hands. I walked over to Main Street, careful not to jostle the box. A gamey fragrance rose up to my nostrils and I wondered if the Asian mushrooms hadn't completely dried out.

When I got to Doe's office, I saw the lights flashing on Chief Cruickshank's cruiser. The EMT's were there as well, running in with bags and a stretcher. Officer Boice put his "stop" hand up. "Can't go in there, Coot, sorry."

"What's going on?"

"Not good." Boice had a more-than-misdemeanor look on his face. He was piss-pants nervous. Two state police cruisers screeched in behind us. Lights flashing, no sirens. One trooper went straight in. The other car was a K-9 unit; the dog, a tall German Shepherd, wiry for his species, paused, looked up, gave my box a sniff, then looked at his handler. The handler, a big putty-white doughboy, gazed at me without pleasure, then went inside.

"Boice, what the fuck happened?"

He was shaking his head like he was trying to deny something too terrible to admit. "Gil's dead, Coot…she killed him."

"Fuck." I backed up and slid down on to the bumper of the Chief's car. "Fuck."

The crowd had pushed in and spilled off the sidewalk. There was another officer now directing traffic away from the scene. "Fuck." I couldn't think. It felt like a column of darkness had engulfed me. My chest was constricted and I struggled to breathe, heaving in and out. Was this really happening? It had to be one of my episodes. I looked around for Mr. Gold Robe. Had he managed to resurrect himself from our last encounter? I was willing to endure some pain for this, take a hit, if it just wasn't true.

She couldn't have done this. But there were the cops, the medics, and most of the town. There was a collective stir and low moan from the crowd as they carried him out. I got up and went around the side so I could see.

The bloodstained sheet that lay over him rippled in a slight breeze, the last flag he would salute. A deafening silence fell over the street. Some folks bowed their heads in prayer. Stony-eyed, always suspicious, the troopers led the way to the ambulance, followed by the EMT's, who didn't look like it was business as usual. This was a bad one.

They hadn't bothered to handcuff Doe. They just escorted her by both arms down the steps. People gasped when they saw her. She appeared to be in a trance. Her mouth wide open releasing a silent scream. They'd put a trench coat over her; but her stiletto heels scraped on the sidewalk. Her face, which is always a puzzle, seemed a decoupage of rouge, blood, smeared lipstick, and black mascara. Her features were scrambled, and the intensity of emotion or whatever it was completed a horrifying mask. If she'd just looked insane that would have been enough, but there was something undeniably preternatural about her. It felt like everything I knew and depended on had just been shattered.

I set the box down on a stoop, kneeled over it and cried until I couldn't see. Then, the thought that maybe I had something to do with this, that I had contributed to this ghastly end with my dallying, dropped hard on my head. And I cried and cried, and repeated, "Doe, I'm so sorry. So sorry."

When I finished my initial grieving, most everyone, including the emergency vehicles, had gone. The forensic team had orange-taped the entrance and was inside still collecting evidence. It was a cool October night, maybe November, cool but not cold, and a spectral mist had moved in off the Rondout Creek as if to complete the scene. I walked back down Route 213 until I came to a recycling bin and dropped the box into it. There must have been something in my tears to loosen the varnish. The leaves and needles and nuts were sliding around in a yellow sauce that made me want to puke.

There would be no celebration, no warm feelings, not a single shred of gladness or hope to be found. Nothing would be the same again. This kind of shit wasn't supposed to happen here. It made me very unsteady.

I stopped in front of The Duchess of Cheese and thought I'd get a coffee, try to clear my head out. I studied the interior to see who was inside. A giant wheel of cheese hung from the ceiling and rotated over the heads of the patrons. It was a cool feature, a rotating wheel of cheese with rubber rats attached by their teeth. Hopefully, the cable would never snap. The Cheese of Damocles, murder and death being the topic of the hour.

If the folks in there didn't know already, I didn't want to talk about what I'd just seen. Word would get out soon enough. The reflection of my face was red, puffy, and distraught. I looked like hell and thought hell couldn't be much worse. As I gazed at my reflection another face slowly superimposed over it. Gil's bloodstained face looked out at me, a mask of horror. His lips were moving as if he were praying or pleading. I could hear his voice. He was begging me to provide solace, to instruct him, to show him what's supposed to happen next. "Shit," I said, "it doesn't take long." This was nothing like Kurt. Worse than a ghost you like attaching itself to you is one you don't feel akin to.

I walked away; his obliterated presence following me down the street, oppressive and desperate. What was I supposed to do with him? How had it come to be that I was the one to usher folks passing into the next world? Yeah, I remembered, my Harriet Tubman brain injury. I turned in to the Box Car and ordered two Firestone Walker Union Jack beers, seven point five alcohol content.

"Waiting for somebody, Coot?" Christine asked, sliding a Slim Jim across the bar—she always gave one to her regulars.

"Got someone," I mumbled. She looked around and shrugged. I felt Gil leaning into me. He whispered, "Coot, what am I going to do?" Shit, *Halloween III*. I closed my eyes and took a long sip. It was cold and crisp, that inexpressible moment of bon voyage a beer drinker craves. The taste that says every little thing's gonna be all right. But all I got was a moment of all right.

When I opened my eyes I saw The Digger sitting across

the bar grinning at me. It was the kind of grin you see in those Southern movies just before they pull the guy out of the car and beat him to death with a trailer chain. I was in no mood for the asshole. Last time we tangled he lost hearing in his left ear. And I, I remembered, brushing my fingertips over my nose, that I could not breathe a clear stream of air up my right nostril. The bastard.

I needed desperately to relax and figure this shit out. It was not an ordinary problem; it was my kind of problem. What was I going to do with Gil? Maybe I could take him up the mountain, and then…what? The Digger kept up that grin; he winked at me. The bastard was trying to taunt me into a fight, which I wasn't up for.

There's something about certain people who exhibit a total lack of humanity, or empathy. You see it on the faces of some badass cops or certain officials sitting behind desks and counters where they are not going to do anything to serve you. They like you to beg them for assistance.

The Digger possessed that lack of kindness to a degree that justified splitting his head open. But one homicide was enough for today. He scuffed his stool back and drained his Bud Lite, incriminating himself further by drinking corporate piss water. Everyone got quiet. He stared at me and announced. "I'm going to the powder room. And then I'm gonna kick your ass. You hear that, faggot?" He strutted confidently into the loo.

There was something kind of flashing from the kitchen service window. It was Clarence, my proud Somali-American friend I'd taken a beating for the last time. He'd written on a paper plate, COOT. NO! GO HOME! I was weighing my options deep into fight or flight mode. But I didn't feel like getting up just then. An asshole like The Digger shouldn't be allowed to get away with this shit. Bullies just inflate more if you don't deflate them with the pushpin of firm resistance.

Everyone at the bar was nervous. None of them liked him, but they were scared to go against him. A few of them got up, threw down some money and got out fast. Gil's presence was starting to freeze my right shoulder. He leaned up to my ear. "I got this, Coot. Let me handle it."

Newly dead, butchered violently, how could he handle anything? Then he was gone, disappeared for good, I hoped. Maybe he was taken in hand by some benign organization that dealt with this kind of stuff. Like a Salvation Army for disembodied souls. I needed just one less obstacle at the moment.

Christine put a shot down in front of The Digger's place. "I'm going to tell him it's on you, Coot." That wasn't going to appease the asshole. It took crunched bone, blood, and a lot of hurt to satisfy him.

The Digger had been in there a few minutes now. Maybe he was applying some dirtbag cologne or ritualistically washing his hands before he came out to mangle me. His scream shocked us. It was high-pitched for a man of his girth and lifted everyone up off of their bar stools. He bounded around the corner of the bar, his usual pig-pink face drained of all color, screaming, glancing in terror behind him, and shoving his palms back in a duck paddle as if to keep something from overtaking him.

He charged out the double door, smashing off a good piece of the frame and upsetting the bench in front of the bar, ripping the chain out of the brickwork. It reminded me of cartoon characters when they'd run through a wall leaving a silhouette of themselves behind. We could hear him screaming and pleading for a long time as if he'd been cornered by a demon. We stared at each other. A few guys snickered in approval. The others observed me suspiciously. I could tell that they thought I'd somehow caused The Digger to freak out. Then it came to me. I was beginning to like Gil more than I had previously, certainly more than when he was alive. Dead less than an hour, and he'd done me a good turn.

Christine said, "Shit, it's like he saw a ghost. I felt something weird in here since…well, since you came in, Coot."

I tried to look innocent and ordered a hardboiled egg and another beer.

That night I got a gift. I dreamt of Kurt. It was a beautiful dream, a reunion. Whoever controls these forces, they were letting me have my friend back, even if it was for just a half hour of REM sleep. They'd even restored him to his robust, youthful self. He wore the same ski uniform he'd worn all those years ago, cleaned up, and pressed. He was really there. And I needed him. We were on the mountain. We stood on the table of a two hundred and thirty foot ski jump looking down at the inrun. The platform trembled in the wind, as a cloud of solid white flakes pelted us, though I wasn't the least bit cold. The flakes felt refreshing on my face and arms, legs, and neck. For some reason I was wearing a t-shirt and boxers—not monogrammed.

He studied the jump and said, "Perfect conditions, Coot."

I was afraid, even in the dream, that I would lose him before we could talk. Or that Mr. Gold Robe would somehow fuck this up. "Kurt, I need to know…" I couldn't remember what it was. I was starting to panic.

"Listen to me, Coot. You remember what I said about Rutsen's treasure?"

"Yeah, I think so."

"I'm not sure now that it is at the horse farm. It's no longer clear to me. I feel like it could be stashed in the rocks facing the trestle. But you have to find it...for Val and Margaret. It'll be college money for Val."

Even in this ultra-rarified dream world it occurred to me, why would a manifestation, a specter, be concerned about my daughter's college tuition? Though, I suppose you can never start planning too early.

"Because you're my friend, you never turned away from me." Holy shit, he was reading my thoughts as well.

"I don't know what to do with Gil." I said quickly. "He's attached himself to me."

"Don't worry about Gil. They've already sent him ahead."

"Where?"

He just smiled. "He'll be alright, not for a while, but he will be."

He took my arm. His hands felt warm. I thought I was out of tears but started bawling like a preschooler. "You can't understand it right now. I sure as hell don't get all of it. How the treasure got moved and whatever. But don't worry about him. He'll be OK."

"She murdered him, Kurt. She just killed him."

He was holding me in his arms like he was protecting a frightened child. I hadn't felt this kind of warmth from another man since the war, when we'd try to comfort each other when one of our guys bought it.

"No she didn't. She didn't kill him."

"I was there. I saw them lead her out of the office—blood all over the place."

"Gerhardt did it."

I was confused. "Brock's father? How could that be?"

"He'd been seeing Doe for over a year. She dumped him when she hooked up with Gil. He was insanely jealous. He came to settle the score, but Gil got in the way. He pro-tected her."

"But he wasn't there. Nobody saw him."

"I saw him. He got out fast before the cops got there."

"Why didn't Doe tell them if she knew?"

"You saw her. She was practically catatonic. She probably still is."

Even asleep it felt like the limits of this dream were stretched beyond what was possible. How could he know this? How could it be true? "They said she killed Gil with a letter opener. They took it for evidence. There was blood everywhere."

"They're wrong. After Gerhardt took care of Gil he was shocked by his own violence, panicked, and ran away. He threw his hunting knife into the honeysuckle bushes in the backyard. Find it and bring it to Cruickshank. Tell him to check it for fingerprints. Be smart about it. He's a cop."

The storm had lightened up and the sky was suddenly ablaze with stars, as if someone had thrown a power switch on. A million specks of light testifying to a previous existence. Like understanding and love, we humans get the news after the fact. Down in the hamlet, there were no lights shining. It was as if it had disappeared. The world, what I knew of the world at this moment, was my friend Kurt and me standing about six hundred and twenty five feet above the town if you counted the mountain and the jump. And he was about to leave me. There was nothing else but us, the jump, and the snow. Kurt fastened his binders and slid back and forth testing his skis for the feel of the snow. He was getting ready.

"Kurt wait, don't go."

We were still standing close to each other. He put his hand on my shoulder. "I'm not going to come back this time. I'll look out for you however I can. You're a good man, Coot. Whether they know it or not. You're a very good man." He slid over to the edge and crouched down, preparing to drop into the inrun.

"Kurt," I blubbered. "I need you here."

He looked back. "You've got everything you need, Coot." Then he smiled. It was a broad smile of such benevolence and confidence that I felt embraced by it. "Watch me, Coot. This one's going to be a record."

He sprung out powerfully over the ramp and raced down faster than I'd ever seen them do it in the Olympics. When he reached the end he adjusted his body and leaned forward in the prescribed position and ascended into the air. He climbed steadily up as if he were being lifted by guy wires. He flew up and up and just kept going. Higher and higher.

I followed him intently, not even allowing myself to blink. He must have reached a height of at least two hundred and forty-five feet. And then...he was gone. There was no arc to his jump. No graceful descent back to earth. Words came to me: *He's jumped out of the world.*

Then I felt myself falling, falling down, dropping from a great height, my stomach in my throat. Descending faster and faster until I was about to smash into the earth. I sat up hard in bed, drenched in sweat, my mouth dry, my heart pounding. I sat and stared at the alarm. Five twenty-two AM. I waited until I finally caught my breath. Then I reached for my pants.

The sun was coming up as I crawled around under the honeysuckle bushes behind Doe's office. I switched off my headlamp and threw it in my backpack. I figured I would have found it right away if it was there. Something caught my eye. It was poking out of the ground and it was shiny. It turned out to be a wad of aluminum foil. I reversed myself and crawled further in toward the fence and felt something hard on my knee. I backed up and saw it. The hunting knife, just like Kurt said.

Then I heard something and shot a glance back toward the driveway. It rolled in slowly, ominously, Gerhardt's Dodge Ram 2500 diesel, blood red. Shit. Quickly, I grabbed the knife with my mini silicone tongs and dropped it in the plastic freezer bag. I threw it into my backpack and began the barbed-wire crawl double time along the fence trying to find a way out. I heard the door slam and I started to panic. I was about to come face to face with Gil's murderer, perhaps mine as well. What else could I expect from him?

The fence was wood and I finally found a rotted portion big enough, I thought, for me to crawl under it and out. My backpack got stuck on something. I could hear his shoes crunching on the gravel as he got closer. With all my strength I shoved myself through as hard as I could, catching a nail and dragging it hard across my scalp. When I got out the other side I rolled down an embankment into a pool of putrid motor oil and other unappetizing liquids, maybe urine or turpentine, some bastard had dumped in there. There was blood starting to trickle into my eyes and I guessed that I'd need at least six stitches in my scalp. I lay there soaking the shit into my clothes holding my backpack above my head to keep the evidence dry, though I figured it wouldn't leak through the storage bag.

I listened as Gerhardt swiped at the bushes. He must have had a machete. He was just slashing away at the bushes to save time. And he was getting more and more agitated every second. He was saying, "Motherfucker. Kill you, motherfucker." Did he know I was there? Was he coming to get me? He must have slashed every bush down to the roots. He stopped and was silent for a while. I could hear him breathing heavily, a desperate animal. He must have been trying to parse out what happened. Then I heard him make it fast back to the truck, start it and get out.

Maybe he thought the police had found his knife. Now it was time to run. But someone else had found it, me. Then a happy thought: I'm going to nail the bastard. For Gil, Doe, and for Brock.

I made a plan. First I'd go to Bebe's and have her sew up my head. I'd seen her expertly stitch up one of her kitchen staff, Alejandra, when she'd cut her arm feeding romaine lettuce through a slicer. Alejandra would not go to the hospital and risk being arrested and deported away from her children. She sat calmly as if she were getting a manicure. Bebe doused the wound with iodine and stitched it up, then wrapped it in gauze. Alejandra refused to go home and finished the dishes wearing rubber gloves, and swept up as well. Bebe provided her "illegal" workers with the unattainable, but inalienable, rights they longed for and deserved. I greatly admired her for that.

Before I left, she made me strip on the back porch and put on a chef's outfit—there was nothing else. White pants, a white tunic, even some rubber-soled clogs. Everything I had on went straight to the dumpster. It occurred to me that I go through a lot of wardrobe. Soon it would be time to visit the Army-Navy store again. Bebe grabbed my arm. "Coot, what are you going to do?"

I gazed into her beautiful, mature face, thought about what she'd been through since escaping Hoboken, how she'd knitted the town together into a fine fabric; well, most of the town anyway. There were still some old bastards who'd never darken her door. My heart tipped with happiness for Zeitzer. He deserved the best, and he got it. "I'm going to get Doe out of jail."

The next thing I did was anonymously contact the Department of Environmental Conservation and turn in the bastard who created a cesspool in the middle of town. The guy turned out to be one of The Digger's crew, an additional bonus.

Next I had to get the evidence to Cruickshank, which made me nervous. Officer Boice showed me into Cruickshank's office.

The Chief had company, bad company from my point of view. He was meeting with two state troopers from Troop T headquarters on Route 209. They were there to meet with the Chief about Gil's murder. But now I was stuck. The troopers, a man and a woman, gave off an unwelcoming vibe. I felt vulnerable.

"Christ sake, Boice. I'm in a meeting. You don't just usher someone in…Coot…what are you doing here?"

Cruickshank seemed agitated, not as friendly as usual. Something had changed. "What can I do for you, Coot?"

"Well…" I hesitated. "I…uh…"

"What the hell is it? I'm busy." He noticed my outfit. "You dressed up for Mardi Gras, or what?"

In my haste to deliver the knife to him, I'd forgotten to go home and change out of the chef clothes Bebe gave me. This wasn't going to help my credibility. I could feel the troopers' eyes drilling a suspect hole in my back.

I was trapped. It's always a mistake when I go to the police. Helpless, not a card left to play, I slid the baggie out of my backpack and placed it on his desk.

"What the hell is that?" Cruickshank snapped. The troopers were on their feet.

"That's the murder weapon."

"What murder weapon?" The Chief was icy and making me more nervous.

"The one that he used to kill Gil."

He looked at me steadily, weighing his options. "They have Doe's letter opener. That's the murder weapon. What makes you think *this* is the murder weapon? And who the hell is *he*?"

Now I was stuck; I hadn't thought this through. I was intent on delivering Gerhardt's knife and clearing Doe. I couldn't tell him that a spook told me about it in dream.

"It's a hunch." My voice was weak and I had no doubt that I was incriminating myself.

"A hunch, Coot? Doe's going away for the rest of her life. And you have a hunch?"

It was clear now, I should have packed it up and mailed it to him or left it in his cruiser. The troopers were standing on either side of me suddenly in full official capacity. They must have thought they'd found a possible suspect without even lifting a finger.

I felt something next to my head. The woman had her service pistol, a Glock 37 with a chambered .45 GAP, barrel length 4.48 inches, tapping my ear.

"Hmm, with love from Austria." I should have kept my mouth shut, but I still felt some pride that I could recall the various tools of the killing trade.

The other trooper, a gray-skinned guy, tall and thin as a straw, pulled out a Taser M26C and held it against my neck. All they needed was a friggin' bazooka.

"Who is this asshole?" The female asked.

"He's Coot Friedman, a veteran, harmless…usually." I was definitely fucked if Cruickshank was taking the low road, and it looked like he was.

The woman leaned over and lifted the bag up and examined the contents. "Where'd you get this, Joe?" Why do they have to be such bastards?

"The name is Coot, and be careful of that. There's prints on it."

"Maybe yours," the guy said.

The tall trooper kept tapping the Taser against my neck.

I was starting to get pissed off now, not the best reaction for my well-being, but I couldn't help it. "Sure you got all eight double A's in there? You look a bit forgetful."

"Wanna find out, asshole?"

In my peripheral vision I could see the black stripe down each of their pant legs in remembrance of their fallen comrades. No such respect for me and my fallen comrades, guys I carry around with me twenty-four-seven.

She said, "I think we should take him in."

"You suck."

She pulled my hair back and slammed my face on Cruickshank's desk. Bloody nose. The chief stood up. "Easy, he's a decorated veteran." Nice, a bit of humanity.

"You're a piece of shit," the skinny guy said.

I didn't care at this point. They disgraced their uniform. "Fuck you. You got what you need. Take it to the lab."

They were about to slam me again. "That's enough," said Cruickshank. "I vouch for this man." There was a brief showdown, and then, curiously, they retreated without the evidence. They must have assumed I was an unreliable witness. The chief slid me some paper towels and I quelled the flow of blood from my nose. That was a lot of blood in twenty-four hours.

The woman stopped at the door. "Don't leave town, Corey."

"The name's Coot, bitch." She started back in after me.

Cruickshank yelled, "No! That's enough." They left.

I stared at my "friend," if that's what he actually was. The Chief seemed concerned. "I'm sorry they roughed you up, Coot."

"You'll be sorrier when they find Gerhardt's prints all over that knife."

"Gerhardt? You're saying Gerhardt killed Gil? That's who you mean by *he*?"

I shoved the freezer bag hard across his desk. "Blood, fingerprints, DNA. Go do your fucking job."

I left; Officer Boice started to mumble something conciliatory. "Fuck you, Boice."

I was woozy from the head banging. I walked through what felt like a mild spring evening, thinking that I needed to find an alternative method of achieving my goals. I only had myself to blame.

I walked on, inhaling my self-loathing and the air in this ill-fated fall night. I walked until I got to Veterans Park on Route 32. I ran my hands over the engraved names on the various plaques and monuments. I pressed their names into my palms and read their lives into mine—my extended family. I stumbled into the gazebo, smoked a roach, then passed out on the bench.

Given Gil's diminished condition they wasted little time planning his funeral—closed casket. Not even the skilled mortician's at Moran's could perform their cosmetic magic after Gerhardt had sliced him up like an Easter ham. They couldn't track down any of Gil's family, but a bit of research revealed that he'd spent a year on a Coast Guard icebreaker in the Great Lakes. This automatically kicked in veteran's honors for his interment, a bugler, Old Glory, the whole nine yards. But the Coast Guard Band declined an invitation to truck down from New London, Connecticut to play Gil's funeral.

This triggered an enthusiastic response from the Shad Town Improvement Association Brass Band and Social Club. They were ecstatic to be called in. Nothing like a random death to get a gig. Beaming Dove in Winter, though not a fan of anything military, created an arrangement of the official Coast Guard marching song, "Semper Paratus," aka "Always Remember." It didn't quite come off with the precision of the Coast Guard Band itself, but was reminiscent of the tune if you'd heard it before, kind of a music box version. They also played the "Battle Hymn of the Republic," for good measure, and of course, "This Land is Your Land."

There had been some material changes in the band since the last time they marched down Main Street for National Yo-Yo Day. I remember that one because Yo-Yo Day can only be on June 6.

They marched with a contingent of yo-yo enthusiasts, walking the dog, shooting the moon, and doing other tricks from the yo-yo repertoire. One of the bandsmen, a Home Depot manager, and a papier-mâché artist on the side, had made a replica of the two-hundred and fifty-six pound World's Largest Yo-Yo, but his only weighed forty-five pounds and they pushed it along on a hand truck.

There was some flap about the occasion as a certain faction wanted to march on Sunglasses Day instead, which rolls around each year on June 27. They thought it'd be cool to wear sunglasses. The yo-yo date won because they could march sooner than June 27. Why postpone pleasure?

The change I mentioned in the band was that now there was a chorus of singing actors, some retired up here from the city. There were at least two minor Broadway stars who expected treatment commensurate with their status, which was over-and-done-with. Their idea was that they could break into song, a capella, or accompanied by the band. They also wanted to insert a dramatic element into the performances in the Greek chorus tradition, commenting on the action taking place, as it were: "Oh, poor Gil, dead before his time. Murdered for lust by the trollop of the town." Or something like that, and as it was soon to be known, was completely false.

One of the new crew was a real pain in the ass named Roger who insisted that he be called Choragus. He'd done small rolls in Shakespeare in the Park and assumed he'd be a big, dramatic fish in the hamlet, but was more like hackneyed herring.

There was a bitching fight between the band members and the thespians. Beaming Dove had her hands full, and her usual steady composure was challenged, leading the band and refereeing the infighting amongst its members. But she couldn't bring herself to limit the membership. A few of the band members insisted that she start auditioning musicians and actors before they could join. She judiciously pointed out to them, that if she did that, there would be no Improvement Association and Social Club at all. None of them would have survived an audition. But all were welcome as long as she ran the show. Hence, it had become an ungainly troupe.

To add to Beaming Dove's caseload, the Senatorial Puppet Bazaar insisted on joining in the festivities. As it was turning out to be a military hero's funeral they thought that their twelve-foot tall, three-person operated Uncle Sam puppet would be an appropriate addition. For some reason they brought out the dragon, unicorn, Sun King puppet, and Ms. Antoinette, a pout-faced, contemporary version of the queen, complete with decapitated head bobbing on a spring. All of them nine- to twelve-foot tall creations, requiring skilled operators who could avoid mowing people down along the route.

The service was officiated by Father Tuey, who'd finally scored big on a twenty dollar scratch-off card, the Win for Life Ticket. He was guaranteed one thousand dollars per week for life, so his credit rating improved tremendously. He used a good portion of the money to send some of the low-income parish kids to college and to have the parish house properly insulated. He also bought himself a late-model silver Porsche with a custom-designed refrigerator to store his energy drinks in along with new beverages he'd discovered that caused him to slur his words at Sunday sermons. But he was a happy man. He was fond of saying, to some disapproval in the congregation, that he had more money than God, if you posit that God doesn't need any money, or he could create some if he wanted it. A "God-zillion dollars."

Given the various competing factions that attended the rites for Gil, there wasn't a recognizable order to the events. It was a bit of a free-for-all. Father Tuey would start eulogizing and the band would crank up, then stop. Roger aka Choragus, had prepared an excerpt from Hamlet that he insisted on reciting. The outsized puppets barely fit in the narrow pathways of the cemetery and were disturbing flower arrangements and assorted mementoes placed about the gravestones. The puppet operators were stumbling over them. There was no opening large enough for the entire band to assemble, so they were scattered all over the grounds. Father Tuey, when he could project his voice over the confusion reminded everyone that this was a sacred Catholic service and that we were on consecrated ground, Saint Peter's Cemetery. It was clear that Beaming Dove had lost control of her sprawling company. What had once been a homespun unit of musicians who celebrated our victories and losses had become, in Wordsworth's words, once again, "a parliament of monsters."

As if on cue in a thrilling Cirque du Soleil performance, the dragon puppet's tail caught on fire. Apparently, it was resting on an anodized aluminum cemetery light, one of those memorial lights that glow eerily in the dark. The red plastic flame guard must have been defective and ignited the dragon's tail that was touching it. It caught fire quickly and sent up a toxic plume of PVC, clay, fiberfill, saran wrap, upholstery, panty hose, and other ingredients used in puppet-making.

The handlers panicked and in their frenzy to get out from under the burning material, they swung it around wildly and it struck The Digger square in the back and catapulted him into the grave. He lay there, cold-cocked, sprawled on top of Gil's coffin, arms and legs hugging it as if he were bidding Gil an affectionate farewell.

I was standing further back with Grady and Todd, the cemetery guys. They were having a private wake, sharing the remains of a bottle of Wild Turkey. Their job was to wait until everyone left, then move in with the front-loader and fill in the hole with dirt. They were laughing so hard they had to cover their mouths with their jacket sleeves. Todd said, "Whaddya think, Coot, should we fill it in now?"

Grady guffawed, "It's just The Digger—no loss."

Todd came back, "Well, The Digger has dug himself in this time."

Grady slurred, "Well done, well dug…well, I can dig it." Their howling laughter wasn't lost on Father Tuey who caste a disapproving eye on them.

Todd continued, "What's dug shall be done and what is un-dug shall remain un-dug."

Grady one upped, "Leave the digging to the living so we can make a living."

Slightly nauseated, I withdrew from them and made a circuitous path over to Cruickshank's car so I could see how Doe was reacting. Of the multitude of emotions I was feeling at that moment, I couldn't come up with vindictiveness or hate, just a devastating pity. My stomach was sick. I looked at her and hoped that Doe hadn't seen The Digger thrown into the grave, but she probably had.

Doe had not been officially charged with a crime. She

had been admitted to the Benedictine Psychiatric unit and was being treated for severe trauma after witnessing Gerhardt make lunch meat out of Gil. They'd administered two rounds of shock therapy to snap her out of it, after which she remembered nothing until she read about it the *Freeman*, staring at the picture of herself being led out of her office.

She was released in time to attend Gil's funeral, but felt too compromised and delicate to stand graveside. Instead, she watched the proceedings from the back of the Chief's cruiser, several rows away, on a video cam he'd placed in a tree just above the action. She was on some serious antidepressants. Bebe, who'd visited her in the psych ward, told me that Doe would not go back to being the town historian. That she felt shattered and that there was no history or future left for herself. Both had been erased. Basically, Gerhardt had killed two people that day, the bastard.

Meanwhile, as we were laying Gil to rest, there was a massive manhunt underway in Sumpter, South Carolina, the third most dangerous city in the fifth most dangerous state in the union. Gerhardt's blood-red Dodge Ram with the Snow Chief plow package was easy to trace, especially in an almost tropical climate where there wasn't any snow to plow.

South Carolina seems to be the preferred destination for fugitive murderers, which is why most of them are easily apprehended. They stay at the Murderer's Motel and eat at the Murderer's Buffet, then drop by the Murderer's Lounge, kick back, have a few, and do a bit of lady killing.

There was actually a place there called the Club Miami, which racked up an impressive number of killings, rapes, and drug activity that finally qualified it for the police department to shut it down. And that's where they'd caught Gerhardt. He'd parked his truck out front and was taking a selfie with Club Miami in the background. He'd taken on the roll of tourist / murderer and wanted to catalogue his experience. He'd have been better off going to Graceland.

He was uber-intoxicated down to his black Doc Martens skinhead boots, and pissing his pants when they took him into custody. The fingerprints and DNA were a perfect match to the ones on the knife I'd turned over to Cruickshank. Gerhardt's arrest and extradition back to New York State resulted in my receiving our town's medal of honor.

At first, I flat-out refused the award. I wasn't in the frame of mind to receive a medal when too many of my buddies had only received them posthumously. It brought back the memories, the bad times. But Margaret insisted I accept the honor. She thought it might provide a firewall against me constantly getting my ass kicked in town.

"Coot Ronald Friedman." The Shirt cleared his voice and looked around nervously to see if he had everyone's attention. His trademark belly inched out under his shirt, displaying an unappealing hairy reddish band. We were in the rec center around six PM, two weeks after Gil's funeral, or whatever form of Roman entertainment it had turned into. "Coot…uh, your action. Your brave action has cleared the name of an innocent person. In particular, Doe Gottlieb. You have assisted law enforcement in finding the guilty perpetrator."

The words "guilty perpetrator," struck me as being an odd construction. And law enforcement was present as I scanned the crowd. My two favorite state trooper assholes were in attendance to honor me. So was The Digger, sneering at me from the back row, his face black and blue, and a patch over one eye. Chief Cruickshank was standing opposite The Shirt on my other side. The Shirt continued his bumbling speech. "You, Coot, single-handedly recovered the murder weapon from the crime scene." He leaned into me and whispered, "How'd you know where it was?"

In the front row, smiling kindly at me, was Zeitzer, Bebe, and the rest of the crew from Bebe's place. In-Su and Aldo beamed at me on the stage. They'd brought a dozen or so yellow happy-face helium-filled balloons, bobbing up and down. Folks sitting behind them changed their seats so they could see the action. Val, sleepy and past her bedtime, snuggled beside them in a sequin cowgirl outfit complete with beaded boots. Margaret eyed me with an expression somewhere between pride and disbelief. I read it from the corners of her lovely mouth, total acceptance. I was the dog she never wanted, but took home, and fell in love with.

This little ceremony was window dressing compared to that. Clark Furey, statue-builder extraordinaire, post-modern rehab devotee, was seated a few rows back and quite obviously had relapsed. His eyes looked like they had sparklers sizzling behind his retinas. His face was a mask of consummate irony and he was smiling to himself, highly entertained by a gaggle of juiced-up thoughts swimming through his brain.

Gathered at the sliding doors was a small contingent of the Shad Town Band and company. I'd made it a point not to invite them to the ceremony, especially after their per-formance at St. Pete's. But it was on the front page of the Blue Stone Press that week. I do not desire celebrity. Just a quiet life in the country.

"And Coot," The Shirt droned on, "you are our hamlet's hero for what you did."

I stifled a laugh because "hamlet's hero" struck me as a special at the Box Car. Something like ham and eggs with hollandaise sauce stuffed in a big boy dinner roll.

"You are a decorated, honorably discharged soldier from the United States Army." I was starting to cringe. "And now, it is my honor to award our town's highest honor…" Cruikshank reached over my head and placed around my neck a sterling silver chain from which hung a crossed pick and shovel, a reminder of our proud mining heritage days. The crowd erupted. I just stood there waiting to go home. I turned to face the crowd; they stood up. They stood up for me. No one's ever done that for me before.

The Shirt pressed an envelope into my hand, which turned out to be a gift certificate for beers and a steak for two at RawHide in Kingston, if I could get myself there. Much appreciated. At least it was located near the traffic circle. I wouldn't have to safari deep into the hipster jungle.

"No hard feelings," Cruickshank said.

"Just keep the bitch away from me," I answered, eyeing the trooper and her skinny partner who still looked none too friendly. No doubt they had more penetrating questions for me. And I wouldn't tell them anything. They could go ask Gerhardt themselves.

It was at this moment Coltaire chose to bring out the *faire plaisir à qn.* He'd been rattling around the kitchen during the presentation running an annoying dialogue with himself. He was not on good terms with anyone in town, so we wondered what he was doing there anyway.

The kitchen door swung open and he rolled out a three-tiered food service cart and parked it at an eight-foot folding table, then got busy. First he took a roll of white paper and covered the table. Then he brought out each tray and placed them on top. The item seemed to have been created in three sections. He ran back into the kitchen and returned with a tub of frosting and a spray can of whipped cream, a few items in a basket, and two large spatulas. Painstakingly, he lifted each section of the dessert with the spatulas and placed them carefully on the paper. When all three sections were snug against each other he cemented them with frosting.

He placed two large redheart plums on the far end and then inserted pieces of what looked like shredded black licorice around them. He took a sieve, placed it at the other end and frosted it in place. Then he grabbed the spray can and performed a finishing touch, laying down a layer of whipped cream from the end of the sieve.

Curiosity took over and people were gawking at the thing. On closer inspection it turned out to be an oblong éclair measuring about six feet in length. It had an unappetizing pinkish-brown flesh color to it. Clark was the first one to get to the table. He studied the object with intense scrutiny as if he were deciphering a Japanese koan. He swayed while he did this. Finally, he turned to us and made the pronouncement: "Look everybody, it's a dick cake. Coltaire made a dick cake—far out, man." He snatched one of the little paper plates and the cake knife and was about to dig in.

Coltaire wrestled the knife out of his hand. "I serve. I serve it." Momentarily, he held the point of the knife against Clark's heart, which was SOP for Coltaire. An infraction such as serving oneself without permission could result in death. This just served to animate Clark to a degree that he would need handling. "Get your dick cake here!" The drug or drugs Clark had ingested were herding into the OK Corral of his psyche.

Cruickshank nodded and officer Boice left the podium and started to escort Clark out of the room, assisted by my trooper friends, leading him outside where he'd probably get his ass kicked, as they couldn't kick mine at the moment.

Clark kept going on the way out: "How much cake

would a dick cake make if a dick cake could make cake?"
The door closed.

There was not an immediate rush to the table as folks
were squeamish about being soon to partake of a pastry that
resembled a six foot penis with whipped cream ejaculating
out of the tip. Coltaire was insulted. He retreated into the
kitchen kicking the door open so hard the small glass shat-
terproof window shattered.

"Speech, speech," the crowd called out. Shit, now they
wanted a speech. This prompted the band, for no apparent
reason, to break into "Just the Way You Are," by Billy Joel.
They were sending us a message that it was OK to be just
the way we are. Not much choice about that anyway.

There was no good explanation for all the crazy shit
going on. The meaning of it all seems to be that there is
no meaning at all, no rationale. The brain, attached to the
stick shift of behavior, has very little to do with what might
be considered as real in our experience. Yet, we make ourselves crazy trying to find out what's real. Then I thought,
what the fuck am I thinking anyway?

"Come on, Coot, talk some talk. Coot, Coot, Coot,
Coot," Brad Breslaw chanted. The guy was a certified pain
in the ass. "Speech, speech," several people called out. But
I wish that they had said, "Think something, Coot." That
would have been no problem. I couldn't stop thinking, even
if it didn't make sense. Public speaking is not my forté.
Besides, it was six forty-five and I hadn't even had a beer
yet.

But there was Margaret looking up at me as if I was
something to look up to. And I felt some kind of reckoning
pulse deep in my chest.

"OK," I started, not too inspired. "This award here," and
I slipped it over my head and held it out toward the crowd.
"This award is…not mine." I wasn't going to tell them that

it really belonged to Kurt, but he wouldn't be claiming it. I couldn't tell them that my spirit brother had given us justice. "I can't just stand up here and take credit..."

Then I noticed Doe standing in the back of the room. She'd slipped in late, probably just to watch and then get out before anyone noticed her. "There's someone else here who deserves it more," I said, stepping down from the stage. As I approached her she looked spent, exhausted, dark circles around her uneven eyes, her other features at odd angles as usual, and looking much older. But she seemed more substantial than the last time I'd seen her. She seemed to be bearing up somehow. I hoped that was the case. People stood in complete silence. She barely nodded, but held me in her gaze. I placed the medal over her head. "This belongs to you." She touched the crossed pick and shovel and pressed it to her chest.

Greatly relieved to be outside of the Rec Center, I wandered over to the pavilion and sat down at a picnic table. The moon cast a soft sixty-watt glow over the playground. The swings and slide, the monkey bars, all looked like bereft creatures waiting for the children to return to animate them in the sunlight. A soft breeze gently rattled the chains that suspended the swings. I noticed a form sitting on one of them. It pushed back and swung forward, pumping and gaining altitude.

I stood up and watched and saw that it was me with a mindless, idiotic look on my face, dumb to everything around me, smiling like a loon. On the swing next to me was my anti-totem, Mr. Gold Robe. He looked bemused and held a lollipop as he swung next to me, the fucker. His mouth was going as if he were chanting as he licked the lollipop. Then he stopped abruptly, grabbed one of the chains on my swing, brought it to a halt, and began strangling me. The bastard just never gives up.

"Coot, Coot?" She shook me hard and I looked into her face and felt mine contort, and I started wailing like a child. "It's no good, Margaret. It's no good. I'll never be right in the head. I'm too fucked up. You can't stay with me."

"Shhh, Coot." She held me in her arms and gently pushed my head against her breasts. She whispered, "There's a little girl in there sleeping on her grandmother's lap. She couldn't dream of a better father than you. Do you hear me, Coot?"

I gave in and pressed hard against her. Her scent, the scent of this woman, has become something as elemental to me as oxygen. I could not breathe without her. I didn't want to.

After the award ceremony, Margaret, Val, and I settled into a brief period of calm family felicity. Margaret was averaging a birth a week with a midwifery group. I still did odd jobs, while I planned another foray up the mountain to find Jacob Rutsen's treasure. If Kurt said it was there, it had to be there.

I was also writing a lot of poems and planning to publish a collection if there was anyway I could. I reread Wordsworth and got all fired up about language, what it can do. And I started thinking that words, especially poetry and stories, can be dangerous things. I wanted to write a poem about that. I thought back about everything I'd ever read and realized you remember it for a reason—because the words are true and maybe dangerous. Phrases and words that stick, that hurt, I call soul-kickers.

So, here's the poem, published for the first time right here because no one else would.

> IN THE END THE WORDS
> in the end
> the words took him off
> into the tall grass

like an angry cat.
we heard bones crack,
the chewed sinew of meaning,
the mastication of end rhyme.
"poetry does nothing!"
we heard him scream,
"poetry does nothing!"
until it ate his mouth,
picking the bone of
no poem, no words, or breath.
it was the words
that ornamented the great tree
of his jungle mind, in the nights of
bright bursting moons,
when he threw words like paint
against an insatiable canvas.
it was the words that
confiscated his tongue,
until nothing spoke, but rumbled
like the low sound of digestion.

It must have been about mid-May. It got warm almost overnight. I decided that Val should have a little pool to splash around in. I dug out a four-foot wide hole next to the garden, about a foot and a half deep, prepared it and cemented it in, manically smoothing it out so she wouldn't get scratched. I placed a slanted flat rock so she could slide in on her bottom. Then I filled it with the garden hose and when it got muddy I filled it some more and the overflow watered our tomatoes, parsley, cucumbers, and hops. I'd planted just one little marijuana plant, which Margaret promptly assigned to the compost pile.

I kept the pool covered with a tarp. Before I showed it to Val I put in a bunch of plastic windup fish and boats.

I threw in a half dozen lemons and oranges because they float. Limes don't float, so I didn't use any. It's weird because lemons and limes are both about one hundred and one grams. It might have something to do with the density of the flesh; lemons are more porous so more air gets in. I also threw in a grapefruit, a symbol for the sun because my life revolves around her.

She screamed with delight. It came to me that a vagrant aspect of my psyche is the need to delight those who are precious to me. To meditate on the object that would most please them, fill their joy tank, and ring their pleasure bell. This little pool with windup fish and boats and fruit was what she had dreamed of her entire three and a half years, but she didn't know that until she saw it.

There were bonus points from Margaret. Sometimes she scratched me under my chin like a Border Collie. I was sporting a little billy goat beard at the time, which suddenly sprang two gray hairs. I clipped them off. Then I had a dream that Baby Val was sleepwalking and went out to the pool in the middle of the night. I installed bolt locks at the top of all the doors of the house and went around checking them at night with a flashlight, and again if I thought I'd missed one. And again if the dream came a second time. Val never walked in her sleep. She slept like a little snorting tank, but I couldn't stop myself.

Now I'm sure it was around mid-May because we celebrated the Buddha's birthday, May 14. Margaret and In-Su decided we would have a feast. There was a lot to be thankful for. And they planned to do it Taiwanese style. Early that week they made a pilgrimage to Flushing and spent about three hundred dollars at the Chang Jiang Supermarket and came home with numerous bags of curious ingredients, including a case of Taiwan Tsing Whiskey Beer, a smoked brew, nothing the lightweights at the Box Car could have handled. It did lead to some regrettable behavior on the part of Aldo and me, and almost Zeitzer, but he's got that built-in self-regulation thing installed by his people. He enjoys seeing me make a fool out of myself—not in a mean way. But all was forgiven; it was a feast day after all. The Buddha would have laughed.

They prepared and cooked for the week before the celebration. Val helped, pouring, stirring, dropping, and spilling all over the kitchen, but it was joyous to see the three ladies in there. It was obviously a female domain and I didn't intrude. The various aromas were intoxicating, some indescribable. Never was a meal more anticipated. The menu: tang soo yook, shrimp tempura, fly's head, conch with basil, sesame oil pork, ma you yau hwa, and loofah with clam. Dessert was caramelized pastry puffs with nuts, and of course donuts; the family loves donuts.

The women dressed in ceremonial robes and danced for us. In-Su hand-made and stitched a little outfit for Val. They must have practiced because they were amazing. Margaret was seductive as hell. Aldo had wrapped colorful scarves around himself and wore tight shorts, probably a vestige of his glory days performing with The Flying Libertinos. He struck a Buddha pose on top of Val's slide. At dramatic moments in the dance he'd do a backflip off the slide and land flat on his feet. He was just a skinny, little Italian guy so the Buddha thing didn't quite come off. But Val laughed until she fell on the ground.

"Kau-gin-a. Kau-gin-a," In-Su shouted: "little monkey." He was like a little monkey. All we needed was an organ grinder.

For some reason Zeitzer wore a flowered Hawaiian shirt, cut off jeans, and sandals with high black socks. He must have been flashing back on Hawaii Five-O, his one time favorite TV series from the day.

Aldo and I wasted no time cracking open the smoked whiskey beer and got silly. In-Su and Margaret shared a pitcher of Mimosas. Z took a sip of the beer and had a coughing fit. After just one brew Aldo attempted another backflip and landed flat on his back. In-Su shrieked and Val cried. He sprung up off the grass slightly embarrassed and strutted over to Val's pool and slid in. "Come on. What you wait for?"

I removed my outfit: torn jeans, retired tennis sneakers, and my Lady Gaga t-shirt—Val's favorite singer. I stepped in wearing my boxers, still not monogrammed, and sat splashing next to Aldo. Val sprinted over and jumped on to Aldo's lap. He moaned, then laughed. "Is OK, I already reproduce." He splashed Margaret.

In-Su pounded her fists on her knees, laughing. "Look that. Look that!" Her grackle laugh: each "ha" was more like a winch squeaking out bits of chain. It made me laugh and give thanks for our little outpatient community where each of us gets lots of passes and a wide berth, say like a quarter of a mile.

In-Su gave an incantation or prayer and we ate. We ate ravenously. Even little Val was putting it away somewhere. She loved it and didn't flinch at the spicy stuff. Neither does Margaret. Z had about six glasses of ice water to counteract the hot spices. We must have been at the table for at least an hour. I think I tried the pastry puffs with nuts. I must have had three more Tsing Whiskey Beers and was feeling a bit trashed.

After this astounding feast, Aldo produced a bottle of Amaro del Capo that he'd been saving, a potent digestivo. "For stomach is good." We sipped and sat around watching the afternoon present a shadow play with plowing white clouds for a roof. It was a perfect afternoon.

I barely remember seeing our guests off. I tucked Val

into bed after telling her the story of the kind ghost who lives on the mountain and shows children where the magical things are and where the good things are to eat. She loves that one. I fell into bed with Margaret and there was an aborted attempt at lovemaking. Still, it was pretty damn cozy. She snuggled against me. Almost as many points as a home run.

The rest of May disappeared effortlessly, but I got antsy at the end of the month. The Memorial Day Parade and the ceremonies coupled with it are not a good time for me. The rampant nationalism against the backdrop of fallen comrades, who've fallen next to you, should not be the stuff of parades. Not when you've cradled them in your lap, and listened as they told you what to say to their loved ones. And it was almost always the same, "Tell her I love her. Tell them I will always love them."

One time a lieutenant took a large piece of shrapnel in his stomach. It must have cut through a major artery. "I have two boys and a wife in Plano, Texas. You will tell them that I died for them. You understand, soldier?"

The problem was I could only report what they said. The Army has its own way of doing things. They send the CNOs, Casualty Notification Officers, to the homes of their loved ones to break the news. The whole process angered me. I kind of rolled up on one of my superiors about it, which earned me a week of KP. Fuck 'em. The only right you really had was a right to die.

The night before the parade it came back, a dream that seemed produced to unhinge me, another Gold Robe dust-up. This time I was sitting in some kind of chrome and glass high-rise office in the city. The intercom burped, "Mr. Gold Robe is here to see you."

"Send him in." A dejected, deflated personage in a gold

robe shuffled in, his shoulders stooped, looking down at the Persian Rug. He slid an envelope onto my desk.

I opened it and scanned for weirdness as if it was not already weird. "I accept your resignation."

He started bawling. "You know that I'm part of you. I was only trying to help."

"You threatened me and drove me nuts when I was barely hanging on to my mind. You disturbed me…a lot." He stood there crying. I felt sorry for the poor bastard, but I'd had it.

"That last time, that dream, you killed me."

"I killed the part of my mind that was killing me. The war is over. At least for me it is."

He lightened up a bit and leaned over my desk extending his hand. "No hard feelings then, ok?"

I thought about it for a moment and should have thought some more. He vise-gripped my hand and yanked me out of the chair and on to the rug where he pushed my face into the plush woolly weave and held me down tight so I couldn't breathe. I struggled, but the strength had gone out of me. Everything looked black and crinkly, and I couldn't get a breath.

I woke up in a panic, my heart pounding. I couldn't see; everything was still black.

I startled Margaret and she pulled away from me. "What's wrong? Coot?" My face had been pressed in her thick hair. I was inhaling it and choking. She held me. "It's all right…just one of your dreams."

"If I ever do anything to hurt you or Val…."

"Shh, Coot. You could never hurt us." We lay there for a while, me in her arms instead of the way it should have been. "You're a good man. You hear me? You wouldn't hurt anyone."

After a few more minutes she slid out of bed. "I'll make

us some coffee." Her long muscular, sandy brown back, hips, her magnificent ass and thighs instantaneously converted my disorientation and fear into pitched animal desire. I was crazed to possess her physical real estate. I wanted to inhale this woman, to swallow her essence into my body. To be of her, part of her, in me—something you can't have, but almost feels as though you can.

We sat in bed drinking coffee, waiting for Val to come barreling in and jump in with us, hugging and kissing, informing us of her itinerary for the day, all the things she wanted to do, make, and see.

Our little girl would soon turn four and Margaret thought it was time for Val to have kids to play with her own age instead of me, twenty-four-seven. I couldn't stand the idea of giving her up, especially to some learning institution that would try to brand her with their philosophy. I hate philosophies. Besides she was learning so much on her own. She had a ravenous curiosity. The truth is I wanted to teach my little precious girl. I wanted to keep her from going down the blind alleys I'd been. She would be the good version of me, not a fuck up.

But Margaret insisted. I knew she was right. Val should have playmates. She should have a normal childhood. Though I may have already forfeited that for her.

Margaret was determined to keep Val out of public school for as long as possible, if not for her entire educational career. She wanted to avoid the mostly patriarchal school boards with their inflexibility and ironclad rules enacted by a board of regents who'd turned education into a retail operation. They gave too much power to the Pearson testing company. All New York State teachers had to go through Pearson to get certified. They were only allowed to shop at one outlet and it was a friggin' scam.

The entire system was designed not to serve the educational needs of the children. It was bad from day one when some assholes conceived the idea that they'd put all the kids in a building and educate them, every grade, in a mandated, regulated bullshit manner, like a ranch where they could brand their minds. Kids learn more from hiking three hours in the woods than all day in a prison/classroom. Better yet, they can hike for three hours, cook out in the open, and read the *New York Times*.

So Margaret made an appointment for an interview at The Little Red House of Nuts and Berries, a somewhat pricey institution with an enigmatic oracular philosophy, up the road in stolid Stone Ridge.

But these were expensive nuts and berries. First, we'd need to see how Zeitzer made out on the real estate deal in Florida and the house in Valdosta, in the clutches of a bank. And that's when the phone rang that morning. Not with a pleasant little chirp, but an ominous bell tolled by a ghoul in a belfry.

It was Z; he sounded terrible. "There's a problem with the condo in Florida, a big problem. It looks like I don't own it."

"Seriously, what the fuck?"

"Coot, what is it?" Margaret stood up and gave me her pre-strike look.

"Listen, we have to Skype with these people at one o'clock. Can you meet me at Bebe's? The connection is better there."

"Z, what happened?"

"Just meet me there. I'm going to take half of a tranquilizer."

That concluded our snuggle session. The next call was her practice. A possible breach birth on the way to Health Alliance Campus in Kingston—an emergency. It was raining shit again. She dressed and bolted out the door, not before she said, "Someone's got to make money in this household." That was a double wasp sting. Why couldn't things just stay on track, even for a week? I determined that I would go back up that mountain and make it give up the location of Jacob Rutsen's treasure. I hoped I'd be able to keep it. I'd looked up the Finders Keepers Law. It's not easy to fence Revolutionary period pewter mugs unde- tected, especially those found on public property. I figured that maybe someone at one of those battle enactment places in Pennsylvania might buy them. I just wanted to drop a chunk of change in Margaret's lap and show her I could provide.

When I got to Bebe's Sprouting Affair, she and Z were caucusing in the back by the kitchen. Given her body lan- guage, jutting her arms out, standing back, stomping her foot with her hands on her hips, I could tell that she and Z were into it bad and I'd better not approach them just yet. I sat at a table near the front window and ordered some cof- fee and my favorite, key lime pie.

Bebe turned a hard shoulder to him, went into the kitchen and slung the door back with such force that it top- pled a set of folding chairs stacked on the side. Z came over to my table and dropped into a seat, a heavily burdened man.

"I really screwed this up. I'm at a complete loss."

"It's not your fault."

"It's precisely my fault. I didn't want to deal with Florida. I wouldn't go there and take care of my own busi- ness." He sighed. "I'm afraid I've let you all down."

"You don't let people down, Z." He ordered a piece of Chocolate Espresso Cake and a glass of soy milk, the appearance of which made my gut rumble. I turned my head to avoid the toxic chocolate fumes from entering my nose. He noticed my caution.

"Are you wearing your bracelet?"

I jiggled my wrist to display it. "Yup, ALLERGIC TO CHOCOLATE."

We ate our desserts pensively and languished over our coffee like death row inmates having a last snack. At five of one he opened his laptop and viewed the keyboard as if it were the contents of a coffin. He dialed in and after a few moments a picture formed of five unsmiling white men seated around a meeting table, the walls, drapes, and furnishings as drab as the men's suits. Except for one; it looked like a Disney character tie, probably Scrooge McDuck, perfect for a banker. The Georgia and American flags were displayed on the back wall.

"Hey there, I'm Mr. Howard, President of Synovus First State Bank. These are my colleagues." He introduced each of the men, three lawyers and a real estate agent. A full house. Yawn. "You are, of course Mr. Zeitzer and you, sir, are...?"

"This is Mr. Friedman, my...associate." Suddenly, I realized I had forgotten to comb my hair back or change my t-shirt.

"Are you a lawyer, Mr. Friedman?"

"No, but I've spent a lot of time with lawyers over the years." A bit of eye rolling, a smug stiffening in their chairs; they seemed to think they had all the cards on this deal.

"I won't waste any of your time, Mr. Zeitzer. We're faxing you a copy of the deed while we speak." He turned his laptop to show us a matronly stall horse with a loaf of blond bun on top of her head feeding paper into the machine. "You will see from this document that the condominium your Aunt Sylvia left you is owned by a certain Mr. Murphy Coleman Shaw, Esq."

Z asked, "And how did Mr. Shaw come to own it?"

"Well, it appears that he bought it as a foreclosure, previously owned by a Stuart Zeitzer of..."

"Nanuet, New York?" Z finished. "He's my brother."

Howard smiled. "Exactly, you and your brother were listed as the owners, but it seems that neither of you responded to the certified notices that were sent out. The property was falling into disrepair. After numerous unanswered letters and summonses from the court it was determined that it would be treated as a foreclosure." Z sunk in his chair. "That said," Howard drawled on, "it seems that Mr. Shaw desires to discuss the matter with you personally."

"Why is that?" Z was tensing his jaw.

"You'll have to find that out from him. Mr. Shaw is a peculiar man. I'm afraid we did not engage well on the phone."

Z leaned over and whispered in my ear. "Because he's Black, no doubt."

"I didn't catch that, Mr. Zeitzer."

Z flicked a chocolate crumb off of the keyboard. It bounced off of my shirt and I almost leapt out of my chair. "I'm still prepared to pay off the mortgage on the Valdosta home."

Howard raised an eyebrow. "Really, why is that, Mr. Zeitzer?"

"Because it's not going to sell any time soon, if at all."

The banker shot a nervous glance at his colleagues around the table. "And why do you say that?"

"Because of violent crime in Valdosta. Your citizens have a one in fifteen chance of being a victim."

Mr. Howard took a breath and appeared whiter than he had at the beginning of the meeting.

Z fired another one. "You have one of the highest crime rates in the country compared to all communities of any size." There was a general ruffling of papers at the table. One of the lawyers got up and poured a cup of coffee.

Mr. Howard was more fang and claw when he responded. "Well, Mr. Zeitzer. Why on earth would you want to own a home in such a crime ridden area as you've painted our city to be?"

"My nephew and his friend just graduated from the Criminal Justice Program at SUNY Ulster College, with honors. They've both been accepted into the prestigious Valdosta Lowndes Crime Laboratory in your fair city. I'd want to provide a place for them to stay during their training. I don't think they'll have any difficulty dealing with the neighborhood, being in law enforcement."

There was a long pause. The lawyer with the Disney tie scribbled something on his legal pad and slid it in front of Mr. Howard, who considered it for a few moments. "Are you prepared to make payment in full at this time? Four thousand five hundred dollars?"

Zeitzer braced his hands on the table. "I'll give you two thousand."

"That's unacceptable, Mr. Zeitzer." I could tell the way he drew his name out with a little lip snarl on the last syllable that he'd didn't like this Northern Jew boy jerking him around. We sat there staring at each other. I was having difficulty following the negotiations. Howard huffed and puffed a bit. The lawyer scribbled something else on the pad. Howard considered it and said, "Two thousand five hundred, not a penny less," the "penny less," was a bit of ethnic code.

Z smiled. "That'll work." There was a bit more haggling back and forth, resulting in the bank agreeing to release the house back to Aldo and In-Su, who would never return to it anyway. The agreement was faxed for Z to sign and fax back. Z promised them a bank teller's check would go out in the morning, and they ended the call.

I sat there studying this remarkable man. "How the fuck did you manage that?"

"NeighborhoodScout.com, a useful site."

"Your nephew and his friend are going to live there?"

"I don't have a nephew."

"Jesus, Z, what are you thinking?"

He picked the remaining crumbs off his plate and popped them into his mouth. He seemed far away now. "I'm still thinking."

Bebe came over and dropped a page on the table. It was a copy of the deed to the condominium in the name of Mr. Murphy Coleman Shaw, Esq.

"How do you know that Mr. Shaw is Black?"

"Because that little piece of White shit told me."

Bebe leaned over and planted a kiss on Z's head. She must have approved.

Z sent the twenty five hundred to the bank in Georgia and gave me two thousand back from my Army policy. I was back in good with Margaret about the house, though Z had done all the brain work. The money would cover the cost of holding a place for Val if she got into the elite school Margaret preferred.

So the next day, or maybe it was a week later, we went to the Little Red House of Nuts and Berries for Val's interview with Ms. Muley, admissions director and resident earth mother. Margaret liked the Nuts and Berries philosophy. Little boys who wanted to dress up as superheroes had to enlist a female superhero and share power equally with her. They had to make up an agreement and present it to the faculty. Children were free to roam around seven pristine acres of fields, hills, and streams, and follow whatever interested them. Student teachers shadowed each child and if that child became fixated on something they'd offer her instruction on it, books, whatever. A kid could spend six years there playing with an acorn and no one bothered him. He might be formulating Acorn Theory. I was new to this, the idea of interviewing four-year-olds for school. It wasn't like she was running for office or anything.

We sat in an overly warm upstairs office. I squirmed as I took in the room. There was a poster that read: Like a butterfly, a child will partake of the flower which nourishes her. The graphic was of a little girl with wings and antennae dipping her tongue into an electric orange flower. The kid looked more mummified than free. It kind of gave me the creeps. From the large window we observed the playground where children engaged in various activities, some just staring at objects of their choice, or contemplating the natural world. One child, a tiny Japanese girl, stood next to a slide examining its pitch. She would no doubt grow up to become a playground designer and make improvements on slides. Perhaps she'd invent one that could propel a child into another dimension. I could already tell it would be a four-beer recovery after the interview.

The educator, Ms. Muley, a matron in a fluffy, white peasant blouse and wide plaid skirt and Birkenstock sandals, from which she raised and spread her toes, a yoga move, peered out at the children with a definitive look of satisfaction spread across her broad face. It was almost as if she could taste them from where she sat. She licked her lips. Probably just dry. Her acceptance and love of her charges was somewhat unsettling, at least it was to me. My father was a proponent of a sharp smack on the back of the head. Not exactly a philosophy, but it got the point across when he was displeased with my deportment.

She asked Val what she liked to do. Val told her she liked to play circus with Grandpa Aldo, throw fruit in her pool, and make spicy noodles with beef. The matron gave her a half melon smile and some eye twinkle. She said, "Val, would you please go and look out of the window." Val complied. You see all the children down there. Is there anyone you'd like to make friends with?"

"Nooo," she said. "I hit boys."

Margaret lowered her head toward her lap. The interviewer, Ms. Muley, stepped over to the window and put her hand on Val's shoulder. "Well, Val, we don't…hit here. We don't hurt our friends."

"They're not my friends." There were three adults in this room and one child, my child, whose words steered her mother's hopes into a brick wall. Secretly, I was proud of her. What education in the world can teach a kid to have her own thoughts if she already has them?

Val squirmed away from Ms. Muley's hand, which might have been resting too heavily on her shoulder. "They're not playing," she said. Margaret's head continued toward her lap.

"They are playing, dear. Sometimes children need to study things to find out what fascinates them." Val considered that for less than a moment, and took up a no-budge position directly behind my chair. I became the barrier, the shield between her and Ms. Muley.

"Are there any other questions?" It bothered me that Margaret's voice was not as direct as usual.

Ms. Muley picked up a ceramic toad one of her little artists had created, painted half white and half black, with an equal sign on it, and set it back on her desk. "No. We'll be notifying parents soon if their child will be joining us."

We sat silently in the car for a minute, taking in the playground and various buildings of the school Val would not be attending. "I'd play with her."

"Who, honey?"

"That girl, in the white dress."

"Where, I don't see her?"

"By the fence."

Shit, I saw her. A waif in a white Victorian dress and buttoned-up shoes. She was waving at Val, who waved back. She seemed so lost in time. It hurt to look at her.

"There's no one there, sweetheart."

"She's there, Mom."

Margaret hissed. "This is you...she gets it from you. Damn it, Coot." Back on the shit barge to Shitsville.

"Can she come home with me?"

Mind fuck, now what? Margaret got in the back seat with her. "Honey, we can't take her home."

The tears started and she pushed defiantly against Margaret. "Why, why can't I?"

"Because she's not there."

"She is there. She's there." She beat her little fists against the window. I suddenly felt an episode coming on. Great, they could bring the whole family to the psych ward at Benedictine. What could I do? I started driving. "Look, she's coming." I checked the rearview. The little ghost girl was following us next to Val's window. Val pressed her hand to the glass. The little girl pressed her hand on Val's.

Margaret shrieked. "Coot...do something...now!" The sound pierced my ears and echoed through my head. I pulled into a gas station on Route 209, got out and started to manically squeegee the windows. What good it would do I didn't know. But there are moments in life, deep, dark pits you fall into and don't really have a way out. So you make something up, even if it's desperately meaningless. You take an action and just fucking hope. When I got to Val's widow the little cloud of a girl was there.

"Excuse me," I said, as tenderly as possible.

She didn't speak, but her words rolled in front of me

like CNN Headline News, the caption at the bottom of the screen. "I'll come back another time. Oh, Kurt says you looked in the wrong place."

Val exhausted herself and fell asleep by the time we got home. We put her in bed and Margaret and I sat in the backyard. I'd taken a beer. Margaret took it and poured it out on the day lilies. "I've had it with you and your ghosts. All the trouble, the episodes, the constant craziness."

She paused. A small piece of meteorite bounced off my forehead, or so I thought. "I think," and she was crying. now, shaking, "I don't know if I can do this anymore… Coot."

And suddenly the world, rather the end of the world, hung above me, about to lose faith in its ability to orbit the sun. It would just drop. I don't know how much time passed.

"Coot, did you hear me? Did you hear what I said?" She was starting to sob.

Finally, I opened my mouth and commanded my tongue to form words. "Yes, you said that I should die… I will if that's what you want. I'd die for you and Val." I thought I was blacking out.

Suddenly I felt her in my arms, her lips on my mouth, her body pressed against me.

"Die? Oh, god, Coot, I love you so much, too much, Coot. What am I going to do with you?"

"Just let me live. You're my life." And like that, we staggered into the house, into the bedroom not knowing which of us held the other up, but so necessary for both of us to keep moving, to keep going where we were going to. In the coolness, the dark, in the sudden primordial paradise of lovemaking, upon the stuffed animals on our marriage bed, we embraced in a manner that bespoke our future.

The future said: you will go forth from this house

together, all your days together, until you shall pass, your souls as one. Sometimes a bit of poetry, which is the currency of the soul, goes a long way. Am I really starting to believe now, my atheism an old beater that only got me halfway down the road?

About two weeks after the Nuts and Berries debacle, Zeitzer called and said, "We have to meet with him."

"Who?"

"Dr. Coleman Murphy Shaw."

"The guy who owns your condo? Meet him, where?"

"At Bard, over in Annandale."

"Seriously, they rejected me for their writing program, the fuckers."

Z coughed. "I know. It was their loss."

"I thought he was a lawyer."

"Coot, I want you to come with me. And...could you...put on...?

"Dress up? You want me to dress up?"

"Yeah, well, he's giving a lecture."

"He's not a lawyer?"

"That's just one thing he is. He's also a professor and he's going to lecture at the Africana Studies Program. He's got some philanthropic institution that benefits underprivileged Blacks. It has something to do with secure housing."

"You think he'd read my poems? I have about thirty now."

"Hmm, that's...not why he's here."

"What's he want with you?"

"He wants to talk about the house in Valdosta. I don't know why. But the man somehow impressed me. I'm not sure what it is. He didn't strike me as a guy who flips properties."

"I'm down."

Wardrobe had always been a problem for me. In the

desert I'd fall out in my green class A service uniform and my steel toed boots, like the ones that fell on my head during the mortar attack. The ones that gave me a skewed outlook on reality. Though it's been enriching at times. Oh, and always, strapped around my waist, was my XM17, a modular handgun system, a real thing of beauty. I'm glad I got one even before it was scheduled to replace the old Army standard Beretta M9 sometime in the 2020s.

Aldo insisted on helping me find the right outfit for my trip to Bard. After the Flying Libertinos disbanded and shut down the act, he'd wound up with all of the costumes. Probably because he was also a trained tailor like his dad was in Sicily. Vinnie, the middle guy in the act, was about the same size as me, but the costume consisted of a maillot, with lower cut leg openings, a silky vest designed to show biceps and chest muscles, and a dance belt underneath, which kind of lifted me up as if a tire-jack was against my nuts. The outfit also included sequined slippers, green, white, and red, like the Italian flag. "Aldo, thank you, but I can't wear this."

"You no like? What you no like?"

"I'm going to a college."

"Yes, college." He pummeled my back. He and In-Su seemed to think that I was getting an honorary degree, which I really wouldn't have minded. I've always regretted my lack of formal education. But reading will take you pretty far.

It turned out I knew the book Dr. Shaw was lecturing on and it was pretty damn serious, an indictment of how the Europeans set out to consciously dismantle the African culture, which preceded theirs, quite brilliantly, for thousands of years. The original African institutions were far superior to the Europeans'. The friggin' Greeks even copied their columns but changed their decorations to Hellenic symbols.

It's like this: White guys with weapons and chains and Divine Right can fuck up an indigenous people faster than it takes to microwave a potato. The stupid bastards were out to torch the cradle of civilization. The same cradle they'd been rocked in. Will the real White European Asshole please sit down.

The agricultural American South at least gave us Robert Johnson, Honey Boy Edwards, Bessie Smith, and the rest of those fine ladies and gentleman. Ironic that the people our race took everything from gave us the music that gives us solace, that we dance to, that we make love to. They gave us our chief export, besides war, as a gift to the rest of the world—back to Europe—music to amaze and entertain their former captors.

Z picked me up at six. "Jesus Christ, Coot. We're not going to a Pride Parade."

"I didn't have time to find anything else." We went to The Duchess of Cheese. Besides cheese and olives and a host of Middle Eastern delights, they sell used clothing in the back, an extra retail boost for their shop. Occasionally, there are complaints about hairs in yogurt or bits of fabric stuck to blocks of cheese, or lint in the baba ganoush. Oh well.

Z ripped through racks of clothing and finally came up with a formal suit jacket with tails, the kind of elegant thing they wear at the Plaza. I put that on over my acrobat attire and looked in the mirror.

"Oh my God. Take those slippers off." He grabbed a pair of scuffed cordovans which were a size too big, but the only ones there. He wadded up paper and stuffed it behind my heels. Now I resembled a Tunisian male prostitute.

Z threw his hands in the air. "Come on. Maybe they'll think you're in the theater department."

We crossed the Kingston-Rhinecliff Bridge, that massive white arched eyebrow spanning the river, with less than reassuring sides that seem to say, "Come closer. Make my day." How could they build a bridge with almost no sides? Was it cheaper? Maybe it's because it's a continuous under-deck truss bridge, and doesn't need higher railings, though they'd be much appreciated. For me, it's seven thousand seven hundred and ninety-two feet of high anxiety.

"You know," I said, "I'm sorry. I didn't mean to embarrass you. I should have gone to Penny's and bought a suit. I'm kind of a loser in that department."

Z stared straight ahead. Having crossed over the highest part we saw the welcoming green on the other side and the solid railroad tracks below. "What you wear, Coot, doesn't really matter to me. You are cloaked in a rare mantle of decency and honesty. Very few men I've known are dressed as you are. I'm proud that you're my friend."

I turned away and looked downriver so he wouldn't see me crying, though he knew I was. I wiped my nose on the sleeve of my dress coat and left a luminous stream of mucus upon it. I stared at the glittering shore lights that were just coming on to welcome the evening. I stared and wondered: how do we get to these places in our lives? What brings us to these moments? I said quietly, "Thank you."

When Z told the kid at the reception desk that we were there to meet with Dr. Shaw before his lecture, he made a quick call and two security guards appeared beside each of us. The kid made another call and reported that: "Dr. Shaw is with President Botstein and other faculty at a reception. He can't take a call."

"You're a pretty official little twerp," I said. The security stirred and suggested that perhaps we should wait outside the building. We were in the Fisher Annex, where Shaw had said he'd meet us. One of the guards placed his hand on my shoulder and I instinctively spun around and locked him in a head hold. The other started reaching for his belt.

Z grabbed the guys hand and thrust it down. "Call him now and tell him that Zeitzer's here." The kid looked stunned at Z's sudden authority. "Call him now." The kid shrugged at the security guys and made the call. I released the one guy, who shuttled back, rubbing his neck.

"Don't touch me again," I said.

The kid reached someone in there who told someone else, and then he hung up and said, "Would you please show these…gentlemen upstairs." So, with a security detail of two we went upstairs to meet one of the most unusual men I've ever met. I wanted to give Z a high five, but thought better of it.

We sat in an office with one glassed wall that looked down over the lobby. The room was loaded with paintings and sculptures and sink-in leather chairs and sofas, and a fancy mahogany veneer conference table, easily twelve hundred bucks. I wondered how I could have afforded the place even if I had gotten in. Even with the post-9/11 GI Bill it still came to almost twenty-eight thousand out of pocket. If I had that much I'd get an RV and take the family out west and hit every national park on the way. "This kind of place is for that little rich bastard we met at the desk." Z nodded agreement.

The door swung open and a gorgeous brunette in a pantsuit and heels observed us carefully for a moment. She smiled at Z, "You are Mr. Zeitzer?" Then she observed me and the left corner of her pixie mouth twitched.

"Yes, and this is my colleague, Mr. Friedman." She nodded, and continued to check me out. Then she opened the door the rest of the way and in walked a tall, elegant Black man whose head and sculpted face reminded me of African princes I'd seen in National Geographic. His color was similar to the conference table. He wore an impeccably-cut gray suit and what I guessed were expensive Italian shoes. Z stood immediately at attention and waited to be introduced. This was the kind of guy you stood up for.

"Mr. Zeitzer, this is Dr. Shaw." Shaw extended a lengthy arm ending in long, willowy pianist fingers. Z took his hand.

"Dr. Shaw, this is my...friend, Coot Friedman." It took me a few moments to respond, such was my immediate regard for the man. When I did shake hands, I found his hand to be quite firm. He could choke an iguana to death with that hand. He looked me straight in the eye.

"I'm glad to meet you, Mr. Friedman." He called me Mr. Friedman. "This is my colleague, Ms. Kerensky. Please, let's sit down." Ms. Kerensky efficiently snapped open two laptops, one facing Shaw, the other facing us.

"Ms. Kerensky, do you happen to be related to Alexander Kerensky?" She looked visibly shocked and exchanged a 'what the hell' glance with Dr. Shaw.

"He was my great-grandfather. How do know of him?"

"I think I read something about him...I'm not sure where. Are you also a lawyer?"

Shaw answered for her. "Ms. Kerensky is one of a team of lawyers who work with my foundation." I could feel Zeitzer's hand squeezing my knee. I should have shut up. Maybe I just didn't want Shaw to think I was the circus freak I looked like at the moment.

"He got pretty high up there, Prime Minister of the Provisional Government." Z squeezed harder. My leg jerked and kicked his chair leg making a low audible thud. No one reacted to it.

Ms. Kerensky displayed a much pained face. "Are you a history buff, Mr. Friedman?"

"Well, yeah. I've had a lot of time to read when I've been..." I was going to say, "in the Army jail." My voice trailed off. I didn't get to say that Alexander Kerensky had achieved that position in 1917 before the Bolsheviks took over. Like who would care?

Dr. Shaw typed in something and a picture of a house with statistics next to it came up. A logo with the letters AAFHF. Under it, it read The African American Fair Housing Foundation. Dr. Coleman Murphy Shaw, President and CEO. "I'll get right to the point. African Americans are systematically shut out of adequate housing in the South and in many places in the North as well. Our foundation raises money, negotiates bank foreclosures, then offers families decent homes at fair prices, not inflated prices and mortgages that Blacks wind up paying about forty percent more for than Whites.

Z nodded approval. "I'm in agreement with that."

"It's an epidemic that we intend to cure." Shaw's pronouncement seemed to echo in the room. He was clearly on a mission. But what could we have to do with it?

He continued, "And our friend, Mr. Howard, at the Synovus First Bank has done more than his share to make it difficult for working Black families to get a fair mortgage."

"I'm not a fan of Mr. Howard's."

"You wouldn't be after he played loose and free with your condominium."

Z looked dumbfounded. "Well, it's not mine. I understand that you own it."

Ms. Kerensky slid a paper to Zeitzer. "I did a complete title search on the property. Our foundation checks out every aspect of a sale. We determined that the property was acquired inappropriately. It belongs to you. Your brother...

Stuart actually signed off on his share for ten thousand dollars. Mr. Howard neglected to mention that. So..."

"You're giving it back to me?" Z was incredulous. "Why would you do that?" We sat there for a few moments staring at Dr. Shaw.

"Because that's how we do business." I wanted to kiss the guy. "But I have a request for you, a bit of a deal you might be open to."

Z nodded yes. He was too overwhelmed to speak.

"You do have a clear title to the Valdosta house. Is that correct?"

"Yes, I paid off the final mortgage for twenty-five hundred dollars. I think Howard and company were glad to unload it."

"Would you be willing to sell both properties at just under fair market value to our foundation? We would in turn help two families own homes they might not ever have access to?"

I couldn't believe this shit was happening. How could this be, in the land of screw 'em and leave 'em? Shaw was the most righteous man I'd ever met. This couldn't be real. "I love you, man." The three of them stared at me for a few moments. "I mean," I said nervously, "most people aren't like this."

Z kind of rested his elbows on the table to support himself. "And I wouldn't have to go to Florida?"

"Not unless you want to." Shaw smiled, an expression that immediately made you feel that you were just the person he wished to see at that moment. He brought you into his world effortlessly, and there was nowhere else you wished to be.

Ms. Kerensky slid another document over to Z. "This," said Shaw, "is a statement of agreement, not a contract. Take it with you and think it over. If you decide you'd like to proceed with these purchases contact Ms. Kerensky. She'll prepare a contract."

Z observed his hands, his fingers entwined. "I don't know what to say."

"I expect you to get advice from your financial person, Mr. Zeitzer. Here is a breakdown of costs and expenses, taxes as well, on both properties. You may find it helpful." Ms. Kerensky slid that one over. The dude was impeccable prepared. Almost scary. I had a quick thought that maybe he was screwing Z worse than Howard tried to. But why would he give him the condo back? Magnanimous was a limp word to describe this guy.

We were at the door now shaking hands all around. I noticed a small red stone around Ms. Kerensky's neck, resting between the pronounced curves of her very white breasts. When Dr. Shaw took my hand, I said, "It's a great book."

"How's that, Mr. Friedman?"

"The one you're lecturing on, *The Destruction of Black Civilization*. Dr. Chancellor Williams' book." His eyes widened as he continued to press my hand in his powerful grip.

"You know Dr. Williams' book?"

"Yes, I've read it. I'm kind of a fan of Afrocentrism."

Shaw took a step back and observed my entire person dressed in that absurd and inexplicable outfit. He made that smile again, warmer this time. Some dentist somewhere must have been thrilled to know him. "Mr. Friedman, we all are still learning how to observe a person without just seeing their exterior. I'm pleased to have met you." I stood there looking down, kind of shuffling a bit, just a hopeful Scarecrow waiting to receive his diploma in Thinkology.

Later on, on the way through the lobby I asked Z for his keys. He was reluctant to give them to me, which was understandable given my history and driving record. I dropped the keys on the desk and said to the little bastard, "President Botstein asked if you wouldn't mind bringing over Mr. Zeitzer's car?" I gave him the description and the license plate number. I could feel the hostility coming out of his eyes like sharp, educated arrows. Slowly, he got up, snatched the keys, and made for the parking lot. Petulant little asshole. We were parked way out there. It would take him a good twenty minutes. That's when me and Z had a very satisfying high five.

Z was starving by the time we left Annandale. We drove into Rhinebeck and had dinner at Foster's Coach House Tavern, old dark wood, with an extensive comfort menu and a piss-poor beer selection, but atmospheric, circa 1890. The best I could get was in a bottle, Beck's, which is Germany's exported gray water. It's lighter than a fly and skirts your taste buds. Well, maybe barbequed fly. We were uber-hungry.

Z got some mixed concoction with Grey Goose Vodka and was almost on his ass when our London Broil Sandwiches arrived. I was getting frustrated with the Beck's and ordered a shot of Jameson. Z was feeling pretty fat after our meeting with Shaw and denied us nothing. We kind of got sloshed and were leaning on each other at the bar. When the food finally came out, a nice looking gal suggested we seat ourselves in one of the horse-stall dining booths. Neigh! We ate like prisoners coming off a hunger strike. And talked.

"Z, I'm fucked up. But did that guy really give you the condo back, then offer to buy it back, along with the house in Valdosta?"

He was weaving a little. "Yes, I think that's what happened. We'll have to see my guy at Ulster Savings. Another drink?"

"Is there a corn in a crow field?" We laughed uproariously. "You know what I mean." Someone kept waving at me from a further booth near the bathrooms. I got up, "Gotta hang the lizard." He cracked up and dove into the second half of his sandwich. Their portions were generous.

"You want your pickle?"

"Go for it," I said.

I got back to the last booth and didn't see anyone, then the lights came on. The booth lit up. There was a guy sitting there... well, a former guy, anyway. He was all dapper and wore a Yankees ball cap. He produced two large mugs. "Knickerbocker, here, and that's Rupert's Extra Pale. Try it."

I tasted both. "That's great beer. Why don't they serve it here?"

"They used to when I came in." He offered me his hand, which I couldn't feel exactly in mine, more like a cool mist. "Colonel Jacob Rupert, the Beer Baron King. And you are, sir?"

"Coot Ronald Friedman, an honor to meet you."

"I noticed that you were unhappy with the beer selection, so I thought I'd offer you my finest."

"Well, thanks, gotta hit the head."

"Did you know I built Yankee Stadium in 1923?"

"No, sir. I didn't"

"I brought Babe Ruth here from Chicago."

I really had to pee, but I didn't want to be discourteous. "Wow, the Babe...one of the great ones." I was about to pee my pants. I looked back down the bar and the scene had turned in to Grand Central Station. People were panicked and running for their trains. One guy in a double-breasted suit and a late 1930's hat knocked into my elbow.

"What are you standing there for? They're coming."

"Who's coming?"

"Martians, were being invaded." I did a quick calculation. Shit, it was Orson Welles radio play from 1938. I shot a glance at Colonel Rupert. He'd morphed into a multi-tentacled space creature with a set of ejecting choppers that sprang out of his chest at my neck. My first inclination was to finish the mug of Knickerbocker, which was the better of the two.

I said to Zeitzer, who was tugging me along now toward the gaping exit, "I don't think I'm done with my episodes. There's a VA Hospital in Valhalla." Then it was lights out, per my standard operating procedure.

But not before I heard Z say, "I didn't eat your pickle. Want it back?"

A few days later Margaret decided we would join a homeschooling group for Val, something I didn't want. But because she wanted it, I embraced it wholeheartedly. It would be a way to make up for Margaret's disappointment at the House of Nuts and Berries. And this was an opportunity for me to be a reading/writing teacher. I didn't think four- and five-year-olds were too young to take on Wordsworth and Melville if explained in simplified terms.

But I was outvoted. The group thought I'd make more of a contribution teaching the kids outdoor skills, camping, and mycology. That was cool, but it wasn't literature. So I designed a private reading program for Val. She loved *Dubliners*, thought it was the funniest thing she'd ever heard. Though we disagreed at the end of "The Dead." Her little woman take on it, to the extent of her budding mind's understanding, was that the guy, Gabriel, was just cranky and should get over what was bothering him. I labored to explain the poignancy of the moment, the snowy tears falling in the "mutinous Shannon," the knowledge of the shades, which we were both somewhat acquainted with.

Just the fact that she'd listened to the story and discussed it was impressive.

The home teaching group was reading *Pippi Longstocking*, the indomitable, independently wealthy, rebel girl, perhaps the first storybook feminist, breaking conventional modes around her. That was OK, but it lacked the Joycean epiphany and the richness of language and irony Joyce spread like Bushmills Irish Honey over soda bread.

The woman who was appointed the literary coordinator, or rather assumed the position, Frances T., was an MFA Writing Program graduate from Bennington College. For us, it was hate at first sight. At the planning meeting, when I said that I'd like to teach writing to the kids, she asked me what my credentials were, *if any*. The sneer in her voice was a snare I allowed myself to get caught up in. I, and I regret this still, took an inappropriate action and was duly ostracized, and banished by Margaret from our bed for a month and a day. I clamped my hand over my groin area and said, "Here's my credentials, Frances."

Frances' partner, Simon, a milquetoasty, overfed new age wombat, lobbied to have the group vote our family out of the home teaching compact. But in fact, most of them couldn't stand Frances' patronizing superiority either. She had a real annoying way of placing any question or discussion into a neat little box and ignoring it unless it was the personal afterbirth of her brain. Since Simon lacked the votes to rescind our membership, I was chastised and forced to listen to Frances as she lamented in detail how I'd injured her, how I'd mentally raped her with an obscene gesture. She said she didn't know if she could work with the group after this atrocity. But of course she would. It would be unfair of her to deprive us of her expertise. I took some solace in composing a quick poem in my head, published only in my head, and deleted immediately afterward.

TO FRANCES T
A mouth with a catch
That made me retch
Into a pan of boiled haddock,
Fourth witch of the other three
That caused Macbeth
To hide in the attic.

OK, that's not nice, but she rendered me inconsequential and sniggered after the fact. She played the higher education card against me and paper-cut my Achilles' heel. I snagged an old copy of the Bennington Review at the library. It was tied up in a pile of outdated journals headed for the recycle bin. It was almost two decades old. At the time she wrote under the name Frances Tegan Tuttle.

Her novella, *Esther in Djibouti,* was serialized in the review and I only got to read the first part. *Esther,* actually Esther of Rye, or Esther on rye with mustard, depending how you read it, is a schlocky romance about a hot Westchester girl's escapades in the Horn of Africa. Ostensibly she is there to study language and culture in preparation for an apprenticeship position at the UN. Her Uncle Sol, who's connected to someone there, is setting it up, and there is something very much Swiss Cheesy about the arrangement.

Basically, the plot of her novella is the holes in the cheese. It gets airy. Unbelievably, she winds up incognito, having fallen in with the nomadic Afar people, who discover her overt whiteness and contemplate dismembering her and broiling pieces of her flesh as an offering/appetizer. But they are stunned by her magnificent beauty and fall into a quandary. She is discovered chained naked in the marketplace by Prince Azzetz as he shops for dates and mangoes. He comes upon her and it's as if an avocado launched from a catapult strikes his heart. He demands her release and they begin a torrid affair. One night, beneath a full moon reflecting off the Gulf of Aden, and after much olive oil-infused lovemaking, he pronounces her his queen, Esther of Djibouti. It's kind of like "Midnight at the Oasis" without the rhythm track.

I continued my private reading program with Val, systematically covering the Russian writers, of whom she found Turgenev's characters to be most appealing. She seemed to have a taste for the realistic novel. Probably because of Margaret, firmly attached to the land and the womb. Not me, helium-filled and likely to float off in the slightest breeze. After a while Frances T became suspicious and warned Margaret that someone was filling Val's head with outlandish literary theory and tainted points of view. Val was becoming a voracious reader and just ran around the sidelines of Frances' stodgy pedagogy. She wasn't interested in the books Esther assigned. It came to a head at a group lesson at Frances' house when Val said that Simon, Frances' partner, reminded her of Chichikov in Gogol's *Dead Souls*.

There was an emergency meeting where I was put on trial, widely reviled, and executed, sort of. Finally, Margaret and I withdrew from the group and just kept Val at home. We handed her books to read. She became intensely interested in the birthing process of farm animals. Z taught her about basic mixtures and compounds. And she was already becoming fluent in basic conversational Taiwanese Hokkien, thanks to In-Su.

Doe, who was somewhat recovered, but shaky, let Val read any of the historic documents of the hamlet, which gave Val the idea, among so many others, that she might want to be a tour guide when she grew up. She wanted to know all about the mountain, and I took her up often. She was a good forager, always accurate, and loved identifying fungi and flowers using her field guide. Fuck education. It's more about interest, attraction, mystery... alchemy. I won't apologize because Val excels at many things. I might have been smarter too if I hadn't suffered so many hailstorms in my brain.

I stopped in to see Z. Val and I had managed to break most of the test tubes and beakers he'd loaned us for our experiments. A lot of them just involved colored water and baking soda. When I got there Z gave me the cue to be quiet. He was skyping with Ms. Kerensky who was holding up papers to the screen. She was saying, "I FedExed them to you this morning. I wanted to walk you through it first and see if you had any initial questions. If you decide to accept the conditions you can sign the contracts when we get back to New York."

"You're coming to New York?"

"Yes, Dr. Shaw will be speaking at Cooper Union." She removed the paper and leaned forward to adjust her laptop. There was the same red stone on a thin white chain she'd worn at Bard, lifting between her commanding breasts, which appeared to be more visible because she wore a loose fitting blouse, much more laid-back than her lawyer's suit.

"Excuse me, Ms. Kerensky, is that an Almandine Garnet necklace you're wearing?"

She instinctively raised her hand to her throat and covered it. "Oh, is that you Mr...?"

Of course she'd forgotten my name, probably a minute after the meeting ended at Bard. "Friedman," I said.

She was suddenly shy. "No, it's a Eudialyte."

"It's really lovely." I could feel Z's fingers clawing into my leg.

"Coot...shut it."

Ms. Kerensky had turned mildly red. "You're quite

observant Mr....Friedman." And I also observed that there appeared to be some tropical vegetation in the background and someone was moving behind her.

"Please give my regards to Dr. Shaw. It was an honor to meet him." It felt like Z was removing flesh from my thigh. Shaw heard his name and came over. She made room for him. He was wearing what looked like a blue silk short-sleeved shirt with swordfish on it. "Hello Mr. Zeitzer, Mr. Friedman."

Shocker! Obviously Ms. Kerensky was more than a colleague or one of a team of foundation lawyers. They were looking ultra-cazh, very relaxed.

Shaw continued, "Take your time with the contracts. If all is agreeable we can meet in New York in..." he glanced at his cell and checked the dates, "...two weeks from today."

"Ms. Kerensky has explained everything to me. Your foundation has been more than generous. I'm delighted to see these families get their own homes."

"Will Mr. Friedman accompany you to New York? I thought perhaps we'd have dinner." The guy was inviting us out to dinner. Why? Then we found out why. "I would like to use you, Mr. Zeitzer." And there was that set of perfect choppers. They looked even whiter on the screen. "There will be a small gathering of folks our foundation has purchased properties from, as well as folks we're presently negotiating with. It will be conducted by one of our people, kind of a meeting to assess quality control and brainstorm a bit on how we can improve our outreach. We want to document the experiences you folks have had working with us. The idea is to encourage new people to get involved."

"Of course I'd do that."

"I'd love to be there," I said, before Z could tell him

that I had other plans. Ms. Kerensky entered the date in her phone. "Will you be lecturing on Dr. Williams' companion book?"

"How's that, Mr. Friedman?"

"*The Second Agreement with Hell*?"

His eyes widened. I had missed the detail that they were more green than brown, well, brownish-green.

"You continually surprise, Mr. Friedman. Actually, I will be speaking about the inequality of housing between the races in America. I gather you've read that one as well."

"Well, it followed the first book. I figured if I was going to try and cover the subject..."

He gave an approving nod. "I see. Well, Mr. Zeitzer, if you have anymore questions I'll leave you with Irene to finish up." Irene? He called her Irene. "You look surprised, Mr. Zeitzer. Irene is my wife."

"Oh, I didn't know that. Congratulations," Z stumbled.

"I didn't mention that at out first meeting as it wasn't germane to our discussion about real estate."

"Of course not. Oh, then don't let me keep you."

"If you don't mind me asking," I said. "Which anniversary is it?" Z looked at me with murder in his eyes.

"It's our second."

"Oh, that's china." Maybe he'd gotten her a Lomonosov Porcelain Decorative Marzin Wall Plate Gothic 7, the elegance of Imperial Russia. That's around three hundred and forty dollars with shipping. And she was worth every ruble. But now it got me thinking, there was something about her voice, very subtle, but something.

What I didn't say to them was that the second anniversary gift traditionally is cotton. Modern is china. Which begs the question: Is irony ever more than a few inches away from our brains? Why irony? Because I'd done my research, the whole line of Shaws had risen from the ranks of sharecroppers in the day. They'd fought and clawed and bought their freedom, worked their way up and educated themselves and their children, one of whom was a great grandson, Dr. Murphy Coleman Shaw, our friend and benefactor. It made me even more proud to know him. I wondered if there was a way I could work for his organization.

Which brings me to my poem, Irony, penned in an ironic moment. I realized after the fact that I wrote it for Shaw, but I'd never show it to him. It was published on a guest check at the Fork in Your Bun Diner, located at the decrepit plaza on Route 32 South.

> *IRONY*
> *Irony is the wild child in the meadow*
> *Who springs up like a June flower*
> *And tells you that what you saw,*
> *What was certainly Duke Blue,*
> *So you think,*
> *Was not, but thoroughly pink.*

After they signed off, I said, "Man, he scored. Goodnight, Irene."

"Jesus, coot."

"What?"

"Just...Jesus."

"Z, did you notice something about her voice? Just the faintest accent. Something..."

"No, Coot. I didn't notice anything. I don't believe I care." He'd never been that short-tempered with me before.

"Z, you're angry."

"No, yes, I'm just tired. I need a break, Coot. Why don't you go home and play with Val?"

Part 4: Facing a Dark Threat

I did go home and play with Val, and Margaret. There was a lull in the baby train and she had time off. Her practice was able to give each of the midwives a month off. We cooked, barbequed, mostly tofu and veggies, and picnicked in the backyard. We had every meal out there and watched the bushes and leaves wither on the trees under intense summer heat, a bit of drought. But we loved it all. I wanted it to go on like this forever. No home school, no babies breaking into the world in the middle of the night. This was the life I wanted.

When summer ended I was at first alarmed, but grateful for an easy transition into fall. Margaret's babies took turns coming, so she wasn't out all of the time. Val was excited to get back to her studies. She started a pen-pal relationship with a little girl in Taiwan. The girl's father was an exporter and was coming to New York in the winter. Val would be able to meet her.

But on the first day of October I felt something pound on my spine. It was like the final minor chord of a demonic concerto, delivered by a pianist of prodigious power. A minor chord suggesting a withdrawal of that soft light we bathed in throughout the summer. And it seemed that the weather followed suit. Huge cumulus clouds hung in the sky without the inclination to move pleasantly overhead. These inert clouds were intersected, almost attacked, by an army of bruise-colored cirrus clouds ripping into their underbellies.

Each day threatened a storm of massive proportions, but nothing happened. Everyone in town felt on edge. There was only one subject talked about—the weather. Finally, at the end of October there was a tremendous thunderstorm that actually rattled the windows and doors. We watched it huddled on the porch. The violence of the storm was Biblical.

Two positive bolts of lightning originating from off the anvil of a huge thunderstorm, considerably more dangerous than negative bolts, struck the faces on the west side of the mountain in what seemed like an assassination attempt. The double-voltage whammy, otherwise known as bolts from the blue, might well have done some cosmetic surgery to the faces I was used to conferring with.

First thing next morning I suited up Val and myself to go take a look. Margaret immediately unsuited Val and was adamant that no one should go up there. There could be stones dislodging—anything could happen. She wasn't about to lose her family in an avalanche. I waited until Margaret went to work and then scooted Val over to In-Su's and Aldo's for a slide show on the Inferno, in Italian, no less. Val liked presentations.

In-Su asked me if I had a job that day, which was a bit grating. I didn't tell her, yes, I have to convene with the stone guardians of our town and see what shit might be flying our way. Not that she would have understood that. For a brief moment, standing in the doorway, I couldn't tell the grandparents apart. They're both small people.

I decided the safest way to make my ascent was to follow the rail trail along Binnewater and then bushwhack up. It was steamy and wet after that intense storm. The ground and the rocks were slippery. The mosquitoes thought they were at the Chinese Buffet. When I got in position I scoped it out with my bird glasses. It looked like more rock had been shifted around than I thought. There were burnt markings where the lightning had left its fury.

Banana nose's nose was blown off and tumbled down

about fifty feet and lodged in a crack which held it vertically in place like a tombstone. Stoner Van Etten's face was split in half. Raging Tom sustained a series of pockmarks on his cheeks. And Vanita, one of her perfectly smooth breasts was shattered, which was most disturbing. The rest of them, Grinder, Hooded Parrot, Jasper, seemed to have sustained little or no damage, just some burn marks.

This was going to require all of my skill and complete concentration. I was out of breath and needed to rest for a few minutes before I rappelled down. I remembered, but really hadn't forgot, that I had a bit of Strawberry Cough in my backpack. One of the conditions of our nuptial was that I cancel my subscription to *High Times*. I did, but not before I'd ordered three quarters of an ounce of the Strawberry Cough, with the highest lab-tested THC at a *High Times* Cannabis Cup: 25 to 28 percent. It has an exquisite berry flavor to it. I added in a bit of Super Lemon Haze to round out the mix. Both of these fine products top the THC charts.

I began my descent as the shit kicked in. I went momentarily blind and clung to the rock face like a salamander. I was looking for increased mental awareness, and enhanced problem-solving skills, not mind-freak THC gumbo. I'd say I was at loose ends, but I couldn't locate an end, loose or otherwise, for at least twenty minutes.

Meanwhile, the mosquitoes had second helpings of Lo Mein Me. I should have listened to Margaret. I should always listen to her. And if they found my sorry-ass body impaled on a Tree of Heaven down below, oh well. Torturously, the initial wave of sky- high high began to wane. I took the remaining bits of Strawberry and let them flutter down the mountain. "I'm done with this shit," I said, my lips pressed against a cool wall, sealing with a kiss my pledge to never smoke again. Beer? Well, that's a whole different allegiance.

Carefully, I continued down, slithering along jagged outcroppings and maneuvering around bushes and trees and vines that could have really played hell if my rope got tangled in them. My plan, as it came to me, was to lower myself down far enough so that I could view them all at once and address them as necessary. That took another fifteen minutes of excruciating effort. When I reached the desired position, I saw that it was not the desired position. I was looking up vertically under them. I'd miscalculated. I needed to be a good fifteen feet out from the mountain to see them. I studied the trestle. If I could somehow attach a rope to one of the girders I could work myself across.

Suddenly there was Kurt's familiar voice scolding me from the other side. "Are you crazy? Do you want to wind up like I did?" I stared at the trestle and suddenly realized that all I really had had to do was walk out there and yell to them from behind the railing, perhaps with a megaphone, when no one was around. The thought of how much easier it would have been made me sick, and the Strawberry Cough that played havoc with my mind turned into a violent retch. The peanut butter chip pancakes with organic raspberry syrup I'd made for our breakfast projected into the bushes.

After about ten more minutes of recovery I realized I couldn't climb back up. I inched my way down, praying I wouldn't run out of rope. When I finally got to within five feet of the huge flat rocks that rested on the bottom like giant toppled dominoes, I ran out of rope. I cut it off and dropped five feet and landed on my ass. I climbed off and stumbled onto the sidewalk next to 213.

Exhausted, parched, defeated, my ass rearranged, horrified that I'd thought to bring Val with me, I hobbled home with seven tails between my legs, one for each of the faces I'd failed to contact. But when I finally did the next morning, they wouldn't speak to me. I called them each by name. I beseeched them to predict what this would mean for the hamlet. What would happen without them as our first line of defense, our firewall? But they were immovable, stone silent. Maybe they were still in shock.

I shuddered. I felt that this was a material change to the coordinates of the town as we moved forward. I thought that I might have seen a tear fall from Vanita's eye, perhaps mourning the loss of her perfect breast. But it seemed that even they had had enough of me, and so had I. Pity the man with the penchant for misadventure, rudder cracked, sails torn, and whose course is set for calamity.

And how and to whom should I report this imminent danger? Without the faces, conscious and watchful, ever looking west, what would become of us in this plate of mixed greens and senses we call home?

I wouldn't trust Chief Cruickshank with this. I knew that Z would not believe it. He'd take it as another one of my fantastic tales stoked from reading too much Washington Irving on weed. And I am way done with weed. I didn't even wean myself from weed; I resigned.

But Z would listen to me. He was the only one who really would listen. Well, Margaret would listen but it would upset her. I had to protect her from my mind. If she ever turned on me like she did on Hamzah, I'd be in a small padded room at Benedictine waiting for my next dose of Thorazine.

If something dark could be coming our way, I'd be left alone to deal with it, whatever it was. I remembered the episode I'd had at Foster's Coach House Tavern, the War of the Worlds, a Martian invasion. Was it a harbinger of what would happen to us? That reminded me of Blades, a martial arts guy I sometimes have a beer with. He swore that spaceships had followed his car out on Route 52. He claimed that he drove up to one the size of a warehouse and it lifted and was gone in the time it took him to blink. Then someone texted me from the South Pole of my brain. "Martians? Really, Coot? What the fuck?"

As it turns out, the only person I can confide in, the only one who would listen attentively to my stories, is Val. At a precocious four, she possesses a deep understanding of the nature of things. I wanted to get her IQ tested at the VA, but Margaret forbade it. She thinks that my pronounced psychic presentation is enough for our household. If Val is special, and she is, it'll manifest by itself, without help from Daddy. Although reading the classics to her doesn't hurt. When I told Val about it, I left out the part about Martians, but described the various injuries the rock faces had sustained. She got out her little nurses play kit and insisted on going right up there to treat their wounds. After my last experience that's the last place I'd take her.

"How about a little gravy and fries?" She gave me her mischievous imp smile. It's our secret. Sometimes, not often, when Margaret's at a long birth, I take Val over to the Fork in Your Bun Diner for a snack. We're both partial to french fries and gravy. Sometimes we share an open-face turkey sandwich with extra cranberry sauce. We're not allowed this kind of salt and grease at home. Margaret is strict that we maintain as close to a vegetarian diet as possible, except on Taiwanese holidays when ocean and land creatures stampede across out plates in puddles of spiced sauces.

The owner of Fork in Your Bun, George, affectionately known as Sir George of Grease, is an excessively happy guy. He always made a big fuss over Val, let her come behind the counter and flip a couple burgers. And he always slides us a homemade baklava at the end of our meal. That afternoon, as we happily sloshed our fries through the brown gravy and into our mouths, he handed me the Freeman.

"You see this, Coot? Pretty crazy." I read the headline: "Naked Man Spotted Running up Joppenbergh Mountain Carrying a Cross." My heart jolted a couple times. My first thought was maybe the naked man could have been me. It had better not be. I wouldn't do something like that, would I? Hell no! I had to put it out of my mind.

"What, Daddy?"

"Oh nothing, sweet, just some crazy man running around the mountain."

"Daddy likes the mountain. You're partial to it." She got that word from Margaret. God, I love her vocabulary.

"Yes, Daddy does." I got the check and paid. I tried to act unaffected, but something about this new development really worried me. The stone faces weren't operational, so all bets were off.

The next day brought some relief. There was a picture of Chief Cruickshank in the Freeman leading a long-haired young man to his car, a coat thrown over the kid's shoulders to hide his nudity. The headline read: "Cross-Bearing Naked Man Apprehended." No charges anticipated. Suspect held for observation. I paid Cruickshank a visit to get the story. He still felt bad about the time the troopers messed me up in his office. He asked me how I was doing, how were Margaret and Val?

"So what's with that kid?"

The Chief stretched back in his chair. "He's a new addition at Melrose Hall. Well, actually an alumni. He's been there before."

"Jesus freak?"

"More than that. This one's a sick pup." He stood and

went to the closet and pulled something out. It was a four-foot tall wooden crucifix with a plush, stuffed monkey nailed to it, palms and feet. The Chief leaned it against his desk.

"Shit." The monkey was smiling. I noticed that he'd even pierced its side and a bit of stuffing was corkscrewing out. "What's his deal?"

Cruickshank read from some paper, probably the transcript from his interview. "This place is evil. The Devil's coming to claim his own."

"Jesus…has he been over to Fay's place?"

"No, you saw his hair. Probably hasn't been to a barber in three years."

"Where'd you get that?" I asked, referring to the monkey.

"Over on the other side near the power lines. That's not all." He slid out some eight-by-ten black and white photographs and placed them on the desk. There were about a dozen images of crucified stuffed animals. There was one of a hippo he'd crucified upside down. All with side wounds, stuffing slipping out.

"Fuck! Bad childhood?"

"They didn't even bother with Benedictine. Took him straight to Burnt Hills, raving all the way."

"What'd he say?"

"Crazy stuff like the town's lost its protection. It's vulnerable. The Devil knows…says it's going to come down from the mountain."

It was like a chilled ice pick to my heart. I knew we'd lost our protection with the stone idols out of commission.

Cruickshank sighed and dropped the file on his desk. "The kid said, no one can stop it. Town's quirky enough as it is. I signed up for straight-up law enforcement, not stuffed animal serial killers."

I don't think the Chief realized how funny that was. But it really wasn't. I replayed the script: the town's lost its protection. It will come down from the mountain. No one can stop it. All that foretelling with Fay, darkness descending, the possible collapse of the mountain, all the crazy shit flying around. Maybe I'd erred on the side of optimism. We could be headed ass-end into communal doom.

Well, I thought, feeling my sweaty armpits soak into my shirt, someone's going to have to stand up to it, be there when it happens. Shit.

And as if on cue, In-Su's sister, Pei-Chun, in Fort Lee, had to have emergency back surgery and would be out of commission at least ten days. In-Su hadn't seen her since moving up north and she insisted on leaving immediately. Margaret felt obligated to go to support her mother and keep Aldo out of trouble. Val begged Margaret to let her stay with me. Margaret declined wisely.

I stayed behind as I had more new odd jobs to handle, but not as big as the one that weighed on my mind. I'd have to find a way to contact Kurt and get some advice or a strategy. I knew of a psychic in Kingston, which I didn't believe in at all. I was prepared to bail if she told me that Daniel Boone was in the room. Also, I'd be taking a risk just going to Kingston; the place seemed to spawn my episodes.

I decided instead to pay Fay Nichols a visit. Besides, I could sweep up for a few bucks. She seemed glad to see me. Since I'd carried her, half-conscious, down the mountain, and agreed that she'd probably seen the virgin, though I didn't believe it, she'd decided that there was something in me worth saving.

"How's business?"

"Good, praise be. I've started shaving some of the menfolk, but I've cut a few. Need more practice." I made a mental note to tell Zeitzer not to go there for a shave.

"So anything new?"

"You're here to talk about that young man, aren't you?"

"How'd you know, Fay?"

"Because we both know it's coming. This town's been due for a long time." She swished her recently used razor across the mirror. The blade was stained red. She wiped it off on her smock. "I've got to practice more. You want a shave?"

"I'm good, thanks. What is it you think is coming?"

"You going to sweep or not?"

I grabbed the broom and started. From the piles on the floor I guessed she'd done about eight haircuts that morning, mainly the older wispy white-haired guys and gals.

I thought for a second. "How'd you know about the naked young man on the mountain?"

"I read the papers."

"I doubt he came in here with a head of hair like that, must be about a half a yard long."

"As a matter of fact, he did." She turned her back and was reading something, acting a bit coy, I thought.

"I doubted he wanted a haircut."

She turned around holding something, folding it over. She got kind of dreamy. She handed me the pamphlet, no doubt some Christian literature. I read the cover, "Are you ready for the next world? Will you be a spark plug or an exhaust pipe in God's Corvette?"

"No, not a haircut," she said. "He wanted me to wash and brush his hair out so it was radiant and silky and shone with the light of God." Her voice was a whisper now. "With the light of God."

I didn't like the way I was starting to feel. Fay was definitely moving toward something unwholesome. "Well, his behavior wasn't too godlike," I said. "Crucifying stuffed animals and poking holes in them...shit."

She removed her smock and unbuttoned her blouse and pulled it apart. A blood-red heart was painted over the left side of her chest. She stared at me, but I was pretty sure that she couldn't see me.

"That boy, that dear boy that you all dragged away, that you locked up, is an angel. He's an angel, Coot." She held open her blouse and stepped closer. "The sacred heart. My sacred heart...do you want to kiss it?" She'd transitioned from a friendly haircutter, witness of Mother Mary, to Carrie at the prom, about to clean house.

The room had grown considerably dark considering I'd arrived there only about four o'clock. The only bright spot, and not a happy one, were Fay's eyes. The usual steel gray marbles with an aura of tiny red flames flickering around them were just flames, some of them starting to shoot out of her eye sockets.

I must have backed quickly out of the shop because the next thing I knew I was at the bottom of the stairs on my back. I was so terrified I couldn't control my limbs. I just crawled away down the sidewalk, the cursed serpent expelled from the garden. I crawled to the post office and lay on the grass.

After I'd recovered a little, I headed home, but stumbled into the Boxcar instead and ordered a DeSchutes Inversion IPA, 7.7% alcohol content. A delicacy from Escondido, California. Truly, it was mercy in a bottle, a liquid nurse tending to what hurt most in my body. Though for me it's always my mind.

I made a bad career choice and had two more DeSchutes. Kind of DeSchuting the falls as it were. I needed some comfort. My thoughts were something like this: I need to brace up a bit. I'll be facing what the fuck knows the fuck what fucking thing tomorrow. So, three DeSchutes later—they should call it conversion ale instead of Inversion because you can really believe in it—I got up to go.

But when I left I stopped because someone held the door open for a wheelchair. When it got closer I saw that it was The Digger, completely fucked up, diminished, slumped to one side of the chair. We looked at each other. He knew it was me. We just looked at each other for a while. Christine came up and took his hand gently. She whispered to me, "He got caught under a trencher, crushed most of his spine. He can't hear too well."

She smiled brightly at him. "C'mon in, we're ready for ya." There was no reason he'd want me to, but I followed him to a little table on the side near the kitchen door. He was done with bar stools. I sat down next to him along with Jason, the man the family had hired to wheel him around town and get him to doctors' appointments. Jason happened to be an Oneida Indian and an expert bow hunter. We'd traded arrows in the past and he'd showed me how to make my own. But since that time with Fay on the mountain I don't hunt anymore.

Christine returned with a mug of Bud Lite with a straw. She handed me another DeSchutes. Then she dropped a few Slim Jims and a bag of barbeque chips on the table. Jason started cutting up the Slim Jims with his Bowie knife. He broke the chips in half. His nimble fingers display a certain grace that added some relief to the circumstances. Then he began to lift the mug to The Digger's lips. I lifted my bottle up and waited. The Digger nodded OK, and we toasted, sort of.

We listened to selections of his favorites: Margo Price, Chris Stapleton, and Randy Travis. I don't know how much of it he could hear, but he nodded to the twang and took in the stories, none as bad as his own. He sipped his beer and soon Christine was there with another one. Jason fed him a piece of Slim Jim and watched to see he didn't choke on it. Clarence came over and set a bowl of what looked like chicken broth on the table. Jason stirred it and checked to see if it was hot.

I wondered how The Digger felt? A Native American, a Black man, and his all-time nemesis at the same table, served cheerfully by a faded blond with sequined butterflies on the back pockets of her jeans. But The Digger wasn't thinking about that. He was just trying to swallow and hold it together. I made a mental note to say "thank you" after every step I took for the rest of my life.

After a while I felt something touch my hand. It was his, misshapen, not too useful, but still some strength in it. So I took his hand and we sat there and listened to country music and drank beer. He'd forgiven me, or he was sorry he kicked the shit out of me a while back. And when it was time for me to go, I let go of his hand and nodded at him, nodded a false bit of hope that he would be alright. But he wouldn't.

He was dead two weeks later. I think I sensed it when he passed. But he didn't come to me. He must have had other business to tend to. About a month later, The Shirt gave me a Bayern Coat of Arms Ceramic Beer Stein with a metal lid, not a trivial offering. It was from The Digger; he'd left it to me in his will. The Shirt presented it hesitantly. I wouldn't have known if he'd just kept it. But there was something about the presentation. He needed to square something. "He was working on my property when it happened...my brother."

"I'm very sorry." There was nothing else to say.

I lay in bed that night missing the hell out of Margaret, stuck down in Fort Lee with her aunt. I could smell her body, which ranged from gardenia to ecstasy, in the moment when she opens up and I enter her inner world, suddenly a raja, a king, not the pauper I am. I must have forgotten to undress. I felt for my house keys and pulled out the pamphlet Fay had given me. I turned on the light. WUAS – Wake Up America Seminars. End-Times Prophecy, Fort Walton Beach, Florida. It figured. It has a few sections in it like: Lucifer is Released from the Bottomless Pit, The Image of the Beast of Babylon, The Devil Appears on Earth, and other comforting tidbits. I read through half of one.

When I couldn't stand it anymore I chucked the pamphlet into the trash and went out to the backyard. I slid into Val's pool. It was a warm evening, a curious softness about it, for late October. The breeze had consciously determined it would be dead still. The stars were slightly out of focus like soft candle flames. Not like Fay's eyes. I shuddered; the water felt soothing. I closed my eyes and thought "Now what is it I'm supposed to do, and how am I going to do it? And really, I'd rather not."

"You'll know what to do when it happens." And there was the little Victorian waif with her buttoned-up shoes standing over me. The same one who'd followed us part of the way home from the Little Red House of Nuts and Berries.

I said, as gently as I could, "If you don't mind, I've had a rough evening." I smiled stupidly at her so she'd know I wasn't a mean man, just an exhausted one, freaked out down to my medulla. "At the moment I just can't..."

"I'm not going to come and play with Val anymore."

"You've been playing with Val?"

"She's my best friend. Even of the girls I knew when I was..."

"Alive," I said. She looked down then wiped her eyes, which I noticed were hazel colored. Little girl ghost tears. I

wanted to pick her up and hold her, but thought I shouldn't.
"Why won't you play with Val?" I asked.

"It upsets your wife. She sees Val talking and laughing
with me and it scares her. I don't want to scare Margaret."

And now I was entertaining the insane thought: where
to go to fill out papers to adopt a little ghost girl? I was in
self-pity mode.

"It's not going to end," I said.

"What won't end?"

"Me, I'm crazy. There's something wrong with my
mind."

"You see me, you can talk to me, can't you?"

"Yes, but that means I'm not all right."

"No, it means you're different. Kurt says you're a good
man and I can talk to you."

"Kurt, have you seen him?"

"Yes, he's sort of my guardian for now."

I felt a sob inching up my throat. "What did Kurt say?"

"He said that you should just go there. You'll know what
to do. He said you were like Odysseus, the man who can
contend with all things, just a little…"

"Crazy?"

"No, just overly imaginative. That's supposed to be a
good thing, isn't it? You know what Val did?"

"No."

"She taught me how to read."

"You can't read?"

"I can now. Our family was just the caretakers of that old
school building. They didn't pay us much and we didn't
have money for me to go to school."

Now I was wiping my eyes. "I'm sorry. You can come
to me any time that you want." It struck me how adult she
was in her presentation. If she were alive she'd be about
one hundred years old, I guessed.

"I have to leave...they said."

I didn't ask her who they were.

"May I...may I put my feet in?"

"Of course." I scuttled back to make room. I thought maybe I should get out. But I was just dead weight at the moment.

She unlaced her boots and removed her stockings and stepped into Val's pool.

"Can you feel it?"

"Yes, it feels cool. It feels good." She lifted her feet up and splashed a bit. She smiled. I watched her moment of happiness and wished I could create a place for her back in the world. Slowly, as if timed by some austere clock, she got out and put her things back on. She thanked me and began to back up. "I wished that you had been my father. Then Val would have been my sister." And she was gone.

Alone, my family gone for the moment, and no one to hear me howl at the moon, my tears so full, my mouth tasting the salt, until I rolled out of the water on to the ground and, I don't know what, prayed, which I don't do, for that little girl's soul. The little girl whose name I'd forgotten to ask. But of course Val would know.

The little waif told me that Kurt said I'd know what to do. But I wasn't so sure. I need some backup.

"No, Coot. Absolutely not." Z hung up.

"I called him back."

"It's five AM, Coot. I'm going back to sleep. I will not go up there with you. Last time I had to be carried down on a horse, you'll remember."

"Z, you're the only one I can ask."

"Coot, maybe you should call Dr. Fung. It might be time..."

"Time for what? To go back to the VA hospital? To get

drugged and lay in the ward until Fung is satisfied? Fuck him, that's not happening. Z…I'm scared."

He got quiet for a minute. "You're scared? I don't think I've ever heard you say that before."

"It's just that I don't know what this is."

His tone softened. "Coot, there's no such thing as the Devil. It's just a device to keep people in line, he's just an old puppet they shake at people to frighten them… medieval."

"Something's happening and I'm going to be there when it does. This is my town, my life is here, my family."

"When are you going?"

"After dark… Z?"

"What?" I could tell that his anger was about resignation. The man couldn't deny me and maybe he should have. I'd been nothing but trouble for him. But I truly loved the man and he knew it.

I spent the day prepping. I dug out an old pair of fatigues, washed and ironed them. I put new batteries in my Black Diamond headlamp, a recent acquisition for caving. Then I went to the attic. It was at the bottom of a trunk where I'd hidden it for safekeeping. My XM17 Modular Handgun System, a little souvenir I'd taken with me after I was discharged. It was like a reunion. I loved that weapon, but I broke out into a sweat because I'd promised myself to never carry one again. And could I make myself use it if I had to? And use it against what?

I cleaned it meticulously and popped off a couple empty rounds. What a fine little machine. I oiled the holster, which had dried out a bit. I sharpened my gutting knife and sheathed it. I knew this was all just dress-up, but I needed to feel prepared. What was happening had less to do with mind and matter, but more with beings who don't give change for your dollar in the material world. In fact, a harsh and perhaps terminal refund could be in the cards. These were forces way beyond my control. All the indicators were pointed toward the mountain. And that's where I was going.

The sun was down by the time Z got to my house and a crisp curve inhabited the air. It seemed that the month was catching up to its typical pre-November temperatures. The sky had cleared and the soft candle star formation had given way to bold lanterns, making the headlamp less necessary, but still useful. Z parked and turned off the engine. I noticed that Bebe was in the front with him. I slid into the back seat.

"Coot, I really think we should go to Benedictine and talk with someone."

"That's what you think?"

"Bebe and I talked it over. We don't want you to get hurt...or anything."

"Drop me off at the park." They looked at each other. She mouthed to him, "No."

"I'm a big boy, Bebe. Just drop me off, please."

"What's with the gun, Coot? This is different than before. You're carrying a weapon." Z reached back carefully, "May I have that?" I understood now that they'd planned a little intervention for me.

I pulled the handle, hopped out, and took off. This was not a night I could afford to spend under supervision. Even as I ran, I forgave them. They're the best friends I've had, but they don't experience things the way I do.

I ran down to Main Street and was surprised by a line of cop cars, including the sheriff's department, slowly cruising along. I noticed some of the houses had toilet paper crisscrossing their fences and trees. There were smashed pumpkins on the sidewalk. Some of the store fronts had been egged, bright yellow yolks oozing down the windows.

A few garbage cans had been overturned. For once I knew exactly what date it was: October 30. The night before Halloween, aka, Mischief Night, Gate or Cabbage Night, or Goosey Night, depending on what part of the country you called home. Or...Devil's Night. Fay's fire-flashing eyes shot through my mind. Devil's Night, shit.

From my vantage point I could see the swirling red lights of patrol cars making another sweep through town. It was just a few eggs and some toilet paper, but enough for a show of force. "Hey you, kid, put that pumpkin down." I noticed a few revelers dropping lines of orange crepe paper over the railing of the trestle. A few more were lowering a large white sheet with Casper the Friendly Ghost looking a bit pensive. Why wouldn't he, this Casper McFadden of Whipstaff Manor, a twelve year old boy who played outside in the cold too late and died of pneumonia? Why didn't his inventor father tell him to come indoors? Or at least invent a vaccine for pneumonia. The poor bastard. If he had lived they would have made fun of his name in school anyway.

There was a large cardboard skeleton twirling wildly in the wind. The revelers were wearing reflective makeup and costumes. One, dressed as a rat, was vomiting over the railing. He must have started celebrating early, this being the Festival Town. Each event is treated with reverence and closely resembles a Pieter Brueghel Tupperware party.

This night's precursor was nothing compared to the pageantry that would take place the next day, beginning with the little ghosts and goblins marching down Main Street. As usual there would be a patrol officer stationed outside of the bakery in case Coltaire went off, which he did on certain holidays. On the last Bastille Day, he stormed the police station in Bloomington and freed Kaiser, the German Shepherd, from its pen. True to his training, the dog chased Coltaire around the parking lot, biting him on his ass and thighs. *Vive la canine*! This was the kind of holiday that he should definitely be kept inside.

The kids would march to the rec' center to fill their tummies with huge amounts of candy corn, donuts, and cider. Then they'd hit the neighborhoods and score additional pounds of candy, weighing down their little arms, and resulting in late night purchases of Pepto Bismol, crying, and attacks of diarrhea. The thought of all that chocolate terrified me.

Four blunt rim shots grabbed my attention as the Shad Town Band broke into a raucous version of "The Monster Mash." No one was singing the words, but you didn't need them. The words were in the air and the heads of everyone who heard them, first penned in October 1962. I thought it was interesting that the writer, Bobby Boris Pickett, sang the song impersonating the voice of Boris Karloff. Boris, meet Boris.

The band must have been practicing at the Senatorial Puppet Bazaar judging from the way the sound carried up the mountain. The Puppet Bazaar folks had planned an exciting new creation for the big parade, designed to scare the hell out of everyone. It was so large they'd placed it on a cart with wheels. It was to be pulled by three motorized shopping carts donated by Hannaford Market. The drivers, three men, dressed as the Three Muses in full kitsch ballerina outfits would add an additional bit of sparkle to the festivities.

I had the good fortune to get a private viewing of the thing about a week before in their giant workspace, formerly the garage that housed the bus that brought people into town. It was a huge, partially clad, almost naked earth goddess, enthroned on a full leather taxicab seat, complete with checker decor. There was something about the plastered make-up job that reminded you of those large ladies from the boroughs, like she was riding into Astoria to have her nails done.

The theme was meant to suggest hunger and fertility. Harkening back to the Greek serpents, she was a man-eater. In her wide mouth would be a squirming, screaming blood-spattered man begging for his life. He'd be fastened in with ropes and Velcro. Two more male victims would be fastened to her hands waiting their turn to be devoured. A female Polyphemus as it were. Her arms would lift them up and down in tempting preparation. It was impressive that they'd designed the hydraulics so well to lift the weight. The guy in her mouth would try to squirm out. Somewhere inside of the contraption was a recording of chomping and gnashing of teeth, punctuated with thunder bolts. This monster, this device, was sure to give a good scare and a happy Halloween to all. The Shirt advised them that they shouldn't roll it out until after eight-thirty PM when the kids' curfew kicked in.

On the next day, the band would follow this creation around town. Beaming Dove had chosen a Stevie Wonder favorite, "Isn't She Lovely." There would be the usual spirituals, the Pete Seeger songbook, which always got everybody going. Pete was a local hero, an international one as well. He's visited the town a few times and campaigned for progressive candidates.

For some reason Beaming Dove decided on a show tune from *Annie*, "Tomorrow." A hopeful blast from the way past, late seventies. Which reminds me of a poem I wanted to share. It's untitled, but best described as a vegetarian knock-off of Macbeth's angst, his speech about the futility and brevity of life. Especially when you're waiting to be charged with murder. My poem is brief as it mirrors life, but not without a bit of flavor, as life offers. It was first published verbally at Scauzillo's Pizzeria where Sal was going on about having the best tasting pizza sauce in the state. After I'd recited it he thought for a moment and said, "That's it?"

UNTITLED
Tamari, and Tamari, and Tamari
Creeps on at this tomato paste.

Oh yeah, that night, Devil Night—I didn't want to be spotted so I got off Main Street as soon as I could. I cut in behind Rejuvenation, once the toll house for the canal, now the new tea house, whose teas and elixirs purported to cure any condition in your mind or body. Anything but thirst. There is only one true elixir for thirst.

I followed the old Delaware and Hudson tow path to the park. A tree cast a perfect shadow of oxen against the stone wall. We nodded to each other. As I expected, Z and Bebe were waiting for me at the trailhead. I did a bit of trespassing by a neighbor's house and started up the mountain. Would they call the cops on me? Not that they'd have far to go. I didn't think they wanted to, but they were afraid for me. Afraid of what I might do to...what?

I jogged up the first section of the trail, the equipment in my backpack flipping around inside the canvas enclosure. The coiled rope slapped against my thigh. The air was bracing and the dried twigs, acorns, and pine needles crunched noisily under my boots. A dead giveaway if I was being followed. Periodically, I cast a quick glance over my shoulder to make sure I wasn't. In the desert, a momentary lapse of consciousness could cost you your life. I got winded before I reached the horse farm and slowed down.

I wondered if the Countess Von Heidelberg might be out for an evening jaunt. I wouldn't mind her company, especially when she chose to be an intimidating presence. The old stream bed signaled the incline, which was steep and featured small polished rocks and boulders designed for tripping you over on your face. When I got closer to the top I stopped at the guy wires that hung from the old tower that was once the place where the television signals were received. The fuse box had been decorated with graffiti, but nothing new since last time. Pieces of wooden platform dangled from the trees. It's always a problem getting the previous generation to tidy up before the next one.

A few more yards brought me to the summit. I gulped ice water and watched a waning gibbous moon with grayish-black indentations rise above the ridge. I made a thorough scan with my bird glasses and determined that not much was happening around there.

Now I'd have to hike down to the plateau that over-looked the trestle and out toward the west above the stone faces that had gone mute and been seared as a result of the lightning storm. The Rondout was gleaming conspiratori-ally as it snaked along its banks to eventually unite with the Hudson. Does a creek know that its purpose is to flow into a greater body of water than itself? Hell no; it just rips along. It's just a ride. But what about, and I don't know why I was thinking this, when a river breaches its banks and floods, like it did here in 1952? Does it know it's flood-ing, causing people great concern? Hell no. It's just what it does. That's what I love about water. And when people sink into a tub or the public pool and say, "This is so refresh-ing," it might be for them. The water could give a shit.

I took up my position against the large boulder and spread out some victuals on it. I was hungry and thought I should eat something. I'm fond of sourdough pretzels and gruyere cheese. With slices of Seckel pear it's a real treat. I didn't bring any beer with me, which I was starting to regret. I pulled a napkin out of my backpack and a vial con-

taining just the tiniest amount of Super Lemon Haze nestled happily at the bottom.

I looked around, guilt-ridden. And the dialogue began.
Dump it. You're done with this shit. Yes, I am, but I could
just finish this up and never do it again. It's a bad idea, I
thought, tapping the stuff into my pipe. This will be the end
of it. You sound like an addict, asshole. Maybe I am. But
I was pretty certain I'd never buy weed again and hoped
no one offered me any. I touched the flame to it and drew
it in; it disappeared. I tapped the pipe out and dropped it
into a crevice never to be seen again until after the next
ice age. At first the Super Lemon Haze wrapped me in a
soft bunting of peace and love. No harm could come to me
or my town. I would defeat my adversary with the greatest
power man has ever known, love. That's what the ministry
of four taught us, that love is all you need.

I was having my pre-game snack when the boulder
cracked open and gobbled up my lunch. A hideous mouth
that hadn't seen a dental hygienist for centuries sucked it
down along with my gutting knife, which I'd used to slice
the gruyere. I grabbed for the handle just in time as a toxic
belch hit me in the face and the rock closed up solid as if
nothing had happened. Except the blade was stuck tight in
the rock, which appeared to be seamless.

I pulled up on the knife as hard as I could. I tried shaking
it back and forth. I hopped up on it and kicked the handle.
Nothing. The blade was stuck solid with little promise of
retrieving it. This was not an ordinary knife. I'd carried it
with me all over Afghanistan and Iraq. A Ruko three and
one-eighth inch blade, gut hook with a deer horn crown,
eight inches total. I'd slept with it. I used it once to cut the
umbilical cord of a tribes-woman in Lashkargah. She had a
boy. I wasn't about to lose my knife to a friggin' rock.

I worked it back and forth, bent down and pulled it with

all my strength. "Fuck this! You want to play Excalibur? We'll play. Friggin' English." I worked at it frantically for about ten minutes, then stopped to douse water over my head. Then I went at it again. I pleaded, "I really need this knife. Don't do this to me."

Suddenly it let loose and I yanked it out with such force that I did a backflip into a beech tree, banging the shit out of my head. I sat at the base of the tree cradling the knife in my arms. But everything was spinning. I hoped I hadn't fractured my skull. The spinning increased and I couldn't maintain my balance, even braced against the tree. I fell sideways and into a familiar state I know all too well. Black out.

They were walking toward me, some being dragged on pallets, some of them carrying children in their arms, some leading them by their hands. As they approached one of them fell to her knees in the sand. She tottered there for a moment and then fell forward and was still. Far back behind them the smoke rose from their village into a graying sky. Their movement caused the dust to enshroud them. Their heads covered, their long black dresses, the children's green clothing, all moving toward me. There were no men. I knew where they were.

The topography told me we were somewhere near Musa Qala. I also knew this was not happening years ago when I was there. It was happening now. I knew in part because I read the news. Fifteen years after we invaded Afghanistan the civilian death rate was over one thousand six hundred in half a year, a new record. And one third of them were children. Where's the pride?

I stood there until they reached me, their faces either black or masks of terror and sorrow and a loss that would never be accounted for. They passed through me as if I wasn't there. But they spoke to me; they listed the sources of the casualties as if reciting a shopping list. The Taliban, sixty percent of the deaths. Afghan forces backed by the US coalition's failure to honor international humanitarian commitments. The mines, the indiscriminate firing near civilians. The militias who answer to no one, the bastards. The US air strikes that miss their target.

"You're killing us...our children." One woman spit on me, but only sand came out of her mouth. Toward the end of the procession, another woman stopped in front of me and removed her head scarf. "You were supposed to help us, Coot. But more of us are dying now than when the great American Army came to save us."

"Abessa, Abessa?" She continued on with the group. "Abessa, it's not my fault. I didn't do this. Bush did it, this fucking endless war. I was just a troop. It's..." I sank to my knees and pleaded. "Abessa, please, please stay."

She turned back and shouted, tears working through the dust on her face: "Yes, you saved me. But not them. They're dead." And the woman disintegrated before me, ashes fluttering down on the sand. Gone.

"Abessa! Please...I'm sorry."

"You should be sorry, Coot. You worried us sick." Slowly, Z's face came into focus. "What the hell are you thinking?"

"The women just vanished, they turned into dust."

"What women?"

"Abessa...Abessa."

Someone gave me a sharp slap across my face. I opened my eyes for real. It was Bebe. She was kneeling beside me, Z on the other side. He held my canteen to my lips.

"Drink." I took a long one, my head throbbing from the impact with the tree. He pushed my eyelids up and examined them with his flashlight. "No concussion." He felt my scalp.

"Ow. Shit!"

"You've got a big bump. Knock some sense into you?" I could see straight now and I knew where I was. They helped me up and supported me on either side. We stood there until I found my legs. Then they began steering me gently back toward the trail that wound down the mountain.

"No, not yet. What time is it?"

"It's just after midnight."

"I must have been out for at least an hour. You didn't see anyone...?" Of course they didn't see anyone. I'm the one who sees them. I scanned the trestle. There was a throng gathered out there and they seemed to be focused on the mountain. Some of them were pointing at it. I couldn't tell what they were saying, but they were excited. Then, as if some mad conductor had brought his baton down to animate the orchestra, emergency vehicles descended upon the hamlet. Not just our own guys chasing pranksters. There were sirens, yelps, European high-low tones, whoops, phasers and air horns. The various emergency sounds meant they were responding from at least three other towns. Their remote vehicle search lights parried each other in the sky, a Hollywood opening of sorts. "What the hell is it?"

Z pulled out his cell. "It's already on YouTube." He showed me the screen. The mountain was bathed in flood lights, but there was something else there. Something that had never been there before.

"Holy shit. Let's go." The fastest way back now would be to bushwhack down the Binnewater Road side to the rail trail. It was dark and treacherous.

"I'm not doing that." Bebe turned and headed the other way.

"I have to go with her. Be careful." Z pressed my shoulder. "Be smart."

Smart, I thought. I don't do smart. I made my way down, stumbling, catching my clothes on branches and thorns, trying to avoid ruts and crevices. The dark hampered me from moving faster. But I caught a glimpse of what I was pretty sure was a copperhead who cordially let me pass. Though I took its hiss seriously, a warning to proceed with caution.

The last part was a dirt slide, still muddy from recent rain. There was no negotiating it on foot, so I slid down and was deposited unceremoniously on my face. I got up, spit out gravel, and sprinted toward the trestle several hundred feet away. There were people crowding on from the Mountain Road side and more behind me coming fast. I worked my way between them until I got a few yards out and took a look.

The cloud of light coming from the vehicles below was almost blinding. It was punctuated by swirling banks of red and white LED lights. The sirens cut off and a semi-silence settled over the scene, the mountain transformed now into a giant postcard: *Come to scenic Joppenbergh for the history. Beware of the future.*

I fought my way to the end of the trestle and sprinted down the hill and over the Keator Avenue Bridge, then west. The road was blocked off, so I took the stairs down to the creek and followed it until I was even with Binnewater Road. I climbed up and took a reconnaissance position on the metal railing. I scanned the mountain with my bird glasses. As I was panning across, all of the lights on fire trucks and police cars and everything else went dark as if a main circuit breaker had been thrown. A collective gasp rose from the crowd and a chorus of "Oh my Gods" filled in the empty space. Cell phone lights flickered, hundreds of electronic fireflies. Then the engines shut down—all of them.

The officers, firemen, paramedics exited their vehicles and walked around blank, shrugging their shoulders. Then their radios quit working. No squelching, shoulder mics, no earphones, voice recorders, or comm kits. Nothing. Just the silence of silence. Maybe five hundred people in the street and up on the trestle staring at the mountain. It was as if they'd been summoned to a long forgotten appointment set many years in the past.

A murmur rose from the crowd as they observed the rock faces, walls, and foliage. Now that the vehicle lights were doused the real light show was in progress. An array of colors was shimmering upon and cascading over the rock faces. It occurred to me that the colors corresponded to the temperament of each face. Banana Nose was appropriately gleaming wet yellow with soft brown spots. Grinder looked subdued in a serious gray-black tone. Hooded Parrot scintillated green, purple, and harvest corn. Jasper sported a muted Southwest, burnt yellow, brown, and green cape. He looked particularly mysterious as his color represented the twelfth stone of Aaron's breastplate, and the sixth stone of the New Jerusalem. How the hell did I recall that? I think I read it in the Bible some years ago when there was no other reading material in that particular lockup.

Raging Tom was expectedly hellfire red, pissed off, but obviously enjoying the light bath and the attention from the spectators. Stoner Van Etten was awash in psychedelic orange moon radiance. He looked like he'd consumed the economy-size bag of Super Lemon Haze. My little hit of the stuff still held about an eighty percent sway on my mind. This stuff is not chuckle powder; it's strong medicine. Vanita shone with the most feminine soft blue-violet I've ever seen. Her face was resplendent.

And then I noticed something that surprised me more than the mysterious lights. Banana Nose's nose had been restored. A two-hundred pound piece of stone, I estimated, that had been hit in the lightning storm, fallen and wedged in a crack far below, was now back in place. The nose job of the century. Stoner Van Etten's face had been split in half, but now it was repaired. Raging Tom's pockmarks from flying debris were smooth again. And Vanita, lovely Vanita, her shattered breast had been replaced, perfectly herself again. How could this be? Was there a master surgeon of nature who performed these works? The others, Grinder, Hooded Parrot, and Jasper were missing the burn spots I'd seen on them. Was it the palette of colors flowing over them, or pulsating from within, that was the healing factor, the restorative principle?

I hopped off the railing and worked my way through the crowd heading back toward Keator Avenue. Then I noticed that the colors were intensifying as if at the end of a fireworks display where they blast everything they've got left into the sky, the finale. Was this the finale of our town, the end of our time on this remorseless earth?

Then I saw it. About twenty feet above the mountain, illuminated by that faint waning gibbous, just enough light to reveal figures like delicate powdered charcoal sketches of exquisite shading and tone, with hints of pastels highlighting them. Skiers! Dozens of them flying in waves, arcing away from the mountain. They glided over the creek and disappeared into the gloom. Effortlessly, they soared out into the western sky. They reminded me of charcoal sketches I'd seen before at some museum. They kept coming, gracefully lifting above us like migrating birds into the night.

They were leaving the mountain for the last time, the final competition, the final jump into eternity, or whatever sphere or distant star you travel to one day. I wondered if Kurt was with them, maybe leading them out.

I looked around to see if others noticed them, but everyone seemed to be drawn by the array of lights on the mountain. I walked on and watched hundreds of folks turned around taking selfies with the light display behind them.

Then I slammed into something hard and unforgiving. It was Coltaire, wild-eyed in the throes of some demented Francophile curse. He was holding two cookie cutters and clicking them together, a pair of bakery castanets. "*Oeil de chat! Oeil de Chat!*"

I only recognized one word, cat. "Cat what?"

"Cat's eye. You see it, cat's eye!"

"You think this is chatoyancy? No way Col." I knew what he meant, like when a stone changes in luster or color with an undulating white shimmer. It's caused by fibrous inclusions or cavities within the stone. That definitely was not happening here. This stuff wasn't tiger's eye quartz. It's ancient bedrock. And this technicolor acid trip was something way beyond simple science. "Look up there," I said. "Up there. Do you see them? They're skiing."

He jerked away from me and raised his fist at the mountain, his eyes widening. "*Nana vagin, de pus.*" You could always count on him for a rational response.

I felt protective of my mountain. I grabbed his big French face and clamped it with my hands. "This mountain is no pussy." He shrieked, pulled away from me, and ran toward the church.

As I walked on I noticed that some people had raised their arms up to it. Some of them seemed to be praying. Other people were holding up their lighters and waving the flames slowly.

I saw two firefighters subduing Fay who was trying to break away and start climbing up toward the light—not a safe choice. She probably thought this was it, the Rapture for sure. I passed her in silence. She was murmuring, "Oh, Jesus, oh my Jesus." How could it be the Rapture when I was still hungry because that bastard rock ate my lunch?

I was overwhelmed and over-stoned, still good and high and had no thought of what I'd do next. I allowed myself to float around the surface of the crowd on the collective energy, a listless waterbug low on consciousness. Exhaustion was quickly pitching its lead tent in my body.

Someone grabbed my arm and pulled me aside. It was Cruickshank. I wasn't feeling exactly simpatico with him after the last go-round with the troopers. Though I suppose he did what he could to keep them from completely trashing me.

"Coot, we need to talk. See that van over there?"

It was a supersized, armor-plated black van with "gov" license plates and other telltale signs. "Homeland Security at your service."

"Yeah, and they want to talk to you. I'm supposed to bring you to them."

"And...?"

He placed both hands on my shoulders and looked me square in the face. I realized suddenly how much he'd aged since he'd taken on the job. I felt sorry for the poor bastard. He was just a cop, not a paranormal investigator.

"I'm going to turn around and walk away. You do what you think is best. But they don't give up." We stood there like that for a few moments. "I don't want to see you get hurt again."

He left me there as another swell of excitement lifted from the crowd. I looked up. The colors were intensifying, moving faster. I made my way toward the van and knocked. I didn't want the assholes showing up at my house.

The sliding door opened and a hand reached out and

grabbed my shirt, yanked me inside, then pulled my XM17 from its holster. An intimate pat-down followed. Not quite a body cavity search, but personal. It was then I realized that I'd lost my knife. It probably had slipped out of my hand when I smashed against the tree.

There were four agents in there. One in a dark suit, the others in full military uniforms, their weapons gleaming in the soft light.

"Sit down," came the command. The same hand pushed me down into a swivel chair.

"How are things at Stewart, guys? Flying straight?" I knew that they were headquartered at Stewart Airport in Newburgh.

"Shut up. Don't talk unless I ask you a question." One of them placed an item on the table before me.

My brain clicked. Hmm, nice. Sigarms Double Action Only, designed for a reliable six-point-five trigger pull. "Good choice, same as the Texas Rangers."

"I told you to shut up." One of them came beside me cradling an AR-15. I almost laughed. They used these babies for personal defense. If a civilian owned it, it was called an assault weapon. And these tools came with a thirty-round clip.

I should have stopped myself, but I was pissed and offended by their discourtesy. "Well, go ahead. You can kill thirty times." He swung the shank of the piece against my head. Now I was two for two after the bang up on the mountain. "You cocksucker." The guy shifted back for another swing.

The Suit said, "No." The guy backed off. The Suit continued: "I know you want to live to piss someone off another day, Sergeant." Of course he had all my shit off of the computer. I rubbed my head and decided it was time to think about how the hell I was getting out of this one.

These guys were the baddest of badasses. The IRS guys were Cub Scouts in comparison. You didn't get in the way of HS unless it was to provide something for them to pulverize in the name of God and country. I could tell that the Suit was nervous. After all, it was a pretty unusual situation out there. Probably beyond the reach of an AR-15.

"I understand that you might know something about this."

"What?" They turned up the lights. The Suit was sweating. He was a slender Asian dude with a mascara line moustache. I didn't ask him if he was born in the US of A.

"What the fuck is going on up there? You spend a lot of time on that mountain, don't you?" He slammed a slim iron bar across the desk. I slipped my hands back before it connected. "You tell me what the fuck is going on."

"I'm a veteran on disability. You're a piece of shit." I told myself to stop, put on the breaks. But if they thought I knew something they might not really kill me too bad. I hoped.

"I hike up there. I do it for relaxation. Got a bit of PTSD. Nothing you'd respect. Whacked vets not honored here."

The Suit shot up like he'd been ejected from his chair. "Thank you for your service."

He came around the desk with a piece that had a barrel opening the size of a silver dollar, designed to do ultimate damage at close range. Basically an execution device, but aren't they all. He pressed it gently to my temple.

"You're going to help me solve my problem, or your fucked up brain is oatmeal." Ah, death, the great equalizer. We're all just hanging around making small talk in the Devil's waiting room. It came to me. He was sporting a Marushin COP 357 Short Barrel 6mm. If he decided to activate it, there'd be no oatmeal or brain. Just splat, just like that. And he wouldn't feel a thing. The unit was designed so there was no blowback, nice touch.

"Fair enough," I said. At least it meant that we were going for a walk, an improvement from the hardware I was dodging in the van. We filed out onto the street and started back up 213. People stared and moved cautiously out of the way. Whatever this procession was they didn't want to have anything to do with it. A short jaunt to Calvary. What was I supposed to do? I had no idea what was going on, but it might be a chance to escape these fascists.

I thought of Wordsworth walking between the emergency vehicles. "Though inland far we be." That's cool if you make it to decrepitude. This shit is sudden death playoff. And I didn't have the friggin' seed of a plan.

"I need Zeitzer." They exchanged glances.

"Who the fuck is Zeitzer?"

"He channels for me." I felt some steel on my back. "Go ahead. Waste me in front of my neighbors. Hey everyone," I shouted, "say hello to Homeland Security. They're here to save your ass."

The Suit leaned into me. "Channels what?"

"Stuff like this." I nodded toward the mountain. We stood next to a Saint Ann's Mercy Medical Unit and waited.

He sent out two of his guys who located and escorted Zeitzer and Bebe in a gruff manner up to me and my guards. Bebe was seething. "If you fuck with this guy, I'll rip your eyes out." They toned down for a moment.

"OK, what's the plan, Sergeant."

I made a plan out of no plan. Actually, an anti-plan. "I have to get up there and talk to them."

The Suit snorted, "Oh, really. Want to take a picnic basket?"

"I need my piece back and a flare."

"The 17? The fuck you do."

"OK asswipe, you take care of it." I turned away. They pinned me against the vehicle.

Zeitzer grabbed the guys arm. "Leave…him…alone. Or you'll be back in Virginia scanning emails that mention ISIS." There was something grand about Z when he asserted himself. People listened. Even these vigilantes.

"Who the fuck are you? Are you military?"

"No, I'm a pharmacist." One of the team cracked up.

"A pharmacist…oh my God."

The Suit turned on him. "Shut the fuck up." The guy cowered. "Get it."

"Get what?" Mr. AR-15 asked.

"A flare…and his piece."

"Sir, are you sure?"

"Now. Get it." The Suit sensed, as we all did, that there was a percolating wave of hysteria sluicing through the crowd. All the burners were turned up high and the stew was about to boil over. It would be a catastrophic dining experience. There needed to be some kind of immediate resolution before the rest of the Eyewitness News Teams descended on the town. I knew the FBI would monitor the situation, which kicked in protocol. That meant that the guy in the Oval Office had to be briefed. It was crunch time. Something had to move or there'd be drones with warheads flying up the Hudson Valley. And what would their target be? The side of a mountain with carved faces as noble, venerable, and replete with state secrets as Mount Rushmore.

He was back in thirty seconds. The Suit grabbed the gun and emptied the chamber, except for one. "This one's for you if it doesn't go well. Save me the time." He held the gun back for a few seconds, reluctant to hand it over. I didn't know what I'd use it for, but I wanted one, wanted to feel it tight back in my holster, a bit of authority. And it pleased me that I made him, Mr. Suit, follow one of my orders. I put the flare in my back pocket. No idea why I'd asked for it. He brushed his pencil moustache against my ear, a peculiar, intimate gesture given the circumstances.

"Who or whatever the fuck you are, if you can stop this event there's some folks in the main office who'll be very happy. You understand?"

An award, how generous. "Yeah, I understand. The government's happiness is usually bad shit for me."

We eyed each other. "What are you waiting for?"

"I need that."

"What?"

I pointed at the fire truck with the extension ladders. "That should get me within range."

"To do what?"

I purposely repeated his question in an irritated tone. "To do what? To do what I have to do." Whatever the fuck that was.

His mind clicked along, cynicism driving a serpentine belt. He scanned the truck. "Let's go."

Chief Larry, the head of our volunteer fire department, climbed up the backside of the unit and took a defensive stand. "You're trespassing."

"No we're not." The Suit flashed him his ID.

Chief Larry didn't flinch. "We're in an emergency situation. Get off the truck." The Suit's crew moved in on the chief.

"This vehicle is now United States property. Stand down." The Chief grabbed for an ax and the guys subdued him. I saw his head bounce off a brass nozzle on the way down. They might have tapped him with it, by accident of course. You had to marvel at what bastards these guys were. But after all they were here to save our way of life, mainly Manhattan Island, make it safe for the multi-nationals to buy it up.

"Let me talk to him." Z climbed aboard. They didn't stop him. They had to let him "channel." We moved up a few feet toward the cab. I was surprised that they let us alone. Z whispered, "What the hell are you doing?"

"I don't know."

"What's going on up there?"

"I don't know... something."

"We should let them take care of this...whatever it is."

"Can't."

"Don't do it."

"I love you, man."

Z's eyes filled with tears. "Don't say that. It sounds...final."

The Suit shoved us apart. "OK, you two want to get a room? Let's go, Sergeant. It's showtime." He escorted me to the platform basket area and I hopped in. I stood there and waited as we collectively recalled that we were out of gas. All the engines and machinery had kicked off mysteriously a while ago. "You, get up here." The young fireman obeyed and joined us on the truck. "How's this thing work?"

"Well, sir," the kid was scared out of his response pants. "This is a hundred foot extension ladder, four sections of metal truss..."

"Skip the tutorial. How's it work?"

The kid was shaking. "It's a hydraulic operation...with a tractor driven propulsion motor."

"Can you do it manually?"

"No sir." The kid rested his hand on the ladder controls as if to apologize for its inactivity. Suddenly the board began to hum and lit up like the tree in Rockefeller Plaza. The kid crouched to jump off the truck. They grabbed him.

Lights were restored on all the vehicles. Everything was flashing and as crazy as it had been before the plug had been pulled, the work of some poltergeist freak electrician who'd hijacked the juice from the power lines and restored it just for fun. The Suit grabbed the kid. "Can you operate this?"

He was crying now. "Yes sir, I think so."

"Do it." The kid looked at me for guidance.

"There's no fire, sir."

"Up there. Take it up there. On the mountain." The kid engaged the control and the basket shot up, almost catapulting me out of it. His hands were shaking. He'd have been a lousy pianist. He struggled to control himself and now the basket was lifting smoothly into the air, the sections of metal truss ladders gliding out effortlessly high.

The lights, the frantic activity below reminded me again of Bartholomew's Fair. And the Lemon Haze showed no sign of releasing its hallucinogenic grip on the mind that had been formerly my mind. I recalled vaguely that Lemon Haze was kind of a round-up drug that attracted previous narcotic guests in the body to convene and hoedown in the recreation room of the brain. Despite this a thrill tickled my synapses as the ladder rotated around to the mountain and I greeted my seven companions with my head bowed and hand on my heart.

The radio chirped. "Is that high enough?"

I found the response switch. "Not quite."

"You can control it from there. Be careful...it's sensitive." I tried the various toggle switches and made adjustments. I took myself up another twenty-five feet or so and made a slow descent about equidistant between Raging Tom and Stoner Van Etten. This situated me about ten feet from Vanita's breasts, bathed in the surreal blue-violet light. From this distance I could feel the light pulsating out and surrounding me, a gauze of sensuous light cocooning my troubled body until the pain from various beatings and stupid shit fell away, spooning me into a euphoric state. I became aware of vibrations and tones that flowed within the lights.

She was singing to me; her voice was pure sorrow and unbearable beauty. It was, I suddenly realized, a siren's song. There were no words, just alluring female voices of an ancient character, like the chant and polyphony of medieval churches. She was harmonizing with herself. Involuntarily the basket inched closer to her breast. For some reason I responded to that by taking the weapon out of my belt. I turned it in my hand, touched the trigger, hung it from my index finger then let it drop hundreds of feet below. In this sudden comforting presence of peace and unearthly soothing music, a weapon was unnecessary.

The basket had reached Vanita's right breast and stopped. Just below it in the center of her chest, a rose color the shape of a fist pulsed in and out. I placed my palm on it and began to cry. Her heart beat against my hand and I felt it through the stone. I don't know how long I stayed there; perched in the basket with my palm placed upon her heart, mine beating the same steady rhythm as hers, one and the same.

When I looked around I noticed that the lights were fading on the stone faces. The colors seemed to disperse into the rock until they were again the gray and black shades they'd been before the transformation. I felt the last beat of Vanita's heart, but kept my hand upon it, solemn tears streaming down my face. "Vanita, what is it? What should I know?"

Reluctantly, I withdrew the basket away from her, regarding each of them in a new way. They would never look the same to me again, but I knew for certain they were there to protect us, as conscious and well-intentioned as any beings in this strange location in the world. Latitude: 41.8402. Longitude: -74.073. Home.

I came about in the basket high over the crowd and thought I'd let myself stay suspended a while longer, lingering in the exchange with Vanita and uncertain what my reception might be on the ground. I was completely straight now; the last vestige of the super-weed had escaped my body. Without a doubt, that was the last thing I'd ever smoke again. I knew it. But I would have donated blood for a cold beer at that moment. And being AB positive, my blood is in demand.

I grabbed my bird glasses and scanned the crowd. I was particularly interested in what the Suit might be up to. He was not an ally. He was easy to pick out, strutting around, an officious cock. He was deep in his cell reporting his success on the mountain, the bastard. He'd probably get a promotion and I'd get a... I focused in on his face. He was expressive and had precise mouth movements. I read two words off of his lips that sent miniature fear rockets through my skull: New Mexico.

The bastards! Now I knew their game. Dulce, New Mexico, the not-so-secret human/alien underground facility far beneath the Archuleta Mesa. That's the reward the folks in the front office had planned for me. Dulce, not so sweet. There were supposedly short "grays" and tall reptilian humanoids patrolling their vast underground web of passages. They had me pegged as an alien because of how I turned out the lights on the mountain. Now they wanted to probe my brain, find out how I did this shit. Which I did not do. It just happened.

I'd read about their Level 4 laboratory. The aliens, it said, taught the humans how to remove the bioplasmic body from the physical body and replace it with an "alien entity" force matrix. In other words, they could remove the soul of a human. Basically, kill the human and insert some paraphysical fuck-up so it could operate secretly in the physical realm. No thanks. I wasn't about to become their soulless man or their canary in a basket. Not in my world.

I scanned the crowd again and saw the Suit sprinting toward the fire truck. The fucker wanted me down, now! I turned back and threw the toggles into gear and came fast into the mountain for what would be a crash landing. Maybe the last one. The ladder froze abruptly and almost toppled me out. They had the master control.

I looked down. I needed just about ten more feet to reach the rock. I'd have to jump. I noticed the tree because it was moving toward me quickly; rather it was growing at a rate of about five feet per second. A tree-of-heaven with a thick bittersweet vine curled conveniently around it. I had just enough time to light the flare, wedge it between the bars to cover my exit. I grabbed hold of the vine, which had graciously extended itself into my arms and slipped out of the basket. My foot slid over the frame just as the ladder withdrew quickly. Fuck you, Suit.

I started working my way down the vine but I didn't have to. The tree withdrew back down into the crack it had suddenly sprung from. I was left sitting on a crag redefining what good luck meant when I noticed something glinting in the fissure the tree had disappeared into.

I focused my Lux-Pro LP480 light in the crack and there it was. A chest with a bronze lock and handles manufactured in the colonial style. Built to last. An ornate burnished letter R was engraved on the oval lid. I'd finally found it, or it had found me: Jacobus Rutsen's treasure chest. Just like Kurt said. But it wasn't near the horse farm. It was almost publicly hidden in the rock facing the tres-

tle and guarded over by these moai, these ancient personages, until the right person stumbled upon them. Was I
the right person? It was surprisingly well-preserved, probably because an overhang kept water from flowing into the
crevice, and good old colonial craftsmanship.

How the miners could have missed it was strange. They
poked in every inch of this place. I marked the spot and
shoved some loose rocks into the opening. It would have
to wait, there were already two helicopters hovering overhead burning holes in the mountain with their search lights.
And no doubt a small army of Homeland Security and
other interested parties beating a hunting path up the hill. A
nice night for a fox hunt. Time to disappear.

Contingency plans: six years in the Middle East taught
me that you had to have them. I had three for this case, but
only one I was really willing to do. One was an underwater airbag with an elaborate oxygen unit I'd assembled in
a cave, good for forty-eight hours. Too claustrophobic, but
great for keeping beer ice-cold. I'd even rigged up a pad I
could watch wrestling matches on.

Or, I could Velcro myself to the top of another cave way
back in the pitch dark and share the space with bats returning from the insect buffet. There'd be lots of guano. I'm ok
going mano e mano with guano, but not with what's in it.
There's a fungus that can give you histoplasmosis. It's OK
if it stays in your lungs. But if it spreads it's permanent bat
time-out.

My third and only desirable choice was the Ruined Cottage, but I'd have to almost be invisible to get back inside.
They'd be all over it. I knew that they carried portable X-
ray machines and would check out the walls. Inside the
wall facing the east was an insulated lead-lined opening,
big enough for a man and a half. A rather comfortable one
with fresh air vents and a small compartment for snacks.

There was even a slightly inclined plank with a quilt on it for catnaps. There was a tube for removing urine, etc. into the ground beneath the crumbling foundation. They would really go over the cottage, so it was more of a challenge. I loved tricking the bastards. They get apportioned millions for technology, but are no match for a demented, but crafty vet. That was my destination.

I accomplished the first part of my approach with ropes. I'd deposited networks of ropes, coiled to look like bird's nests, in some of the taller trees. When no one was watching I swung my way down about seventy-five yards, then did the barbed-wire crawl until I reached the back wall of the cottage. I hid there salamander style, then crawled in when it was safe. Judging from the boot prints outside, stubbed-out smokes, and crappy cologne residue—they all like No. 9 Team Force By Adidas or No. 6 Driven By Derek Jeter Eau De Toilette Avon. Jeter's about as French as a matzah ball—I knew they'd already been there. It didn't mean that they wouldn't be back. Standard operating procedure.

But, I thought as I wedged myself into the wall entrance I'd constructed to blend in flawlessly, this was not standard procedure. If these bastards caught me, it'd be a one way ticket to Dulce, Level 6, aka Nightmare Hall by the zombie employees. I could wind up having my brain transplanted into a seal, catching three-headed chubsuckers for lunch. I scrambled out of the wall, peeked outside, studied the terrain, and ran like a weightless entity down to the boulders surrounding the kilns. They should have been all over the place. Not a single vehicle, but one: Zeitzer's.

I crawled to it, slithered up the back door, hopped in, and lay on the floor. My sudden appearance frightened him and he burned rubber spraying gravel out behind us. "Just drive normal. Pull out next to the Zen shop and head to 32. We'll have to go to Kingston." Not my favorite destination, but I figured they'd be stopping every car north and south on the Thruway.

"Jesus Christ...Coot, this is it. This is the limit. They're going to kill us."

I didn't tell him what they might actually do, though a pharmacist's brain might not be all that interesting to them. And I'd be goddamned before I'd let them take his soul. I could feel his body shaking through the seat.

"Not good. This is not good. It's the government, for Christ sake!"

I tried to think of something to calm him. "Where's Bebe?"

"I put her on the bus to Hoboken. She's with her sister. Jesus Christ, Coot. Say something."

"I might have a plan."

"That's a bad something. Do you have any tranquilizers? I can hardly drive." I felt the car swerving.

"Don't draw attention to us."

"I need a drink...something."

"OK, I know a bar off the main drag."

This helped slightly. "By the way, I found it."

"What?"

"Rutsen's treasure, remember? It's supposed to be a fortune in gold coins, pewter spoons, period buttons, deeds, which are probably worthless, and jewelry, fine ladies' jewelry from the day."

"I don't care...really?"

"You'll be able to live wherever you want to."

"I'm not going to Florida."

"No," I confirmed. "Not Florida."

"I was thinking we could buy a compound and all of us live there."

"I don't think so. When they're looking for you I don't

want them to find me. Besides, Margaret would never go for that."

"She's very fond of you, Z."

I directed him down to the Kingston Caves area of Delaware Avenue. A somewhat low-end neighborhood with a vintage pizzeria and home to the White Eagle Hall that rents out for dances, weddings, and parties. We passed the fences that block the entrance to the caves. I'd heard that it was an underground marvel. There were still industrial swings and chains from the mining days. There were even some pickaxes hidden in nooks and crannies. One of the guys who's been in there told me there was a magnificent ice pillar that looked like a Roman column. I wanted to get in there and see it for myself, but there was a pressing matter at hand. Drinks.

We parked and waited until there were no cars going by. Just a random hearse creeping through the intersection, the driver scanning the sidewalk as if he'd lost his fare. But the dead get one last ride, just one. Then we slipped into Riccardi's Hideaway and were momentarily comforted by the Neapolitan bouquet of garlic fumes doing the tarantella above pots of steaming marinara sauce.

We sat on the back deck. Colorless leaves blanketed the floor. Faded, slippery, and large, artifacts from decades of autumns I'd walked through and forgotten.

The waitress immediately brought us out half a loaf of warm bread and olive oil with garnet gems of balsamic gondolas navigating the surface. I told her we were just there for drinks.

"Everyone has to eat something. We're celebrating Carmella." She explained that many of Riccardi's long-term patrons, some for thirty years, put in their wills that they be remembered at the restaurant, an after-party of sorts. She told us that Carmella was just shy of ninety when she passed last week and had dined religiously after church at the place for twenty-one years. So everyone had to eat and drink something.

With that, Z ordered a Double Gin Gimlet and one on the runway after that. His hands shook as he dipped bread in the saucer. The beer list was disappointing; basically crap you'd drink at a golf course. I settled on a double Old Fashioned with two Maraschino cherries, sacrificing hops for sweetness.

She brought the drinks on a tray with an order of calamari with marinara sauce and a glass with celery sticks. She said there was salt in the water. We toasted...to what? Death by Homeland Security. We downed the drinks in record time, at least a silver medal, then ordered two more. Half way through the second one a sly smile settled on his mouth. "You know, my people...Jews don't usually eat squid."

I toasted him. "Go for it, baby. Squid pro quo." We laughed until we choked. "What are we doing here getting hammered when one of the most sophisticated law enforcement agencies is out to detesticle us?"

"Squid pro quo." He doubled over laughing and slapped his thigh.

The waitress appeared with two more drinks. I stared at them momentously as they represented a trap door into a pit of binge-eating crocodiles.

"Go ahead. They're on Carmella. Her estate is paying for everything. She wants that you should eat and drink."

We toasted Carmella, so generous in the afterlife, two men without an apparent care in the world. "L'chaim," he said, reverting to a roots pattern. Somehow we never get rid of them. It was easier for me being a kind of nothing in particular. We both agreed: no more cocktails. We were too far gone, poster guys for AA. Z's cheeks were puffed out in classic pre-barf mode.

"Maybe this was a bad idea."

"Probably was. But look, you're not nervous anymore."

"No, I'm sick."

I was spiraling into a void, despite feeling rather gay. "Look, Z, if we were elks and were at an AA meeting, I'd say, 'My name is Coot and I'm an elk-aholic." It took him a few moments to process my vacuous humor. When he did, his laughter released in tight-throated torrents, followed by a coughing fit. Then he gagged and rocketed partially digested chunks of squid into my face, hair, and my favorite Anthrax t-shirt. The waitress returned with wet warm towels, a broom and a dust pan, followed by the sous-chef with a mop and pail. There seemed to be no lack of accommodation at Riccardi's no matter how fucked up you got.

I helped Z into the men's room to finish unloading his meal. "How are we getting out of here?"

"Not sure yet." I went back to the table to apologize to the cook.

The waitress was holding the hundred Z had tipped her. "This is too much."

"You earned it." I took two twenties out of my wallet and handed it to the chef. "So did you."

"Muchas gracias." He bowed.

"Maybe you guys should have a designated driver. Which way are you going?"

"No, no thank you. You've been very kind."

"I just don't think...maybe you shouldn't drive." For some reason she seemed to be pleading with me. She needed something. Zeitzer joined us and we stumbled through the dining room where the post-funeral gala was still in full swing. They were playing a video on the wide screen of Carmella holding court at the restaurant for her eighty-fifth birthday party. Seated next to her was an emaciated, miserable-looking guy, probably her husband.

The bartender, an eggplant-shaped dude with coarse black hair sprouting from any part of his body that showed skin, stepped out and blocked our passage. "Where ya goin', Gina?" She was visibly shaken by his presence. A Saint Francis medal glinted off his packed chest, seemingly without conveying the qualities of humility and love to its owner.

"Um...nowhere. Just giving these guys a ride home."

He edged in closer to us for effect, some bristles twitching. "I'll call you guys a cab. Go relax, Gina." The strength and resolve ran out of her quickly, a reverse transfusion. She desperately feared this man.

"We're good, thanks, got a car outside."

"All right, then." He stepped out of our way. And suddenly it was daytime. Not just daytime; the curtained windows of the place lit up with blinding summer whiteness, casting our shadows on the far wall.

Z squinted. "What, a movie shoot?"

"Don't think so." I heard the unmistakable whoosh and shuffle of helicopter blades idling in momentary rest, waiting. Everyone, including Mr. Eggplant, ran toward the windows to see what was happening.

Instinctively, I grabbed Gina's hand and pulled Z along as fast as I could, considering I was mondo intoxicated. I dragged them through the kitchen, sliding over the night's scraps and out the back door. The only plan was to make it to Z's car. When we got to it, it was sitting on a flatbed truck awaiting transport to some government garage, the tires secured with chains.

We stood there and gradually became aware of the wall of hedges on both sides of us. But they weren't hedges;

they were Homeland guys, state troopers, local cops, and more guys in suits. And they were locking and loading, as they closed in on us—a Bonnie and Clyde moment.

"You know these guys?" Gina asked.

"Kind of."

"I think I'm pissing my pants." Poor Z, I'd done it to him again. And I shouldn't have grabbed Gina on the way out. But I couldn't leave her with the Eggplant. He was out to harm her. Maybe she'd spent some time with him and decided to change her diet, allergic to nightshades.

"Good evening, Sergeant. I trust you had an enjoyable dinner." It was the Suit, speaking through a megaphone. We were completely encircled now by a small army, very close. They escorted us individually to the prisoner-transport helicopter and strapped us in out seats.

"Please, mister," Gina pleaded. "I don't know these two. Just giving them a ride."

"Then you won't have anything to worry about." She whimpered, "Please don't hurt me." What the fuck had I done? I looked down and watched Riccardi's, the street, houses, cars, and lampposts become a miniature nighttime neighborhood of a small town.

The hearse reappeared and flashed its high beams in an ominous salute. Then darkness as they slid the blindfold over my head, followed by a sharpie in my arm, and it was double blackout. Just before oblivion set in I hated myself because I couldn't do anything for Z and Gina.

It was the smell that brought me to consciousness. Bleached sheets and linens, the aroma of institutional cafeteria food and well-done coffee. That and the faint smell of rubbing alcohol. And the sound of voices reverberating off of high ceilings. I sensed an unmistakable presence in the room, a lugubrious entity seething with pomposity and pretension. I said as I opened my eyes, "Fung, you quack, they haven't fired you yet?"

"You remember me, Sergeant Friedman." He seemed delighted to see me. Why?

"I'm afraid you've had a breakdown. You're going to need some time to recover." He was shorter than I remembered. His head barely reached as high as my pillow.

"Put in the paperwork. I'm signing myself out."

"I'm afraid you can't do that."

"You know I can."

"Not if you're on suicide watch."

"You're full of shit. I'm not suicidal."

"You've been taking quite a few risks."

"Fuck this." I tried to sit up, but couldn't. The bastards had restrained me to the bed.

"Where's Z and the girl?"

"Your friends were released and sent home. But there are more here waiting to see you." He stepped into the hall and had a brief muffled conversation. He returned with the Suit, Chief Cruickshank, and some academic-looking guy, stooped and apologetic. A get-well committee of sorts. They stood there observing me, waiting for me to do something. Fung made the introduction. "This is Doctor Auchmoedy. He's in charge of New York artifacts at the state museum."

I knew the museum. I'd taken Val there to see various exhibitions. She loved the carousel on the fourth floor. "I'm not talking to anybody until you take these fucking straps off."

Fung looked at the Suit for permission. He nodded. So they were working together. The Suit was running this game and my old friend Montaigne Fung was assisting. So much for the suicide crap. Fung returned to the hallway and two attendants followed him in. They undid the restraints, slid them off, and retreated. "I want black coffee and three Advil unless you have something stronger."

"I'm sorry you're not feeling well." Auchmoedy kind of bowed while he spoke.

"Yeah, a little too much *carnevale*."

"Oh, you speak Italian." He bit his lip and continued nervously. "Well, Mr. Friedman, as Dr. Fung said, I'm in charge of artifacts at the state museum. There are some particular items said to have belonged to Jacobus Rutsen. You might know that he founded your town. Well, our research indicates that this might be the case. A description of the items turned up in his papers. If indeed these items do exist they are the property and heritage of the state. I understand that you're quite familiar with the mountain he named after himself…"

Holy fuck. They knew about it. They probably thought I'd stashed it somewhere. I chose some careful words. "I'm not aware that Rutsen had any…items."

The Suit leaned over me, his pencil moustache transmitting threat. "Given your circumstances maybe you could become more aware."

OK, I smelled the deal coming. I didn't know how it would go down, but there could, I hoped, be a deal and I'd walk. I'd actually walk away one more time. And I would never, ever, I promised myself, get into shit like this again. A young nurse came in with a tray. I sniffed the coffee to reassure myself it was the same bad over-cooked VA brew. I checked the tablets for printing. "It doesn't say Advil."

"We use generic medications now. It's cheaper." Fung eyed me. "They work the same." I took them. After all they thought I had something they wanted. And I did. But I wanted it too. Reparation for my time spent with Homeland Security.

"Well," Auchmoedy stuttered, "here's my card. Please

contact me if you should come across anything." Fung nodded at him and he left the room. I was starting to get the feeling that this whole thing was orchestrated. Now it was the Chief's turn.

"So, Coot, you and I are going to take a little stroll up the mountain and do our civic duty."

"You take a stroll, Cruickshank. I'm not your problem-solving tool."

"He seems irrational. Maybe he needs to go back on suicide watch," he told Fung.

"OK, OK, we'll take a stroll, but I don't know anything about Rutsen's items."

"Zeitzer says that you do know something."

Fuck they must have worked Z over and scared the shit out of him. Otherwise he never would have said a word. I couldn't blame him. I'd gotten him into this shit.

"OK. Leave Z alone. He's a better man than you bastards will ever be." Cruickshank smiled. Checkmate. He'd probably get an award or something from the state if the governor could keep his sorry ass out of prosecution long enough to do it. We have the most corrupt state government in the country. Two of the party leaders who ran their caucuses like a flea circus are serving long-term sentences. Corruption is us. The Chief made ready to leave, his part in the play over with.

"See you in the hamlet, Coot."

That left the three of us. The Suit thanked Fung for his expert medical attention. Fung gave me an artificial solicitous look. "Let me know if you ever want to talk. You really should be in long-term therapy with medication. PTSD doesn't cure itself."

Neither does sleeping with the enemy, fuck-face, I thought to myself. The Suit circled the room thoughtfully, considering his next approach. I judged it to be late afternoon from the slant of light at the window. My head was pounding as I tried to stay focused. He came back to the bed and placed a small briefcase with buckles and a lock on my lap. "It never happened."

"What never happened?"

"The whole thing on the mountain. It never happened. Right?"

"All those people saw it. It happened."

He unlocked the case and flicked the buckles up. "Crazy little town. A bunch of hicks. Something in the water." He leaned over me. His teeth were small, like a kid. He repeated emphatically. "It never happened." He opened the case. It was all green inside, choking with green. Hundred dollar bills, new and pressed tight, each wrapped in bands of ten thousand dollars each. I ran my hand over them. There were fifteen of them, stiff and real US currency. So this is what he meant when he said the folks in the main office would be very happy if I was able to make it go away, which of course I hadn't. I didn't know what happened.

He waited. I felt myself kind of sink into the mattress; I sank down with the weight of how my government, the country I'd served, conducted the state's business. It was just a payoff. Corruption and bribery. Bangs, lots of them, whimpers, and cash. I didn't want to be dirty like this guy, whoever he was.

I asked him: "What do you believe in?" He was easing toward the door, almost sliding, greasing his way, a snail in a suit. He wasn't going to answer me. I shouted, "What do you believe in?"

He turned back. "Keeping the homeland secure." Then he was gone.

I lay there holding the case in my arms and asked myself what I believed in. Not God, not country, maybe some. But

I believe in my family. And it seemed like months since I'd seen Margaret and Val. I had to get home.

The nurse returned with my clothes and more hot coffee and two more tabs of generic Advil for the road—very kind. For some reason she asked if I needed help getting dressed. She watched me drink the coffee. "How's your headache?"

"A little better, actually. Thanks."

"I'm sorry."

"Why?"

"I don't know…whatever they were doing to you…didn't seem right."

I dressed slowly, monitoring the debate in my head. Why not keep the money? I didn't do anything wrong. They're all fucks anyway. I have a wife and child to support. Besides, now that they knew I might have stashed Ruten's treasure, I wouldn't be able to keep it anyway. Some of that money was Z's. I owed him big time.

Yeah, the money came from good people who paid taxes so the government could spend insane money on shit like this. People want to believe their government does the right thing. But is it possible for any government, even the least murderous one, which is not us, to do the right thing? Well, I'd paid too, plenty.

I slid a couple hundreds out and stuffed them in my pocket. By the time I passed the nurses' station I was feeling fat. Just the prospect of stepping outside, away from the stale oppressive air of the hospital and Fung's gravitational pull, seemed like an award. I slipped out a crisp bill and handed it to her.

"Oh no."

"Please take it." The other nurses stared.

"Why?"

"Because you were nice. Because I have it."

It was five o'clock in some season in the capital city of New York State. The seat of government, some decent ethnic restaurants, old Dutch homes, old-money mansions, soulless condos, and about as many churches as there are McDonald's. Standing there on New Scotland Avenue, I felt a crease of cold wind against my chest; maybe it was November. I was wearing a pea coat so it must have been cold.

And I was suddenly aware of how alone I was. I felt that cold steel hook of loneliness in a town I'd never willingly return to again. My people were an hour and thirty minutes south of here. I needed them. I headed for the bus station. All of that cash, and I didn't even think to take a cab to the station. Shit, I could have taken a cab all the way home.

When I got there I found Margaret in the kitchen drinking coffee, which was unusual for her. I felt an icy draft flowing off her body, which halted my approach. I thought I'd escaped the chill I'd felt in Albany.

"Where's Val?"

"Sleeping at Mom's." I ached for her, the desire to be alone with her.

"Oh."

"You didn't even call me." She dumped the cup in the sink.

"I was tied up, well, strapped down actually."

"Zeitzer told me. What the hell were you doing in Riccardi's? Damn it, Coot, I need sanity to raise my daughter."

"I...we were hiding from Homeland Security."

"They were here. They came to our house, your daughter's home!" Margaret screamed this. She'd never screamed at me before. My throat closed, descending fear, a lethal plunge down an elevator shaft.

"What'd they want? Did they threaten you?"

"He said to remind you that it never happened, or they'll come back. What the fuck is this about?"

She'd never sworn like that before. I lowered my forehead on the table. "It did happen."

She began to sob. Each of her sobs, her cries, a hacksaw severing my intestines and drawing them out through my navel.

"OK, it didn't happen. What's it matter now?"

I waited, a frightened child, desperate, having lost his mother in a department store. "What do you want me to do?"

She didn't answer. Was this going to be it? My last chance to be a human in the world? A fucked-up one whose brain was a no-go zone? Life canceled out just like that?

"You don't want me, Marg? Is that it?" She bit her lip. "Do you want me to go now?"

"Be quiet."

We sat there for a long time. She seemed to be listening for or to something. I was dead weight in my chair and sweating. I needed to vomit. I was trapped. I didn't have a card left to play. Well, maybe one. I picked up the briefcase and set it in front of her.

"What's this?"

"It's yours." She opened it and looked inside; her eyes widened.

"What's this for?"

"It's for what didn't happen."

"They gave this to you?"

"They think I helped them."

I was struggling to piece together the thoughts. Something didn't happen. I didn't make anything go away. It was just what they wanted it to be. Strange thoughts, passing clouds. But the hundred and fifty thousand inside was real, minus a hundred and thirty dollars for the nurse and the bus ride home. And $2.50 for an egg salad sandwich I'd got from a vending machine.

Margaret sat in front of the case of money that existed because something else didn't. She stared at it.

It felt like we sat there for an hour. The case open, a symbol, a curse, something that answered essential needs, security, goods and services, death benefits, whatever?

"You have to give it back. It's not ours."

"It's for you and Val...no matter." I didn't finish the sentence. "And if I give it back, if I don't play cheat ball with these guys, I could wind up in a freezer in New Mexico."

She closed the case and slid it across the table, and gave me a long, thoughtful look as she was deciding something.

"I'm afraid, Coot. You make me afraid. For you, for Val..."

"Marg, it's different now. I know what I did seems crazy. But I'm not crazy. I'm not like I was—I'm past that. Don't be afraid. What I did on the mountain was to protect you and Val...to protect this place. It's just that I see and feel things...different. That's no reason for you to be afraid. If I thought for a second that I'd be dangerous to you and Val I'd go away and never come back."

"Coot..."

"No, please listen. It's real. The money's real. This home is real. You and Val are the only real thing I have. We're here now and we'll be here. It's real...Margaret?"

I don't know how long we sat there. Finally, she got up and went to the fridge. She stood there transfixed. She seemed to be lost, floating in a reverie. She was so far away yet so real before me, a supernova contained in a woman's body, in a kitchen somewhere in my immediate universe. She placed some leftovers on the counter.

The impossible knot of my body, the sickness in my stomach, the fall into the elevator shaft eased and loosened.

I watched her warming up the food at the stove. Suddenly she turned and held me in her eyes, those curiously brilliant eyes, eyes I would never completely know the depths of and how they connected to her heart. I hoped she was thinking what I wanted to allow myself to think. That I'd provided for her. For her and Val. However fucked up I am, despite the absurdity of the circumstances, somehow, inexplicably, I provided for them. The smallest movement of her lip, her eyebrows, showed me she understood.

And then she said, her voice flat now as she issued a directive. "Don't ever ask me again if I want you to leave."

Later that evening, in the steaming cup of a winnowing November night, or whatever month it was, we made love upon our holy bed blanketed in thousands of hundred dollar bills, unwrapped, starched and scratchy, the cash crinkling beneath our wrangling and rolling bodies. And when she finally fell asleep with her head on my shoulder, I drank in the tea of her sweat, of her womanhood. I started to drift off, but first swore a sacred oath to this woman, in the name of the goddess of the earth, and the muscular gods who hold up the sky, the words of which I will not tell.

We'd managed to achieve status quo again. It had been my plan to retrieve Rutsen's treasure chest and deposit its contents into Z's safe deposit box until we could figure out what we should do. But after the close call with Margaret when I got back from the VA hospital, I stayed home. Also, Margaret seemed to have become the most sought-after midwife in the valley. She was averaging three births a week, some taking up to forty-eight hours a pop. She'd come home exhausted. I'd feed her, draw her a bath, and she'd sleep until the phone rang again, another woman casting off into the eternal stream of labor. Margaret seemed determined to help birth every baby in a fifty-mile radius.

The good part, besides the baby bucks pouring into our account, was that I spent more time with Val. She was determined to teach me all the Taiwanese language she knew, but I was a bad student. I think I have a foreign language deficiency disorder. She became impatient with me. I made a deal with her: first we'd read *War and Peace* and then go back to Taiwanese lessons. I figured by the time we got through the novel she'd forget about Taiwanese. The choice was selfish on my part. I'd read the book years ago. The idea of reading it again out loud to her young mind was exciting, a guilty pleasure—to enter Tolstoy's world again! The ever-developing characters. The guy took life and hurled it upon the page for the rest of us to marvel at. For some reason she insisted on calling him Toad Stool.

There was the risk that she'd be bored as hell, but not my little girl. She immediately connected with Natasha. She went around the house saying: "I have had so little happiness in my life." She could say it in Taiwanese as well. Margaret became alarmed when she first heard it. I told her that Val and I were writing a funny story together. She didn't think it was funny.

So, as Val and I read the story, she was Natasha and I was Andrei. And we spent cozy afternoons sipping cocoa and reading a great book. We agreed that "Toad Stool" was the best book I'd read to her. I was so thankful that she had failed the admittance interview at The Little Red House of Nuts and Berries. I wouldn't have to pick her up at the end of the school day to find out she'd stared at pine cones for five hours and arranged them on project paper. Education in the hands of the assured educator, packing a six-gun loaded with pedagogy, is just tyranny. Like I keep saying, hand the kid a copy of the *Times*, a backpack with a healthy lunch, and they're on their way.

On the following Thursday the Chief showed up.

"Unlock the screen, Coot." It was Cruickshank and Boice. "We have an appointment, remember?" He was too god-damn serious.

"We didn't wake you up?" Boice seemed actually concerned.

"No, I'm always up at 6:30 in the morning. Calisthenics."

Cruickshank snorted. "Let's go get it." My dilemma was, should I lead him up the mountain to Rutsen's booty and turn it over, or pretend that I don't know where it is and spend three hours sweating him up and pissing him off for coming up empty-handed.

Now that the Suit was out of our lives, I hoped, maybe I could make this work. Of course I didn't know how adamant the State would be in pursuing their rightful historic property. How much trouble could I get into?

I needed to buy some time to think, so I led them through the horse farm. "I don't really know where it is. You know that."

"Try a little harder."

"What's in this for you, anyway? Since when are you a fan of state antiquities?"

Cruickshank said, "Don't give a rat's ass about it. I just don't want anymore weird shit coming down here. That means keeping your ass on the straight and narrow. Comprende?"

We poked around for another hour or so, then I decided, screw it. I felt I deserved to see what was in the chest. It was more about my attachment to the place, the time I'd spent up there, all the crazy shit that happened, or didn't happen. But I didn't need it. We'd done well enough on the real estate deal, which reminded me that we still hadn't sat down with a calculator and figured it all out completely. And how much would be left after taxes. I led them around the mountain, past the old antenna and cables until we could see the trestle down below. "We should look there."

"Why?"

"I don't know. Just a feeling."

"Damn it. We'll need equipment. We can't climb down that."

"I can. I'm used to it." I knew a way around the steepest rocks, plus I had some rope and tools stored just about twenty-five feet below our location.

Cruickshank checked his watch. "We've been at this for three hours. You better have it when you get back. Or I'll have to make a call to your friend at Homeland Security." An ominous offer.

I worked my way down until I was out of sight. I grabbed some rope and tied an end on to a piton I'd driven in previously. It would hold tight. I worked my way down slowly, feeling for familiar foot holds. I realized again that this place was as important to me as any sacred shrine in the world, except the holy shrine of my girls. I stopped and thought: I have everything I could ever need. That sudden unannounced bequest of happiness, a flight of doves carrying you by your shirt sleeves and pants cuffs over a frost-rimmed blue lake.

I slid down the last rock face and crawled on to the crag, then looked for the spot I'd memorized. The place where the tree-of-heaven had deposited me from the fire truck basket, on that night that didn't happen. I shined my Lux-Pro flashlight into the crevice. The dirt and pebbles I'd swept into the opening were gone. I reached in the length of my arm...nothing. I held the light and pushed my face into the crevice...nothing. It was gone. No chest with a bronze lock and handles, no letter "R". Nothing! It was gone. Rutsen's treasure was gone. And I'd be gone when I got back without it. Cruickshank had nothing to lose. He'd throw my ass to the wolves just to show that he'd done his job. The bastard.

I decided that the best direction for me was down, not up. As usual I ran out of rope. Couldn't remember to store a longer line. I had to jump the last five or six feet and it hurt. I landed on some acorns and slid into a crevice and twisted my knee; a sharp throbbing pain took over. I was hobbled, limping, a compromised contestant too far from the finish line.

I texted Z. He got right back. "Jesus Christ, Coot. Try to make it down to 213. Ten minutes." I grabbed a straight sycamore branch for a staff and staggered forward. If I stepped into another crevice it would be over with. And there was still the embankment and metal guardrail to contend with. It must have taken a lot longer than ten minutes. Z was there. He hopped over the railing and ran down the embankment, an athletic feat I wouldn't have expected of him. He dragged me up the incline, sat on the railing, hauled me on to his lap, swung around and dropped me on the brush and gravel. "I didn't mean to do that. You all right?"

"Just shoot me for Christ's sake."

He dragged me up to his car, threw me in and took off. He took a circuitous route up Cottekill Road, down Sawdust Road, over Breezy Hill Road, back to Route 32, and right on Main Street. He slid into Bebe's parking lot and parked behind the garden on the pathway that led back to Willow Kiln Park and eventually the library. We made it to the basement stairs. "I can't do that."

"Sit down." I sat and he bumped me as gently as he could down each step on my butt. He helped me up, positioned me on a hand truck, leaned me back, and rolled me up to the front of the basement near the walk-in cooler. He got me a chair and told me to wait. I was kind of amazed at how quickly and thoroughly he'd managed my situation. It reminded me of steer wrestling.

He returned to the basement with Bebe. He took a chopping knife, cut my pants leg and wrapped a bag of ice tight around my knee, which began to numb it and relieve the initial pain. He offered me three Advils and a Ginger Brew. Much appreciated, but I knew that Bebe had recently tapped a Six-Point Bengali IPA, a hoppy and fruity brew with pine overtones. And I would have busted my other knee for one.

Bebe reprimanded, "You're not Spiderman, Coot. Time to get real."

"I didn't have a choice. Cruickshank was all over me. And it's gone, Rutsen's treasure. Some fucker got it."

Bebe went in to the walk-in to get some kale or something. She came out and kicked the door shut behind her. She held the treasure chest in her arms, Rutsen's treasure. "You looking for this?"

"Holy shit. How'd you get it?"

Z lifted the chest from Bebe and sat it on two milk crates in front of me. "I went up and got it as soon as I got back from Albany. I figured they'd find it if I didn't get it out of there. I didn't know what they were going to do with you, or when you'd get back."

"What's in it?"

"I don't know."

"Z, you didn't open it?" I couldn't believe he hadn't.

"You went through a lot to find it, Coot. You paid a price. The honor should be yours."

Bebe ran her hand over the engraved R. "Go ahead, let's have Christmas early."

"Is it December? I'm kind of done with months. They keep changing every…"

"Month?" Z finished my sentence. I pulled on the lock.

The key must have been lost years ago. But it wasn't locked anyway. Why wouldn't it be locked? The hinges creaked and complained, but lifted up.

It felt strange. I was sitting in front of about three hundred years of history. And maybe, rightfully, it wasn't mine to open. Maybe I should just pack it up and deliver it to Dr. Auchmoedy at the museum.

"What are you waiting for?" Z asked.

"I don't know. It's weird. And I don't know why it's unlocked."

"Maybe the lock rusted out."

I tugged on the lock. "Brass doesn't rust. It should still be locked. Unless someone unlocked it. There was no key, right?"

"Unless it fell out when I hauled it up. But why should there be a key. Whoever hid it there, Rutsen, if it was him, would have kept the key."

I started to lift the lid up. "Wait." Bebe went back in the walk-in and returned with a bottle of champagne. She uncorked it, aimed the spray at Zeitzer, who spun out of the way, so the fizz covered my face. Then she took a long gulp. She handed it to him and he did the same.

I had some too. It wasn't beer, but it was cold and dry. "Let's hope there's something in here worth celebrating."

They stepped beside me as I raised the domed top. Z shined his penlight into the opening. I lifted out a GI Joe Action Figure, US Army. Then three cans of Silly String, red, white, and blue, piles of Monopoly Money, a Classic Magic 8 Ball, and dozens of gold foil wrapped Hanukkah coins. There were also small plastic cowboys and Indians, the kind I played with as a kid.

I dumped them out onto the floor. Shredded comic books fluttered down followed by a dated Good Housekeeping magazine, the cover advertising: How to Make a Perfect Holiday Sponge Cake.

"What the fuck?"

"I'm sorry, Coot." Z put his hand on my shoulder.

"Whoever did this made it personal to me. The bastard made it personal."

Bebe started picking up the items off the floor. "Who else could have known it was there?"

I noticed something on the magazine cover. "Can I see that?" The perfect sponge cake on the cover of Good Housekeeping had been altered. Someone had scribbled or rather drawn over the picture of the cake a pink glaze with fleur-de-lis delicately sketched in. I turned to the page the recipe was on. There were notations next to some of the directions and some of the directions crossed out and others added in, with bizarre ingredients for a sponge cake. And comments like: *Va te faire encular*, aka go fuck yourself; *tu me gonfles*, aka you're pissing me off; *merde* and *putain*, aka shit and fuck. "Motherfucker. It's Coltaire. He did this."

"Coltaire, how could it be him?"

"Look, *parlez-vous Francais*?" Z studied it for a moment.

"It's like the writing he did on Margaret's cake, remember? But how could he know about the treasure?"

"For all his hate and fear of the mountain, I've seen him up there foraging. He uses morels and other stuff in his pastries. It's a free grocery store. He might have just stumbled on it."

"What are you going to do?"

"I think I'll have to take a look in his house."

"That's crazy. He lives upstairs from the bakery. He'd kill you. And he'd be within his rights if you trespass."

"I have a plan, sort of."

"It had better not involve me. I'm not doing this one."

"You're out, Z. I promise. Maybe just a phone call."

It took a few days until I could put full weight on my knee. I hoofed it into Le Raide E'clair. The bell tinkled its usual alarm. He would never allow himself to be taken by surprise. Coltaire was carrying a tray of colorful mini-pastries up to the counter. He leaned over them maternally and whispered, "I gave you life. Now you will give yourselves to the mouth of the world."

"Well," I said, "the town anyway."

"What the fuck do you want?" Ah, the retailer of the month award.

"A buttered hard roll and a coffee."

He set the tray down gently as if it were a donated organ. He turned and went to the basket of rolls. "You know where the coffee is."

"Is it fresh?"

"Fuck you."

He didn't bother to offer to heat my roll. He dumped it on a piece of wax paper and slid it across the counter. "Three seventy-five."

"Remember the cake you made for Margaret? The one with the midwife stuff on it?"

"So?"

"She loved it. It kind of sealed the deal for me. Except for the chocolate lettering. I got sick."

"I don't give a fuck about your allergies. And that was mocha anyway." How could a master baker not know that there was cocoa powder in mocha?

"Yeah, well, I really am grateful. I'd still clean out your basement if you want me to. Or maybe…the attic?"

His eyes widened. Suspicion and sudden nervousness formed sweaty beads on his forehead. OK, so if he did have Rutsen's treasure it had to be in the attic. "There's nothing in the attic, nothing, just some old furniture. Why would you want to clean my basement out?"

"I owe you for the cake."

"OK, when?" He couldn't turn down free labor.

"Wednesday at seven. Work for you?"

"In the morning?"

"No, I've got another job. It'll be seven PM."

"I close at six."

"Won't you be here?"

He sneered, "You think I'd take my eyes off of you?"

I bit into the roll and butter squished out the sides. At least he was generous with butter. "I wouldn't want you to. My cleaning is like performance art."

I arranged for Z to call about seven fifteen the following Wednesday. I was in Coltaire's basement tying up stacks of cooking magazines and pornography of a type I will not describe, but just say that it involved scantily-clad female "bakers" ranging from petite to wrestler, wielding phallic tools of the trade such as rolling pins, oven thermometers, and rubber spatulas, positioned near their orifices.

Z called from the Coastal gas station on a pay phone with a paper towel over the mouthpiece reading from a script I'd prepared. He told Coltaire that he was calling from the Planning Board meeting in real time. There was a proposal on the table from two hipsters straight out of Williamsburg. They wanted to renovate the vacant furniture store building on Route 32 and put in a mega-bakery and bistro. The Au Courant Croissant Company and more.

I could hear Coltaire jumping up and down in rage. Then the door slammed and the bell jingled his departure. I figured I had about twelve minutes while Coltaire drove to the board meeting, broke in on them and to find out that there was no such proposal on the table. They were actually arguing the pros and cons of a dog park, which was going mostly con because their chief concern was always liability. They wouldn't even approve a community garden because someone might get whacked with a hoe.

I sprinted up the cellar stairs, ran through the kitchen, then up the stairs to his apartment. I found the attic door and pulled. It didn't budge. I pulled harder and it opened. I flew up the stairs. There was, like he'd said, some old furniture and a large table with a sheet draped over it and various items poking up from underneath. I took a deep breath and very carefully lifted the sheet.

And there it was. Rutsen's elusive treasure, but with more items than expected. There were piles of gold colonial coins and bills, silver buckles and hair pins, snuff boxes, and of course lots of pewter mugs and more buttons. But how the fuck did he know how to find it?

I heard the door jingle and then slam. He couldn't have returned that fast unless he suspected something. I dropped the sheet and looked for a way out. I could hear his heavy steps on the apartment stairs. I shoved open the back window and climbed out to find myself hanging from the sash on the second floor. I slid the window down as I grabbed onto a thick drain pipe and hung on like a monkey. There was a slightly protruding façade, fortunately a decorative building, and I made my way along that until I scuttled around the corner, then hung on to another window. He lifted the window so hard I heard glass break.

"*Bâtard*! You *bâtard*," Coltaire hissed.

I kept going until the next drain pipe and I shimmed down as fast as I could, then ran around to the front of the building and reentered the bakery making sure the bell was audible all the way up to the attic as I'd heard it. I yelled, "Coltaire, are you here?"

He barreled down the stairs and through the bakery,

coming for me, a fleshy linebacker. Then he slid on some cooking oil. He slammed into the display case and groaned.

"Are you OK?"

"I'll kill you."

"Why, I'm just cleaning your basement."

"You were in the attic," he blubbered and groaned.

"What are you talking about? I was cleaning out the cellar when the bell rang. I came up and couldn't find you. I went outside to look around. I just came back in. What's so special about your attic anyway? You got live porn up there?"

"You motherfucker."

"You want some ice or something? Or should I just leave?"

"You weren't up there?"

"Fuck you and your attic."

He calmed down somewhat. He seemed to be buying my story. He took hold of the case and dragged his thick frame up, about two hundred and seventy-five pounds I didn't want to have to invalidate if he attacked me. There's a certain move I learned in hand-to-hand reserved for big guys like him that renders them incapacitated, or possibly dead. Neither of which would polish the apple of my local reputation. "You didn't go up there? You swear?"

"I did not. But you're making me curious about what I would find."

"I told you, old furniture." He slid open the case and took out a Russian Style Mille Feuill and shoved the whole thing into his mouth. He sighed. No wonder the guy was so big. He baked them and ate them as well. He didn't offer me one. I remained as calm as I could, as my internal organs exchanged 911 calls. "Come back tomorrow and finish."

"OK, see you at nine-thirty." I walked out slowly, feigning ultimate relaxation, hearing the goddamn tinkle of the bell for the last time.

I called Dr. Auchmoedy and filled him in. I told him that my friend Coltaire was hiding the stuff in his attic for safe keeping. A favor to me. There were, I said, unscrupulous characters around town who were after it. The good doctor was thrilled and promised he'd thank Coltaire.

Promptly at nine-thirty the next morning, Dr. Auchmoedy arrived with a contingent of Albany State Troopers and several antiquities specialists just in time for coffee, pastries, and treasure.

Coltaire deserved to get thrown under the bus but it would have disrupted the twisted algorithm of the community. I figured if Coltaire didn't take a hit for it he'd be grateful to me for that much, as grateful as he gets. He'd forgive me for not getting him charged with unlawful possession of state property. I laid low and waited. A day or two passed and nothing from Cruickshank or Coltaire, so I figured all was well, I hoped. As well as it gets around here.

Part 5: Tidying Up

Zeitzer called early the next morning.

"Did I wake you?"

"No, having tea with Val. What's up?"

"We have an appointment."

"Why?"

"You don't remember? Tomorrow evening, Cooper Union, in the city."

"Why?"

"Jesus Coot, did you forget? Dr. Shaw."

"Yes, I remember him." It seemed like a millennium since we'd met with the guy. The whole thing that didn't happen on the mountain had changed my internal sense of time and direction, compromising it more than usual. If I were a migrating goose I'd fly straight into a billboard.

Z paused. "Coot would you mind…"

"Dressing up?"

"Well…"

"I'll go to Penney's and get a suit, shoes, and a tie."

"Good, nothing too flashy."

"Don't worry. I won't ask Aldo for help with my wardrobe this time." He seemed skeptical.

When I came downstairs the next afternoon I was wearing a Stafford Travel Brown Sharkskin with a vest. I had on a Van Heusen No-Iron Lux Sateen dress shirt that felt like silk. And a pair of brown plain-toe dress shoes. I found the tie in the Wave shop, which offered multiple types of paraphernalia. It was a Garfield & Sunflowers Novelty Tie for just twenty dollars.

Val stared at me. "Where's my daddy?"

"I am your daddy."

Val said, "Daddy, those are not your clothes." She was right. I felt stiff. If anything went down I wouldn't be able to move freely, though why would that be necessary? Even so, the training stays with you.

Margaret stared as well. She'd never seen me in a suit.

When Z arrived to pick me up he took pictures with his cell phone. Margaret pushed my hair back off my face and kissed me.

"Just don't do anything to attract attention. Don't get arrested. Behave, for our sake."

Z drove us into Manhattan, then downtown. He sprang for a parking garage because he was there to pick up a check. And Dr. Shaw had graciously invited us to dinner. I still couldn't figure that out. Why would a high-powered, connected guy like Shaw feed a couple of upstate hicks? And not just burger and beer. He and Irene were staying at the Bowery Hotel, a bastion of fine taste and luxury. The housing market must have been good. That plus his lecturing fees.

We checked in at the desk and the clerk said they were expecting us and directed us to the twelfth floor. Z was perplexed. "Why aren't they meeting us in the lobby?"

"Maybe he wants to do the business stuff in private."

"That makes sense."

The elevator was decorated better than any room I'd ever lived in. The place was no barracks. Floor-to-ceiling factory-style windows, personal trainer and massage service, four hundred thread count Egyptian cotton sheets, and shoeshine service, to list a few amenities.

The last one caught me in my gut. A detail, but significant. Shoeshine reeks of the good old days in the South. It's sickening. Remember the song "Chattanooga Cho-Choo"? The White passenger asks the "boy" if he's at the right train. The "boy" assures him that he is. Then the White dude rewards the "boy" by letting him shine his shoes, Christ! I figured that with all Shaw had going on he wouldn't notice that a shoeshine was just one of the amenities they offered. But if I was the grandson of a sharecropper and had to fight my way through that Jim Crow wall of shit they tried to block these folks with, I'd tell them to go shine their own shoes. Or shove them up their white asses.

I admit to a certain other disorder I have besides a strain of PTSD. It's self-diagnosed and I call it RDD, which stands for Reverse Discrimination Disorder. I make sure that I am attentive and respectful to people of any shade of color other than white, which of course includes Taiwanese. It's something innate in me.

I saw a bumper sticker once that said: WHITE PEOPLE JUST DON'T GET IT. They still think that the world was created in God's image in seven days. What if it turns out that God is a black hole of monstrous, destructive energy? Or just a chance combination of chemicals or random atoms attaching for the sake of mutual comfort and profit?

My greatest prejudice is against people who won't read some history and educate themselves as to what happened to the folks they put down, how the Native Americans wound up on reservations with their sacred land and monuments decimated by white imperialism. And the Black travesty, still active today, and not so subtle. There's a movement to pay reparations to the descendants of the victims of the Atlantic slave trade. Good luck getting that one passed through.

Physics is succinct: Black and White are not colors because they don't have specific wavelengths. But White contains all wavelengths of visible light and Black is the absence of visible light. Ergo, all things being equal, as

they should be, White is Black as Black is White. Fuckin'
A.

I was snapped out of my internal revolution when Irene
answered the door, dressed in a red pants suit, all business
and chic female power. She showed us in. Dr. Shaw was
uncorking a bottle of wine. He greeted us like old friends.
I hate it when guys give you the fish hand shake and don't
even take hold of your entire hand. Shaw knew how to
shake and he looked you right in the eye as he did. And
that smile; the man radiated the pleasure he took in those
around him, and the joy of his mission, which was huge.

We sat at a table overlooking uptown, the Empire State
Building, a beacon sparking with prosperity and possibility. The city, the place where young people come to follow their dreams. And are not always so successful. How
many of these young dreamers had crashed against those
skyscrapers and fallen into the canyons below.

On our second glass of wine, not cheap stuff, I refrained
from saying, "but here's a bit of nectar and ambrosia!" I
caught myself and gave a stern warning. You just better
keep both eyes open.

Irene efficiently distributed the paperwork and pens
around the table. She explained the purpose of each document and even had little red arrows showing where to
sign. Nothing was left to chance. Shaw asked us if we had
any concerns or questions. It wasn't too late to change our
minds. Though the deal was mainly with Z. I was along for
the fringies, wine and dinner—a night out in the city. I was
starting to feel as lit-up and freewheeling as Times Square.

We signed here, here, here, and here, and initialed multiple times. She passed the stack and he signed everything
quickly. He opened a leather-bound book and handed Z a
check. Z considered it for a moment and said, "This is more
than we agreed upon."

He explained that after all the financials were reconciled it came out to a slightly higher figure. "Our accountants are perfectionists." He added, "Our foundation was very pleased to purchase two homes at once."

Then he opened another bottle of something equally dry, delicious, and heady. We toasted and soon after, he announced that we were due downstairs for dinner. Then off to Cooper Union. He reminded Z that he was still counting on him to meet with a small group of folks and talk about his experience with the organization. I was curious as hell to peek at the check, but hung back as if this was a standard evening for me.

And so it went. Dinner downstairs at Gemma Frutti Di Mare Trattoria, in baronial splendor and more great wine served in pitchers. The food, the bread, everything was to Di Mare for. When I check out of this world hotel I want to be thrown into a vat of their Angel Hair with Clam Sauce and be left to marinate into the next dimension.

Then we were off to Cooper Union. I was feeling way magnanimous and handed a homeless vet a ten-spot on the way in. This was not lost on my companions and Z gave me his just-don't-do-anything look. I was a little bit looped and nodded out a couple times during Dr. Shaw's speech, inviting Z's elbow into my ribs.

What I heard of it was penetrating. Dr. Shaw quoted from The Fair Housing Act, Title VIII of the Civil Rights Act of 1968. Not much had actually changed. Discrimination was alive and well and growing like cancer in America.

As promised, Z attended the gathering of future home providers, well-off folks who could manage with one less property, and every one of them had nothing but the utmost respect and admiration for Shaw. And then it was over.

Shaw thanked us; we shook hands all around. Irene held

back for a few moments. She seemed uncertain at that moment. I thought maybe she'd been put off by my comments about her grandfather and her jewelry. She took both of Zeitzer's hands in hers and said, "There should be more like you in the world." I loved that she said that to him. He was visibly moved and coughed nervously. Then she took a step toward me and offered her hand. Her beautiful face glowed, not from the crass auditorium lights, but an inner intelligence and depth of character that startled me. I held her hand for that brief moment without words of my own. Her tone was conciliatory, and open-hearted, but mischievous, a bit of payback perhaps, "Farewell, comrade."

We were heading for the parking garage and Z decided he needed coffee before the drive. We walked west toward the river and were in view of the garage when two young men passed us, turned around and held steel to our backs. They relieved us of our wallets and took off. "Son of a bitch." I started after them but Z grabbed my coat. "Don't bother."

"They got the check. The little bastards." And they were already way gone. We got in the car and locked the doors. Z slipped the lid off of the cup and took a sip, offered me some, then put it in the holder. He slid off his shoe and pulled it out. He handed it to me. A check for three hundred and seventy-five thousand dollars.

"Holy shit. You put it in your shoe."

"My father and mother came from a country in Eastern Europe with no name. It was a place where our people learned to run for their lives. They taught me well." We pulled out our cells, which the young thieves, unskilled and nervous, forgot to take, and made the appropriate calls. The credit and debit cards, Home Depot, were dead in ten minutes. I'd given my only cash to the veteran. Z slid a fifty out of the glove compartment and we paid the attendant.

The rest of the ride home would be courtesy of E-ZPass. We twisted on to the West Side Highway and he put on one of his favorite CDs, C. "Gatemouth" Brown singing "Ventilator Blues." He opened the windows and tapped out two Pall Malls. We lit up. Ventilators and unfiltered cigarette smoke, a nice combo. The highway was uncharacteristically sparse—hardly any cars. We passed by thousands of lit-up windows, some just soft as candle light, others blazing with activity, the hyper life igniting the rooms. The buildings shooting up into the sky, concrete monuments in a vast garden of bedrock, primo Manhattan schist, gifted from deep in the earth a half-billion years ago.

Z leaned back and steered leisurely with one hand. I noticed a new nonchalance about the man. He'd loosened up some; he was chill and in control. I admired him without exception. The lights shimmered with promise as we neared the George Washington Bridge. I leaned back, confident in the man who motored us forth—my confidence, at least in the immediate future, bright as the full Hunter's Moon, a Super Moon, that scraped its butt lifting over the Palisades, then bounced a playful beam off the windshield.

When Z dropped me off we made a plan to meet at my house to figure out what to do with the money. We needed to be smart about it. That kind of cash draws attention. Between the three hundred seventy-five thousand for the homes Shaw bought, and the hundred and fifty thousand, courtesy of Homeland Security, for the *nonevent*, there was much to talk about. It would be a relief because I'd stowed the briefcase under our bed, which was no way to do banking. And after that night Margaret and I romped on our bed, I kept pulling hundreds out of the pillow cases and mattress cover. I couldn't chance walking into a bank with that kind of money. Z had put Shaw's check in his safe deposit box until we could all meet and talk about it.

I'm pretty sure we all assembled on a Saturday morning. I made vegan raspberry lemon poppy-seed pancakes, so sweet we didn't need maple syrup, but it was still available in a quart jar. I served them with vegetarian sausage links and a huge pan of home fries, cooked to perfection in canola oil with garlic and onions. The trick to make them come out good is paprika and a handful of sea salt. That and Full Circle Organic Tomato Ketchup. The meal was served with Audubon whole bean coffee, Shade Song French Roast, and Dongding Tea, with a cinnamon stick—In-Su's favorite.

I also attempted donuts and burned my fingers repeatedly with hot bubbling oil. Aldo had three of them while they were still steaming hot. To add to the confections, Zeitzer brought two containers of gourmet ice cream from Zora Dora's Micro Batch Ice Cream in Beacon. A party.

I got some nice compliments about my cooking. It feels good to feed people, especially your family. After we cleared the kitchen table Z passed out some small calculators so we could all follow the numbers. Z quipped, "Ladies and gentlemen, start your calculators."

In-Su shook her calculator and turned it over. "What for?"

Z opened a small notebook. "So, we have five hundred and twenty-five thousand dollars to think about."

"Minus one hundred and thirty I used from the hundred and fifty thousand," I added. "Plus the egg salad sandwich for $2.50. I'll replace that."

Z gave me his "For Christ sake, Coot" look. "Coot, forget the sandwich. We have some serious decisions to make here. I've been reading up on the tax laws. I'm trying to figure out how to legally avoid turning over most of it to New York State."

"What money, need money." In-Su looked under the

table to see if there was any money. Z and I had already agreed that we should donate some money back to Dr. Murphy Coleman Shaw's foundation for the good work he was doing. The guy had been completely straight up with us. There were no objections to that. And everyone voted for a 529 college savings plan for Val. But at the moment she had other ideas.

"Can I have fifty dollars?" We all looked at Val. She was peering at us through the hole in her donut.

Margaret stroked her hair. "What for, sweetheart?"

"A camp." She got shy and didn't finish what she was saying. But I knew what was coming and tried to intervene, but I was too late.

"For ghost children."

Margaret continued stroking her hair and gave me a dry ice look. "Honey, let's talk about that later."

"Just three. Mama, can't I?" Apparently, Val had collected a couple more ghost children who used to live in the neighborhood. Despite Margaret's consternation, I was almost moved to tears. My little girl's heart was so open, her spirit so big and beautiful. I grabbed her donut and held it up to my face and stuck my nose through the hole. Val broke into ribbons of laughter and it eased the tension about the ghost thing. I decided then and there that I'd take Val to the park more often and find living children for her to play with.

"Firenze, I go Firenze. See Casa di Dante." Aldo wanted us to budget in a trip to Florence. He wanted to see the Dante Museo. He planned to donate his copy of the "Inferno" to the museum. He thought they'd be glad to have the notes he'd scribbled in the margins. We nodded appreciatively as if that was the most logical thing to do. Poor guy, I understood how he felt. I still wanted to publish my poems in a book if anyone would ever give a shit about that. And was his dream or mine any less realistic than a ghost camp? Everybody's got a dream.

Zeitzer lobbied hard that we should all get Roth IRA retirement accounts. None of us ever heard of them before. He said he'd make an appointment with his money guy and we could all go and have a tutorial on them.

Margaret, the other voice of reason besides Z, said she'd like to get replacement windows for our house. She'd researched it and wanted Wood Casement Anderson 400 Series windows. They're top of the line windows and run $400 a pop. We have twenty-four windows, so the whole thing would come out to about nine thousand six hundred and change.

We'd answered to the Northeast winters for a long time dressed in layers and sometimes down vests as the frigid air seeped into our old house. It'd be nice to be warm. I desperately wanted to install a woodstove, but Margaret thought they were dangerous. She said we wouldn't need a woodstove if we replaced the windows. Z agreed with her and said we'd save a fortune on heating fuel. I was out-voted and as I thought about it, our discussion had taken on a way practical tone.

It was only fair that Z should get the money for his Aunt's condo, and even more because he'd figured out the whole deal—and it had worked! Z was clear about his needs. He only wanted enough to ensure he'd never wind up in a retirement community in Florida. Besides, he had a successful business to sell when the time came. Then, quite embarrassed, he said, "I took out my fold-up map of the United States and cut off Florida."

Curious, the mania, the fear, and the night terrors we all have. Each one different but manifesting from that frightened child's castle that was more of a slum. But we didn't know it at the time. I didn't say what I knew to be true. That

Z and Bebe were moved in together and neither of them was going anywhere but deeper into each other. They were burning it up and my pride meter was pinned on a hundred for Z.

I hit the head to relieve myself from too many cups of Shade Song French Roast. I couldn't stop drinking it. The buzz was intense. I could have recited the Greek alphabet in one second, but I don't know it. Pig Latin, maybe. When I came back through the hallway I heard my name. They were talking about me. I tiptoed up to the kitchen entrance.

"He's fine. He's never been better. Don't worry about him." It was Z talking to Margaret. The words caught in my chest.

"He's good boy, good boy. Generous boy." Aldo said.

"Who he?"

"Coot, mama. My husband."

"Coot good. Good mam."

"Man," Margaret corrected.

I rested my forehead on the door jam and closed my eyes.

"He's a brave man, Margaret. He's been through a lot. To be his friend…" Z's voiced cracked.

The look on Val's face, the light that shone from my girl's eyes, vanquished the darkness and pain in the world…in my world.

"This is my family. The only one I will ever have and the only one I'd ever want." In silence, I placed a soft blessing on each of their heads. "Thank you." I took a few moments to compose myself then cleared my throat so they'd know I was returning. They looked at me as if, I thought, they were seeing me for the first time. "How about some more donuts?"

Epilogue

It's late, so late it's early, about three forty-five AM. Margaret and Val are tucked in tight and warm. I couldn't sleep. I leave the heat on sixty-eight. I hear the radio tell me it's November. It feels cold; looks like snow. I'm on my old Schwinn Cruiser pedaling through town. There is no one else on the road and the road itself seems lonely, lacking any commerce.

The Super Moon tonight, aka the Beaver Moon, is so bright that the Rondout Creek is an illuminated landing strip. I can see my shadow from the glow. The Beaver Moon is also the Frost Moon. A gaggle of geese complain as they wait to check out at sunrise.

I ride without thought or effort because my mind is a blotter. A blotter that absorbs every color, nuance, pulse, and heartbeat of this place. This hamlet, in this late moment in a tired century that's kept a brave face to the world as circumstances beat its back bloody. I am the witness, the altered being, the one who sees all that is here. The recorder and the reporter, imperfect, mistaken, but with indescribable affection.

I coast by homes and storefronts, and commune with each soul in restless slumber or merciful peace. The porches shimmer; the windows yawn. The chimneys release the vapor of failed effort, the effluence of exhausted dreams. None of us will carry away what we cherish most when we're gone. This darkness is also what animates this place, and every other desperate village, burgh, and city in the world.

But this particular one is mine. I dwell here and am part of each tree, plant, and rock. I inhabit the structures that

312

hold it up, and the cells of its animals and humans, minute particles, desperate and swirling, sparks shot from flint, then fading in the air.

Margaret understands and allows me these occasional sojourns into the night. She loves me beyond reason, though undeserved. She understands that though I am hers, I am also owned by other things I cannot erase or forget. This mountain. This street, this shotgun highway that leads only east or west. This creek that divides the quadrants of the town, as it makes its way to the river that calls its name.

And the endless black and white newsreel that spins in my head, the desert, and the faces of my comrades. The eyes I watched close, to never open again. My dead. But still alive in the front compartment of my simmering brain, where they will live until someone or something flicks the switch off on the way up to bed.

Automatically, the thick front tire turns down the alley into the park, crunching over the gravel and sand. Here is the earth-moving equipment, stored since the water main repair. They wait, crouching iron beasts, insatiable for the street and earth beneath it when their time shall come 'round again.

I stop pedaling. My old Schwinn enters the trailhead and begins to climb. Mice and other creatures stir in the weeds and romp across the frosted fields. The path is bright, the trees illuminated. The Beaver Moon announced to early inhabitants the time to set the traps before the swamps freeze. The beaver furs kept Algonquins and colonists alike warm, a rare time of peace and cooperation.

I pass the Ruined Cottage and recall my nights there, my sorrow, my tears for a woman named the same as mine. Wordsworth's grief, the poor bastard worshiped youth until it betrayed him, hope ebbs. It comes back to me like a song: "Though nothing can bring back the hour / Of splendor in the grass...the primal sympathy..." The poor bastard. All of us poor bastards. Yet, for some reason, I feel a keen euphoria budding in my chest.

Higher up now on the mountain just past the turnoff for the horse farm, I wouldn't mind some company. I hear, or think I hear, the Countess Von Heidelberg grunting, snorting, and farting in her stall. She is perhaps dreaming of Pegasus, his powerful wings hovering above; that he might fly down to pleasure her.

There are other creatures that greet me as night fades. A Barn Owl hoots and a Great Horned answers. They begin a protracted conversation. Hooting owls, I've read, scared shit out of the Romans. An omen of impending disaster. Owls predicted the deaths of Julius Caesar and Augustus.

Native Americans called it "Crossing the owl's bridge," making the journey from life into death. But the hooting adds to my feeling of exhilaration. Hoot on my feathered brothers and bless my ascension and safe return.

The snow begins to fall. Just light flakes at first, thin and pale, suggesting a greater festivity to come. And here finally, the precipice, the final, dramatic drop below. A few street lights have faded out under the moon's glare, and pre-dawn's fingertips, painted pink like my little girl's, streak into the sky.

My front wheel rolls out over the abyss. The bike stops, but maintains its balance, even though my weight should topple it down. Science is confounded, logic withheld. I balance upon air, extended out over the owl's bridge. And then the word, "Jump." Just one word.

And time withholds its relentless moments. As I balance between...and wait. I count something I cannot calculate.

Slowly, the front tire rises up off of nothing. It lifts up until the bike is balanced on the back tire. An icy current of air brushes my face. The tire edges forward. A decision is to be made.

Gradually, the rear wheel rotates and faces the trail. The bike settles down to its normal position. Oblivion stretches behind me, tingles the back of my neck. I move forward. Soon the old trail becomes steep with rocks, boulders, loose gravel, and snagging roots that vie to disrupt my balance.

But they can't. I am solid and secure. Finally made whole. I ride ahead, exalted, euphoric, tasting the world, its flavors of earth, blood, and sugar. I feel its anchoring grasp; its compelling muscle holds me here, holds me hard. I see the world before me now, wide open, luxurious, and grand.

∞

About the Author

Mark Morganstern is a native of Schenectady, New York. He studied at the Manhattan School of Music, played bass fiddle, and toured with jazz and classical ensembles before deciding that music was not his best choice of profession. An avid reader and writer, he switched majors and graduated from the City University of New York with an MA in English/Creative Writing. His fiction has appeared in *Piedmont Literary Review, New Southern Literary Messenger, Hunger Magazine, Expresso Tilt, Mothering Magazine, Scarlet Leaf Review*, and other journals, and was anthologized in *Tribute to Orpheus II*. He received an honorable mention for his story, "Tomorrow's Special," published in the *Chronogram* 11/06 Fiction Contest issue, selected by guest judge, Valerie Martin. His collection of stories, *Dancing with Dasein*, is available from online booksellers.

Mark subs at the local high school (everything from physics to gym, occasionally even English) and books concerts for The Rosendale Cafe, a vegetarian eatery he owns with his wife Susan and their children.

Contact Mark at markmorganstern@gmail.com.

A Request

If you enjoyed this book, its publishers and author would be grateful if you would post a short (or long) review on the website where you bought the book and/or on Goodreads.com or other book review sites. Thanks for reading!

Please see the next few pages for other offerings from Recital Publishing.

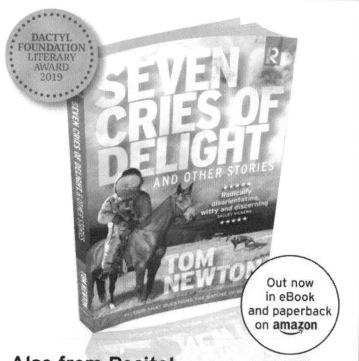

319

Also from Recital

"Ponckhockie Union is an alchemical exploit in which trauma and synchronicity operate as elixirs, ennobling ordinary lives. Its elegant clarity presents two kinds of detective story, one unfolding in the New York's Hudson Valley and the other in the mind of a man who finds his own sense of self getting in the way of his highest aspiration, which is to transcend the world of category and convention and dissolve into the primal material of the cosmos."

Djelloul Marbrook
Award-winning poet/novelist:
Far from Algiers, The Light Piercing Water Trilogy

Out now in eBook and paperback on amazon

Reweirding the world
www.recitalpublishing.com

Made in the USA
Middletown, DE
04 June 2020